Praise for Michael J Malone

'A terrific read . . . it makes the hairs on the back of your neck stand on end. Loved it.' **Martina Cole**

'Strong female characters, honest, pithy dialogue and ever-present empathy for the victims make this a deeply satisfying read.' *Sunday Times*

'Bristling with unease . . . twisting the thriller into a new and troubling shape.' **Eva Dolan**

'Malone is a massive talent.' **Luca Veste**

'Vintage Malone. Pitch-black Glasgow noir with a conclusion that hits you like an express train.' **Mason Cross**

'Twisted, sharp and just a little bit heartbreaking. Nicely plotted . . . Malone's characterisation is fantastic.' **SJI Holliday**

'*Dog Fight* is . . . an outstanding thriller . . . truly gripping . . . The story is beautifully crafted and perfectly paced . . . set against the background of an issue that truly matters.' *Undiscovered Scotland*

'Malone gives us his customary mix of humour, insight and darkness to produce a slick thriller with a killer punch..' **Douglas Skelton**

Also by Michael J Malone

Michael J Malone

CONTRABAND

Contraband is an imprint of Saraband
Published by Saraband
Digital World Centre, 1 Lowry Plaza
The Quays, Salford, M50 3UB
www.saraband.net

ISBN: 9781910192771
ebook: 9781910192788

10 9 8 7 6 5 4 3 2 1

*All characters appearing in this novel are fictitious. Any
resemblance to real persons, living or dead, is purely coincidental.*

Typeset by Iolaire Typography Ltd.
Printed and bound in Great Britain by Clays Ltd, St Ives plc.

MIX
Paper from
responsible sources
FSC® C018072

I'd like to dedicate this novel to the memory of Margaret Thomson Davis. Of the plethora of celebrities who passed away in 2016, she was the one who was my hero. She was a wonderful woman and a hugely talented storyteller, and I count myself extremely fortunate to have had her as friend and mentor. She was always ready with a smile, a piece of advice and/or a witty comment, and I probably quote her every time I speak to an aspiring writer. The world is a lesser place for her passing, but I'm sure she's looking down on me as pleased about my success as she was about her own.

MJM, January 2017

PROLOGUE

They came for him at midnight. Approached him as he huddled in the doorway in his sleeping bag. Two guys. Stocky, in collar to toe black. Had the look of ex-squaddies.

'Want to earn a few bucks?' one of them asked as he crouched down. Getting eye to eye.

'Piss off,' he said.

'Don't be like that, mate. Just trying to help a brother out.' He held out a hand. 'Name's Dave.'

'Yeah?' He squinted into Dave's face, looking for an agenda. Saw nothing but an open and friendly face. He still wasn't taking the hand. He'd learned caution since being forced onto the streets.

Then he caught sight of a tattoo just above the neckline of Dave's black t-shirt. Ornate lettering across both collar bones that read: *Sapper*. He was right. Saw the guy, instantly thought: army.

'Gavin,' he said, but kept his hand inside the sleeping bag and pulled it tight around him, like a defence. Wasn't giving too much away too soon. He'd met a lot of wankers in the army.

Dave shuffled in his jacket pocket, Gavin stiffened, then relaxed when he saw it was a packet of cigarettes. 'Smoke?' Dave held out the packet with a smile.

'Sure.' What can it hurt? he thought.

Dave's mate held out a lighter. Gavin hung the cigarette on the tip of his lips, stretched towards the flame. Pursed his lips and sucked greedily on the flame. Felt the warm smoke fill his lungs

1

and savoured the familiar calm and light-headedness. Hello, Mr Nicotine, he thought. Long time no see. Cigarettes were a luxury on the street. Food was his priority, although he was often tempted to forego a stale Greggs sandwich for a smoke, but the gnawing in his gut was the more difficult form of hunger to ignore. That and the booze.

'What happened, mate?' asked Dave as he squinted through his exhaled smoke.

'Shit happened, mate,' answered Gavin, as he was reminded of the camaraderie of the smoker. It always amused him how a pair of smokers could quickly become a community. Conversation flaring up with the strike of a match.

Dave said nothing, just nodded. His expression showing he understood.

Gavin looked at him, assessing. Dave appeared to accept the judgement. Expected it. And Gavin saw someone he could actually speak with. Usually, he was invisible, but this guy *got* him. And ciggies were always something that loosened his tongue.

'You'll have heard it all before, Dave,' said Gavin before taking a long toke. 'A shit childhood, you fight your way through your teen years 'cos you're angry with fucking *everybody*, you see a recruitment officer at one of those high street stands, you wonder what it might be like to have some routine and then the army becomes the only family you ever had. Then active service and some *seriously* bad shit happens. You're invalided out and civvie street just can't deal with you. You don't have that set of skills, you know?' He sat up and allowed the sleeping bag to fall from his shoulders and drape around his waist. This was probably the longest he'd spoken in months.

'Then the drink and drugs become your family. The only thing that makes any sense. That and the violence.'

'Yeah?'

'Apart from when I'm high, the only other time that life makes sense is when I'm in a scrap.' He gave Dave the once over. As if measuring him for a chibb. 'You're lucky I'm so tired, or I would have had you the minute you started speaking to me.'

'Hey,' Dave held up both hands, 'I'm a lover not a fighter.'

Gavin snorted an 'Aye, right.' Looked over at Dave's mate. 'What's his deal?'

Dave turned his head. A silent signal passed between them and the other guy left.

'Strong and silent make me nervous,' said Gavin. Then looked at the packet of cigarettes resting in Dave's hands. 'Any chance of another one for later, mate?'

'Sure,' said Dave. Threw him the packet. 'Keep the lot.' He grinned. 'I'm supposed to be giving up.'

'Me too,' Gavin shared the smile. Felt a connection. 'So,' he bit. 'You mentioned earning a few pounds? How much we talking about?'

'Two hundred and fifty. At first. Could become regular, mate.'

Gavin thought about the hard weeks of winter he'd just lived through and calculated how many nights' bed and breakfast that amount of money could pay for. Felt himself fall into the cushion of a soft bed, dressed in clean sheets. Then his mind moved to the sight of him handing a portion of it to the guys who hung about outside the train station, and accepting a small white package as a trade.

A small voice chimed in his head: if it feels too good to be true it usually is. He ignored it. He had the whiff of a high. Oblivion.

'There's this guy,' Dave began. 'Bit of a pussy. Fancies himself as a promoter. Basically he's got this underground fight thing going on. Lots of city types who wouldn't know an AK from an air rifle get off on watching other guys fight.'

'Right?' Why the hell not, thought Gavin. He loved a scrap. And this way he got paid.

'It's all hush-hush,' said Dave. 'The guy has connections, and he's scared that the vanillas get to hear about his love for a fight. So we have to take you in with a blindfold on.' Dave examined Gavin as if for his reaction. 'Still interested?'

'Two hundred and fifty?' asked Gavin.

Dave nodded

'Count me in.'

'Sweet,' said Dave and held out his hand. Gavin took it and shook. 'Tomorrow night at twenty-two hundred hours. We'll pick you up here.'

Dead on ten, he was collected in a black BMW. Dave apologised as he put a black cloth bag over his head.

'We really need to protect our guy's anonymity,' he explained. 'Sorry, dude.' Then a pause. 'Now I'm going to fit you with some headphones . . .'

'But . . .' began Gavin, and his words were cut off when he lost his hearing to a U2 tune. No point in getting antsy, he thought. This is like the hazing training he heard about from some of his mates in the Special Forces. They could deal with it, so could he.

He lost track of time in the car. Ten minutes? Twenty? Felt the car brake and he was guided out of the door. A hand on his shoulder and he was taken a few steps. He felt a shift in atmosphere. Must be inside some kind of building.

The headphones were pulled off.

Dave said, 'For your own protection we're going to keep the bag on. It also helps with the sense of theatre for the suits.' There's a chuckle woven through his words. 'Wankers.'

'When do I get it?' asked Gavin. He heard a tremble of fear in his voice. Coughed. He couldn't come across as a pussy. He added some spine to his words. 'When do I get the money?'

'Hold out your hand,' said Dave.

He did and felt some paper being placed on his open hand. Rubbed his fingers over it.

'Put it in your jacket,' said Dave. 'You can count it later. First we need to get you ready, ok?'

'Ok.' Gavin instinctively spread his weight over a wider stance, after he pocketed the cash.

4

'You're going to feel someone taking off your jacket and your top – and don't worry, we'll keep them safe for you until you get back after the bout.'

The use of the word "bout" reassured Gavin. Gave this whole strangeness a feel of truth.

Once his top half was bare he felt a chill. Shivered.

'Don't worry,' said Dave. 'Once you get started you'll soon heat up.' Then, 'Hold out your hands, palms face down.'

Gavin complied and felt a stirring of a warning. This had gone far enough. Who were these people? What had he got himself into? As he felt the questions collide in his mind, Dave spoke.

'You are going to love this. You're a scrapper, right? I can see it in your shoulders. In the way you stand.'

And Gavin allowed himself to be reassured. For the twentieth time that day, he asked himself, what's the worst that could happen?

'We're putting some wraps on your fists. Don't want you breaking a knuckle just as the fight gets started, right?' Pause. 'And Gavin, once we're done? I'm taking you somewhere for a shower. Man are you rank.'

Gavin laughed. Welcomed the switch in mood and the release of fear.

'Just, no funny business,' he said. 'I know what you paras are like.'

'Fuck you,' said Dave. 'Who knows what shit you Royal Latrines used to get up to.'

Again Gavin felt reassured. There's nothing like the exchange of insults to get the juices flowing before a fight.

'Right,' said Dave. 'That's you.' And Gavin felt a tug on his hand. Flexed his fingers. Punched one hand into the palm of the other. Felt good, he thought. Someone knows what they're doing.

'Going to put the headphones back on,' said Dave. 'And the next thing you hear will be the call to get on with it and fight, ok champ?'

Gavin nodded as Bono once again filled his aural canal. Fucking hate U2, he thought. He felt a hand on his shoulder. The pressure of it was different. This wasn't Dave, he realised. Felt a stirring of fear. Tamped it down. Dave's a good guy, but he can't keep him as a safety blanket.

Man the hell up.

He was guided into another space. Felt another change of atmosphere, the naked skin on his torso registering a change in the heat and the hand pushing him on was transferring a sense of urgency. The feel of anticipation.

Then a hand on the middle of his chest stopped him dead. A hand on each shoulder positioned him. Automatically he resisted. Trying to keep his own stance. Then realised this was part of the show and complied.

His headphones were removed. His ears adjusted instantly, and the air around him was alive with loud, hungry male voices. A discordant choir urging violence. Some of the voices nearby emerged from the urgent thunderous rumble.

'Fuckin' yes.'

'Get intae 'um.'

'Kill the bastard.'

The bag was removed from his head, and he shielded his eyes from the sudden blare of light, blinked rapidly to help his eyes adjust.

His knees buckled. Adrenalin surged through his system.

The first thing he saw was the other man. Similar height. Cropped hair. Wearing nothing but a pair of combat shorts and strapping over his knuckles.

The limbic brain took over. Assessed the risk. Flooded his system with chemicals that put his body in the best position to fight or flee. This was an occasion, thought Gavin, where flight was out of the question. This crowd wanted blood and pain.

Keeping one eye on his opponent, he scanned the room. Noted the low ceiling, the flickering bulbs, concrete floor. Then the men standing in a circle around them. Most were in suits with ties loosened. Some middle-aged, some in their twenties. Some were puffy-faced and grey, others tan and tight. Some were holding fistfuls of cash and waving them in the air.

All of them were roaring. They wanted to see a spray of blood. Hear the crack of bone on bone.

Gavin processed this in milliseconds. He saw his opponent move into a fighting stance and instantly did the same.

He thought about his sleeping site. Sure, it was as far from a palace as you can possibly find, but right now it had its appeal. He pushed this thought aside. Mess this twat up and you get a clean bed for a few nights, he told himself.

He acknowledged the churn in his gut. Fear was healthy. Fear had kept him alive all these years. Courage was not the absence of fear, but the willingness to carry on despite it, he remembered his first army sergeant telling him.

It's me or you, mate, he thought as he looked at his opponent and received the same look back in return.

He read the other man's face and body. Ribs showing, cheekbones like ridges on the sides of his face. Read how he favoured one leg and offered his stronger side in defence. There used to be muscle there, he thought, but now it's stringy, out of power and condition.

Much like himself.

He ignored the hunger gnawing at his stomach, regretted his decision not to go to the soup kitchen the day before. He lowered his hands to his sides. Skipped from one foot to the other, tried to control his energy stores, but letting just a little out to warm his muscles. He rolled his head, trying to loosen his shoulders. Such as they were. If only this had happened a year ago. When he was still fit. He'd kick this guy's arse.

Gavin ignored the negativity of this thought. He *would* kick this guy's arse. You or me, mate, and it ain't going to be me. Allowed the certainty of this to inform his facial expression and his stance. He knew from long experience that most fights were won or lost in the mind.

He bared his teeth. Growled.

The shouting around him intensified. The audience working itself into a grim lust.

The guy who removed his blindfold stepped to his side. Gavin turned quickly to see a tall man, cropped white hair and small round black-framed spectacles.

This man moved his head closer to his. His breath hot and urgent in his ear. Through the din, Gavin heard three words.

'To the death.'

1

She wasn't Alexis, but she'd do just nicely. For now.

Kenny O'Neill was in one of those hotel bars. All chrome and glass with black leather seating. Like they were going for a cosmopolitan look, but falling short and winning the try-hard award instead.

He'd stayed on after a meeting. Some wankstain from Edinburgh trying to sell him a delivery of iPhones that "just fell off a container down at the docks, mate". The price? "Going for a song, big man."

The cops would be all over that like fleas on a dead pigeon, so he passed, giving the guy a "don't darken my door again" warning. The "or else" part of it referring to the potential loss of teeth. Or maybe even a testicle. Depending on his mood.

Said wankstain didn't let the door hit his arse on the way out.

Kenny had a reputation. A reputation he was living up to these days. He caught his reflection in the mirror behind the bar. The lower half of his face was obscured by a row of malt whisky bottles, but he had a decent view of his eyes and a look so cold it could chill your liver. Warming them up was a problem these days. Ever since . . .

He brushed off the thought. Not going there.

But he couldn't close it off entirely before an image of Ray McBain slipped past his guard. A picture that twisted his gut. His oldest friend, lying on his back, naked, with a knife sticking out of his chest.

Music being piped into the bar was slow, smooth jazz. Lazy vocals and easy rhythms. He allowed himself to go with it, prayed the effortless beats would distract him. Then he looked over at her.

She was working the room, but you'd have to know the signs to recognise this. Kenny knew the signs. He read them keenly. The flick of the hair, the half-smile, a look that managed to be light, yet heavy with invitation.

This, Kenny was interested in buying.

The bartender was standing to attention within earshot. Wearing a white shirt, black waistcoat and pale-face combination.

'Glayva on ice,' he ordered, wondering briefly about the guy's vitamin D situation.

'Fancy something sweet?' Her voice low and soft in his ear.

'I sure do.' He turned to face her, letting her know he had been aware of her approach. 'And the lady would like . . .'

'Sloe gin, please. Heavy on the tonic,' she said with a smile and slid on to the stool beside him with practised ease, despite the tight, knee-length skirt and high heels.

She was subtle with her makeup. Just a touch of mascara and a shine on her cheekbones and lips. Any more would have been a waste of product. She didn't need it.

'My day has been low on the tonic element. Perhaps I should join you,' he said. The barman paused in his movement. 'Just carry on,' Kenny said and turned back to his new friend.

'Productive meeting?' she asked, tilting her head to the side. It was a tiny movement and suggested her interest in the answer was sincere.

'I've had better,' Kenny replied. He felt a flutter in his stomach. That was rare these days. Since Alexis, few women managed to engage him, past the obvious. He was flattered by her interest despite being aware it was purely professional. 'You just can't get the customers these days.'

'Oh, I don't know,' she said, flashing a smile.

The barman arrived with their drinks. Went through the pantomime of placing a paper napkin down on the bar, over which he rested the filled glasses. Then he tilted a small bottle of tonic over the gin and poured half of it in. Then paused as if waiting for approval.

'Just give me the whole bottle,' she said, moving her straw out of the way of the barman's aim. 'The evening's too young to scrimp.'

The barman placed the bill in a small leather folder and slid it across the bar to Kenny. He fished his card out of his wallet and placed it on top. 'Just keep my tab open for now.'

Kenny turned back to her and raised his glass. 'What should we toast?'

She stretched over to pick up her drink. Her white silk sleeve moved up the pale of her skin, displaying a gold bracelet. Delicate and tasteful. 'A long and happy life?' she replied.

'I'd settle for either one of those,' said Kenny and raised his glass to his lips for the first sip, keeping his eyes on hers as he drank. When the alcohol hit his stomach he realised how hungry he was. He ignored it. Food could wait.

'Is this a regular meeting spot for you?' she asked. Subtext: I haven't see you here before.

'No,' he said and looked around the room. 'I prefer something a little more business-like. But my associate had heard great things about this place.' He looked her full in the face. Raised an eyebrow. 'Seems like he had a point.'

'What line of business are you in?' she asked, accepting the compliment with a small nod.

'Buying and selling. This and that.'

'Successfully, I would venture.' She looked pointedly at his suit jacket. The suit was bespoke. Made for him from the finest Italian cloth, and it took someone with a good eye to spot the difference between this and your higher-end John Lewis special.

'The clothes maketh the man,' he replied, accepting the compliment.

'I don't often get quoted Shakespeare of an evening.'

'Given how much he contributed to our use of language, that's a surprise.'

'I do like a brain in a man,' she said and leaning forward pursed her lips around her straw and drank. Kenny watched the flow of fluid, up the straw and then the movement of her small Adam's apple as she swallowed. Felt a charge.

'Have you eaten?' he asked.

'I was just going to go up to my room to order room service.'

'What's on the menu?'

'Whatever sir cares for.'

Next morning, Kenny woke up to the vibration of his phone in his jacket pocket. As always, when roused from sleep, he was instantly awake and ready for the day. The light coming in through the curtains was sufficient to see that his jacket was hanging where he put it the night before. On a hanger, hooked over the wardrobe door. You don't pay two grand for a suit and then allow it to be crumpled into a ball.

He moved her arm off his chest and slid naked out of the bed. The phone stopped ringing when he reached it. Typical, he thought. He looked at the alert. Two missed calls from Aunt Violet. He felt a surge of guilt. Damped it down. It had been a year since his father had come back into their lives, and since then he'd only visited Vi twice. Each time it was all he could do to stop himself from punching Vi's husband, Uncle Colin, in the throat. The man was imprinted into his irritation circuit.

He heard some movement behind him as she sat up in bed. He turned to face her. She smiled and modestly arranged the quilt over her breasts.

'Nice view,' she said, looking pointedly at his morning erection.

He returned her smile and realised, for the first time in many months, that his smile was genuine.

'Does madam have a card?' he asked. Giving last night a score, it would be a ten out of ten on the need-to-be-repeated scale.

'Of course.' She leaned over to the bedside cabinet, pulled her bag over on to her lap, opened it and pulled out a small rectangle of card. 'Here.' She offered it to him. All the while she protected her modesty, which Kenny found strangely endearing considering what they'd spent the night doing.

He walked over, sat on the bed beside her and read the detail.

'Nice to meet you, Christine,' he held out a hand, 'I'm Kenny.' They shook. Her hand small and warm in his. She giggled at the absurdity and Kenny felt a thaw beginning. And an increased urgency in his groin.

'Would Christine like to have a little more fun before she goes off for the rest of her day?'

She allowed the sheet to fall from her breasts and reached for him.

'I think that would be perfectly acceptable.'

2

Ian "Mabawser" Ritchie was a changed man. Since he completed his service and returned from Afghanistan he'd found comfort in the mind-cocoon of a variety of substances. Some were even legal.

Physically, he was the same person who first put on a uniform for his country, but mentally he had craved time-out, and that was why he chased the dragon, the herb or whatever could help press the pause button on the reel that seemed to go through his brain on a never-ending loop.

Shame at the person he had become meant he did everything to avoid family and old friends. Even his cousin, Kenny – especially his cousin, Kenny - received a rubber lug. He could cope with texts or phone calls at a pinch, but he refused to meet any of them face to face.

A variety of treatments failed, and he even found himself self-censoring when talking to a pleasant, well-meaning counsellor from the NHS who couldn't handle hearing about the violent deaths he'd witnessed.

Then his caseworker introduced him to Combat Stress and a stay at Hollybush House in Ayrshire. He responded to the old sprawling house, the extensive gardens and the other ex-squaddies there. A chance to speak to other people who *understood* what he was going through.

Had his first full night's sleep in an age. Felt there was enough energy in his thighs to go running again. Cracked out a few press-ups, got working on a punch-bag and even started to notice the ladies.

Couldn't approach any of them, right enough. What would they see in a basket case like him? Besides, they had their own issues. What would that be like? A car crash meeting a train wreck? Best to be avoided.

One of the other guys struck a chord. Dom Hastie. He was only twenty-five. Grew up in a rough part of Glasgow. The only child of addicts and a second-generation benefit baby, all he could see in the black, shit-stained carpet rolling into his future was a life of drug abuse and benefit fraud. White male privilege, my arse. So he joined up. Got a bullet in the head for his trouble.

'Friendly fire, my hairy hole,' was how he described it. 'Fuck that for friendly.'

He got caught in cross-fire while out on patrol in Helmand. Took an American bullet in the brain. He was supposed to die. He didn't. He was told he would never walk or talk. He did both, after a fashion.

'The docs say I'm a walking miracle,' he told Ian the first time they met. 'A fucking miracle, mate.'

The bullet with his name on it mashed the part of his brain that regulated emotional and impulse control. It also left him partially paralysed. He had little sensation on his right-hand side. When he smiled, only half of his mouth moved. His right hand hung, useless, at his side and he couldn't move his right foot.

'See learning how to do stuff with my left hand, mate?' he said to Ian. 'Try brushing your teeth, wiping your arse or even having a wank wi' the wrong hand. It's tricky as hell,' he added with his trademark lopsided grin.

Ian made the initial mistake of going for the visible injuries and allowing them to engage his empathy button. Soon, however, he learned to understand the younger man's emotional injuries.

'Tried to commit suicide twice,' he offered over a late night illicit smoke, hanging out of his bedroom window on the second floor. 'Before I learned to walk I took a trip in my wheelchair to the top of a set of stairs. Hoped I would break my neck on the way down.' He squinted through the cigarette smoke. 'Couldn't even get myself out the chair.' He coughed a laugh. 'Pathetic. Then there was the time I tried to chew through my wrist.'

'What?' asked Ian. 'That would take a bit of effort.'

'Aye. Was painful as fuck, mate.' He scratched the right side of his face, under his eye as if testing for feeling. 'What about you? Ever try to check out?'

'Sure,' said Ian and looked away, over the top of the tree canopy, to a glittering night sky. That was as much as he would say. He'd worked through that demon with his counsellors. Didn't want to go tickling its chin while talking with a mate. You never knew what might wake it up.

Dom looked at him. Silently acknowledged that he could read the signs. That part of the conversation was over.

Fair enough.

'What about that Meg lassie? She always seems to be in the hallway the same time as you. The one from Dundee? She's lovely. No fancy getting to know her better?' asked Dom, changing the subject.

Ian knew exactly who he was talking about. Short, auburn hair, a ready laugh and both legs blown off below the knee by an IED.

'Nah. She's one of the guys.' Ian had difficulty seeing beyond the camouflage gear to the gender beneath whenever there were female soldiers in his unit. Kept things simple. And now when they were all recovering ex-service personnel, that mental block remained. 'Would be like shagging a brother.' He shuddered.

'I'm calling bullshit on that, mate,' said Dom with a twinkle. 'Beautiful eyes and a nice rack. No way she's a brother.'

Ian playfully swiped at the back of his head. 'Away an' chew on your wrist, ya wee bastard.'

Dom ducked his head and giggled in response, as if delighted someone he trusted didn't treat him like an infant.

'I see you're wearing a wedding ring,' Ian said, looking over at Dom's hand. 'A bit young, aren't you?'

'Got her pregnant, didn't I? First time an'all,' he grinned, grabbed his crotch with his good hand. 'Super sperm, me. One shot. Bang!'

'Yeah, that was *real* lucky,' said Ian with a grimace. 'How's that working out for you?'

Dom took a long draw on his cigarette, exhaled and screwed his eyes against the smoke. 'Could be better. Missus can't deal with my . . .' he adopted a posh doctor speaking voice, '. . . my anger management issues. And the wean is feart to look at me. Keeps running away.' He smiled, but it was clear from the haunted look in his eyes that this pained him more than anything. He'd bought the line: fight to keep your country safe, and now to his own child he was the bogeyman.

3

Kenny was sitting on a pine bench in the changing room of The Hut, a damp towel round his waist. Enjoying the feeling of having worked his muscles. Hard. He pushed his wet hair back away from his eyes and looked at his cousin Ian as he pulled on a pair of jeans over his faded DC comic-themed boxers. Gave a mental nod at the definition appearing on his abdomen. Big cousin was getting his act together.

'Superman?' he asked.

'Got a problem wi' that, cuz?'

'Just might,' he made a face, '. . . let the ladies down. You'll get done under the Trades Descriptions Act.'

'Very funny,' said Ian as he pulled on a grey t-shirt.

'They'll think Superman will be powering your arse. And they get the Joker.'

'The Joker's from a different cartoon, and I just kicked *your* arse, by the way.'

Kenny stood up. Grinned. And turned to the battered grey locker that held his clothes. A blue paper towel on the floor caught his eye. He picked it up, balled it in his grip and threw it into the bin in the corner. The previous owner might have been a lunatic, but at least he kept the place tightly run.

He and Ian were the first people in that morning, so the towel must have been left there by someone the previous evening. He'd have to have a word with the cleaners. The Hut might not be the fanciest gym in the city, but they could at least keep it clean and tidy.

As he dressed, he considered the change in Ian since the last time they spoke. Clear skin, bright eyes and a purpose behind every movement was a big improvement on the man who was released from service a couple of years earlier.

He bit back on a retort. Ian hadn't kicked his arse, but it had been closer than it should have been. At one point while they were grappling on the mat, Kenny thought his cousin had him pinned, but a butterfly guard, a sweep and he had him in a submission hold.

Ian was not a man who gave up easily, but Kenny's superior strength and fitness levels told and eventually Ian tapped out.

Ian towelled his long, blond hair. Plucked an elastic band from his pocket, pulled his hair back and arranged it into a demented mother's version of a ponytail. Kenny smiled in response. Personal grooming was never Ian's forte.

'So,' Ian said as he leaned over to tie his laces. 'Are you the boss here now?' He looked around himself, showing he was talking about the gym. 'What's happening with this place, since you know . . .?'

Ian was referring to the disappearance of the previous owner, Matty the Hut. The only people who knew what really happened, and who Matthew King really was, were dead or could be trusted to keep quiet.

Happy that no-one was around to overhear, Kenny answered. 'Since Matt did a runner, I got my lawyers involved. Found out this place is owned by a trust, and it looks like we can satisfy their requirements and keep the place open.'

'Sweet.'

'Which reminds me,' Kenny spoke before the idea was fully formed, but as it shaped in his mind, he found he liked it. 'We haven't yet replaced the old man. Fancy becoming the new Matty the Hut?'

Ian cocked his head to the side. Sat down on his side of the bench.

'You serious?'

19

'As cancer.'

'But . . .' he said. A single word laden with so much that didn't need to be said. His drug problems and how he had effectively hidden from society – polite and otherwise – since he was decommissioned.

'None of the old stuff matters,' said Kenny. 'You're getting back on your feet, aren't you?' He grinned, the idea growing on him with every passing second. 'And look at you with your Superman boxers and a six-pack. You'd be a natural.'

'Piss off,' replied Ian, but his expression displayed interest. 'I could do this,' his voice was quiet. Then more firmly, 'I could totally do this.'

'I'll clear it with the trustees and you can start . . . right now,' said Kenny. He looked at the bin. 'And your first job is to have a word with the cleaners.'

A couple of minutes later, they were in the former owner's office, and Ian was sitting on the only chair.

'But . . .' he started to speak. His innate sense of caution and recent lack of confidence about to reassert its position as his default behaviour.

'It's just common sense, cuz. You've been in the place often enough over the years, you'll know what needs done. And we'll get you enrolled in a fitness instructor's course,' Kenny said, rubbing his hands together.

Ian sat upright in the chair, and Kenny wondered why he hadn't thought of it before. The ideal solution.

'One thing,' said Kenny. 'Don't cock it up.'

'Not going to happen, dude.'

'And another one thing,' Kenny added. 'When are you going home to see your mother? She keeps phoning me, wondering what's happening.'

'Aye, aye,' said Ian, now slumped in the chair. He hated to disappoint his mother. 'I wanted to wait until I was really back

20

on my feet, you know? When she could really see the difference I'd made.'

Kenny nodded. He could fully understand the impulse, but it was unnecessary. There were few people more accepting than Ian's mother. 'Your mum wouldn't care if you walked in her door with a joint stuck to your bottom lip and a syringe hanging off your arm. She just wants to see her son.'

'Aye,' said Ian. 'Aye.'

'We'll need to talk wages,' Kenny exhaled. 'I'll have my guy look at the books and see what we can pay you.'

Ian's expression showed he would do the job for free.

'We'll pay you,' Kenny repeated. 'But will it affect your benefits?'

'Don't get any,' Ian replied.

'What do you mean?' Kenny asked, knowing his cousin's reluctance to get involved with any level of bureaucracy. 'You must've been due something?'

'Dunno. Never applied. I get a wee pension. That's enough for me.'

'But . . .'

'But nothing.' Ian bristled. 'I went in to the DSS for some help with the forms and stuff when I was on the gear and in full PTSD mode. Man . . .' He shook his head at the memory. At the man the war made him. 'I was hyper vigilant. Every loud noise was an explosion. Every sudden movement was somebody coming to kill me. Sitting in those waiting rooms was a nightmare. Ended up making a complete arse of myself.' He lowered his tone. His version of an apology. 'Most difficult place I've ever been. And I've been in Helmand.'

'It's all moot now anyway,' said Kenny. 'You've got a job.'

'Aye.'

'So when are you going to see your mother?'

'Soon.'

'When?' Kenny's tone suggesting it better be sooner than that.

'Tonight. I'll go tonight.'

'Great,' said Kenny, bringing his phone out of his pocket. 'I'll just send her a text before you change your mind.'

Ian sat back in his chair and crossed his arms. He's said he was going, so he would go.

Once he'd finished thumbing out the message, Kenny stepped closer to Ian and put a hand on his shoulder. Gripped it hard.

'Excellent stuff. Mabawser Ritchie is back.'

4

On the way to his parent's house, Ian decided on a detour to see how Dom Hastie was doing since his time at Hollybush House. It had provided the necessary break, and kick up the arse that he needed, but the younger ex-squaddie's situation had the added complexity of a serious head injury, and Ian needed to see if the younger man's time with Combat Stress had any lasting impact.

He parked his ancient red Ford Escort in the car park at the side of the high-rise flats in the east of the city he'd been told was Dom's address. He didn't bother locking it. If any of the local scrotes wanted to steal it they were welcome. That would be a joy-ride feeling more like a yawn-ride while they waited for the engine to heat up and the accelerator to get anywhere near the legal speed limit.

A child appeared at his side.

'Watch your car for you, mate?'

If this had been a Dickens book, thought Ian, he'd have called the child an urchin. Tattered canvas shoes, baggy shorts and a tracksuit jacket were topped off by the ubiquitous baseball cap. This one was dark blue, bearing the legend NYC, and Ian guessed the kid hadn't been outside a mile radius of their current situation, never mind visiting the Big Apple.

'What's your name?' he asked, feeling in his pocket for some change.

'Whit do you want to know that fur?'

'I like to know who I'm doing business with.'

The child brightened beneath its dirt-smeared face. *Doing business* meant cash was going to change hands.

'Myleene.' And Ian realised she was a girl.

'What age are you? And who's supposed to be looking after you?'

'I'm eleven and a half and that's nane o' yur business. Last guy who asked me that was well dodgy.'

Ian could only guess at what this girl's life entailed, but he felt relieved at the street smarts she was showing. She'd need them in this place.

'Right, Myleene,' Ian said as he looked over at his car. 'What's it worth?'

'A fiver.'

'Piss off,' said Ian. 'It's a battered old Ford. Try again.'

'That's the going rate, mate,' Myleene said while holding out her hand. Her small face was pinched with determination, and Ian realised there was an imperative here. She looked barely fed. He pulled his wallet out of his pocket, plucked out one of his last fivers, and handed it over with the stray thought: thank God he had a job.

The note was exposed to the air for seconds before it was plucked out of his hands and disappeared into one of Myleene's pockets.

'Anything happens to my car, I want that back,' he said trying to be as stern as he could.

She stretched to the top of her four feet ten inches height and adopted her most serious expression. 'It's a fiver an hour, mate. If you're not back before then I'm off.'

Ian turned away from her before his amusement at her was too obvious and she was slighted. He walked up the slope to the entrance and felt the gradient work his lungs. How did the elderly manage up this with their weekly shop? he wondered. And how the hell did Dom manage with a gammy leg and a walking stick?

He stood outside the double glass door, craned his head

back and looked up the wall of the building. Columns of small windows set into grey brick and horizontal lines of concrete, like brutal steps, drawing his eyes up to the release of a rare clear sky.

Noticed the CCTV camera.

Inside, the lobby was dark with a strip light flickering on the ceiling adding moments of light. There was one red door with the legend *Stairs* in print above the lintel and a similar sized single aluminium door for the lift.

Another CCTV camera. On the one hand this was reassuring. On the other it was a concern. What was going on around here that needed a constant vigil?

He pressed the button to call the lift. A small light shone and he settled in to wait. Minutes later there was still no lift, and he looked over at the stair entrance and debated whether or not just to go for that. Dom was on the tenth floor. He could run up the stairs. Give his heart and lungs a mini-workout. Christ, he thought, Kenny O'Neill was a bad influence. Just a few months ago he wouldn't have considered the stairs for a second, instead wishing he'd brought a newspaper with him to help wait out the lift's arrival.

If it ever did arrive.

He moved closer to the lift door, put his face to the small glass window set at head height, and looked up in a vain attempt to gauge if there was any movement in the lift shaft.

Giving up, he walked over to the stairs. Pulled open the door and stepped inside the stairwell. Bare concrete with dark blue railings. He ran up one flight, walked the next, and kept this pattern going until he arrived on the tenth floor. High intensity interval training for anyone who can't afford the gym fees, he thought.

He passed no one on the stairs. The only sound was the echo of his feet hitting the solid surface and his strong, even breathing. His legs felt strong and he savoured the feel of blood surging into his thighs. This wouldn't have been possible even six months ago, and he thanked whatever gods were responsible for the change in his fortunes. There's no high like a natural high, he thought with the conviction of the recently converted.

On the floor in front of the door leading out to the tenth landing lay a crumpled, empty can of coke and he realised this was the first piece of litter he'd seen. Over the years he'd heard so many stories about Glasgow's high rises and how they'd suffered from, at best, bad management and at their worse, the public spaces like the stairwell and landings acting like drug dens. For Dom's sake he was pleased that things seemed to be well managed around here.

The door squealed a protest as he pulled it open and walked out onto the landing. Two guys brushed past him. Then another.

'Hold the lift,' a stocky bald guy shouted, ignoring Ian's presence. Another examined Ian from head to foot in the manner of someone assessing potential risk. This guy looked like he was tall enough to stretch up and touch the ceiling. The lean state of his figure highlighted by the way he was dressed, all in black: shirt, jeans and dress jacket. His hair was bleached white and a pair of small eyes studied him from behind a pair of Harry Potter spectacles. It was a look Ian was well used to. When he was growing up, violence was only ever a milligram of testosterone away, and you had to be aware where the next threat might come from.

He felt himself react to the look. Tightened his core, broadened his stance and held his shoulders wide. If this guy was looking for an easy target, this would broadcast the opposite.

The man's eyes skimmed off him with an expression that suggested he'd been dismissed as a concern. Which was fine by Ian. He'd be happy to mix it if need be. He rarely walked away from a fight, but he was here to see a mate and it wouldn't do to be caught up in something just outside his door.

Behind him, he heard the lift arrive with a slight whine. The door opened and he heard the footfall of the three men as they made their way towards it. He turned for another look. Saw the tall, skinny guy incline his head to listen to what the bald guy had to say. He was more worthy of note to Ian. There was something about his gait that suggested army. He'd met hundreds of guys like him over the years, and if he spotted him in a crowded room full of civilians he'd recognise him as such.

Ian turned away before Baldy became aware of his scrutiny, but locked his image in his mind. He was not only army, but he was a scrapper. It was there in his stance, the lightness of his tread, the way his eyes roamed the space.

For sure, he'd spotted Ian and was going through the same mental process he was. Speccy had been much more obvious, but the bald guy had surely taken more in.

What it meant for Dom, he wasn't sure, but his gut was telling him it wasn't good. This was too much to be a coincidence. These guys on the same floor as Dom?

Ian looked for flat E. Saw it was at the far end of the large square landing and made his way there and knocked.

He heard Dom shuffle to the door. One foot being dragged and the regular knock of his cane on the floor as he moved closer.

'I fucking told yeez, you'll get your . . .' Dom shouted as he opened the door. When he saw it was Ian his expression changed, but not before Ian could see that there was a real note of concern there.

'Told yeez what, Dom?' Ian asked as he looked over his shoulder at the empty space in front of the lift. 'Get what? What's happening, buddy?'

'Ach, nothing, mate. Just some arseholes.' He worked a muscle in his jaw and lashed out with his walking stick, hitting the side of the door with some force. 'Fuckers,' he spat.

'Dom, what's going on?'

'Are you coming in or are you going to stand out here asking daft questions, for fuck's sake?' Dom asked, his eyes large, face bright with anger.

Knowing from his short time with Dom in Hollybush that it was best to let the gale of his anger blow over, Ian swallowed his irritation at Dom's tone and smiled.

'And it's nice to see you too, wee man,' Ian said. He stepped forward and pulled Dom into a hug. Felt a tremble. Thought, need to get to the bottom of this. Walked past him into the flat, down a dim corridor into the main living space.

While Dom caught up with him, he had thirty seconds to look around and assess how his friend was living.

The living room was a good size and was kitted out in the nearest charity shop chic. A brown velour covered sofa with wooden arms and legs. Two matching armchairs. A small coffee table with coasters placed on each corner. A small flat-screen TV sat in the far corner, on a glass table. On the floor beside it a PS4 and a tall pile of games.

The walls were covered in a geometric print wallpaper that had probably not been on display in any wallpaper shop for at least four decades. Orange and brown. They were bare of artwork, but the panoramic window offered a view over the city that would have put any pictures to shame. To the side of the window was a door, which led out to a small balcony. Ten months of wind and rain being perfect balcony weather, thought Ian. Did the architects who built this for Glasgow city council not read the brief?

A gas fire and dark pine fire surround was the only other piece of furniture in the room. The top of it bearing some framed photos of a small boy.

The floor was covered in a fawn carpet that looked as if it had been hoovered to within an inch of its life. The flat was functional without being cosy. It was also spotless. Looked like Dom was on top of that at least.

'Have a seat, mate,' Dom said as he limped into the living room. 'And I'll put the kettle on.'

Ian leaned forward towards the fire surround and studied the photos. They all showed a small boy in various growth spurts. From the just-out-of-the-maternity-ward pic, swamped by a padded suit, to what Ian judged was a more recent photo. He picked it up and felt himself smile in response to the huge toothy grin on the boy in the photo. Blond hair, blue eyes and delighted that his daddy was there by his side. No one would ever doubt the parentage of this kid, thought Ian. The resemblance between the two of them was striking.

'Let me, dude,' said Ian. 'We both know I'll only have to carry it through after you've made it.'

'Wait . . .' Dom started to protest, but Ian was past him, back into the corridor and pushing open a door he guessed would lead into the kitchen.

'Jesus,' he said as he took in the sight. He heard Dom arrive just behind him.

'I had a wee episode,' he said.

Sure you did, thought Ian, and wondered if the guys on the landing had anything to do with it. He stepped inside the small square room and picked the kettle up from the floor. As he put it on its electrical rest, he looked around himself. The appliances and the sink were all spotless. And this re-assured him. What worried him was the crockery spread in shards over the floor and the cornflakes that crunched underfoot. Looked like the box had exploded.

'Can't control it, mate,' Dom said. 'I get angry and can't stop myself.'

'Fair enough,' said Ian. 'It's the bullet, not you.'

He watched as Dom picked up a broom and began to sweep the floor and had to restrain himself from helping. Instead, he picked up the kettle again and carried it over to the sink where he filled it up. Then he put it in the electrical dock and switched it on.

'The mugs are in the cupboard above the kettle,' Dom said. 'Along with the tea and coffee.' He managed a smile. 'If I stick stuff in cupboards it means when I go mental I don't sweep everything onto the floor.'

He was handling a long-handled broom and shovel combination with a one-handed dexterity that was impressive. Ian guessed that this wasn't a first.

Drinks made, Ian carried them through to the living room and set them on the low coffee table. Taking care to use the coasters. The table top was so scarred it wasn't worth the effort, but they were obviously there for a reason, he judged, so best use them.

He sat and fell into the deep cushion of the sofa. Thinking he'd need a crane to get him back out, he stretched forward for his coffee and took a sip.

'So, who were those wankers?' he asked when Dom sat down.

Dom made a face. 'Och, you don't want to know, mate.'

Ian studied his friend. Knew he was hiding something and thought he'd let it pass but keep an eye out.

'The wee man's your spitting image.' He changed the subject and Dom was like a different man. Lighter and brighter.

'Yeah, handsome wee bugger, eh?'

'See much of him?' Ian asked.

'Every other Saturday afternoon.'

Ian nodded, not sure what to say, but thinking if he was in Dom's shoes, and that was the only time he was allowed with his child, he'd be knocking down social services' door and demanding a recount.

'They want to see me settle in and settle down. See how the head injury affects my behaviour. If I show some improvement they might let him stay over.'

'Great,' said Ian, thinking that was shite. 'What about this place? How's it suiting you?'

'S'fine,' Dom answered, hiding the lie behind the act of putting his mug to his mouth and sipping his drink.

'The tenth floor?'

'S'fine.'

'Does the lift ever break down?'

'Only every other day,' answered Dom with a what-can-you-do half-smile.

'Dom, that's shit,' said Ian. 'You're half paralysed and you're

30

on the tenth floor of a building where the lift often breaks down. Mate, you need to do something. This is not good for you.'

'It's only temporary, Ian. The whole block is scheduled to come down at the end of the year. Then I'll be re-housed.' He gave a small laugh. 'Think I'm one of the few white faces in this building. It's full of them asylum seekers. Poor bastards.'

'You getting help, buddy?' Ian asked. 'There's loads of organisations set up to help ex-squaddies. Need any help with any of that shit?' He mentally reviewed Dom's situation. It just wasn't good enough. The tenth floor of a doomed tower block for a young man who was partially paralysed and emotionally incontinent? 'The help's there, Dom. You just need to ask for it.'

'Aye, I know. I'll get on it tomorrow.'

Sure you will, thought Ian. If it comes to you, you'll take it, but you won't go looking. Won't want to be a pest or a burden. Won't want to do anything that will dent your pride.

Ian recognised the increase in the pitch of Dom's voice and thought he'd better stop questioning him. It might start to sound like constant criticism rather than genuine care for his well-being.

'How you filling your time?' he asked.

'I got the PlayStation for the wee man.' He nodded towards the corner of the room where it sat. 'And I'm utter shite. So I'm practising for his next visit, so he doesn't show up his old man.' He laughed.

'I've never been one for computer games,' said Ian. 'They're for spotty geeks who can't get laid.'

'Piss off,' said Dom. 'I'm getting plenty.'

'Sure you are,' said Ian. 'Pulled it off yet?'

'It's red raw, mate,' laughed Dom.

'What about your missus? Any chance of you two patching things up?'

'Doubt it,' answered Dom. 'She can't handle the change . . . the way I've become. Who can blame her, eh? She's only twenty-four.

She's got one five-year-old. Doesn't need an adult who also acts like a five-year-old.' He stared into the distance. Looked as if he was seeing nothing but his own uselessness. Tears flowing down his face. He wiped them off his cheek with his sleeve. Looked everywhere but into Ian's eyes.

Said, 'Shit. I can't control nothing.'

Ian stayed a few hours, trying to learn how to play games on the PlayStation and failing like that was his mission in life. Once he judged that Dom was sufficiently diverted from the giant lump of shit that was his life, he left with a promise that he'd be back soon.

His car was still there. Undented and without its mini chaperone. She did say she would only be there for an hour.

Ian looked around. The only people he'd seen since he arrived were Myleene and the three bozos outside Dom's flat. Where was everyone?

He jumped in the car and drove off. Passing the tiny supermarket at the bottom of the road, he recognised a small figure leaving the shop carrying what looked like a bag of groceries.

He braked and rolled down his window as he drew up alongside Myleene.

'Told you I would only be there for an hour, mate,' she said, with the subtext: you're not getting a refund. She continued walking.

'I'm not bothered about that,' Ian said while kerb-crawling alongside her. Realising this might not look too healthy to onlookers, he parked the car and stepped out on to the pavement. When Myleene saw this she started to run.

'Oh, for . . .' Ian chased after her. Realising that this might look even worse than the kerb-crawling he slowed down and shouted after her. 'Ok, if you don't want any more cash, keep running.'

She slowed, turned when she was about twenty yards away and studied him from under the visor of her cap. Ian couldn't see her eyes in the shadow, but he could make out the line of her lips and the point of her chin.

'Whit do I need to do for the cash?' she asked.

There was a low wall halfway between them. Ian walked to it and sat down, making himself smaller, less of a threat.

'I need you to keep an eye on a mate. Run errands for him and stuff.'

She said nothing.

'You got a mobile?'

She snorted as if this was the silliest question she'd ever been asked.

'What floor do you live on?'

'Whit's that got to do wi' you?' She took two steps towards him.

'My mate lives on ten.'

'The soldier?'

'How do you know?'

'There's a few old families in there. Most of the others are . . .' she paused while she sought the words, ' . . . on an asylum thing. The other one wis a soldier.'

'Right. That's my mate, Dom. He might need a wee hand now and again. You up for it?'

'It'll cost you.' She took another few steps towards him. Reached the end of the wall and sat, placing her small bag of shopping on the ground between her feet.

'What you got there?' Ian asked. From his angle he could see the red and white squares on the cover of a Mother's Pride plain loaf and the corner of a box of cornflakes.

Myleene shot the bag a look of longing. As if she couldn't wait to get inside and eat the contents. 'Stuff,' she answered.

'I love stuff,' said Ian. 'Especially in a big bowl of milk.'

Myleene giggled and Ian caught a glimpse of the child beneath the carapace of street. He pulled a tenner out of his pocket and handed it to her. It disappeared into one of her pockets. 'There will be more when I hear you've been a good help to Dom.'

'Whit's wrong wi' him? Is he no just young? How can he no do stuff for hisself?'

'He got shot in the head.'

Myleene's mouth fell open as she digested this. 'My da's brother was in the army. Got killed in one of them *'stan* places.'

'Yeah, Dom should have died, but the bullet went right through. Mashed his brain and affected lots of things. Made him paralysed down one side of his body.'

She pushed her cap back on her head so she could see him more easily. 'How does a bullet in the head do that to somebody?'

'Parts of your brain control different parts of your body,' he replied, and stretching forward pressed a finger against her forehead. 'That part affects you when you go to the toilet. If you get shot there, you pee the bed.'

'Eh?'

Then he pressed the top of her head. 'This bit affects the way you like chocolate. If you get shot here you'd rather eat mud.' He lifted his hand to the back of her head. 'And if you get shot here you walk like a penguin.'

She grinned. 'You're daft.'

'Aye,' he chuckled. 'You up for it then?'

She nodded, her head moving back and forth fast to demonstrate her eagerness to help.

'Get your phone.' She did. 'Save this number.' He gave her his number, and with her tongue sticking out she dialled it in. 'My name's Ian.'

'Saved,' she said.

'Right. Call me.'

She did. His phone rang and he saved her number.

'Cool,' he said. 'I'll tell him if he needs any shopping done to call you and you'll fetch it for him, for a wee fee?'

She nodded again, her eyes bright with the possibilities.

'Before I go,' said Ian as he stood up. 'Some guys left just after I arrived.' He described them. 'Did you see them?'

Myleene said, 'Aye. My maw says I've to run soon as I see that bald guy. Says he's bad news.' She studied her feet and gave a little shiver.

'What have you seen, Myleene?' Ian took a leap. There was more to her reaction than just a warning from a protective mother.

'Got to go.' She got to her feet as if moving to some silent signal and ran before he could ask her anything more.

5

'Dimitri and O'Neill Investigations – let us find the bastard for you.'

'Dimitri, remind me. Your phone does have caller recognition, yeah?' asked Kenny.

'Course it does, boss. You think I speak to actual customers like that?'

'We have actual customers?'

'Not really.'

Kenny grinned, enjoying the banter. The "investigations" side of the business was purely for his own use. Part of his trade was in information. The right detail in the wrong hands could make him a lot of money, and Dimitri was as skilled as they come in ferreting it out.

They met when Dimitri was half-heartedly selling him stolen goods. Kenny realised he was probably the worst would-be criminal he'd ever met, and when he heard what Dimitri's real skills were, he took him on.

'I need you to do some research for me.'

'Fire away.'

Kenny fished a business card out of his wallet. 'Her name is Christine . . .' He read out her telephone number.

'That's it?' Dimitri was incredulous. 'Her first name and her telephone number?'

'That's all I have.'

Kenny preferred his girlfriends to come with a price tag. Kept things uncomplicated. Everyone knew where they stood. Except with his last "girlfriend", Alexis, things had become very complicated indeed. He had fallen in love with her, tried to protect her from her pimp boss and ended up being betrayed as Alexis was used as a pawn to get to him and his "disappeared" father.

The motive was revenge for past sins, and he and his father almost paid the ultimate price. Subsequently, Alexis was told to get out of Glasgow, and whenever he felt an urge for one of his girls grow beyond just getting his dick wet, he vowed he would know everything about them first.

He recognised that his interest in Christine had a little bit more of an edge, and before he saw more of her, he wanted to be confident her agenda was nothing more than a payday.

'Where did you meet her? Let's start with that,' said Dimitri.

'In Circus, the downstairs bar in that new hotel on Great Western Road. Hotel Pasha.'

'I take it her affections were, how can I say it? Negotiable?'

'She's a working girl, Dimitri. No need to go beating about that bush.'

'Pun intended?' Dimitri giggled, sounding a lot younger than his fifty years.

'Jesus, you're way too alert this morning.'

'Sue me.'

'If only,' Kenny mumbled. 'Right. You know everything I know. Go to it, my good man.' He hung up.

Next order for the day was a workout. A challenging hour-long circuit of body weight exercises left him drenched in sweat and pleasantly aching. A hot shower followed by a high-protein breakfast and a black coffee and he was braced and ready for the rest of his day.

And the first item on the agenda was to go and spend some time with an old friend in a graveyard.

6

Kenny pulled his collar up against the late autumn chill. Stuffed his hands in his jacket pockets, wishing he'd remembered to put on a pair of gloves. Even for Glasgow at this time of the year it was cold.

He'd only been here once before, at the funeral, and he hoped he would be able to recall which grave he was looking for. Gravel crunched and popped underfoot, and the little boy in him couldn't resist kicking up the crisp, brown leaves that piled together at the side of the path. Perhaps it wasn't the done thing in a burial ground, but if McBain could see him, he'd only laugh.

Judging by the shine on these memorial stones, it was a fair bet that Kenny was in the more recent part of the cemetery. He read a few of the names and began a series of calculations. Couldn't help it. The numbers were all spelt out, and it was amazing how young most of these people were when they died. Graham was 44. Mike 48. And Lucy was only 38. Shit, that is young, he thought and began to come up with reasons why they might have died so young. He was aware that people of Glasgow had lower life expectancy than any other British city, but these people hadn't even reached a middle age, never mind an old age.

Jesus, you're getting melancholic, Kenny. Give it a rest. He kicked another pile of leaves and walked on. He recognised a tree at the far end of the path. The fork in its trunk and the crazy lean on the heavier right branch sparked a memory of him noticing it last time he was here.

He paused as grief and guilt hitched a twist in his gut.

He should have been there. He should have done something.

He took a left at the end of the path and knew that the grave he was seeking was just twenty or so yards further on.

Kenny picked up his pace when he saw the simple stone and a familiar figure standing before it. They turned when they heard his footsteps and gave a little nod in acknowledgement.

'Awright, Kenny?' the man said.

'Sure, Ray,' he replied and looked at the stone. It was pink marble and had a simple carving. Maggie Gallacher. R.I.P. and the date of her death.

Kenny offered his old friend a smile and said nothing. What could he say? Then as Ray crouched down to arrange the bunch of flowers he brought with him, Kenny studied his oldest friend. He seemed to have aged in the last year. His skin was the pallor of putty and the two-day growth on his cheeks was almost white.

Looked like he'd lost a few stone as well. For most of their life Ray had been a yo-yo dieter. Gaining and losing the same thirty pounds on a seemingly annual cycle. If only he'd known grief would have provided a solution, he wouldn't have bothered.

After Maggie died, Ray retreated from the world. Was given time off work to recover from his own, almost fatal wounding and avoided most attempts at contact from his friends.

Kenny flashed back to that scene. He'd never forget walking into that bedroom and seeing Ray lying there on his back, naked, with a large knife sticking out of his chest.

Once he'd dealt with the attacker – at this thought Kenny pulled his hands out of his pockets, made a fist and examined his knuckles; he'd broken bones on both hands when he methodically beat Leonard to death – only then, once the mist of his rage had passed, did he think to check if either Ray or Maggie were still alive.

He tried Maggie first. There was nothing. No pulse, no breath and her flesh was cold. He'd never forget the chill from her skin when he put his fingers to her neck.

Ray was pale, but there was a faint pulse. He worried that pulling the knife out might cause greater injury so he left it in while he called 999.

Kenny shook his head as if trying to slough off the image. 'Why . . .' The words were stuck in his throat. He coughed and tried again. 'Why are we meeting here, Ray?'

'It was a year ago. Can you believe it?' Ray stared at the tombstone as if seeing a universal truth. Swallowed. The corner of his mouth twitched as if his brain had sent the order to smile and his lips had forgotten how to form that shape. 'She'd laugh if she saw how maudlin I'd become. Tell me to get a grip.'

'Yeah,' said Kenny, more from a need to acknowledge his friend than to offer agreement. He didn't really know Maggie well enough to know if that's what she would say. 'Don't know if she had any time for me, to be honest.'

Ray raised his eyebrows in agreement. 'You were my mate, so she was fine with that. Thought you were incredibly vain. What was it she said? If he was made of chocolate . . .'

' . . . he'd have nibbled his knob down to a nub.' Kenny finished the sentence with a smile. Maggie did have a memorable way with words at times.

Ray stood up, put a hand on Kenny's shoulder. Looked deep into his eyes. Whatever he saw there satisfied him, and he said, 'C'mon. Let's go somewhere warm. We need to talk, and I have a powerful thirst.'

7

The bald guy was called Barry Gibbs. And yes, his mother was a fan of the music from Saturday Night Fever, and if the daft bint had survived the heroin overdose she took to celebrate his fifth birthday, he'd never have got tired of slapping her for saddling him with such a fucked-up moniker.

Still. People learned. Sing the opening bars of 'Staying Alive' in his hearing and a broken nose would be the least of your worries. The last guy who did it was permanently wearing an eye patch.

He shortened his name to Baz.

Part of him was grateful to his mother. The near constant slagging he got as a kid and his increasingly violent reactions had turned him into the man he had become.

The army had finished the job. Given him the necessary skill set. Let him work with his natural aggression: taught him to savour knuckle on bone. Until he was even too much for his commanding officers and given a dishonourable discharge. This lead to a happy few years as a soldier for hire working in some of the planet's most dangerous places.

See the world. Get to kill lots of poor people.

He should get that printed on a t-shirt, he thought with a grin.

Now he was back in his home city for a wee break. Things had become too hot in his last tour. A local warlord had put a reward on his head after he had, quite accidentally, shot his son. A pitiful ten thousand dollars. An insult, quite frankly, but to the people in that region it was a princely sum and he had to get out.

Home. He looked out of his riverside penthouse flat, along the dark ribbon of the Clyde, towards the silver, space age shapes that had sprung up on both sides of the river. Progress, he sneered. The city fathers might have grand ideas as to how the city should move towards the next century, but its inhabitants would always bring them back down to earth. He laughed at how the Clyde Arc had been re-named *The Squinty Bridge* even before it was open to traffic.

Glasgow. You got to love it.

He kicked his legs away from the quilt that twisted itself around his legs as he slept. What was that all about? Was as if he'd been jogging in his sleep. He could remember part of one dream that had been on repeat since he came home.

In his dream he had a bull mastiff as a pet. Which was nonsense as he was terrified of dogs. He was bitten as a kid. By one of his mother's druggie friends' dogs and had never got over it. Couldn't even remember it happening, but the fear remained.

As he walked across to his en-suite bathroom and aimed a stream of piss into the bowl he thought about this dream pet. It was a huge bastard, but it loved him. Wagged its tail like it was trying to shake it off. Slobbered all over him.

Baz shook off the last few drops, flushed and moved over to the mirror. Examined his neck. Almost expected to see tooth marks, so real was the repeated moment in the dream when the dog would lie on the bed beside him and open its mouth wide, holding his neck in its maw. There he would hear the dog's heavy breathing and feel its teeth on either side of his neck, pressing with just enough force to reduce the blood flow to his brain. Letting him know that with just a little effort it could pierce skin, muscle and ligament and tear out his throat.

He turned on the cold water tap and placed his hands there and sluiced the water over his face, hoping the chill would banish the dream from his mind. Then walked into the open-plan kitchen-living space. Filled the kettle and looked at the mail he received the day before.

One of the first pieces of mail he'd received after he picked up the keys to his flat was a letter from a fellow mercenary. Jean-Claude was Belgian, living in London, and his version of a congratulations on your new home card was an excerpt from The Economist, no less, saying that Glasgow may have a higher concentration of psychopaths than any other city in Europe. Jean-Claude had scribbled with a sharpie across the top of the page, *Welcome Home – there goes the neighbourhood*!

A text alert sounded on his phone. It was Harry. Wasn't his real name, but it suited, what with the Potter spectacles. *Time to go*, he was saying. So Baz dressed and in jig time he was out the door and heading towards Harry's BMW in front of the building.

There was something about the man, thought Baz as he made his way down in the lift. Something not quite right, and that was saying something after all the fucked-up characters he'd dealt with over the years. But he'd been sent by the London bosses so had to put up with him. For now. But first chance he got, the guy was history.

He climbed in the car and Harry drove off without a word. And by the time he reached his destination, near Partick Cross some twenty minutes later, he still hadn't said a word. The car stopped outside a tenement building on the main drag.

'Number 18,' said Harry. 'Flat 6B. Give him a fright.' He handed Baz a small gun, complete with silencer, and Baz knew what was needed.

A former soldier was dealing for them. He'd allowed his junkie customers to do him over instead of paying their inflated prices.

His name was Billy and just a few minutes later he was on his knees in front of Gibbs. Begging.

'I'll get the money, big man,' he said, terror bleaching his expression.

'Too late,' said Baz, pulling the gun from his pocket and aiming it at the man's right knee. He thought of The Economist article and grinned. *Psychopath*. That was one label he was more than willing to live up to.

Back in the car, Harry held a hand out for the gun. Felt the heat.

'This has been fired,' he said in that deadpan voice Baz was learning to hate.

'Aye.'

'He's not dead is he?'

'No. What do you think I am, a bloody idiot? A wee bullet in the kneecap sends a message, don't you think?'

Baz looked over at Harry. His expression a challenge. *What the fuck is your problem*? If it was possible, Harry's face was even paler than normal. His lips an angry line.

'I've got some big fights coming up. I had my eye on Billy. No way he's gonna be fighting now.'

'Should have said the gun was a prop, you arsehole. Somebody hands me a gun, I use it.'

'My guys know what I mean when I hand 'em a gun,' Harry replied. Behind his glasses his eyes were mostly black, and despite himself Baz felt a chill. 'You owe me, Gibbs,' said Harry. 'Find me a fighter. And soon.'

'What kind of fighter do you need?' Baz asked as he mentally scrolled through the guys he knew.

'When I say fighter, I mean a patsy. A pulse and the ability to stand upright will do.' Baz formed a smile and had an image of some poor sap bent and bloodied while men in suits stood around screaming for more.

'I think I know the very man.'

8

A couple of days later. Ian approached Dom's door, his knuckles prepped, ready to knock when he heard a scream coming from the inside. He was about to put his shoulder to the door when it was followed by a cheer and then a high-pitched giggle.

His shoulders sagged in relief and he shook his head in self-mockery. It's been a long time since you were in a warzone, Ian. There's no need to jump every time you hear a loud noise.

Heart rate slowing to normal, he rapped on the door. Heard a shout.

'Coming.'

Then the drumbeat of a child running before the door opened. A familiar face peered up at him.

'It's you,' said Myleene with a grin.

'And it's you,' replied Ian.

Myleene stared up at him, her eyes bright with the need to have fun. 'What?'

'Letting me in?'

'What's the password?'

'Celtic,' replied Ian.

Snort. 'You're *never* getting in.'

Then a voice sounded from behind her.

'If it's Ian, Myleene, just let him in.'

Ian stuck out his tongue.

'You're Ian?'

Ian nodded.

'Awww,' she responded and stepped aside. 'I wanted you to guess what the password was.'

As he strode past her, Ian thought about some of the PS4 games he'd noticed in the pile beside the TV the last time he was here. 'Lego,' he said.

'How did you guess that?' asked Myleene as she trotted behind him on the way along the short corridor to the living room.

'Easy,' said Ian. 'I'm a total genius.'

Myleene made a noise through pursed lips. Then said, 'Yeah, sure you are.'

'You are far too smart for your age, young lady,' said Ian and reached out to muss up her hair. Then feeling like that was possibly the most patronising thing he'd ever done, he jammed his hand back into his pocket. Just how do you talk to children these days?

'Ian,' said Dom with a big smile as Ian walked in. And for the first time since he'd met him Ian realised how young his friend was. 'Myleene is just showing me how to play these games.' His grin widened. 'The wee man's coming over day after tomorrow and I need to get ready.'

He was sitting on an armchair. On his lap was a cushioned tray, much like the one he imagined lonely and elderly people might use to rest their dinner on while watching soaps on TV. In this case, resting on the tray was a control for the game console.

Dom read his glance and explained. 'Got myself a one-handed control. It helps to have something to rest it on when my arm gets tired.'

'Cool,' said Ian. 'Who's winning?'

'Me,' said Myleene.

'Only 'cos I let you,' replied Dom.

'As if,' was Myleene's easy retort. 'You're rubbish.' Then when she read Dom's expression of disappointment. 'But you're getting better.'

Ian laughed. He was impressed that the two of them had already struck up such a relaxed relationship, and delighted that his hunch was working out. He moved over to the sofa and sat down. Myleene picked up the other remote and sat on the floor at Dom's feet, resting her back on the side rest of his armchair.

'Get you a drink, mate?' asked Dom, keeping his eye on the screen. 'You can have anything as long as it's coffee.'

'Water will do,' said Ian, looking at Dom and thinking he needed to get him on his own for a minute. 'Myleene, would you mind getting me a glass?'

'Jeez, what did your last slave die of?'

'Please, Myleene?' asked Dom. 'I should really do it, but . . .'

Myleene jumped to her feet. 'Sure, Dom. You asked nicer.' She stuck out her tongue at Ian and left the room.

'Brilliant idea, mate,' said Dom, nodding his head in Myleene's direction. 'She's been a godsend.'

'Aye,' said Ian, 'she's a wee character.' He paused. 'Did you check that this was alright with her mum? People can be funny about this kind of thing.'

'Ian, mate, that's sick. She's just a wee lassie.'

'You're one of the good guys, Ian. But there are some dangerous people out there and folk might not like the idea of a single, adult male having a vulnerable wee girl coming in and out of his flat. They'll put two and two together and come up with something twisted.' Ian felt like a prick, but it had to be said.

Dom's mouth opened as he considered this. 'To be honest, I never gave it a thought. She's done some shopping for me, like you suggested, but then she spied the games and asked for a wee shot. What was I to say? No, in case folk think I'm a kiddie-fiddler?'

Myleene entered the room, carrying a glass of water for me and a packet of crisps probably for herself. 'Fiddling what?' she asked.

Dom picked up his controller and waved it in the air. 'This.'

She made a face. 'That's a weird word.' She looked at me. 'And my mum knows where I am.'

Right. Of course. She'd heard every word.

'If you're going to be teaching Dom how to play this stuff, it wouldn't hurt for him to meet your mum and let her know what you guys were doing,' Ian said.

Myleene made a face. A shadow forming over her expression. 'Doesn't care. She just sleeps off the Buckie all the time. As long as I'm no under her feet.'

Dom waved the controller at me. 'Fancy a fiddle?' he asked with a smile.

'I've got no interest in this crap,' Ian said. 'Gaming has completely passed me by.'

'That's 'cos you're old,' said Myleene. 'My mum says she hates it 'cos she's old.'

Dom laughed at the expression on Ian's face.

'Owned, mate,' he managed to say between splutters of laughter. 'You were totally owned by a ten-year-old.'

Before he knew it, the three of them had dissolved into giggles.

When the laughter abated and Dom and Myleene had once again become lost in the Lego gaming world, Ian watched his young soldier friend and was cheered by the change in him. There was optimism for the first time in a long time. He had a home. His son was visiting soon, and if people had minds that were too ready to go to that sort of place, then fuck 'em. Fuck the lot of them.

9

The Blue Owl was a late-night jazz club at the wrong end of the city centre. It didn't ever get a licence to sell alcohol beyond midnight and never managed to book any decent jazz musicians. Yet it managed to make a profit.

This was one part of the legal side of Kenny's business empire. A crucial part that allowed him to access the cash made from the side – the cash that gave legal the finger.

The titular owl was perched on the wall over the bar. A giant installation made from car bumpers, fashioned loosely into a shape that would please only the most relaxed of twitchers. To help satisfy anyone who had hopes of listening to some actual jazz, Al Jarreau was wittering on about moonlight over the sound system.

Kenny approached the bar, leaned on it and looked at Ray. 'What you having?'

Ray looked at his watch. Gave it some thought. 'Coffee?'

'Piss off,' said Kenny. 'You a poof?'

Ray gave a small smile in reply. 'What are you, twelve?'

'Just yankin' your chain. Coffee it is,' replied Kenny. Then he looked along the bar for a member of staff. 'Hello,' he shouted. 'Anyone there?'

A voice came from the corner of the room. 'She had to go to the loo. Said to tell anyone who came in she'd just be a minute.' Kenny turned round to look at the only other customer in the place.

Sitting in the far right corner was an old man, a pint of Guinness and a folded cloth cap on the table in front of him. His small head seemed to float above a heavily cushioned jacket, and fine lines radiated over his face like the contour map of a particularly hilly location. He was hunched in his seat like he'd come in off the street to dodge a coffin.

'Like your jazz?' Kenny asked him.

The old man screwed up his face in reply. Asked for clarification. 'Whit?'

'Thought as much,' mumbled Kenny. 'Need to do something about this place, he said to Ray. 'This isn't going to convince anyone.'

'Eh?' said Ray mimicking the old man, but his expression told Kenny he knew exactly what he was talking about. The Blue Owl would need to have more of a buzz than this to convince any stray money-laundering investigator that the income coming through this place was legit.

They waited for another thirty seconds.

'Fuck this,' said Kenny and walked behind the bar. The coffee machine was similar to the one he had at home, so he set about serving himself and Ray.

Carrying their drinks, they made for a seat at the other end of the room from the old man.

Ray sat down with a low groan.

'Getting old, Ray,' said Kenny.

Ray took a sip of his drink. 'Just what the doctor ordered.' Looked up at Kenny. 'For my old age.'

'What prompted this then?' asked Kenny. 'It's not every day I get a summons from the great Ray McBain.'

'Like I said. It's the anniversary today,' said Ray. He swallowed, looked up from his coffee to meet Kenny's gaze, and Kenny read the weight of his friend's grief, in his eyes, in his skin and in the pale of his lips. He looked like he'd aged ten years in the last twelve months.

'Aye,' said Kenny. What else could he say? He leaned back

in his seat and waited for Ray to continue. Whatever it was he wanted to say, he'd get there in his own time.

'You've no need to feel responsible, Kenny.'

And it looked like he wasn't going to waste any more.

'Who says I do?' Kenny swallowed. He was way too sober to go into this.

Ray pursed his lips. Blew over the top of his drink. 'I know you too well, Mr O'Neill. We've barely spoken in the last year . . .' Kenny opened his mouth to speak, but Ray didn't give him a chance. ' . . . and don't give me the just-giving-me-space routine. I needed you, mate, and you were posted missing.'

'I . . .' Kenny sat upright and looked anywhere but into Ray's face.

'So, I thought it was time. I need to start living again. And we need to get this out in the open. I was the one who fell asleep on the job. Quite literally.'

'Aye, but . . .'

'But, your job that night was to watch over Alessandra Rossi. We knew that Leonard would come after one of the girls before he came after me. So, you had to be there while I . . .' Ray coughed, 'tried to protect Maggie.'

'Fuck,' said Kenny. A single syllable that was drawn out and laden with his guilt and disappointment at himself. He leaned forward on the table, chin propped up on one hand.

'I can't handle your guilt as well as mine, Kenny, so get over yourself, eh?' Ray adopted a similar posture to Kenny. 'Besides, *you* got the bogeyman.'

'Aye.' And Kenny was back in that room, out of breath, arms like lead, winding up for just one more punch.

'I saw the medical report.' Ray raised an eyebrow. 'Brutal.'

'How does that fit into legal procedure?'

'Alessandra thought it might help me to see what kind of number you did on Leonard.'

'Who says I was even there?'

'Ale didn't,' answered Ray. 'Or you'd be doing life at Her Majesty's leisure.'

Kenny raised his coffee cup. 'Here's to DC Alessandra Rossi.'

'She says to tell you not to get used to it. Next time she'll have you in handcuffs quicker than you can say Police Scotland.'

'She wants me, she really does.'

'In your dreams,' laughed Ray, and for the first time that day Kenny caught a real glimpse of his old friend.

Ray looked at Kenny. 'We're good?'

'We're good.'

'What about you? Any word from Alexis?'

'Jesus, you're really in a talkative mood today,' said Kenny.

'I've barely been out of the house for the last year. Making up for lost time,' Ray replied. His voice heavy with irony. 'Don't worry. Normal service will be resumed shortly. I'll be as talkative as a church gargoyle.'

'That's a suitable metaphor. What with you being an ugly bastard,' said Kenny, relaxing a little now that the real business of the day had been conducted.

Alexis. For a man like him who had issues with trust, forgiveness for her betrayal of him was simply not up for debate. 'Last I heard she was in London.'

'That it?'

'What more do you want? She fucked me over. End of.'

Ray made a face.

'What?'

'Nothing,' answered Ray.

'That's not nothing,' replied Kenny. 'That's something with a silent, ugly gargoyle face.'

Ray grinned. 'Piss off. And you know what I mean. You had something with Alexis. Isn't that worth working through the shit for?'

'So now you're going to give me the "I've been close to death" speech? Life's too short? Bugger that for a game of soldiers.'

Kenny took a last sip of his coffee and placed the cup on the saucer. Hard. 'Where is that barmaid, for fuck's sake? What am I paying her for?'

Ray sat back in his chair. Looked at Kenny.

'Aye. Ok,' said Kenny. 'I'll calm down.' He gave a small smile. 'It still hurts, you know? I don't let the walls down easily.'

'Why is that, do you think?'

Kenny cocked his head, the way a dog might look quizzically at its human. 'What is this? Bored with gazing into your own navel, so you're peering into mine? Piss off. And anyway, that's a ten-whisky question.'

'And that's the problem right there, Kenny. 'cos after only six whiskies, you're under the table.'

'True,' said Kenny with a grin. 'My Scottish credentials are shot to shit when it comes to handling the drink.' He scratched the side of his face. His neck. Felt the heat building there. Needed to get the conversation away from him and Alexis.

'What about the job?' he asked. 'You back at work?'

Ray shook his head. 'I'm leaving the police.'

'Wait. Really?'

Ray nodded his head.

'You're leaving the police?'

'Aye.'

'Won't it like, fall into a terminal state without you? Won't the criminal underclass take over the world without you being there to sort them out?'

'Something like that,' Ray answered quietly, and Kenny saw the change in his friend. He was calmer, centred: notwithstanding the weight of his grief. He'd run the gauntlet, let it tear away much that darkened his mind and come out the other side with a different appreciation of life and what really mattered.

Kenny grew serious. 'Man, this is big. You sure about this? Police work is your life, Ray.'

'It *was* my life. Nearly cost me my life on several occasions.'

He looked over Kenny's shoulder as if all of the arguments and counter arguments floated there. 'I'm done, buddy. Can't stomach it anymore.'

'What are you going to do?'

'Dunno.' He shrugged. 'Do I need to do anything? Can't I just *be* for a while?'

'You've been reading that Buddhist mind-shit again, haven't you?'

A half-smile response. 'Something like that.'

'Well, roger me with a baseball bat and call me Sue. Ray McBain is no longer a cop.' He looked at his watch. 'That must be cause for celebration. Whisky?'

'If you are insisting.'

'I'm insisting,' Kenny said as he stood. Paused as a thought hit him. 'Does that mean I can tempt you over to the dark side?'

'As long as I get to be the woman in this relationship,' Ray said, primping his lips.

'Piss off, dafty. I mean the *dark* side. You could be my right-hand man. No one is going to mess with O'Neill and McBain.'

'Yeah, that's never going to happen.'

'Aww. How not?'

'You know, conscience?' Ray laughed. 'Anyway, where's that whisky?'

Kenny turned. 'Coming right up.' Then mumbled, 'Just as soon as I find a member of staff.'

Just then a small, slim woman in a black shirt and faded jeans walked through a door at the far right of the bar. She pushed her long, black hair back out of her vision and blinked as if the light was too much for her. Once her eyes had adjusted, she formed a smile as if she'd dredged it up from the place where lost greetings go.

'Can I help you, buddy?' she asked.

Kenny walked over to her, pausing just beyond where most people's personal space was set. Saying nothing, he looked at her as if summing her up.

54

'Eh, can I help you?' she asked again, suddenly unsure of herself.

Kenny lowered his voice. 'If I was to do a tox test on you right now, sweetheart, would I find anything untoward in your blood?'

'You the polis?' she bristled.

'No. Worse than that,' said Kenny. 'I'm the owner. You've got five minutes to grab your things and leave.'

'You're the owner? How come I've never met you?' She pulled herself up to her full five feet of outrage.

Kenny pulled out his wallet. Found a card. Waved it under her nose.

'Blue Owl Enterprises,' he said. 'Recognise that from your payslip? See the bit that says Managing Director? That's me. Now kindly fuck off.'

She turned. Walked back through the door she had just come from. Returned moments later, walking with one sleeve in her jacket and the other arm reaching behind her struggling to find the space for her hand. She paused in her walk long enough to find it and, shrugging the jacket into place, walked over to Kenny.

'You owe me two days' pay,' she said, jutting her chin out.

'I owe you bugger all, darling. You were through the back office getting jacked. Now piss off before I kick you out.'

'Charming,' she said, and with as much dignity as she could muster she turned and walked out of the door.

Kenny then walked behind the bar. Had a scan through the malt whisky shelf. Picked one starting with Glen, because basically any whisky with Glen in the title was good shit right? Poured himself and Ray a stiff measure, filled a small jug with water and returned to his seat.

'Seems like we have a vacancy,' he said to Ray. 'Ever worked behind a bar?'

10

After the fight, Gavin was again hooded and led through into another part of the building. Stunned at what he had just experienced, at what he had just *done*, he allowed himself to be moved as if he were on casters.

As he walked, he held his eyes shut tight. His breathing amplified within the confines of the cloth bag.

Injuries he didn't realise he had started to register. Ribs on his right side. The point of his chin. His top lip. One eye was so swollen he could hardly open it. Points of pain that throbbed in a metronome to his pulse.

What had just happened?

Felt like it was all over in seconds.

He knew he had it in him to protect himself. After all, that had been his motive throughout his military career. Get in and get out with as little damage to himself as possible. Don't seek out the violence, police it. That had been his mantra. And it worked. Mostly. Any deaths he had contributed to had grown from that situation, but to actively set out to end someone?

Didn't know he had *that* in him. Perhaps it came from a year of living on the streets? Combine that with his military training and he was something to be reckoned with.

That moment at the end, before they pulled him off, felt so good.

Glorious.

There was no society. No restraint. Shackles shorn. Just him and the other guy and the need to stay alive.

And *he* was alive, with the tang and taint of blood in his mouth. Whose blood was it? His or the other guy's?

A flash and he saw himself biting down on the other guy's ear. Tightened his jaw. Sharply twisted his head and tore.

That wasn't him. Was it?

Man, it felt good.

A fucking delicious delirious glorious high. Someone got to pay for all the shit he'd been through over the last few years.

Now the low.

He felt drained. Surprised that he still had the energy to keep upright. All he wanted was to slip into his sleeping bag and hunker down in his doorway. But this guy was pushing him to keep walking. He prayed they'd stop soon and allow him to rest.

Then he remembered the money. It was in his jacket pocket. Still better be there.

He realised he hadn't been paying much attention to where he was going, his one available sense, his hearing, turned inwards. Drawing attention to it, he heard a beep, a door handle being turned and the swoosh of a door on carpet.

A few more steps, a hand on his chest, then the bag was removed. He blinked against the sharp light. Looking around himself he saw that he was in a small room. There was a large double bed and a sofa. One wall was curtained and the other held a desk area and large television. A hotel chain? Hotel Bland, judging by the lack of colour. Vanilla walls, blue bedspread and curtains.

'Take a seat, mate. Looks like you need one,' he heard and turned to face the speaker. It was the white-haired guy with the specs. Standing beside him was Dave who was wearing a grin like he was especially pleased with himself. Made Gavin think: just who the hell was fighting, mate?

He caught a look between the two of them. A look that was

all about self-interest. We've found something we can milk here. Some *one*.

Gavin would park that for the moment. Come back to ponder on it some more. In the meantime he needed a shower, food and sleep.

A long sleep.

As if he read his mind, Dave spoke. 'Bet you'd love to step under a shower right now, eh?'

Gavin could only nod.

'Cool,' said Dave and walked across to the desk. Picked up a piece of card. Looked like a menu. He handed it to Gavin.

'Have a look at this. See what you fancy and we'll order room service. By the time you've showered the food should be ready.'

Gavin took the menu. Read. Opened his jaw. Assessed his ability to chew without too much pain.

'A steak,' he said. 'Rare. And a big plate of chips.' Didn't bother with a "please". These guys owed him. He saw how much cash was moving about in that, what, underground car park?

'Shower,' he said and got to his feet.

'Throw out your clothes,' said Dave. 'And we'll get them cleaned. There's a bathrobe behind the toilet door.'

The water was wonderful. Hot and powerful, the jets of water stung at first, but then he gave into their promise of healing. Let it pour over his head and shoulders. Leaned back to get it full in the face, then his chest. Moved forward again so that the water could cascade down his neck and shoulders. Felt the pressure on his muscles. An easing.

He looked down at his legs. Bruising the length of his left thigh. That would really hurt in the morning. Still, it would be better than what the other guy was feeling. If he was feeling anything.

Was he even still alive? He examined his conscience and found that he didn't much care. You or me, mate, he thought.

There was a knock at the outer door. It opened. Low voices. Must be his food.

At the thought, his stomach issued a growl.

Reluctantly, he turned off the water, stepped out of the shower cubicle and grabbed a towel. He roughly dried himself, spotted a white, towelling robe hanging on the door and put it on.

The mirror was steamed up. He considered wiping it clean to have a look at himself. Decided against it. He would face that in the morning.

He opened the door and walked into the room. Spotted a tray of food on the desk. His stomach issued a groan. He knew, because of his limited access to food over the last months, he would have to take the food slowly and leave some of it on the plate or he'd suffer. He sat down. Picked up the knife and fork.

Before he could start eating, the white-haired guy leaned forward into his vision.

'Tomorrow,' he said. 'You and me do some talking.'

11

The weather was Glasgow grim. A uniform dark grey sky gravid with the intent to harm. Using wind to throw sheets of rain at the long-suffering inhabitants on the ground.

Water sliding down the outside of the window in solid bars reminded Kenny that often in his childhood his uncle Colin made this house feel like his own personal prison.

On the sofa, Kenny was surrounded by pink and frills. Doilies and china dolls. Throws and cushions. His aunt Violet was in complete control of this space, and it amused him as he sat on the sofa beside Ian, feeling like they must look like a pair of grizzly bears in a flower bed.

Ian shared the feeling and sent him a half-smile and a wink. Aunt Vi sat on her armchair, like it was her throne, her tiny frame swamped by cushion. The only person in the room who was not entirely comfortable was his uncle Colin. He looked like he had a bee trapped behind his teeth and a wasp stuck up his arse.

'At last,' chimed Violet. 'I thought I'd never get you two over here.' She looked from one to the other. 'My two big boys.' And she couldn't be more proud if they had been astronauts or brain surgeons.

At her use of the words "my two big boys", Kenny sat rigid. Checked Ian and Colin for a response and relaxed when he realised that for Vi this was just an expression. She wasn't making an announcement. She and he were the only ones who knew that Ian's father was not her husband, Colin, but Kenny's dad, Peter.

The man who was married to her long-dead sister.

Peter disappeared the night she died – forced into suicide to protect her son, Kenny, from a local gangster who promised to murder him in retaliation. His father didn't surface again until just after Kenny turned thirty, when the same local gangster reached out from the past to try and kill them all. Revenge truly was a cold dish for this guy, but Matty the Hut, as he was known, was foiled in his plans, and after some incredibly difficult events he was put firmly in his place.

Six feet under. In an unknown, unmarked location.

Kenny's reintroduction to his father was difficult. How can you overcome eighteen years of absence? The adult can reason that it was enforced and it saved his life. But the inner child remembers the missed birthdays and the endless nights thinking, what was he worth if even his father didn't want him?

He was still working on that relationship. In theory. Thinking about taking occasional trips to Peter's home in the central Highlands. But he had a new family now, a young son and daughter to his new wife, and rightly, they were his priority.

How Kenny fitted into that dynamic was a puzzle they'd need time to work out.

In the meantime, he had to make sure his aunt Violet was reassured that he was still "her boy", and if sitting in her nest of pink and cushioned comforts waiting to eat a stodgy meal of stew and dumplings was the price he had to pay for that: so be it.

'I just need to check on the potatoes,' Vi announced as she stood up. Both Colin and Ian stood as she did as if to help her in the process, but she waved them down. She'd fully recovered from her stroke of the previous year, with only a slight twist on the left side of her smile as a reminder.

'I'll come with you,' said Ian and walked out of the room with her. Kenny wanted to hang on to his shirt, force him to stay, rather than be required to make conversation with his uncle Colin. But, as soon as they were out of the room, the older man reached for his remote and turned on the television. Set it to the sports news channel and fixed his sight there.

Feelings were a long time mutual.

'You better not be turning on that television,' Vi shouted from the kitchen.

'Sorry, dear,' said Colin with a twist in his expression. He pointed the remote at the TV and turned the volume down and mumbled, 'If she thinks I'm talking to the family criminal . . .'

'Still going down the bowling club every night, Uncle Colin?' asked Kenny as he chewed on a grin, thinking, may as well play the part.

Colin looked at him as if to ask, talking to me? Kenny noticed his right hand, resting on the arm of the chair, tighten into a fist. Thought, someone's simmering.

'Never saw the attraction really,' Kenny continued. 'A bunch of old people with dodgy backs and knees, making them even worse, throwing one wee ball at a group of other wee balls.'

'It's a game of finesse,' answered Colin with a sniff and a sneer. 'Not that you'd know anything about that.' The word "you" was loaded with spite. Like he'd hawked it up with a chunk of his lung.

Kenny raised an eyebrow. Round one to Uncle Colin. He'd give him that. The miserable old git had little else in his life. Might as well allow him his small victory.

'Ian's looking good, eh?' he said

Colin grunted. And Kenny noticed his jaw muscles tighten. Then Colin rubbed at his bottom lip with the fingertips of his left hand as if holding back the words he was desperate to say.

'Can't remember the last time I saw him so well,' Kenny carried on. 'Back at the gym. Looking after himself . . .'

Colin shot forward in his seat, eyes shooting spite at Kenny.

'Why don't you piss off and crawl back into . . .'

'Dinner's ready, guys,' Violet sang as she walked in the door. She read her husband's body language. 'What's going on?'

Kenny stood up. Rubbed his hands together. 'Not a thing, Aunt

Violet. Just waiting patiently for dinner. I am starving.' He put a hand on her shoulder and pulled her into a half hug. 'Bloody starving.'

As Violet turned and led the way into the dining room, Kenny shot his uncle a look. Whatever's eating you, it said, lock it up. This is for Vi.

Every Sunday for as long as he could remember, his aunt Violet served up a plate heavy with homemade steak pie, potatoes, carrots and peas. Dessert was always chocolate fudge cake. And this meal was just like every other one he'd ever sat through. The middle of the table laden with condiments and sauces, and the air above their head heavy with his uncle Colin's unspoken resentments.

As usual, Aunt Violet's light chatter managed to mask the underlying currents, and he and Ian chipped in with inconsequential comments: TV programmes they'd watched, the latest fitness fads, who had the worst taste in music.

Ian was full of chat about his mate, Dom. How he'd been helping him work his way back into civvie street.

Violet's eyes were shining with love and not a little relief at the change in her son. This was the best version of him she'd seen for years, and with the looks she kept sharing with Kenny, it was clear to him that she was giving him a huge share of the credit.

While this was going on, Colin sat at his end of the table and attacked his food as if it might leap off the plate and escape back into the kitchen.

As this thought hit Kenny, he looked at his uncle and thought his cutlery was hitting the china with a little more force than usual. What was going on in that man's head? he wondered. If he could help amp it up a little more, that would add to his pleasure in the meal. He decided not to. Today there was something else at play and he could sense that Colin was close to an eruption.

From memory, it happened about twice a year. His carefully constructed appearance of near civility would crack and he would let fire. Both barrels. They'd be aimed at Kenny.

On the majority of occasions he would satisfy himself with

a series of passive-aggressive grunts and mumbling.

"Just like his father."

"Leached off me for years."

"Waste of space."

Kenny would take it all for his aunt Violet's sake, until she stepped in and cut Colin down with a single word. "Enough."

Then Colin would eat the last piece of his cake. Wipe his mouth with his napkin. Stand up and say, 'Delicious meal, Vi. Thank you.' Then he'd turn and walk out of the room as if his spine had fused into a steel rod while he was eating.

Kenny could write the script.

Today was different.

Today was building up to his bi-annual explosion.

Ian was completely oblivious. Chuntering on about Dom and how he was hoping to see his son more often and how it was ridiculous that a disabled ex-squaddie had been dumped in a high-rise flat but a neighbour's wee girl was helping him with his shopping.

Kenny felt himself smile. It was so good to see Ian so animated. And so healthy.

'And you've got your new job at the gym,' Vi beamed. 'I'm so proud of you, son. How you've cleaned up and got yourself sorted out.' She looked across at her husband. 'Isn't it great, Colin?'

'Yeah,' he replied as if he'd just taken a bit of gristle in with his meat. 'Wonderful.' He lifted a corner of his napkin and wiped his mouth. Then he tucked a corner of it into the V of the neck of his jumper.

Violet shot him a look. Decided to leave it and put a hand on Kenny's. 'Thanks, son. You've been a good help.'

'Yeah, bro,' said Ian, aiming a wink at Kenny. 'Cheers.'

'Bro?' asked Colin. 'That's short for brother in your lingo?' He stared at Ian, waiting for a response, his face unreadable.

And Kenny felt a chill. Where was this going?

'It's just an expression,' said Violet. 'Eat your steak pie, Colin, and let the adults talk.'

'What's that supposed to mean?' Colin threw down his cutlery and sat back in his chair.

'It means you're behaving like a child, Colin. I don't get my two boys together very often, and all I ask is that you sit on whatever is eating you and show some civility.'

Kenny caught a quizzical glance from Ian and looked to the ceiling in response.

'Civility,' said Colin and speared a slice of potato with his fork, shoved it in his mouth and swallowed as if it was edged in shards of glass. 'With one of Glasgow's biggest criminals and *that* . . .' he assessed Ian with a look of thinly disguised disgust.

'Enough, Colin,' Violet said sharply. 'I don't know what's got into you today. Can't we have a nice family Sunday dinner? I haven't seen the boys for ages.'

'You say that like it's my fault?'

'Isn't it? You're either miserable and mumping about nonsense or you are downright rude.'

'S'alright, mum,' said Ian, reaching over and holding her hand.

'I only wish it was, son,' she replied, her eyes sparking with tears. Then back to her husband. 'If you can't at least be polite, you know where the door is.'

'That would please you, wouldn't it?' demanded Colin, his voice rising in pitch. 'I've done my job. Provided for you and your . . .' he looked from Kenny to Ian, ' . . . boys all these years while their father fucked off and . . .'

'What?' asked Ian.

'Colin!' Vi shouted a warning to her husband. 'What's got into you?'

'You know, they say that a man can never understand what a woman goes through when she is raped by a man. Yes we can. This is it. Being lied to for years. Having no other use to the woman other than his ability to earn. Saddled with another man's child for over thirty years.' He paused. Searched Violet's eyes for something. 'That's a non-physical form of rape, isn't it?' Colin was now slumped

65

into his chair, sadness having momentarily overtaken his anger.

'What are you on about, Dad?' Ian was completely mystified. He looked at Kenny for guidance, and all Kenny could do was study his plate. The only person in the room who didn't know the truth was Ian.

'You know, don't you?' Colin looked at Kenny. Kenny looked at Ian. Found it difficult to meet his gaze.

'Dad?' said Ian. 'Mum?'

'How long have you known?' asked Violet, her voice little more than a whisper.

'I think I've always known,' said Colin. 'Then when Pete was here last year.' He looked at Ian. 'The similarities were . . . striking.'

'Colin,' Violet held a hand up as if to stop her husband from doing . . . anything. 'I'm sorry. So sorry. I didn't mean to lie to you. It was . . .'

'Difficult? Tricky? Convenient?' Colin was on his feet, leaning forward, jaw tight with anger.

'Colin, please . . .'

'Dad, what the hell is going on?' demanded Ian.

'Work it out . . .' Looked like he almost said "son". Stopped himself. 'You're not a bloody child. And you're back on your feet, thanks to your *bro* here. Time you knew the truth.' He plucked the napkin from his jumper and threw it on the table. He looked at Ian as if studying him for the first time.

'What a waste of space,' he said. 'The best bit of you dripped down your mother's leg, boy.'

Violet and Kenny both gasped at the cruelty of his statement. Kenny wasn't sure Ian had heard it, so unfocused was his stare as he fought to take in this new information.

Colin left the room. Moments later the front door slammed shut and then they heard his car roaring along the street.

'Someone tell me that Jeremy Kyle is in the kitchen with a film crew?' demanded Ian.

12

Ian was on the balcony in Dom's flat. Elbows on the rail, breathing in heavy night air. The sky was a dark sea of cloud, the ground lit up far below him like a carpet of stars. The world turned upside down.

What the hell?

Colin wasn't his dad.

He and Kenny were *actually* brothers?

After his dad . . . Colin . . . stormed out of the house, he, Kenny and his mother just stared at each other. Minds a jumble of thought. None of them sure what to say.

His mum's face said it all, to be fair. Her expression slack with a secret revealed. The weight of it replaced by the fear she would lose two of the most important people in her life.

'I'm so sorry, son,' she said, her cheeks shiny with tears.

'You knew?' Ian said to Kenny, the question an accusation.

Kenny nodded, his eyes conveying his commiseration. 'Just found out recently. But it wasn't my secret to share, Ian.'

Ian wasn't listening. Couldn't listen.

'My dad is your dad?' he asked.

'Aye.'

'Ian, please, son, let me explain,' pleaded Violet.

'This is . . .' Ian placed a hand on either side of his head as if trying to still the whirlpool of thought. He stood up and without another word followed Colin out of the door.

He couldn't go back to his own place. A bedsit with a view on to a grey brick wall. He felt lonely there at the best of times.

Driving aimlessly for an hour, he recognised a block of flats stretching into the sky just ahead. A column of light. And soon he was knocking on Dom's door and wordlessly accepting the mug of coffee his young friend thrust into his hand.

Myleene was cross-legged on the carpet in front of the TV, a controller in her hand. Dom read Ian's expression and asked her to leave.

'Do I have to?' she asked, eyes on the screen. She was wearing a pink t-shirt and dark jeans. The ubiquitous baseball cap was missing and her brown hair was tucked behind her ears and resting on her shoulders. Actually looked like a wee girl.

'Aye,' said Dom. 'It's late. Your mum will be worried about you.'

'As if,' said Myleene. Dumped the controller on the floor and stood up. 'See you tomorrow?'

'Sure,' said Dom.

She left.

Ian made his way on to the balcony. Dom joined him, leaned his back against the rail and turned his head to the side to face Ian.

'I cannae look down. Makes me feel dizzy.'

Ian simply stared into the space in front of him.

'Imagine putting a balcony on a high-rise flat in Glasgow. You get to sunbathe twice a year, and it's the perfect place to throw your drug-dealer from,' Dom said.

'My dad's not my dad,' said Ian.

Dom crossed his arms against the chill. Shivered. Offered a quiet "Fuck" in support.

Then, 'What happened?' he asked.

Ian explained.

Dom repeated his supportive "Fuck" every time Ian paused in the telling.

'Mate, that's some serious shit,' he said once Ian fell silent.

'How did you get on with your dad?' Ian asked. More from a

need to get someone else to talk, to get away from the jumble of his own thoughts, than a request for information.

'Rarely see him.' Dom used his walking stick to balance as he moved over to a small chair in the corner and sat. 'When I was a kid, he was mostly on the needle. Now he's on the methadone. Lives about five minutes from the chemist he gets it from and is terrified to be five minutes beyond that five minutes.' He squinted up at Ian. 'Isn't worth a fuck.'

Ian noticed that Dom was shivering with cold.

'C'mon inside,' he said.

They slumped on the sofa, side by side. From somewhere Dom produced a spliff, lit it and began to smoke. He offered it to Ian.

Ian stared at it. Debated with himself. Heard the man he'd always thought of as his father discount him as "that". Thought, bugger it, might as well live down to his expectations, but when he sent the command to his hand to reach for the joint, he found he couldn't move.

'No thanks,' he said.

'Good for you,' said Dom, eyes screwed up against the smoke.

'How can you afford that shit anyway?'

'Always a way,' he answered. 'It's not a luxury, mate. Only thing that keeps me calm apart from the wee man. And Myleene,' he added with a grin. 'Fancy a beer?'

'You've got beer?' asked Ian, wondering how his personal shopper – aka Myleene – would have managed to get a hold of that.

'Nah,' Dom answered.

Ian reached across and lightly punched his arm. 'Prick.' Felt a surge of affection. 'Thanks, mate. Didn't know where else to go.'

Dom's face pinked. He looked away. Uncomfortable in the moment, but clearly pleased that he was of use to someone. 'Any time, brother.'

'Brother,' Ian repeated and thought of Kenny. They were like brothers. Lived in each other's shadow throughout their youth. Too many shared experiences to count. Now they could add being abandoned by their father.

'What kind of guy was your dad?' asked Dom.

'Which one? The sperm donor or the one who put in a shift?'

'The one who looked after you.'

Ian shuffled through his thoughts like they were a pack of cards. Found a couple that suited. 'Knowing this, it all makes sense, you know? He did the practical things well. Paid the bills. Cut the grass. Decorated the house. But mostly gave off a silent feeling of disappointment.' Ian shifted on the cushion of the sofa so that he was facing Dom. Felt the give of a large spring as he moved. 'There was this one time. I was about twelve or thirteen. I broke my arm falling out of a tree. Doing daft kid shit. I might be misremembering this, but his car was in the garage, getting a service or something so he had to carry me like a couple of miles to the hospital. Too mean to pay for a taxi.' He paused to organise his recollection. 'They put a stookie on my arm and kept me in overnight, in case I was concussed.

My dad . . . Colin . . . slept on the chair beside my bed, and I woke up in the middle of the night and he was leaning over me. He kissed my forehead and then stroked my hair, and even in the dim light I could see that he was worried about me, you know? I remember thinking, fuck me, he *does* love me.' Ian crossed his arms. 'That sort of thing should be taken as read, yeah? But I remember being surprised by the thought.'

Ian looked at Dom. 'Shit. Look at me feeling all sorry for myself. At least I had someone there for me.'

Dom shrugged. 'Everything's relative, mate.' He grinned. 'My parents messed me up. Your parents messed you up. Different reasons, same result.'

'You make much sense, grasshopper.'

'Grasshopper?' Dom was mystified.

'An old TV programme,' answered Ian. 'Makes me feel very old that you don't follow.'

Dom yawned, his mouth wide in a long note of fatigue.

'Sorry, mate,' said Ian. 'I'm keeping you up.'

'It's alright,' replied Dom. Leaned forward and, planting his stick on the floor, he eased himself into a standing position. 'If you can't face going back to yours, you're welcome to stay.'

Ian nodded, finding that this was an agreeable notion.

'Sofa's comfy for a seat,' said Dom. 'But sleeping on it, not so much. And I don't have a spare quilt. The wee man will just have to share my bed.'

'No worries,' said Ian. He'd be happy just to have another human within hearing distance. Couldn't face going back to his own place. Too bleak. Too many bad habits had sifted into the fabric of that space, and they'd only whisper to him in the dark. Call out the relief available from that next hit.

'There's a king-sized bed through there,' said Dom. 'You're welcome to share.'

Right, thought Ian. Found that he would be quite comfortable with the idea. 'You're not going to try and shag me in the middle of the night?'

'Don't worry, mate,' said Dom. 'I'm firmly in Camp Vagina.' He looked at Ian's crotch. 'Unless you've stashed a pussy in there somewhere?'

'Ha! Now wouldn't that be interesting,' replied Ian. 'Afraid it's just your bog-standard meat and two veg, mate.'

'Ok, sweetheart.' Dom grinned. 'Time for bed.'

Minutes later, both men were stripped to their boxer shorts and lying side by side in the dark. Ian inched away from Dom, concerned to make sure that not one part of him touched one part of Dom.

'Well, this is awkward,' said Dom.

Ian could hear the smile in his voice.

'Piss off,' he said.

'Night, night, honey.'

Ian turned on to his side, faced the wall and realised he was smiling.

He woke with a start. Could have been hours later. Or minutes. He had no idea of the time. Then he became aware of a noise. A sniff. A gentle movement in the dark beside him. Surely not, he thought. Then another sniff and a high-pitched gurgle, and he realised that the movement was coming from too far up the bed for Dom to be enjoying a moment of onanism. The man was crying.

'Hey,' Ian turned to him and moved closer. Then as if he was speaking to a child, he asked, 'What's up, buddy?'

Nothing.

The movement stilled momentarily, and then as if the dam had been breached the sobbing began again, but with more force this time.

'Mate,' said Ian and felt a pang of guilt that the previous evening had all been about him. He was so caught up in his own drama, he hadn't even asked Dom how he was getting on with his attempts to see his son.

Lying on his left side, he shifted closer in the bed, lifted an arm out from under the thin quilt and placed a hand on his friend's shoulder. Patted it a couple of times. Almost said: there, there.

Jesus H, you are pathetic, Ian Ritchie.

What would a woman do in this situation? She'd coorie in and offer as much unconditional support as she could, that's what.

He remembered his old sergeant. Gun. His initials spelled Gun Shot Wound. Ian never did find out what they stood for. GSW was in time shortened to Gun. And this guy was hard. Glasgow-street hard with old leather for added toughness. But he knew when to adapt his approach to the needs of his guys. One minute he'd be kicking someone in the balls. The next, he'd be drawing a recruit into a hug, whispering reassurances in to their ear. He'd call you a pussy one minute, tell you that you were the best soldier in the army the next. What would Gun say? What would he do?

Ian took a breath. Be a man and do what's needed, dude.

'Hey, hey,' he said again, aiming for a soothing tone. He shifted closer in the bed and held Dom close. Part of his mind pleased that enough of the quilt had fallen between their bodies so that there wasn't any skin-on-skin action.

Dom responded. The speed of his crying reducing until it stopped with a sniff. And Ian was back there in the hospital with his dad on the bed beside him. He felt his throat tighten with emotion. Pushed away a cry of his own.

That had probably been the last time another male had touched him without the intent to harm. And here he was, all but spooning into the back of a broken friend, caught up in the warmth and comfort of the touch of another human being. He parked a lifetime of social conditioning and gave in to the nurture of it.

He'd face the hurl and heft of his thoughts another time. This was a moment to enjoy the presence of another sentient being. No agenda. No twisting of the truth. Dom's breathing slowed as his emotion subsided and Ian closed his eyes, feeling the other man's rhythm pull him into sleep.

13

Gavin allowed himself to be guided to a car and driven through the city. What did it matter? All he was good for were his fists, if that meant he got food and shelter that was a decent trade in his book.

The car stopped in an unfamiliar part of the city, and Dave said, 'That's us.' And climbed out.

Nice car, thought Gavin as he followed Dave on to the pavement. A smooth ride and it gave a satisfying thunk as he pushed the door shut. Then he turned his attention to the building he'd been dropped off at.

It was grey, small windows, three floors, flat roof. Looked like it was designed by a council worker rather than a qualified architect. Functional and with no ambition.

A small fir tree adorned either side of the red front door as if someone at the council had the word "pretty" on his tick-box list of design marks to hit.

'One of my mates told me about this place,' said Dave as he walked towards the door. 'It will get you off the streets until you get yourself enough cash for some rent.'

Gavin gave a yeah, whatever, shrug and followed in through the front door, noticing the CCTV camera aimed at the entrance, and another one in the spacious hallway pointed towards the reception area.

Actually "reception area" was an exaggeration. There was a desk that looked like it had been lifted from an abandoned school, the dirt wiped off its surface and a piece of white card was folded with the word "Reception" written in black felt pen and placed on the middle. The only other thing on the desk was a phone and a notepad.

Behind the desk sat a woman whose complexion was as grey as the building outside, black frizzy hair piled on top of her head and frameless spectacles perched on the edge of her nose. Gavin fancied that if anyone bothered to fill out a piece of card for her, the black felt pen would be used to scribe the word "harassed".

'Help you?' she asked with visible effort.

'This is Gavin Smith,' said Dave, and leaning forward he slipped an envelope across the desktop.

Smith, thought Gavin. A beat too close to the truth.

'Right,' said the woman. Before she reached for the envelope she gave the camera overhead a furtive glance. The envelope quickly disappeared into the folds of her voluminous black cardigan.

Interesting, thought Gavin. Looks like this isn't formal.

She put both hands on the top of the desk and pushed herself to her feet. Add weary to harassed.

'Hi Gavin,' she leaned forward and held out a hand. 'My name is Brenda and I'm the day-shift supervisor.' In contrast to her initial demeanour, her tone was welcoming. 'This is not the ideal place . . .' Her pause was laden with the subtext: for either of us. ' . . . But we will do our best to make sure you are comfortable and safe while you are with us.' She managed a smile of reassurance and looked by his side.

'No luggage?'

Gavin shook his head.

'Ok,' she responded as if that was the usual response. 'Let me show you to your room.'

'Before you go,' said Dave, holding out a small, black rectangle. 'Here's a phone. There's one number on it. Mine. We'll be in touch. Meantime, get rested up, eh?'

Brenda moved round the desk, and when she neared Dave she pulled her cardigan round her capacious bosom as if he carried his own personal chill around with him. She avoided his eyes, keeping her gaze on Gavin.

'This way, please,' she said and pointed towards the stairs in the far right corner of the space.

As they climbed the stairs – slowly – she maintained a breathless monologue on the rules and regulations of the establishment.

'No visitors in your room, please. No music after 10pm. No smoking either. There is a smoking area out back if you need a puff.' At this she looked back at Gavin over her shoulder and smiled, as if this was a regular haunt of hers. 'Your room key is in the lock in the back of your door. If you lose it there's a ten-pound fine.' This was added with a tone that suggested she never expected to receive the fine. 'If you need to wash your smalls you can use the sink in your room. For larger items we have a washing machine just behind reception. You can book in a time to use it. There's also an iron there. That also needs to be booked.'

They reached the top floor. Brenda took a right and walked along a corridor. Dark blue carpet, pale blue walls and a series of Formica-fronted doors and Gavin was back in the hotel chain he'd just left. He noted the doors were much closer together than they had been in the hotel, suggesting the rooms were small.

Brenda reached a door with 21 marked on the lintel. 'Here we are.' She pushed it open and then stood to the side to allow Gavin to pass her.

He stepped inside. Took in its entirety in a glance. A single bed lined one wall. On top of the mattress lay a folded quilt, two pillows, a sheet and a quilt cover with washed out red and blue stripes. On the other wall was a double cupboard and a small door.

Brenda stepped in and pushed open the door. 'Here's your toilet and shower cubicle. Word to the wise. The hot water usually runs out just before 8am, so you need to get in quick.'

Then she brushed past him to reach the white doors of the cupboard.

'This is your kitchen.' She opened it to display a small sink and worktop. The worktop housed a microwave oven, a kettle and a hotplate. 'All the mod cons.' She added with a smile, 'How lucky are you?'

She watched him as he took everything in.

'Any questions?'

'Nope,' said Gavin and realised that was the first thing he'd said to her. He didn't want her to think him rude, so he added, 'Thanks.'

She nodded as if he'd answered a silent question of hers. 'Most of our residents leave the building during daylight hours. That's up to you. Always puts me in mind of my holidays in Blackpool when I was a kid. Had to get out of the bed and breakfast in all kinds of weather.' She shook her head. 'Why did we put up with it, eh?' She coughed out a laugh as if she had just located her sense of humour. 'Anyway. Most of the residents are refugees. From all over, poor bastards. So, you'll maybe learn a few foreign words. Brush up on your language skills.'

'Any questions?' she repeated, hands on her wide hips.

'Nope.'

'Don't know if you noticed, but there's a wee shop at the top of the road. Might want to get yourself up there. Get some tea and biscuits or whatever. Some washing up liquid? Toothpaste, eh?' Then realising she was overstepping some kind of mark, a flush rose on her cheeks.

'I'll . . . eh . . . I'll leave you to it. Let me know if you've got any questions, eh?' She turned and left the room.

'Thanks,' Gavin called after her and then closed the door.

Right enough, the key was in the lock, so he locked it, turned and fell on to the bed. Feet crossed at the ankles, head resting on the folded quilt, he considered his change in fortunes. Okay, it wasn't the Hilton, but it was warm and dry. That was all that he needed.

He realised that this was the first time he was on his own since Dave picked him up for the fight . . . and he was back in his spot on the street, Dave leaning down towards him, offering a cigarette. He was a nice guy. Was looking out for him. Or was he? He felt a dull ache on his thigh where the other guy caught him. At the same time the knuckles on his left hand flared a twinge.

He had allowed his self-preservation instincts to be tamped down by Dave's friendly demeanour. A moment of weakness. The need for a break from the cold drudgery of life on the street.

Why him?

Of all the guys living rough in that part of the city, why did they home in on him? Did they know who he was? Were they aware of his past?

A knock sounded on his door. Three quick raps with a knuckle. Almost polite. Thinking that it might be Brenda or Dave, he jumped to his feet, took the four steps to the door and opened it. He saw a tall, lean figure.

'Hello, my neighbour,' the man said. 'My name is Mo. Like the runner.' Then he turned to the side and made a running motion with his arms. He was wearing a red t-shirt and black leggings. 'I love to run and I'm from Somalia too.'

Taken aback, Gavin offered his own name in reply.

Mo repeated it. Savoured it as a child might enjoy a new flavour of sweet. 'Ga – vin.' Then, 'Welcome, Ga – vin. My neighbour.' He held out a hand. Gavin took it and shook. Then made to close his door.

'Does Gavin have food?' Mo asked with a small bow.

Here we go, thought Gavin. Muttered "fuck off" under his breath. 'Sorry, mate. Haven't had a chance to get to the . . .'

'No . . .' Mo reached forward and pulled at his sleeve. 'Come.' He turned and pushed open the door facing him from the other side of the narrow hall. He turned back and motioned Gavin towards him.

'Food,' Mo said and pointed to his open cupboard. On the work top there was the remains of a plain loaf, a square of butter and a half-empty jar of strawberry jam. 'I welcome you to our wonderful home.' He held his long arms out to indicate he was talking about the entire establishment. 'Food?'

He was so earnest in his wish to offer hospitality that Gavin didn't have the heart to refuse.

'Ok,' he said and braced himself for a possible punchline. In his experience, people were rarely this friendly without an agenda of some sort. But Mo simply flashed his large white teeth at him and turned back to his "kitchen". There he pulled out a plate from the cupboard under the sink and deftly made Gavin a sandwich of butter and jam. Once finished he held out the plate and gave a small bow.

'Please, my new friend, Gavin. Enjoy.'

'Sure,' said Gavin, completely unsure where to put himself. He reached out for the plate with his right hand, brought the bread to his mouth, tore off a chunk and began to chew.

Mo was beaming. 'Allah says kindness to every living thing is reward.' He was all but hopping from one foot to the other in his pleasure at being able to give this stranger a gift. 'The jam ... it is jam, yes? Is delicious. So sweet.' He giggled as if this was the most delightful thing he had ever encountered.

Gavin chewed and swallowed and smiled in response. 'Yes, Mo, it's delicious.' Once he finished he handed back the plate. 'That was ... great. Thank you.' Unsure what to do next, he brushed his hands against the sides of his trouser legs. Was there a protocol for this kind of thing?

He felt shamed by the man's kindness. He gave a small bow and then cringed at himself. Jesus fuck, Gav, what are you doing?

'Cheers, mate,' he said and turned to walk back to his own room. Once inside, he turned to give another smile and bow to Mo. Then he shut and locked his door.

Back on his bed, he felt a small piece of wetness on the corner of his bottom lip. He checked with his tongue. Jam. He licked it off. Gave himself a mental row for not handling the situation better.

He examined his actions and his thought process to ask himself why the situation had been so awkward for him. It was not because the guy was foreign.

Was he so unused to acts of kindness?

Dave *had* been good to him. Got him cash and shelter, but with him there was a purpose.

Mo was being kind for the joy in doing something, however small, for someone else. With that thought he closed his eyes, sent his inability to accept such a small gift with grace to a corner of his mind, to ignore it, and fell asleep.

Hours later, he became instantly alert when he heard the heavy tread of two pairs of feet along the corridor outside.

It was dark. He pulled the phone Dave gave him from his pocket. Pressed a button on the side and it told him the time was 1:15.

A door crashed open, and it was so loud he thought it was his own. He was on his feet before he could blink. Realised his door was intact. Cocked his head to the side to hear what was going on.

Light filtered in under his door.

He heard the noise of a scuffle. A voice.

'Please, no. Please.'

Mo.

Without thinking, he unlocked his door, opened it and stepped forward into the corridor.

Mo was pinned up against his bedroom wall by one man, while another stood to the side watching. The fighter in Gavin assessed the strengths and weaknesses of the men in an instant. Both looked strong and well fed. Possibly well off as well: both were in jeans and leather jackets, and were clean shaven with trim haircuts. The one pinning Mo against the wall was almost as tall as the Somali, but the width of his shoulders suggested he had much more heft. The other man was of average height and build.

'What the fuck is going on here?' demanded Gavin

All three men faced him.

'It's okay, neighbour,' said Mo, eyes large with fear. 'I ok.'

'Yes, listen to the nigger,' said the smaller man, his face a snarl. Gavin couldn't place the accent. Possibly Eastern European.

Gavin took another two steps forward and leaned on the lintel of the door as if there was nothing more stressful going on here than a discussion about the merits of a greenhouse as opposed to a polytunnel.

'You want watch?' the smaller man said. 'The nigger has not paid protection last two weeks. He must learn this is not possible.'

'Is that right?' said Gavin, crossing his arms and then his legs at the ankles. 'Just terrible, eh? People not paying up for stuff. What exactly is protection?'

The taller man turned away from Mo, but still kept him pinned against the wall with his meaty arm.

'What the hell?' he turned to his smaller friend as if for an explanation. *Who is this crazy guy? Is he for real?* Then he faced Gavin. 'Don't worry, friend. We come see you next. Tell you all about it.'

'Lovely,' said Gavin. 'That'd be really neighbourly of you. Do you guys live here or something?' He waved a hand down the corridor. Caught the sight of movement from there, turned to see a couple of faces peering out from behind doors. When they saw him looking they retreated back into their rooms and quietly pressed their doors shut. There would be no help there then, thought Gavin.

'Friend, we finish soon. Come see you next. Go back to your room.'

'Sorry, buddy.' Gavin screwed up his face. 'I don't think I can do that. I have a thing about bullies. Cannae stand them.'

And that was all the warning he was prepared to give them.

The big guy's hands were full with Mo, but he judged him to be the biggest risk. The small guy was on the way to the big guy. Two steps to him. Then three to the big man.

He covered the first part of that in the time it took the small guy to change his stance. Gavin's right fist shot out. Adam's apple. Bullseye. The man fell to his knees, choking.

'What the . . .' the big guy said, threw Mo at Gavin. He stepped to the side, twisted and allowed Mo to pass him, but enough contact was made for Gavin to lose balance. He stumbled onto the bed but this had the happy coincidence of helping him avoid the swing the tall guy made.

Gavin landed on the bed and spun to the side as he rose. This gave him speed and leverage for a kick. Catching big guy in the stomach.

He grunted.

'Please, fellows. This man is hurting,' cried Mo.

Don't worry about him, thought Gavin. We don't sort this out now, they'll be back another night, weapons a-go-go.

Gavin was on his feet. Easily dodged another swing, like it was telegraphed. The force of the man's flailing made him twist too far. Gave Gavin an opening. He crashed a fist into the man's solar plexus.

Breath exploded from his lungs and fell forward. Gavin caught his head in both hands and as he brought it crashing down, he thrust up his leg.

Nose, meet knee.

This is much more fun, Gavin thought, than those *to the death* things that Dave got him involved in.

Big guy collapsed to the floor.

Small guy was wheezing, hands at his throat, eyes bright with panic.

'Oh, calm down, buddy,' said Gavin. 'I barely touched you.' Then he looked at his face. Remembered hearing about a guy who had to have a tracheotomy after being hit in the throat. Thought: oops.

He picked up the big guy by the collar, got him to his feet.

'Better get your mate to hospital,' he said. 'These things can be downright nasty.'

Big guy rushed to small guy and said something in a strange language.

'Hurry up, mate,' said Gavin. 'That doesn't look good.'

With a look that promised retaliation, big guy ushered small guy to his feet. Gavin stepped in to stop him from leaving the room.

'Next time,' he warned. 'I'll be less friendly.' Then he stepped to the side and allowed them to leave.

When they were gone Mo gave a whoop. Jumped from one foot to the other. 'Man, you kick assed. That was most awesome.'

Gavin shook his head. 'You're crazy, mate, if you get off on that.'

'My friends . . .' he held his hands out as if including everyone in the building, ' . . . will be loving you. Those bad men hurt us.' He struggled to find the right words to explain. 'Make us steal things.' He drew himself up to his full height. 'I am not a thief. I run.'

'Good for you, mate.' Gavin patted him on the shoulder. 'Now I sleep.' Then thought, jeez, you're speaking broken English now?

Back in his room, lying on his back, he considered that the men might return, looking for revenge. Good, he thought. That'll keep me in practice.

He was woken in the morning by a polite knock on the door. He squinted his eyes open to check the time on his phone. 6:45. Mumbling *forfuckssake*, he opened it to find three men, all in t-shirts and jogging trousers, all African, all wreathed in smiles. They bowed in unison, said "thank you" and walked away. For the next twenty minutes a procession of men bowed to him and offered him their thanks. After the first couple he became decidedly uncomfortable. Told the rest to bugger off.

He slammed the door shut. Wasn't for opening it again. He'd pretend he'd left the building.

Minutes later there was another knock. Much firmer.

He pulled it open with, 'Give us a break, eh?'

Standing there was a small, white man in red cord jeans and blue checked shirt. Matching jowls and paunch. He was flanked by a couple of uniformed police officers.

'Mr Smith, I have had reports of a disturbance last night. Fighting is forbidden. I'm going to have to ask you to leave.'

This must be the night guy. He had a badge. Jim Bent. If the hat fits, thought Gavin.

'Wait a minute, you wee prick.' Gavin stepped forward in to the man's face. Bent blanched and stepped back.

'He's being violent. Arrest him, officers.'

Gavin assessed the situation. This guy was probably in on it. Was probably receiving a payment to allow the other men to come in and extort the residents. Heat rushed to his head. A morning of being told he was a hero meant he had to live up to it, right?

He stepped forward and crashed his forehead down on Bent's nose. A scream. High-pitched like a teenage girl.

'Right, Mr Smith.' One of the policemen grabbed him. 'We can't have that.'

'What the hell?' Gavin struggled as one of the cops twisted his arm up his back. 'This guy's a fucking extortionist.'

'Shut up, mate,' the other officer said as they forced him out of the room. 'Go quietly, or instead of just losing your room, you'll be in a cell.'

Gavin made a calculation. He could take these guys, but going toe-to-toe with a pair of police officers, armed with batons and pepper spray, was a different thing to launching himself at a couple of thugs. Could they be in on it? If so, they had the weight of the law behind them.

Besides, he'd done what he could, no?

Not my monkey, not my circus.

'Right, right,' he said. 'Going quietly.' He groaned at the strain on his shoulder muscles as the officer continued to apply pressure. 'Going quietly, mate.' He eyeballed the young cop. 'I don't have much. Can I at least get my stuff before you throw me onto the street?'

His partner gave a nod and he was released from the hold.

Gavin rotated his shoulder, assessed if there was any damage. 'That was good,' he said to the policeman. 'Need to teach me that.'

As he walked back into his room and picked up his jacket, Bent was holding a hand over his nose and shouting. Keeping a noisy dialogue going that would mean Gavin couldn't be heard if he made another accusation.

Blood dripped from Bent's nose. A line of it down his shirt.

'We can't have people like you in this place. You're a disgrace. This is a safe haven for these poor people. Imagine having to flee danger in your home country to come here and face even more violence? People like you should be shot. Shot, I tell you.'

'No one's going to get shot, Mr Bent,' one of the officers said. To Gavin he said, 'Let's go.'

Gavin nodded. Slipped his jacket on. Felt the reassuring weight of the cash he'd stashed in the lining. A few good meals there, and if he slept on the street, more than a few highs.

He checked the pocket of his jeans for the phone. Still there. When he ran out of cash he'd maybe use it.

Before he left, he faced Bent. Put some snarl in his face.

'I'm on to you, mate. This isn't over.'

14

Kenny looked at his aunt Vi. She looked small and lost, tucked into the deep cushion of her sofa.

'Don't worry. The old codger will be back,' he said.

She shook her head. 'This time, I'm not so sure, Kenny.'

'This has been stewing in his head since he saw Pete last year. If he was going to leave, he would have left then.'

'And what about Ian?' She hugged herself. Her face tight with worry. 'He's been doing so well recently. 'This could send him back over the edge.'

'Don't worry about Ian,' said Kenny. 'A few rounds on the mat down at the gym will keep him right.'

'I'm not so sure, son,' replied Vi. 'Ian's a thinker. Goes deep. You saw his face. This is a huge shock.' She shook her head slowly. Swallowed as if the taste of past sins was coating her tongue. Her face soured at her own silent acknowledgement of painful mistakes. 'What a mess I've made of things, son. What a bloody mess.' Her head slumped forward and she gave in to her tears.

'Here,' said Kenny and sitting down beside her, pulled her into a hug. 'I promise you, six months down the line and you'll be wondering why you were so worried.'

'Don't think so, Kenny. This is bad. Really bad.'

'Hey, hey.' Kenny held her tight. He could feel the bones of her shoulder through her cardigan and was reminded of the stroke she suffered just the year before. He'd always thought of his aunt Violet as being indomitable. One of those doughty Scots women who would face the world, hip cocked to the side, a half-smile on their face and the words "Come ahead" on their lips. Whatever the world and their menfolk threw at them, they'd endure and come out of it stronger and wiser.

For the first time, he felt a stir of worry for her. 'It will all turn out fine, Aunt Vi. I promise you.' How he would make good on that promise, he had no idea.

After Vi stopped crying, she disappeared into the bathroom and reappeared with her makeup reapplied and her shoulders square to the world.

'I'm fine, son,' she said. Her smile was weak. 'Probably best if you go. Colin won't come back in if he can see your car outside.'

'If he does anything . . .'

'Don't worry about Colin. He's a grumpy bastard, but he'd never hit me.'

They kissed. His lips against the cool paper of her cheek. He left.

Kenny climbed into his car. Pulled out his phone and called Ian. No answer. Sent him a text. *Need to talk? Geezabell?*

He drove to the end of the street. Looked straight ahead when he passed Colin's car at the end of the road. Indicated, checked for traffic and turned left. And looking in his rear-view mirror could see Colin beginning the manoeuvre that would see him complete a three-point turn and return to his home.

Kenny parked. Should he go back? Colin was never the violent type, but he'd never seen him quite so angry. His aunt Vi was safe surely? She could handle Colin.

This time?

Resentment against Kenny's dad, Peter, ran deep in the man. Peter got the woman he was in love with and then impregnated the woman he settled for. Sure, Colin had come to love Vi, even Kenny could see that, but the cool indifference with which he'd treated Kenny, even before he took up his current career path, suggested that Colin had taken up nursing grievances as a life-long hobby.

Kenny drummed his fingers on the steering wheel. Should he just let them deal with it themselves? Colin's face flashed into his mind. The moment he'd let rip. Bug-eyed and furious. Veins popping on his forehead and down his neck.

He'd never forgive himself if anything happened to Vi.

What to do?

Kenny looked at the time on the dashboard. Chrissakes, he'd been sitting prevaricating for at least twenty minutes. Anything could have happened.

He waited until the only car on the road passed him, then he turned and made his way back to the house.

Kenny parked a few doors down and then jogged to the front door. Saw that the living room light was still on. And the one above it: Vi and Colin's bedroom.

He pressed his head against the door and listened. Nothing. Should he stay, or should he go?

He had to make sure, so he turned the handle as quietly as he could and stepped inside. Heard the quiet rumble of his uncle's voice, then a short reply from Violet.

Then a crash.

Without thinking, he pushed open the living room door. Facing him, his aunt Vi was upright, holding a heavy quilt and a pair of pillows. He could quickly see that Colin had tried to pull them off her and in doing so had knocked over a lamp on the table at the side of the sofa.

'What's going on?' he demanded.

'What the hell is it to you?' Colin was in his face as if Kenny had re-stoked his anger.

'Kenny, I'm fine,' said Vi, dropping the bedding on to the sofa and then pulling the hair from her face. Her voice was slightly slurred, as happened when she was tired. Her hangover from last year's stroke. 'I'm just going to have a wee sleep on the sofa here.'

'There's no need,' said Colin. 'Come to bed, Vi.' He looked defeated. 'I can't sleep . . .'

Kenny looked from one to the other. He needn't have worried. Vi's quiet dignity always seemed to cast a spell over her man.

'Right. I'll be off then,' he said. 'And let you two kids deal with things from here.'

Vi sent a smile of thanks that was dimmed by fatigue.

Colin followed Kenny to the front door, mumbling as he did so. Kenny turned to face him as he stepped out of the door. With effort, he quelled his dislike of the man and tried to reason with him.

'You know, part of me recognises and appreciates that you gave us a roof over our heads . . .'

'I don't need your thanks, you little prick,' Colin interrupted.

Kenny stepped up to him. Face inches from his.

'If it wasn't for that wee woman in there . . .'

'That's your answer, is it? Violence?' Colin raised his chin as he spoke, as if presenting a target. 'Well, come on, give it your best shot. Let's see you punch an old man.'

Kenny stuffed his clenched fist into a pocket. That was close.

'You had a chance to do a good thing. Two wee boys in need of a father, but you let your sad wee ego get in the way. There's more to being a dad than keeping someone fed and sheltered, you know.' Kenny looked Colin up and down. Noticed how old he had become. Eyebrows thinning, tufts of hair growing on his earlobes, thick lines pressing down from either side of his mouth, giving him a permanent scowl. 'Nothing ever pleased you. Your dislike of us both affected everything you said and did.' Kenny shook his head. 'You might have been here, but really? You were absent.' Without waiting for a reply, he turned and walked down the path and back to his car.

Once inside, he pulled his phone from his pocket and sent Ian a quick text.

You ok?

He knew Ian wouldn't respond straight away, so he scrolled down for another number. The way he was feeling right now, there was no way he could go back to his flat and settle down for a quiet night in. He needed to go for a run or organise himself a good hard shag.

He found the number he was looking for and sent a quick text. There was no way he was going for a run at this time of night. That was for losers.

He received an instant reply from Christine.

I'm all yours. A second text arrived shortly after, giving him her address.

Ignoring a faint bell of warning that reminded him he hadn't received any intel from Dimitri about Christine's background, but enjoying the charge of anticipation in his groin, he slipped the car into gear and drove off.

15

Ian woke and realised the bed was empty. He opened his eyes to bright sunlight. Dom's bedroom curtains being as effective as tissue paper. He felt sleep tug at him, but knew that the light would prevent him falling over again, so he sat up, rubbed at his eyes and listened for any clues that might suggest where Dom was.

The flat was silent.

He stood, lifted his jeans from the floor and pulled them on. When he lifted his arms to put on his shirt, he caught a nose-full of his own aroma. Nice. Thought it was a good job he didn't get lucky last night. No self-respecting woman would put up with that.

He walked through the hallway, the living room door was open and he could see that there was no one on the sofa. A few more steps and he could see that the kitchen was also empty. He made for the kettle, filled it and switched it on.

A full mug heating his hands, he walked through the living room and out to the balcony where he found Dom sitting in the far corner, huddled up within the thick cushion of a ski jacket that was several sizes too big for him.

The younger man smiled when he saw him and then looked into the distance, over the rooftops of the city. 'I love this time of day,' Dom said. 'The humans are all in their hutches, and I can pretend the world is a benevolent place.'

'Oooh,' said Ian. 'Benevolent. Good word.' He took a sip of

his drink. 'Wait until I've finished my coffee before hitting me with big words like that.' He bent forward and leaned against the railings, cold hard steel against his elbows. The cool air chilled his shirt, despite the sun. He shivered.

'Want my jacket?' asked Dom. He took a puff on his roll up.

'Nah,' replied Ian. He exhaled and watched his breath plume in the air. 'I'll survive.' He looked over the city, his gaze skimming over rooftops, treelines and strips of asphalt. Traffic was already lining up on the motorways. Orderly queues of drones waiting to punch their clocks for another day of thankless, low-waged toil. He felt equal amounts of envy and disgust towards them. *They have purpose. They're looking after their families. Keeping a roof over their heads and then filling that home with shite. We used to talk about Generation X,* he thought. *Now we have the X-Factor generation.*

He caught the sweet musky scent from Dom's cigarette.

'Is it not a bit early for that?'

Dom squinted through the smoke. 'Only thing that helps the headaches, mate.'

'Fair enough.'

Dom held out his smoke. 'Want a hit?'

Ian felt a pull of expectation. The knowing that temporary mental peace was just a few short inhalations away. He ignored it. Shook his head. Couldn't trust himself to actually voice the word "no".

'There's some cornflakes if you're hungry,' said Dom.

'You're alright,' replied Ian. 'If I want cardboard I'll just eat a box.'

'Aye, but will your box have enough salt and come fortified with iron?'

'Naw, but it will have some nice words on it.'

'Prick.'

'Fud.'

They exchanged a grin.

'The wee shop down the hill does a nice bacon roll,' said Dom with a hopeful expression.

Ian felt his mouth fill with saliva. 'Good call,' he said. 'The vegan's gateway drug back to meat.'

Twenty minutes later he was back in the same spot holding two paper bags. Each filled with a pair of bacon rolls. He was considerably warmer having run all the way back, but the bacon had lost some of its heat. He apologised to Dom.

'Don't care,' he replied, his mouth full of half-masticated meat and bread. 'This is the tastiest thing I've had for days.

They munched in companionable silence, and then Ian sorted them both out with another cup of coffee.

Ian plucked his phone from his pocket and checked his messages. Two each from his mum and Kenny. Looked at the power bar and noticed it was getting low. Hadn't thought to go back to his for the charger.

'What kind of phone you got?' he asked Dom.

'Samsung.'

'Great. Need a wee charge here.'

Dom pointed out where his charger was. Still stuck in the multi-point extension lead with all the other electrical equipment in the living room. Ian located it and plugged his phone in. He discounted the messages. He'd answer later. Needed some time first to sort this all out in his head.

Colin wasn't his dad.

Kenny was his brother.

Two of the people he trusted most had been lying to him for years, and he felt the injustice of that burn in his gut. And as for Kenny saying he only recently found out, he wasn't buying it. The man's stock-in-trade was information. He found out stuff faster and easier than anyone he'd ever met.

Why didn't he tell him?

Sure, he'd been in a sorry place for a good while, and might have reacted badly to the news. But fuckssakes, they were brothers. Actual brothers. How could he sit on that?

As if on cue, his phone buzzed an alert. He bent down to look at it on the floor. A text from Kenny.

It read: *Going to The Hut today? Fancy sparring with me?*

Ian recognised this for what it was. An apology and an attempt to make it right between them. Getting down and sweaty on the mat stripped away all pretence. They would be all sweat and sinew, grunt and strain. You have the truth of a man when you're pushing them face down on to the floor.

Imagining himself in that situation, he felt a thrill in his muscles. It would be great to make the prick pay. He discarded the thought easier than the temptation of the joint. Felt a surge of anger. Saw himself and Kenny circling each other. Knew he wouldn't stop until one of them was a bloody mess.

He needed space before he saw his cousin again. Time to think this shit through.

'Time?' Dom asked, shooting a look at Ian's phone.

Ian told him.

Dom stood. Said, 'Cool. Time for Jeremy Kyle on the telly.'

'You watch that crap?'

Dom shrugged. 'Reminds me there's folk worse off than me,' he said and shuffled into the living room, pointed the remote at the TV and fell into the armchair. Thinking he'd nothing better to do, so might as well join him, Ian followed and sat down.

The TV blared into life. An audience baying for tears and snot. Across the bottom of the screen read the legend – *Abandoned by my mother. Three potential fathers – which one is my dad?* A young man sat in a chair in the middle of the stage. Red and blue checked shirt and gelled hair. Looked like this was his best clobber. This was offset by the plaque of acne on his cheeks. It was as if he'd been sprayed with tomato sauce in hair and makeup.

'Jesus Christ, this is a pile of shite,' said Ian as he got to his feet. 'Where's your dry towels?'

'Yeah, go for a shower, ya manky bastard. You're minging,' said Dom with an unrepentant smile. 'Towels are in the hall cupboard.'

Ian walked to the cupboard. Opened it and found that Dom's military habits were still strong. The contents were meagre but everything was firmly in its place. An ironing board was tucked to one side. Shoes were in neat pairs on the floor as if waiting for a foot and a march. Three bath towels were on the shelf facing him. By their side was a pile of hand towels looking as if a ruler and a protractor had been used to check the angle on the small cotton tower it made.

Some people might see this as OCD'ish behaviour, but Ian recognised the habit and the compulsion, and he was reassured on behalf of his young friend. Whatever else was going on in his life, he was retaining control over this small part of it, and that would surely be a help.

In the bathroom, he stripped off, pulled the shower curtain to the side and turned on the water. He waited until the heat built and then stepped under the cascade. Let out a groan of pleasure as he felt the water power over his shoulders and down his back.

He spotted a bar of soap sitting in the corner of the bath, picked it up and began washing under his arms and between his legs. As the water washed away the resultant suds he thought again about his family.

What would his mum be thinking? Would she be worried about him? He'd given the poor woman enough to worry about through the years, and he felt a pang of guilt. Quelled it. This one was on her.

Then he felt guilty about the impulse to ignore his guilt.

Fuck. What a mess. He ran his fingers through his wet hair. Stood with his chin tucked into his neck so that the water hit the back of his head and neck. Groaned at the simple pleasure. If only life could be this simple.

He heard a noise. Some shouting. He shook his head, trying to get the water out of his ears. Had Dom turned up the TV?

He turned off the water. Nothing. Must've imagined it. Turned the water on again, reluctant to leave the atmosphere of steam and cleansing.

Another shout. A crash. He turned the water off again. That wasn't the telly. Was Dom having another rage episode? With reluctance, he pulled back the shower curtain and stepped out of the bath. He picked up the towel and wrapped it round his waist, thinking fondly: better check on the wee prick.

Pulling his wet hair away from his face, he walked into the living room.

'Dom, what's up . . .' He paused in his speech when he saw two men standing over Dom. He recognised them as two of the men he'd seen on the landing the first time he'd come over to visit Dom.

'Now this is more like it,' said the tall, slim one with the round-framed glasses. His eyes roamed down Ian's naked torso in the manner of a farmer assessing a beast at market.

'What the fuck is going on here?' demanded Ian.

16

The policeman drove for twenty minutes then pulled up just beyond a bus stop. The cop on the passenger side climbed out of the car and opened the rear door to let Gavin out.

'You need to look into that guy,' said Gavin. 'There's something dodgy going on in that place.'

The look the cop gave Gavin shamed him, judged him and found him wanting. Nothing he could say to this guy would reach his attention. He thought about telling the cop who he was. What he'd done. Signed up. Gone to war. He could give him the ex-squaddie down-on-his-luck story. Shook his head. Nope, not going there. As the song should say: too proud to beg.

'Think yourself lucky we're not locking you up,' the cop said.

'Fuck you very much,' said Gavin. Imagined the crunch of his knuckles on the cop's face and walked away before his temper got the better of him.

He took a couple of steps away from the car. Waited until it drove off and took his bearings. A constant flow of traffic: cars and pedestrians. A long stretch of straight road, flanked either side by sandstone buildings. The ground floor of each of them a shop. Charities, beauticians, tanning salons, fast food eateries and convenience stores as far as the eye could see. He looked up and read a sign. Dumbarton Road.

His stomach groaned. He'd had nothing to eat since the sandwich he'd been given by Mo. Should find a coffee shop and get some food. As the thought hit him he reached into his pocket and fingered the wad of cash. He could eke that out for some time on the street. Or he could find a cheap hotel, live it up for a few days and then go back to his usual haunt.

A car pulled up beside him. The low, sleek black shape of a BMW.

The window slid down and a voice sounded, 'Get in.'

He looked. It was Dave.

Considered bolting.

Dave repeated, 'Gavin, get in.'

With a sigh, he complied. Dave looked over his right shoulder, judged the traffic and drove off.

'How did you find me?' Gavin asked.

'We've had eyes on you since you went in that place. Did you think we'd allow ourselves to lose an asset?'

An asset. Gavin heard that. Parked it for examination later.

'No. I mean when you approached me the first time. How did you find me?' Gavin asked and watched Dave's response. He didn't blink. Answered quickly. Too quickly.

'We're always on the look-out. We drive through places we know men live on the street.'

'So you got lucky when you found me? I just happened to be a scrapper. Just what you needed.'

'Yeah,' said Dave with enthusiasm. 'How lucky was that?'

Gavin turned to face the traffic. Thought about debating the point, but reconsidered. Why bother?

'Where you taking me?' he asked. No point in diving deeper, he could tell when he was being stonewalled.

'Want to earn another couple of hundred?'

Gavin assessed his knuckles, his various aches and pains from his first fight. If it was as easy as that one, it would be no fight at all.

'Has the price fallen?' he asked.

'You were too good the last time. The odds will have gone down. We don't earn as much? You won't earn as much.' Then as if thinking out loud, 'Might need to get you out of the city. Fight you somewhere else.'

'Let's see how this one goes first, eh?' said Gavin. Thinking: bugger it. What else was he going to do? Find a street corner and stare at his feet?

'Good man!' Dave said and thumped the steering wheel.

Two hours later, Gavin was stripped to his combat trousers. The flesh on his naked chest and back stippled against the chill. He rolled his neck, circled his shoulders and then flapped his arms against his chest. Willing blood and heat into his muscles.

'It's a lunch-time fight,' explained Dave. 'The cops expect this kind of stuff only to happen at night. This keeps them guessing. And the suits working in their office batteries around here love a bit of blood and gore with their chicken wraps and sparkling water at lunch break.'

Gavin zoned out the crowd that circled him and focused on his opponent. On first sighting he thought it was Mo the Somali runner. This guy had the same cropped hair, dark skin, height and lean build, but his face was missing any of the warmth that shone from Mo's.

As Dave had wrapped his fists he explained that the lunch-time crowd were looking for a different form of entertainment. A knockout would do. No need to go for the kill. They would be sober, and too much would push them over the edge of excitement into a clear-headed fear when they had to go and stare at a computer screen for the rest of the day. Which would surely mean a lower audience and less money being bet the next time.

'But again, no referee, no three-minute rounds,' said Dave. 'Last man standing kinda deal.'

A big guy with hands full of cash and a hypnotically large double chin waddled into the space between the fighters. His belly strained the buttons on the vast expanse of his shirt, and his piggy eyes shone at the prospect of more cash coming his way.

'Gav the Grinder,' he shouted in a high pitch, pointing at Gavin. The crowd picked up his name and started shouting. Gavin considered giving them a brief show. Caught the expression of a young guy in the crowd. Looked like he was about to piss himself from a mix of fear and excitement.

Fuck that, thought Gavin. I'll save my energy.

'Rahman the Reaper.' the man pointed at the other fighter. The crowd then picked up his name and started chanting it. Rahman showed his teeth, held his arms out and flexed his biceps. Needn't have bothered, thought Gavin. Seen more meat in a veggie burger.

Rahman began gearing up for the fight. Bobbing on the tips of his toes. Shot a couple of jabs into the air in front of him. Not bad, thought Gavin. Some speed there. Let's see how he does with a real human being.

He stepped up to the guy. Planted his feet. Swung and crashed a low hook into Rahman's lower ribs. Then he took a step back and, before the other man could react, jabbed at his jaw.

The crowd went crazy.

Rahman stumbled back out of range. Shook his head as if clearing sparkled vision. Gavin gave him the space. Notice was served. This wasn't going to be a pleasant lunch break for you, mate.

Gavin kept light on his feet. Felt hate heat his arms, legs, gut. Aimed it at everyone. Ex-wife, her parents, his kids, every bastard who'd ever slighted him. Channelled it into the bag of bones and skin who was gearing up for another go at him.

Rahman windmilled his fists.

Thinking: is that the best you can do, Gavin waited until the last minute, stepped to the side and brought his knee crashing up into the other man's gut. He bent double and Gavin clasped both hands, raised them over his head and brought them down on the back of the other man's neck.

Rahman collapsed to the floor. Gavin followed in with feet. Kicked ribs, stomach, tried for the balls, but Rahman had curled up, so he changed focus and went for his head.

Sweat was coming now, clear odourless drops collecting on his brow and back. Breath ragged. He stepped back took a couple of breaths. Willed his lungs to slow. Shit, he was so out of shape. Should be able to do this all day long.

His pause allowed Rahman time to get back onto his feet, and Gavin could feel the crowd willing the other man back into strength. He was now the underdog and they would love to see him land a punch or kick on Gavin.

That ain't happening.

The noise of the crowd blended into a deep throaty babble. Came at him as if through thick cotton. One young guy, white faced, bug-eyed, collar and tie loose, stood silent and unmoving. Mouth open as if the hinge of his jaw was stuck. Looked like he was now realising that violence wasn't pretty, wasn't anything like those games on computers. Gavin sent him a look of pure loathing.

Welcome to my world.

The blow came out of nowhere. Dropped him to his knees. Chill wind poured through his ears, metal tainted his tongue. Knowing the other guy would sense the opportunity, Gavin took a look, saw him coming back in swinging. Managed to curl his toes to gain purchase, and when Rahman was within reach he shot up at him, caught him in the midriff, like a rugby challenge.

The force carried them several feet and they both fell to the ground, Rahman on the bottom. Gavin tucked his head into the other man's neck to keep away from his teeth and landed several punches: ribs and stomach.

Rahman kicked out with his knees. Bony. Sharp. Caught Gavin on the side. He pushed away, twisted and clambered to his feet. Trying to disguise his fatigue.

The other guy climbed to one knee. Then stood. Breathing hard.

They were facing each other, swaying slightly. Vision narrowed, they circled in a dimming circle of light, feet spread, fists balled, knees bent. The crowd faded. The only sounds that registered in Gavin's mind were a distant pounding and his own heavy breath, like a giant was in his ear.

A breeze, and the coldness on his skin felt good. Reviving.

The other guy moved on to his lead foot, left hand rising as he telegraphed an intended blow. Specks of blood dripped off his swollen lip. Gavin came forward on to his right foot, stepped inside the other guy's reach and shifted his head away from the blow. Knew that to get his strike in, he'd have to take a hit. Tensed for it while his right hand exploded up. He threw everything into it. From his feet, to his core, shoulders, fist. Shooting *beyond* the target. He connected with the solar plexus. A comical ooo expression from the other guy as air shot from his lungs and he fell forward.

Gavin repeated his earlier move and brought his knee crashing up into Rahman's face as he fell forward. Felt the connection: thigh on jaw. Rahman crumpled to the floor. And Gavin was on him. Kicking, punching, biting, snarling. Enjoying a surge of energy, knowing the fight was his.

He felt hands on his arms, shoulders, neck. Pulling him off.

The crowd now silent.

One voice reached him through the blare of fury in his mind. Dave was in his ear. 'You won, mate. You won.'

Gavin shook his head and returned to himself as if the violence had sent him elsewhere. Looked around himself at the pale faces in the crowd. He snarled. He was beast. Dog. Wolf. A creature none of these men had ever been faced with. Felt a renewal of hate. Of them.

Himself.

He launched at the men nearest him. Windmilling fists, kicking, snarling, biting. Caught someone with a head-butt before he felt an arm wrap around his neck and pull him away. He felt the strength in this man. Arms of corded steel.

He had been a beast, now he was like a child. Couldn't fight this man. Felt Dave's breath, hot in his ear.

'Fuckssake, man, cool it.'

Allowed himself to be pulled away.

Rahman groaned. Raised himself on to one knee. He was breathing like he'd just sprinted a marathon. Lungs struggling to take in enough air. His face a mask of blood from a cut above his eyebrow, bottom lip already hugely swollen. His right arm cradled the lower ribs on his left side.

The fat guy was in Dave's face.

'Fuckin' animal . . . needs to be put down . . . don't bring him back.'

Suits me, thought Gavin. Felt Dave's grip on him loosen slightly. Willed himself to relax. Saw a group of men in the crowd squaring up, fists clenched as if waiting for a silent signal to attack him. But most of the crowd wanted nothing more than to return to their coffee and Kit-Kats. They'd come here for a bit of a scrap and were taken aback by his ferocity. Since the time most of these men left adolescence their only probable link to violence was shouting at other men in the opposite football terracing. The odd punch up out the back of the local. Or the comic violence of the movies. Lunch-time fight club brought them back to that dreaded moment at school where they might be called out to fight another boy. Gave them a shot of adrenalin to get them through the rest of the day.

Gavin looked at the remaining audience. Made eye contact. Shuffling through them one by one until they broke the link and, slumped with shame, turned away. He had taken the unwritten contract that he be nothing but a lump of muscle willing to bleed for their entertainment, pissed on it and reminded them he was a human being.

The crowd began to disperse. Silenced by what they had just witnessed. Their shoulders hunched as if in acknowledgement of the difference between TV and real life. But Gavin knew once back in their office, they would each sift through the last few minutes, forget the pain inflicted, reduce the combatants to two dimensions. Consider their worth and scale it down to nothing but dirt and crumb.

Then they'd be back next week for more.

17

Kenny woke to a warm hand on his cock. A light stroke and he was hard and ready for action. He felt a pleasant ache there after the previous night's action. Thought: hell yeah. Turned on to his side, smiled at Christine and shifted so he was leaning above her.

He slid inside her easily and moving slowly, felt every inch of him push deeper until he was grinding pubis to pubis.

She was in his ear. Soft lips pressing. The heat from her breath as she moaned.

His phone trilled from his suit pocket.

He ignored it and continued to grind, savouring the sensations.

The phone stopped.

Then started up again.

'For fuck's sake,' he said.

'Pun intended,' said Christine with a laugh. 'I don't mind if you need to get it.'

Kenny pushed himself up into a press-up position. Savoured the connection. The heat. The wet.

The phone continued to ring. Was probably his aunt Vi worried about Ian. And the spell was broken.

'Sorry,' he said and disconnected from between her legs.

When he reached the phone it stopped ringing. He looked over at Christine with a would-you-believe-it look. She giggled.

Kenny read the display. Yup. Aunt Vi. Felt a charge of worry that his uncle Colin might have turned on her. Quickly discounted the notion. The man was many things. A wife-beater wasn't one of them. Besides, when he'd walked in on them the previous night it was quite clear that despite his faults he loved Vi, and she him.

He held the phone up to Christine. 'Mind if I . . .'

She sat up in the bed, pulled the quilt up to cover her breasts. Smiled. 'You're the customer . . .'

'True.' Kenny grinned. 'Why am I being so polite?' He sat on the edge of the bed, and with his back to Christine called his aunt. She picked up immediately and charged straight in.

'Kenny. Where are you? No, don't answer that. I don't want to know. I'm worried about Ian.'

Jeez, thought Kenny. Take a breath. 'He'll be fine, Aunt Vi. He just needs some space.' Kenny felt the bed springs shift as Christine inched closer to him. Then her arm snaked round from behind him and her fingers found his cock. He had fallen flaccid on hearing Vi's voice, but now re-stiffened. Christine held her thumb and first finger in a circle and her hand began to pump slowly.

He let out an involuntary groan.

'What did you say, Kenny?' Vi asked.

He exhaled. Coughed. 'Nothing. Didn't say anything.' Wanted nothing more than to plunge between Christine's legs. Closed his eyes against the driving need.

'Could you check on him for me, please, Kenny?' Vi begged him.

'Yes,' he managed to say. Eyes shut. Jaw all but clenched.

'Promise me?'

'Yes, I promise,' he all but shouted. Regretted his tone. Softened his voice. 'Kinda distracted here, Aunt Vi, but I promise you I'll go and see him and report back. Ok?'

'Ok. Thanks, son,' she said, and Kenny felt shame at her worry. Christine's hand continued to move. Then she moved round, knelt in front of him and placed his cock in her mouth.

'Got to go,' he squeaked into the phone. 'Bye.'

Some time later, Kenny walked into The Hut. Opened the door

and shouted, 'Ian?' His cousin's car wasn't in the car park, but he still felt the need to check.

Inside the space, he scanned the room. Caught the familiar smell of sweat, old leather and wood, and cheap air-freshener. Saccharine notes of berry sifted in among the more masculine scents. A couple of guys on the mat stopped circling each other long enough to shout, 'Kenny!'

He nodded in response and walked over to the changing room door. Pulled it open. Caught sight of the naked, hairy crease of arse and swinging balls as a man leaned over to pick up his towel from the floor.

'Jesus. Things you see when you don't have a gun,' he said. Thought: I need to go back and see Christine so I can banish that from my mind forever.

The man stood and held the towel in front of him. Too late *now* for modesty, thought Kenny.

'Ah, Kenny. How's it hangin'?' His name was Richard Fortey. A regular at the club. A grunter when laden with a heavy barbell and now imprinted in Kenny's memory.

He shook his head as if trying to dislodge the picture from his mind and then responded. 'Christ, you're an ugly bastard. Think I prefer the view from the back.'

Rich grinned. It was all part of the game. 'Whatever floats your boat, mate.'

Enough with the banter, Kenny thought. 'Seen Ian today?'

'Nope,' Rich replied. 'Ain't nobody here but us chickens.'

Kenny nodded his thanks and turned to leave.

'Hey, mate,' said Richard. 'Water's freezing. Near froze my nuts off.'

Wouldn't that have been handy, thought Kenny. 'Sorry, Rich. I'll have a look at the boiler before I go.'

His phone buzzed. He had a look. A text from Vi.

Caught up with Ian yet?

For chrissake, Kenny thought. Give me a chance. He thumbed a reply as he walked back through the changing room door.

Not yet. Just heading over to his place.
Sorry to be a pest, son. Let me know asap, eh?

Ian's flat was just minutes away. Ground floor of a typical Glasgow tenement building. Four floors of blond sandstone. Kenny parked and, as he walked to the entrance, thought that at the end of each working day parking here would not be quite so easy. He pocketed his key, and before he dropped the keys into cloth he fingered the one that was for Ian's front door. Best to knock first. Wouldn't do to go charging in and interrupt him at something.

The front door wasn't locked, so he was able to push it open and then approach Ian's door. It was a distressed blue, the paint cracked here and there, with a spy-hole at face height. He knocked, and as the noise filled the narrow, high-ceilinged hallway he tried to remember the last time he had been here. Shook his head. Nope. Couldn't remember.

That's ridiculous, O'Neill, he thought. Must do better.

No answer.

He knocked again. Listened for a response from inside.

Nothing.

He pulled the keys from his pocket. Located Ian's, slid it into the lock and pushed the door open. He stepped inside and instinctively knew the place was empty. Still, better check, he thought.

'Ian?'

Silence.

He stepped further into the narrow hallway. Looked right to the living room and from his vantage point could see a battered old, brown velour sofa. Not so much lived in, as suffered through the travails of a series of squatters.

Three steps and he was in the living room. Couldn't help but contrast it against the plush luxury of his own place. Shrugged. He could offer Ian all sorts of cash and stuff, but he simply wasn't interested. He'd always thought life was about *doing* rather than *having*.

Still, thought Kenny, taking in the TV in the corner of the room, the time came when you had to get rid of the TV and VHS cassette combo. No DVD: *cassette,* for fuckssakes.

He made a mental note: get Ian a flat-screen TV and a Blu-ray player. Pretend that it fell off the back of a van. And seeing it would be coming from Kenny, Ian might even fall for the lie.

That was all well and good, but where was the prick?

He backtracked to the hallway and beyond to the bedroom.

In pride of place was a double bed, with low pine effect railings at either end. The quilt was bundled up in the thin pile at the foot of the bed. Weren't these ex-army guys supposed to be tidy?

The room was so small there was little space to walk round the bed, but as he did so Kenny could see that Ian's belongings were just as meagre as he remembered. There was a single bedside cabinet, built from the same pine as the bed. Sitting on top of that was a lamp, bearing a purple shade that went with nothing else in the room. And beside that a phone charger.

Well, wherever you are, thought Kenny, your phone could die on you. But he took its presence as a good sign. Meant he wasn't planning on being away for long.

Kenny walked to the window, the view mostly made up of a red brick wall. He craned his head to the side to see, yup, another red brick wall. But this one was faced up with a row of green and blue wheelie bins.

Nobody's going to be looking out that window and writing poetry, that's for sure.

He turned and shuffled back round the bed to the door. As he did so, he caught view of a small piece of paper and a pencil at the side of the lamp.

The paper was a napkin. Cheap, thin paper that looked as if it had originally come with a Happy Meal. He picked it up to see that a series of numbers had been scribbled on it. It read like a phone number.

Kenny smoothed it down on the pine surface. Read it through again. Yup. Must be a telephone number. He dialled it.

Three rings and a female voice answered.

'Good morning. Hollybush House, how can I help you?'

'Right. You're Hollybush House. Of course you are,' said Kenny as he tried to place the name.

'Yes, we are, sir,' said the voice. 'How can we help you?'

'Sorry,' said Kenny as he failed to come up with something. 'Not who I was looking for.' He hung up.

Dialled Dimitri.

'Good morning, Dimitri and O'Neill Undertakers. We put in a shift. How can we help you?'

Kenny groaned at the man's cheer.

'Do you sit up all night thinking this shit up, Dimitri?'

'Kenny. How the hell are you? If you are on about Christine, I've . . .'

'Nope, not Christine,' he replied. 'Hollybush House. Find out what it is and where it is. Soon as you can.' He hung up without waiting for a response.

He walked back through towards the living room and on the way peered into the bathroom and then the kitchen. Both were clean and tidy and looked as if they hadn't been used for a good while. Or, Ian was a clean-as-you-go kinda guy.

In the living room, he had a look through Ian's collection of video cassettes. The usual suspects, including *The Shawshank Redemption, Reservoir Dogs* and yeah, *The Usual Suspects.*

The sum of his brother's life was right here, and it filled him with an ineffable sadness. And a nagging sense of guilt.

Ian goes missing. Yeah, it had only been for a brief time, but he was back on track, back in their lives and a new man. So, something about this was all wrong. And he realised, apart from the gym, his mother's and Ian's sad little flat, Kenny had no idea where else or who else to check out.

Over in the far corner, behind the sofa, a small pine dining table was tucked in, leaving two edges available for a person to sit and eat. In the middle sat a tower of rattan coasters and table mats, and beside them a pile of brown envelopes. He picked them up.

They were all pre-printed Royal Mail postage, paid and stamped on the back with the address of the government office that had sent them. And they were all unopened.

Kenny ignored the temptation to open them. If Ian didn't want to go there, what business was it of his?

His phone rang.

Dimitri.

'Hollybush House?' he asked.

'Yeah?' replied Kenny.

'It's a retreat kinda place for ex-servicemen. I checked. Ian was a resident there for a few weeks.'

Right. That's why the name sent off a note of recognition, thought Kenny.

'Ian did mention if briefly,' he murmured, thinking aloud. Then, 'He mentioned a young guy. Badly injured. A brain injury of some sort. He was helping him out. Keeping him company.' He scoured his memory for a name. 'Donald . . . Don . . . Dom.' It came to him. 'Dom. The young guy was called Dom. Any chance you could get in to their computer system? Track down a Dom who was there at the same time?'

'That's why you pay me the big bucks,' said Dimitri. 'Over and out.'

He hung up.

18

If it was possible, Dom had shrunk, his chin slumped on to his chest. Ian read shame there and could see his young friend was struggling to contain his emotions.

'Who the fuck are you guys?' Ian demanded. As he asked, memory shifted and sifted and presented an image of these two entering the lift just outside Dom's door the first time Ian came to visit.

The tall guy with the spectacles took a step towards him, indicated the other man that Ian could see had ex-army written all over him. 'This is my mate, Baz . . .'

Somewhat incongruously, given the circumstances, Baz nodded a hello, before moving forward to grip Dom by the neck. His large, meaty hand having no problem with Dom's slight frame.

' . . . and we have business with Dom that ain't no business of yours.'

Ian stepped to the side, getting back into Dom and Baz's line of sight. 'Leave him alone, you prick.'

Baz's features bunched into a snarl. 'The wee shit owes us money, and we've figured out a way to make him pay.'

'Talkin' about?' asked Ian. 'What money?'

Dom shrunk into himself even more.

'What you spend the money on, Dom, my old son?' asked Specs.

Dom mumbled.

Baz gave him a shake. 'Aye, ya wee tosser, what did you splash the cash on?'

Ian thought, do that one more time . . . and caught Dom's gaze towards the TV and games console. Added in the cannabis that seemed too rarely to be out of reach.

'I'm guessing some wacky baccy has been smoked. Added to yoghurt. Whatever,' Specs filled in with the manner and tone of someone who was one step up from boredom. 'He owes us money. Can't pay. We have to find something else to get our money back.' *Somefink*.

'How much is it?' asked Ian, thinking he'd get it from Kenny and work to pay it back.

'Never mind, Ian,' said Dom, a tremble in his voice. Squared his chin. Looked at Specs. 'You'll get your money.'

'Yeah, but how?' Baz leaned down into his face. 'You're getting shit all as a pension. Haven't bothered your arse claiming any benefits. This way . . .' he pushed Dom back and onto the sofa, ' . . . you get to pay it all back on a one-er.'

'How much do you owe?' asked Ian.

'Ten grand, give or take,' answered Specs.

'Ten grand?' Ian and Dom both asked at the same time. Ian looked at Dom, who had now gone several shades paler.

Specs looked to the ceiling and pursed his lips as if making a calculation. 'See, there's interest, then we bought out the debt from Baz here . . .' again Baz gave a strange nod of acknowledgement, ' . . . and we have to add interest on to that. Call it a mark-up if you will.' He paused. Nodded his head a couple of times as if he had completed a mental calculation and just agreed with himself. 'So that's ten grand.'

'You bastard!' shouted Dom. 'You fucking bastard. I've barely had a grand off you.' He tried to get off the chair, but Baz leaned forward and pushed him back down.

'Touch him one more time and I swear I'll . . .' Ian stepped forward.

'Let me show you guys 'ow serious I am,' said Specs, reaching into his pocket. He pulled out a gun. Both Ian and Dom reared back. 'He . . .' he used the gun to point at Dom, ' . . . owes us ten grand by my reckoning. Now either he pays up in cash . . . or in blood.' He waved the gun about. 'Or in blood. If you see what I mean.'

Ian watched Specs handle the gun. Noted how at ease he was with it. Considered there was no real threat at the moment, but read the cold certainty in the man's eyes and knew he wouldn't hesitate to use it. He looked from Specs to Baz and read his eagerness to mix it. Specs would resort to violence: extreme violence, of that Ian had no doubt, but there would have to be good reason. Baz, on the other hand, had the look of a man who would be more than happy to scratch that itch for no reason whatsoever.

He had to get Dom out of Baz's reach. But how, he asked himself as he suddenly remembered he was just a threadbare piece of towelling away from being bollock-naked. He checked where the towel was tucked in on itself around his waist and was momentarily pleased that it wasn't about to fall to his feet. Not that he cared about being naked in front of these guys, but if things got tasty it might put him at even more of a disadvantage. He wondered how he could disappear from the room to get dressed.

Ian looked over at Dom, sent him a silent signal to keep still and quiet and prayed that he understood.

'Mind if I . . .' Ian pointed at his naked chest.

'You ain't going nowhere, mate,' said Specs.

Ian moved closer to Baz and Dom. 'Blood you said. What do you mean?' As he asked, he calculated distance, possible movement, pieces on a board. How to save Dom from danger while not getting too hurt himself.

'We've got this fight thing, see?' began Specs.

'A fight thing?' demanded Ian. 'Are you deranged? He can barely stand on one foot.'

'It's no' that bad,' Dom said, looking about ten years younger. His male pride injured.

'We have serious fights and then for a bit of fun, see, we 'ave a couple of geezers, much like your mate here, square up to each other. Knock each other about. Put some sausage and mash on him. Everyone's a winner.'

Sausage and mash. Ian took a moment to translate. Cash.

Ian had never been to an underground fight, but he could picture the scene. Saw a bunch of drunk guys sneering at a broken, bruised and bloodied Dom in a heap. Felt his mouth sour at the indignity of it all. Get a bullet in the head for your country and end up as prey to these wankers.

'You're ex-army?' Ian took a step closer to Baz.

'Aye. What of it?'

'You're a fucking disgrace, that's what. You should know better.' Ian felt his anger rise. Turned to Specs. 'And you, you can take your gun and piss off. You're getting nothing but the money back that Dom actually borrowed.'

'Shut the fuck up, prick!' Baz shouted at Ian. Then he launched himself. Ian read his movement and smartly stepped to the side. But the towel was wrapped too tight to move as far as he hoped and Baz got more on him than he should. Still, Ian managed to catch the other man's chin with a right hook before they both went crashing to the floor.

'Oi. Oi!' Specs shouted above the sound of their brief fight. 'I have a gun and I will use it.' A click. A sound that Ian knew well. The safety was off. Then he heard the front door crashing open and the sound of heavy footfall. Ian caught a glimpse of another guy. This one filled the doorway. Black jacket, black slicked hair. He tried to scramble away from Baz's fists and booted feet and realised his towel had come loose. He sent himself a note of caution: this wasn't a fight he was going to win.

Ian felt himself being lifted to his feet. His arms pinned behind his back. He didn't bother trying to resist. Three men and a gun against one and a half with a walking stick.

Fight over.

He caught a glimpse of Baz's face and had a moment's pleasure at the swelling already showing on his bottom lip.

'Fuckssake, what are you, Baz? Twelve? Get over here.'

'Don't talk to me like that, you English prick.'

'If you 'aven't noticed, fuckface, I'm the one with the gun. And the guys in London sent me up here to keep an eye on you. So do one and shut the fuck up.'

Baz growled. Actually growled.

'Mate. We ain't in the jungle now,' said Specs. 'So lose the attitude. And while you're at it . . .' he gave Ian a look over, his expression twisted with distaste, ' . . . go get this guy a pair of trousers or something. Can't be looking at another man's junk.'

Baz left the room. Returned a few moments later with Ian's jeans. Threw them at him, and the bozo behind him released him from his grip so he could get dressed.

'Good,' said Specs. 'You're decent.' He showed his white, uneven teeth. 'Put me off me breakfast that did.' He looked over Ian's shoulder at his other mate. Gave a nod and Ian was once again pinned with both arms behind him.

'Now,' said Specs. 'The man is a wanker, but he's my wanker and I can't 'ave you taking a swipe at him.' He stepped forward until he was in front of Ian. Without warning, he punched him in the gut. Ian's breath exploded from his lungs, and if he wasn't being held up, he'd have fallen to his feet. The force of it took Ian by surprise. This guy didn't look like he had that in him.

Once Ian recovered, Specs was in his face, nostrils flaring with cold intent.

'You need to learn how serious we are, fella. Your mate here owes us and we want payment now. Tough love, innit?'

Ian nodded. And coughed.

'Understand?'

'Yes,' replied Ian.

'Good.' Specs slapped his cheek with his gun-free hand. Hard. 'Observe.'

Ian chilled in response to those two syllables. Wondered what the guy was up to.

'Balcony,' Specs said to Baz.

Baz grinned. Moved towards Dom and picked him up from the sofa as if he was nothing. Marched him out of the balcony door and over to the railings. Dom bucked and squealed like a pinned rat.

'Help, Ian. Help.'

'What the hell . . .' Ian could only watch as Baz pushed Dom over the railings . . . but caught both his legs before he disappeared from view. Dom's screaming echoed in the air around them, high and shrill with terror.

'Now.' Specs turned to Ian. 'Do I have your attention?'

'Get him back in, you bastard. Anything happens to him . . .' Ian's mind was a whirl of panic. How could he save his mate? But he couldn't move. The guy in black had him held solid. 'I'll have you . . .'

'Do I have your attention?' Specs repeated. His voice loud, fighting to combat Dom's screams.

'Yes, yes, let him back in.'

Specs gave Baz a nod and he reeled Dom back in to safety, as if his weight was no more concern to him than a life-sized doll made of rags. Once back on the right side of the railings, Dom collapsed to the floor. A heaving, sobbing mass of quivering bone and limp muscle.

'Do you 'ave ten grand anywhere on your person?' Specs asked, looking at Dom. He was locked in to the moment of terror and couldn't do any more than heave lungfuls of air.

'What about you, mate?' Specs looked towards Ian and tucked the gun into the waistband of his jeans. Ian hoped the safety was still off and he might shoot himself in the balls.

He bit on a sarcastic reply. That would get him nowhere. 'Nope.'

'Then we 'ave ourselves a little problem.' Specs rubbed his hands together. 'A problem-ette, if you will.' He made a loud smacking noise with his lips. 'We need the money. You ain't got the money, but we 'ave a solution.' He tucked his chin into his neck and looked at Ian over the top of his spectacles. 'Fight club.'

'That was a shit movie,' said Ian.

'Wot you on about?' asked Specs. 'That was Brad's finest moment. You Jocks know bugger all. No wonder there was a "No" vote. Can't 'andle all that responsibility.'

'Oi,' warned Baz. 'English cunt. You don't know what you're talking about.'

Specs gave him as much attention as he might a fly buzzing aimlessly around the room. 'Anyway, this fight club thing. Our guy has to go out of town for a little while. He's too good. Peeps are beginning to think he's a ringer . . . which of course he is,' he added with a grin. 'We need another guy.' He looked pointedly at the lean muscle on Ian's chest and abdomen. 'Looks like we have a ready-made replacement.'

'What's in it for me?' Ian asked, knowing he wasn't in the best position to be negotiating.

'Either you do that and help pay off Dom's debt. Or we have to use Dom.' He looked over at Dom who had crawled into the corner of the room. He was on his backside, knees pulled up to his chest and doing the thousand-yard stare, locked into the trauma of his recent near-death experience that had clearly unlocked the horrors generated by his time at war.

As if aware that everyone in the room was looking at him, Dom looked up from his crouch. Wide-eyed. Teeth bared. Slowly he made his way to his feet. Gathered his walking stick to him. Ian was watching and thinking, please Dom, sit down, save yourself from being hurt by these twats.

'Fuck me. Anybody seen *The Exorcist* recently?' asked Baz.

With a yell, Dom brought his stick down on Baz's head.

'Bastard,' said Baz and reached out to grab the stick from him before he could repeat the action. 'That was bloody sore.' He rubbed at his head and pushed Dom back down on to the floor.

'Done by the cripple, you wanker,' said Specs to Baz. 'Good job you ain't got no sense,' Specs said, cracking a huge grin. 'Would have been knocked out of you.'

'Anything happens to him,' Ian looked over at Baz, '. . . and I will kill you.' He looked at Specs. 'Can I fight him?' He pointed at Baz. 'Arrange that and you're on.'

'Now, now, now, me old son. Can't be 'avin' my business associates getting involved in all that.' He looked at Baz and laughed. 'Tempting, right enough. But look at him. Far too healthy. You, however, look like you need a good feed, are on the right side of rehab, and you can 'andle yourself. Perfect.'

'And if I say no?' Ian asked. 'It isn't my debt.'

'Maybe not, but we just made it your responsibility.' Specs grinned. A cold, feral light growing in his eyes. 'Besides, say no and your little friend here best grow a pair of wings.'

19

Kenny sat in his car and, looking out of the window, craned his neck to see to the top of the tower of flats. A grim stretch of grey, with a regular glint of glass reflecting an ash-coloured sky. The windows on the bottom floor reflected nothing, as they had been filled in with plywood and painted a fetching shade of, yes, grey.

Just off to the left of the building was a small seating area. The grass around it looked as if it had been recently clipped and the seats, in an effort to introduce some colour, were painted yellow. Daffodil yellow. Would save the council planting any actual, you know, flowers.

Two men sat on the seats. Jeans and bomber jackets. Baseball caps. Faces darker than the usual Glasgow residents. That will be some refugees then. Kenny reconsidered his initial reaction and recoil to the building. It would be much preferable to a bombsite and a government intent on murdering its own people.

As if he had read his thoughts, one of the men looked over at Kenny in the car and gave a small nod. Then he breathed out a plume of smoke that formed in the still, cold air above him like an ostrich feather. The smoke hung there for moments before shifting, expanding, human torso shaped, like the refugee had exhaled a bad memory. Then it dissipated like it had never been there.

Dimitri had been as good as his word, and with an ease that disturbed Kenny, found the necessary information. It was only a matter of a few minutes' work before Kenny had an email in his phone with Dom's address and recent medical history.

Poor bastard, he thought as he considered what he read there. Get a bullet in the head and end up ten stories high in a building that was on reprieve from demolition.

Kenny stepped out of the car and before he had taken two steps away from it a small child appeared at his elbow.

'Watch your car for you, mister.'

Not a question. A demand.

That was more like the Glasgow Kenny knew and loved.

'Piss off.'

'Your funeral, mate,' the child said. Both feet planted. Not for moving.

Kenny grinned, reached into his pocket and pulled out a fiver. 'Don't spend it all on the one packet of fags.'

'Cheers, mate,' the child said, and when they smiled Kenny could see it was a girl.

'What age are you?' he asked. 'Should you not be in school?'

'It's the holidays, and only perverts ask a girl her age.'

'Perverts and caring adults, sweetheart. But sadly, you can't tell a wolf for the sheep's clothing.' Kenny thought of his own childhood and the neighbours who wouldn't think twice of chipping in on the parental duties, with a cuff around the ear for bad behaviour and a consoling word when a child was found with a skint knee. Do so nowadays and you'd end up in court quicker than you could shout paedophile.

The girl tilted her head back to look at him from under her cap, her mouth open as she tried to work out what he had just said. Kenny could see a row of bad teeth. Looked like she'd been weaned on Irn-Bru and bars of Cadbury chocolate.

He winked at her. Thought this could be the most patronising thing he'd ever done and tapped her a couple of times on the head. Which was possibly just as bad.

'Won't be long,' he said, taking a couple of steps away from her.

'You get an hour, mate. Then I'm gone.'

With a grin, Kenny walked away from her and towards the entrance. Noted the CCTV cameras above the door and once inside, the CCTV cameras in the lobby. One pointed at the lift door and one aimed at the front door.

He checked his email to remind himself which floor he was going to. Pressed the button to call the lift, thinking: fuck the stairs. After a couple of minutes the lift settled on to his level with a groan as if it had exhausted itself on the way down.

He stepped inside. Pressed the required floor number and took in a mixed smell of aftershave and bleach strained through with a note of vomit. Interesting people who live here, he thought.

The lift announced its arrival on the requested floor with the customary ping, and he exited and looked at each of the door numbers until he saw the one he wanted.

He gave it the knuckle treatment. Waited. No response.

Knuckled the door again.

Nothing.

Thought: fuckssakes, all this way for nothing.

Knocked again.

Same response.

Ian, where the hell are you?

He pulled his phone from his pocket, thinking might as well give him another try. Located Ian's number and pressed the call button.

It rang for the usual number of rings and then went to answerphone. He cut the connection before something registered. He had heard a phone ringing in the distance at the same time he heard it in his ear from his own phone.

Before he could think this through, he thumbed call on Ian's number again.

There.

A phone was ringing again. And it sounded like it was coming from this guy Dom's flat.

He bent down, pushed open the letterbox and heard it clearly.

Ian's phone was inside. If so, was Ian with it and why wasn't he coming to the door?

'Ian,' he shouted through the letterbox. 'It's Kenny. Let me in.'

Nothing.

'Ian, I'm not leaving until you speak to me.'

Nothing.

'Dom, if you're there, tell my eejit cousin to come to the door,' he shouted.

There was a pause, then, 'I thought he was your brother.' Sounded like it was coming from just inside the door.

'Is that Dom? Could you let me in, Dom? I need to find Ian.'

'Go away,' said Dom. His voice was weak and sounded like it was shot through with disappointment. At himself or Ian, Kenny wondered. 'You just missed him.'

'Dom, you might be a friend of Ian's, but if you don't let me in and explain why his phone is ringing from inside your house, I will kick this bloody door in.' Too far? thought Kenny. Nonetheless he took a step back as if he was going to go through with this action.

'Go ahead,' said Dom. 'The house is a bloody mess anyway.'

Kenny moved back to the door, bent forward, pushed open the letter box and peered inside. To the left, he could see a pair of legs and a walking stick. Dom was leaning against the wall. From his posture, Kenny got the impression he'd been there a while.

Thinking about some of the information on the young man's file, Kenny moderated his tone.

'You alright there, Dom?'

Silence.

'Anything I can do to help?'

Nothing.

'Look, let me in, will you? I'm worried about Ian.'

'Your brother'll be fine,' said Dom. His voice weakened as he finished his sentence. Kenny was alert to the nuance. What it might mean, he'd need to find out.

'Dom, I will kick this door in.'

'It's open, you arsehole. Just push it open. It's not like every other fucker just doesn't come marching in.'

Kenny turned the handle and pushed. The door opened easily.

'That can hardly be very safe,' he said to the young man leaning against the wall.

'Aye, well,' was his response. 'C'mon fucking in.' With that, he turned and walked along the short corridor to the living room.

Once there, he flopped on to the armchair, from where he could see the length of the corridor back up to the front door. He let his walking stick fall to the floor. Kenny ran his eyes over the guy's short, slim frame. Also took in the large eyes, soft pale skin, and the weak growth down either side of his cheeks that in his day older men used to discount as bum-fluff.

Holy shit, he thought. This boy was in a combat zone?

'Ian's phone is on the charger, over by the telly,' Dom said. His eyes flitted about, avoiding Kenny's gaze.

Kenny walked over and picked it up.

'And as you can see, Ian isn't here,' said Dom.

'How did his phone get on your charger?'

'He was here last night. Came over after the . . .' He looked like he was trying to find the right words. Settled for '. . . family dinner.'

'And where is he now?'

'No idea.' Something about how his eyes shifted to the side made Kenny think the boy was misleading him.

'Dom, where is he?'

'Dunno,' he replied, eyebrows cast in a shape that was meant to suggest honesty. He even managed to meet Kenny's look. For a moment.

'I'm not buying it, Dom. Where is he?'

Dom leaned forward, his face pale and tight with anger. 'I don't fucking know, ok!'

A line from his medical notes popped into Kenny's head. *Poor emotional control.* Kenny dropped into a crouch so that he was at eye level.

'Dom, I know Ian's a big boy, and he's more than capable of looking after himself. But his mum's worried . . . after the big reveal last night . . . and she wants me to check on him. Make sure he's okay. So if you can tell me what you know, that would be a big help.'

Dom looked at him as if beseeching him. Begging him: don't make me say any more. His face turned pink, his eyes moistened.

Dom mouthed, 'I don't know.'

'He was here. Then he left. You don't know where he went?' Kenny tamped down his irritation. Getting annoyed with this guy would just make things worse.

Dom managed a nod.

'Please help me here, Dom. I'm only trying to find him so his mum will get off my case.'

'His mum,' Dom repeated. His eyes changed focus. 'His mum. Fuck. His mum's coming here with the wee fella. Oh, my fucking Christ.' He looked at his watch. 'They'll be here soon. They can't come over now. Not when I'm like this.' He leaned forward and groped for his walking stick. 'Need to calm down. Need to calm down.'

'Dom, mate,' Kenny interrupted. 'What the hell are you on about?'

'The wee man.' He looked at the photographs on the mantelpiece. 'He'll be here in a bit, with his mum. She'll never let him stay over with me if I don't manage to calm down.' He looked at Kenny. 'Please, please, please, you have to go.' He was gulping in oxygen as if he'd just been on a yomp with a fifty-kilo load on his back.

'Aye, ok.' Kenny held a hand out to try and placate him. 'I'll go. But let me know if you hear from Ian, yeah?' There was no point in pressing him any longer. It wasn't going to get him anywhere.

'Aye,' Dom said and fixed a grin on his face. A desperately enforced calm.

'Take a deep breath, Dom,' Kenny said. 'You'll be fine.' Thinking, no way will he be fine. 'Why are you so anxious?' he asked. 'Does your wife not let the wee fella stay over so much?'

'She's just worried, you know?' Dom said. 'I'm . . . I'm not the best at coping with shit, and she's scared I'll lose it and hurt . . .' To Kenny it looked like Dom's bottom lip was trembling at the thought of hurting his son. 'Thing is, he's the one thing that does keep me calm. The only thing.'

'When are they due?' asked Kenny, thinking he didn't have time for this. Then he wondered what Ian might do if he was here.

'About an hour,' Dom managed.

Kenny thought about how he centred himself before a fight.

'Sit on your arse,' he said. 'Take a deep breath.' To his surprise, Dom did as he asked without question.

'Close your eyes. Think about your son. Think about how being with him makes you feel.'

'Aye.' He opened his eyes. He looked like he'd been bitten by a spot of panic. 'What if . . .'

'We're not thinking about what ifs. We're thinking about what is. You love your son. He keeps you calm. Close your eyes. Be with him in your imagination.' As he was saying this, Kenny was thinking: Jesus, how did he get to be an anger management consultant? This was ridiculous. But, it was what was needed in the moment.

Dom sunk a couple of deep breaths. He was breathing slower. Maybe this was working, thought Kenny. Better leave before he goes off on one again.

'Keep with it. Think about the wee fella. How much he means to you. Where do you feel it?'

'In my chest,' said Dom as he opened one eye.

Kenny raised an eyebrow, which was a command. Keep both eyes shut. Dom did so.

'Now let that heat spread down to your stomach, down your legs and along your arms to your fingertips.'

'Aye, mate,' said Dom. 'Feels like that advert. The Ready Brek glow or something.'

'Exactly,' said Kenny. This was a version of what he went through before he went into a fight. An old fight instructor was fond of telling him the relaxed body and mind makes a better fighter. Conserves energy and helps the fighter be the best version of himself. Surely that would work for a stressed-out combat veteran?

If only life was that simple. But it might help Dom face the next hour.

'Stick with that feeling till the ex and your son arrive and you'll be tickety-boo.' He looked at Ian's phone and considered taking it with him. Decided it might be better to leave it in case he came back for it. 'If you hear anything from Ian, let me know, eh? My number's on his phone.'

20

Baz and his mates managed to get Ian out of Dom's flat and passed over to their fight handler, Dave, by promising Ian that a couple of bouts on Dom's behalf would see his mate's debt being written off.

They lied. Or, more correctly, Baz lied.

He had no intention of letting the little shit off with passing his debt on to someone else to service. Besides, alongside the main bout, the guys were keen to have a little bit of comic relief. Get a couple of – he searched his mind for the right term – *challenged* scrappers to fight it out and the punters lap it up. Whets their appetite for the real violence to come.

And at least the little prick had shown some spark when he'd attacked him with his stick. Sure it was made of a light material, but it still hurt when he caught him on his napper.

That was the real reason he was back here, climbing these stairs. Nobody hits Baz Gibbs and gets away with it. Nobody.

He arrived at the correct floor and pushed open the door just as the lift sounded an alert. He caught a glimpse of a tall, stocky guy before the doors closed and the lift descended. Even in that moment he could see that this man would be handy in a scrap. He wondered who he might be. Another mate of Dom's who could be of use to them?

Baz pushed this to the back of his mind to examine later and walked over to Dom's door, took his baseball cap off and put it in his jacket pocket. Then pushed open the door.

A voice sounded from down the hallway.

'What are you back for?'

Then Baz came into view.

'What the fuck do you want? You can't be here. Beat it.'

To his credit, the wee guy looked more angry than scared.

'Now, what kind of way is that to speak to an old friend?'

'Piss off. Beat it,' Dom repeated, his face tight with anger. 'You can't be here.' He looked over Baz's shoulder as if desperate to see someone.

'Your mate's gone. So he's not going to be any help.'

Dom leaned on his walking stick and pushed himself upright. Then he moved over towards the TV and leaned down to pick up a phone that was being charged there.

'Ah,' said Baz. 'Not happening, buddy. You're phoning no one.' He stretched forward and plucked the phone out of Dom's hand. Then he located the off button, pulled the battery from the back and handed it back to him. 'Put that in your pocket. And if you're a good boy we'll let you have the battery back.'

'You need to go. You need to go. Why are you still here? Beat it!' Dom shouted and moved towards Baz. Once he was within striking distance, he tried to brace himself on both feet before lifting up the stick to strike.

'Oh for . . .' Baz said and easily caught the stick as it fell towards his head. Anger spiked in him as he twisted the stick from Dom's hand, swung it round and caught the younger man on the side of the head. Without a sound, Dom crumpled to the floor. He didn't get a chance to draw his feet up to protect himself before Baz swung again. And again. And again.

Baz was breathing heavily, such was the effort he was putting in to striking the body at his feet. He stepped back once his fury had spent itself and looked down at Dom.

That's your problem, he thought. Just don't know when to stop.

He hefted the stick on to the palm of his left hand. It was lightweight, but solid. Some kind of special wood, but not strong enough to kill someone, surely. Looking down at the guy, he tried to work out if he was alive or dead.

Found he didn't much care, now that he had exercised his bad mood. Served the wee prick right.

He looked over his shoulder at the balcony. There must have been a few folk who'd taken a tumble from one of those over the years.

And these ex-servicemen had a terrible record for suicide.

Just terrible.

Baz bent down and picked Dom up. He manoeuvred the boy into a fireman's lift, and with a few strides he was at the railing. Dom let out a groan. A moan of recognition.

'No,' he said. 'No.'

Don't worry, mate, thought Baz. It will all be over soon. He positioned the light body on the top of the railings, easily ignoring the boy's faint pleas and weak scrabbling at his jacket and with a faint note of regret – he could have made a few notes out of this one – he let him fall.

21

Ian was allowed to dress fully and was then led to the outside of the building and loaded into the backseat of a black BMW. Specs entered the opposite door, the big guy climbed in front and fired the ignition. He couldn't see where Gibbs had gone.

As they drove off, Ian contemplated asking where they would be going and when he would have to fight. Decided not to. He'd find out soon enough.

Worst case scenario? He'd get a kicking.

He'd had a few of those over the years, and he was still here.

Best case scenario? He'd win and these pricks would get all of their money back.

In the meantime, Dom was safe and he'd get the chance to see his kid and hopefully a wee dose of healing. And he'd get some distance from his mum, dad and Kenny.

Dad.

Uncle Colin.

He remembered the last time he'd been with him. The twist of his face. The snarl of his statement – the best bit of you ran down your mother's leg.

The man he thought of as his father didn't like him. *Hated* him.

So, bugger the lot of them. This fighting thing could be the best thing to happen to him for ages. He was fit, clean and motivated. He could do some damage. Then once he was ready he could go back and visit his mum, Colin and Kenny and get the whole story.

He was distracted from his thoughts by some movement from

Specs. He'd leaned forward and pulled a small piece of black material from a pocket in the back of the seat in front of him. He handed it to Ian. By reflex Ian held a hand out and took it from him. Opened it up.

'What's this?' he asked.

'A hood. You need to put it on.'

Ian shrugged. Not bothered, but he didn't want these guys to think he was a pushover. 'What's this, a wee spot of hazing?' he asked.

'We need to protect our sponsors,' Specs answered. 'You can't see where you're going at any stage of this whole thing. Call it plausible deniability. If things go tits up, the filth get involved? You're limited as to what you can tell them.'

'Fair enough,' Ian replied and pulled the material over his head. It cut out the light and he leaned his head back on the headrest. Fine with him. He'd try to get some sleep.

It was difficult to tell how long they'd been driving for, but it would have been at least an hour before he felt the car roll to a stop. For much of the journey – when he was awake – he noticed that they were driving on straight, fast roads. Motorway. They could have gone out of the city somewhere. Perth? Ayrshire? Or they could have just driven on the M8 for a while, turned and come back to try and disorientate him.

He blinked at the light when the hood was pulled from his head.

'This is your home for the next few days,' said Specs. 'Until we arrange your first bout.'

Ian blinked some more, tried to focus on his surroundings. Tried to make sense of what was happening. Hadn't they said they had a fight lined up for him? He assumed that meant almost straight away. Why were they stashing him here?

Once his eyes adjusted he could see that they were parked in front of a low, long building of two storeys. Looked to his eyes like the local council had attempted to build a hotel. With small windows and a grey stone cladding, it appeared cheap and not very cheerful. From his vantage point he could see a small set of stairs up to the main door with a pair of stunted fir trees guarding it from either side.

Specs pulled out his wallet and selected some bank notes. Handed them to Ian.

'The receptionist will meet you and guide you to your room. This money is for her.'

Ian accepted the cash, still trying to process events. 'What's going on?'

'Say, thank you,' said Specs.

'Thank you. And what's going on?'

'In good time, my son. All in good time. Right.' He clapped his hands together. One of us will be by later with some stuff. Coffee, crisps, cornflakes, that kind of shit. This place is what you might call self-catering.'

'Do you only go shopping for stuff beginning with the letter "C"?' asked Ian.

Specs gave this a moment's thought. 'Funny guy,' he said. 'I like that. Now piss off.'

Ian got out of the car and walked towards the hotel's door. As he passed, Specs rolled down his window.

'Hang tight. Your first bout should be in a couple of days. Just chill until then, 'k?'

'Sure,' Ian replied and walked to the door. Thinking, we play this your way.

For now.

22

When Kenny got back to his car, the girl was still there, leaning against it, studying her phone as if the meaning of her life was scribed there. Or at least instructions as to how she might reach celebrity status.

'You stayed,' he said.

'You paid,' she replied. 'Just doin' my job.' She looked at the time on her phone. 'And you're early, mate. You've got 'nother five minutes.'

Kenny nodded, amused by her attitude. 'What could I do round here for five minutes?'

She shrugged. Gave it some thought. Then said, 'Nothing.'

'Just as well I don't live here then, eh?'

He turned away from her and considered hanging about and extending his time beyond the five minutes to see what she might do. If she would charge him for more time. As he turned he looked down the line of cars, following the array of wheeled metal in the arc that the road took. There, closest to the exit was a black BMW. New registration. Big bastard. Saying this was out of place was like saying the Glasgow winter weather could be kind of damp.

He followed the line back until his attention was snagged by a red car. He could see just the wing mirror and a stretch of side panel, so he moved out a couple of paces. And there it was: Ian's beat-up car. He walked over to it, with the girl following.

'You know, you're over your hour here, mate. I'll need to charge you another fiver.'

Kenny reached the Ford. Peered inside. Nothing there but empty seats.

'Ever watch out for this car?' Kenny asked.

'Of course,' she replied. 'I look out for every car.'

'Know the owner?'

'Ian? Aye. He's okay. Rubbish at computer games but.'

'How do you know?'

''cos I played him, up the stairs. In Dom's place. *He's* quite good. Well, a bit better than his mate. Ian cannae play for toffee.' She looked at Kenny as if trying to work out how this information might earn her more money.

He pulled out his wallet, found a twenty and handed it over.

'Wow. You're totally rich,' she said and held it up to the light as if she'd never seen a banknote of this colour before. 'What do you want to know?' she asked, crossing her arms and squaring off her body position as if she was preparing to be there for some time.

'I need to adopt you,' Kenny said, feeling a large smile warm his face.

'Eh. Don't think so, mate,' she said and reared back. 'My maw would totally kill me.'

'Don't worry,' Kenny said, trying to mollify her. 'Just a figure of speech . . .'

'Yeah, for a pervert.'

'Right. Cut it with the wisecracks, missy . . .' He paused. 'What's your name?'

'That'll cost you another twenty.'

Kenny pursed his lips and blew. 'Yeah, right. You've got enough cash out of me, sweetheart. What's your name and what can you tell me about Ian?'

'Myleene, and how do you know Ian?'

'He's my . . .' his mouth formed to say the word "cousin" but he caught himself in time, ' . . . my brother.'

Myleene peered at his face. 'Yeah, you're like twins.'

135

'Really?'

'Nah.' She grinned. 'He's a bit skinny, and his hair's a bit longer. And he looks poor. You look rich.' She said the word "rich" with relish.

'Wee shite,' Kenny said under his breath. Then. 'When did you last see Ian?'

'Today'

'And . . .'

'Got into a big black car with two guys.'

'Kind of car?'

She shrugged. 'It was black. It was big. It was a car.'

Right, he thought. Status symbols like that are going to be lost on her. 'Can you describe the guys?'

She looked at her feet. Then up at him from under the visor of her baseball cap. Large eyes, snub nose, plump lower lip and pointed chin. She looked scared while going for tough. Reminded Kenny how young she was. Back down to her feet.

'I've saw these guys before. They annoy Dom.'

Kenny set that to the side of his mind for later. Softened his tone. 'Can you describe them?'

She nodded. 'My mum says they're bad men. To keep away from them.'

'And . . .'

'There's a bald guy. A big skinny guy wi' specs and a big wide guy.'

A wide guy, a baldie and a skinny guy with specs. That won't narrow it down much, Kenny thought. There's half the population of the city right there. He looked at Myleene and tried to work out if he could get much more out of her. Doubted it. She might be gallus, with enough attitude for ten ten-year-olds, but she was still just a kid.

He heard a scream.

He turned towards it.

And heard another noise he would never ever forget, as a body crashed down on to the unforgiving concrete.

23

The sky was leaden, bruised, pressing down on him as he made his way in to The Blue Owl. He shivered against the chill of a Scottish autumn and against the memory of what he'd witnessed that morning.

The noise played in memory. The scream rising in volume, then cut off by a bone-crushing, skin-rupturing, wet thud.

He tried to shield Myleene from the view, but she was too quick, looking beyond him despite herself. Her eyes were big as plates, her mouth a shocked "O". Kenny pulled her to him, trying to offer her comfort. Her whole body was shaking.

'Ohmygod, that's Dom. Dom. Ohmygod, Dom,' she said. On a loop. Then she started crying.

Kenny picked her up. She tucked her head into his neck. He held it there with his hand. Made soothing noises while his mind raced. Tried to make connections.

The two men who'd been sitting smoking over in the seating area walked round to see what the noise was. Wished they hadn't. One of the men looked almost resigned. Terrible things happened in life. He's seen worse: much worse. The other, younger man began to tremble. Looked to Kenny for guidance. He was the white man. The local. He'd know what to do.

Kenny's mind raced. What the hell?

He shifted so that Myleene was still in his grasp, then pulled out his phone with his free hand. Thumbed out an emergency call. Asked for an ambulance. Thinking, too late, but somebody needs to take this body away. He put his phone back in his pocket satisfied that someone was on their way and that no one would have any idea that it was he who'd called it in.

'Myleene.' He spoke softly. 'Where do you live?'

She was inconsolable. Unable to speak. He had to get her away from the body. 'Where's your mum?' he asked while walking towards the entrance. All the while holding her head into his neck so that she wouldn't get sight of the body as they passed.

One of the men removed his jacket and almost tenderly placed it over the body's head. Kenny offered him a silent nod of thanks and entered the building. In the foyer he spotted something he hadn't noticed when he'd first arrived. A door marked "Concierge".

He knocked it.

Nothing.

Knocked it again.

Nothing.

Part of him was relieved. The fewer people that could tie him to this situation the better. He was the last man to talk to the deceased. The authorities would want to speak to him. Suicide or murder?

If they thought it was murder, he'd be in the frame. There was nothing to prove the guy had been alive when he left him.

Still. He had to get Myleene home. No way could he just leave her here. Not with her friend lying out there like that.

He lowered himself, placed her on her feet and bent into a crouch, eye to eye.

'Myleene, I need to find out what happened here, but first I need to get you home. Can you tell me where you live? Is your mum going to be there?'

The lift door pinged open. A man got out. Wearing the ubiquitous baseball cap.

'Hold the lift, mate, will you?' Kenny asked over his shoulder.

The man ignored him. Walked away.

'Very nice,' Kenny said.

He took Myleene's hand and led her to the lift. Thankfully no one had called for it, so he pressed the button and the doors opened. He hoped that as he walked inside, the familiar aluminium shell would serve to announce some sort of normality to Myleene's shocked mind.

When the doors closed, she looked at him. Mouthed, 'Nine.'

He gave her a reassuring smile and pressed the button.

Soon he was at her door with her and she pushed it open and ran inside, shouting "Mum", without as much as a backward glance at him.

He made himself scarce.

In the car, as he drove off, he noticed two things. The black BMW was gone, and a small, blue Peugeot turned into the car park. A small boy was straining at his seatbelt, face bright with excitement.

It was just a glimpse, but Kenny was certain it was the wee boy he'd seen on the photos, pride of place on the mantelpiece, in the dead man's flat.

*　*　*

He took a seat at the bar of The Blue Owl, head in his hands.

'Morning, or is it afternoon?' asked Ray McBain as he walked out of the store room. Looked at his watch. With some surprise he settled on, 'Evening? Want to see our dinner menu, sir?'

'We do dinner now?' Kenny asked, raising his head.

'Shit,' said Ray. 'Seen a ghost? Spent too long looking in the mirror this morning?'

'Something like that,' Kenny answered with a weak smile. 'Not sure I could stomach any food.'

'Just as well,' said Ray. 'It would either be salted peanuts or sweet-chilli coated peanuts.'

'Coffee?'

'Coming right up,' said Ray. He turned to set the machine. Looked over his shoulder. 'So, what's eating your gusset today?'

Kenny told him. And as he was talking he realised that for the first time he'd told Ray everything. Held nothing back. If Ray had still been in the police he wouldn't have told him he was present when Dom fell or that he'd been in his flat beforehand. Preferring to use "the friend" legend. He felt a faint prick of worry. Could Ray ever lose the policeman in him? Can he trust him completely?

'Shit,' said Ray. 'I saw loads of car crashes in my time. Only saw one jumper. His head and arms were like a display in a butcher's window. It was as if . . .'

'Oh for fuckssakes,' moaned Kenny.

'Too soon?' Ray offered a smile of commiseration. 'You get a bit matter of fact over the years if . . .'

'Where's that fucking coffee?'

'It's fucking coming,' said Ray as he placed a white mug, full to overflowing with today's drug of choice. He made himself one and walked round to the other side of the bar and sat on the stool beside Kenny.

'Oh, fraternising with the customers?' asked Kenny, trying to locate his sense of humour.

'Did you pay for the coffee?'

Kenny shrugged.

'Not a customer then.'

Ray took a sip. Swallowed. 'So this black BMW?' he asked.

24

Ian took the key for his room from the woman on reception, followed her up the stairs, avoiding the threadbare patches as if he might somehow fall through them, and then waited quietly as she stood at his door and went through the idiot's guide to his new living space. This is the bedroom. This is the shower room. Blah.

A redundant description when you have a pair of functioning eyes.

'Thank you,' he said when he'd had enough and offered a half-smile. She sighed when she read his cue and walked to the door.

'If you need anything, son, just . . .' she said and tailed off as if she'd just run out of energy.

He closed the door behind her and locked it. Then he made up the bed, kicked off his shoes and lay down.

He looked round the space. Felt as welcoming as a giant spider web to an arachnophobe. The walls were a washed-out blue, the ceiling stippled and painted an off-white. He craned his neck back to catch a glimpse of the small set of curtains – blue – whose next function would surely be as landfill. They weren't thick enough to dry off a recently washed plate, never mind the weak sunlight presently showing outside.

At least the mattress – single bed – was comfortable, he thought as he shifted position.

Still. You've made your bed. Have a wee sleep.

He let his eyelids slide to close.

Tried to sleep.

Acknowledged how unsettled he was feeling and tried to locate the source.

Caught sight of Specs in his recent memory. This wanker's version of fight club?

Nah. He'd been in plenty of scraps over the years. Didn't particularly enjoy them, but he didn't mind getting hurt or dishing it out if need be.

His mother and Kenny? Nah, 'cos bugger them.

His wee soldier mate, Dom?

Aye.

Those pricks had their claws into him. Taking a loan of a grand and turning that into ten k? That was evil shit. He'd do what he could to help out by offering his ribs and fists as payment, and if they came looking for more he'd think about what to do then.

He thought about getting in touch with Kenny. He'd be able to sort these guys out, but he quashed it as soon as the thought developed. All through his life he'd turned to Kenny when things went tits up. It was time to look out for himself. Manage this kind of shit on his own.

Hands supporting his head, legs crossed at the ankles, he savoured this clarity of thought. That wasn't something he had much of a track record in.

There was a knock at the door.

He opened it to be faced with a beaming smile and large eyes in a handsome black face.

'Welcome, my neighbour. My name is Mo. Like the runner. Can I welcome you to this wonderful home with my delicious food?' He half turned, arm out, palm up as if he was the head waiter at the Ritz. Behind him, his door was open and Ian could see a small white tray with a loaf of bread, some butter and some jam.

Ian looked at the food. Looked at Mo. Thought: I've no idea how long you've been here, mate, but it's best you get used to the West of Scotland abrupt charm here and now.

'Leave me alone, eh?' he said, shut his door and went back to his position on the bed.

Two days later. There was another knock on his door. Two days of sleep, coffee and cornflakes and an unremitting boredom that was only relieved by the occasional wank. And thoughts of his erstwhile family. Liars the lot of them. That was what burned. People you trusted lying to you for the whole of your life.

He opened the door to a face he'd never seen before.

'Dave,' the guy said and held out his hand.

Ian let it hang there. No point in making it easy for them. The guy was tall and well set, with an open expression that looked like it would fall into a smile. Like Baz, this guy had ex-army written all over him. It was probably not something a civilian would pick up on, but Ian could read it like he could read a street billboard.

Everything about him said: solid, capable, best-mate material. Which was why he was chosen for this role, obviously. It all said *Trust me*, which was why Ian instinctively didn't. Dave might be a good guy, but his bosses were only interested in two things: cash and pain. Which meant Dave was guilty by association.

'Let's go for a run,' Dave said with a smile. He held up his hand with a set of car keys dangling. His way of telling Ian that his version of a run didn't include any sweat or cushioned footwear.

At the car, Dave asked Ian to sit in the back. He did. Saw the hood when he reached to the side to fix the seat-belt. Without a word, he put it on.

'Good man,' said Dave. 'I like a quick learner.'

Ian felt the car move smoothly out of the parking space, drive a few yards to the street and then take a left into the traffic. He'd barely looked out of the window while he stayed in that establishment, having no interest in trying to work out where he was.

Why bother, he thought. That's the game they want him to play? He'd play it for now. By now Kenny would have worked out several strategies to extricate himself from the situation. He'd know all the exits from that building and he'd know exactly where he was.

Kenny could go and do one.

'Let's have some music,' said Dave. 'Get you in the mood.'

The first tune was the theme from Rocky.

Dave laughed. 'Just messing with you, mate. What do you want to listen to?'

Ian ignored him. Let his head fall back onto the cushioned headrest.

'How about some radio then?' asked Dave. 'Saves us from having to make a choice.'

Yeah, whatever, thought Ian and closed his eyes. He put his hands on his lap and made sure his feet were planted on the car floor, the small of his back pushed into the seat.

One thing Kenny did know about was preparing to fight. Was always banging on about being relaxed and centred and all of that accessing the best version of yourself blah. One kind of advice he'd be happy to take from Kenny right now. The prick.

He'd known instantly what Dave was referring to when he invited him out for "a run". It was fight time. He simply didn't want to announce it in that semi-public space in case someone was listening.

Ian felt the surge and tremble of adrenalin in his limbs, ignored the impulse to drum his feet and fingers. Breathing deep, bringing his awareness down to his core. The time to release energy was not here yet.

His attempts at pre-fight relaxation were disrupted at one point by a news announcement on the radio. Ian caught the tail-end.

"... *possible suicide ... Police will release the young man's name once his next of kin have been notified.*"

Something about the announcement called to Ian's subconscious. Poor guy, he thought. Wonder what drove him to it. It's happening to too many young people. Too many young men.

Dave switched the radio off. 'Nothing but bad news, eh?' he asked.

Ian gave it little thought. At least Dom was safe. A thought that warmed him, and he returned to his ruminations.

After some time of straight, fast roads, the car was manoeuvred round short roads and sharp turns before coming to a stop.

'Keep the hood on, will you, mate?' asked Dave. 'Sorry.' He got out of his seat and walked round to Ian's door and guided him out. 'This way,' he said and took a hold of Ian's forearm. Relief that he hadn't taken his hand mingled with a second's pleasure at having contact with another human being. He quelled it. The warmth of a fellow human was not his reason for being this particular day.

Minutes later, judging by how sound didn't travel, Ian guessed they were in a small enclosed space.

'I'm going to take your hood off now,' Dave said.

He did, and Ian blinked till his eyes adjusted.

'Need to get you ready for the bout, mate. First thing. Taps aff,' he said as he tugged at Ian's t-shirt. 'Seems like the fight mob like to see a naked chest. Some homo-erotic shit right there, if you ask me.'

Ian shucked off his jacket and t-shirt. Shivered at the cold air on his skin. Exhaled as adrenalin began a re-surge into his gut and muscle.

'Don't worry,' said Dave with a chuckle. 'You'll soon heat up.' He moved to the corner of the room where there was a small table and chair. On the table was a blue plastic bag.

'Have a seat,' said Dave. 'And hold up your hands.'

Ian did as he was told and Dave pulled some material from the bag.

'No gloves,' he said. 'But it's not exactly bare-knuckle. No point in you guys breaking a bone on your hand minutes into a fight. We wrap them up. Gives the fight more life, eh?'

With practised ease, Dave wrapped his fists. Stepped back to examine his work.

Ian stretched the fingers in each hand. Formed a fist. Punched into the palm of each hand, and with a nod pronounced himself satisfied.

A phone beeped a signal. Dave pulled his out of his pocket. Checked.

'Right. That's the signal.' He leaned down and placed a hand on each of Ian's shoulders. 'Ready?'

Ian looked into his eyes. Nodded.

'Good. The sooner we get this over with, the sooner we get these guys off your mate's back.' He paused. Looked at Ian's head.

'Do me a favour and take the rubber band out of your hair?'

'Eh?'

'You do speak? Good,' Dave said and leaned back. 'On you go.'

Ian shrugged. Stretched back to pull off the band. Shook his head. Ran his fingers through his hair. Had no idea what it might look like.

'Excellent,' said Dave. 'Gives you a wild-man look. The punters will love it.' He clapped his hands once. 'Let's do this.'

Moments later Ian was inside a circle of baying men facing another shirtless fighter. This guy obviously hadn't read the memo that lots of fights are won in the mind, 'cos he looked like he was working on a volatile bowel release.

Ian spread his feet, got onto his toes and started bouncing. This space was warmer. The air spiced with a mix of flatulence, piss, blood and testosterone.

The other guy copied him, slowly shifting from one foot to the other and then doing a wee bobbing kind of dance. Then he gave a wee kick with his right leg. Had all the menace of someone trying to dislodge a flip-flop from the end of their foot.

Ian gave him the stare. Saw the other guy's Adam's apple bob as he swallowed.

A small, fat guy walked into the centre of the space. Pointed at Ian. Announced, 'The Bellshill Bomber!'

Ian screwed his face. He lived nowhere near Bellshill.

'Sorry,' Dave said in his ear. 'It was all we could think of.'

'Desperate Dan!' the fat guy shouted and pointed at the other fighter, who, on hearing the name tried to look a little less actually desperate. Failed.

He was average height. Face streaked with dirt and fear. Ribs showing but carrying a large frame that suggested he'd once carried a bit of muscle. The stuff that was for show.

This should be easy, thought Ian. Stilled the thought. It wasn't over till the fat guy said it was over.

Out of the corner of his eyes, Ian could see fistfuls of notes being swapped. He'd never gambled. A mug's game. But who was the biggest mug at this point?

'There's no rounds, guys.' The fat referee motioned for them to move closer. 'No tapping out. Just keep fighting till one of you can't stand anymore.' He looked from one to the other, checking for understanding. 'Got it? Anything goes. Kicking. Punching. Biting. Aye?' He stepped back out of range. 'Go to it guys. Fight!'

Dan lunged towards Ian. Windmilling. No control. Which Ian thought he should be able to deal with. He'd fought guys like this before. They could be tricky. Could get lucky if he allowed his concentration to slide.

He slipped to the side out of range. As he did so, he sent a testing uppercut into Dan's side. Connected. Dan snarled at the pain and turned to face Ian again. Lunged again, telegraphing his swing. Ian moved to the side, caught him with a jab.

Dan grunted. Faced up to him again. His expression a mask of hate. Adrenalin would be surging in him right now. He'd be feeling little of the damage Ian had inflicted.

Just need to make sure I put more into my strikes, Ian thought.

Dan rushed in again. Ian wasn't quick enough this time. Caught a glancing blow on the right temple. His pause was enough to allow Dan to grab him into a bear hug, pinning his arms by his side. From there he tried to drive his pointy knees into Ian's midriff. Going for his balls, his gut.

Ian brought his forehead crashing down. Caught Dan just above the right eyebrow. Not knowing what to do next, Dan planted his hands on Ian's chest and pushed hard. They both staggered back.

Ian's breath was coming hard. Dan looked like his was harder. His chest heaving, struggling to fill his lungs. He bent forward, resting his hands on his knees.

The crowd screamed for Ian to take him. They could easily see he was the more skilled fighter here and they wanted to taste blood, smell it in the air.

Ian charged him, throwing a haymaker, trying to take the guy's head off. Startled at the change in Ian's approach, Dan fell back and more by luck than design avoided the blow. His change in movement caught Ian by surprise and he lost balance.

As Ian struggled to correct himself, Dan steadied himself and pulled off an uppercut that caught Ian flush on the left temple.

Knockout central.

Ian's legs folded beneath him and darkness flooded in.

25

Kenny thought about Ray's question.

'Tell me about the black BMW.'

Taking the man away from his job is much easier than taking the job away from the man. Especially someone like Ray McBain. Lived and breathed police work. He'd immediately hooked into the area of probable suspicion.

Kenny made a face. 'Thought about looking into it, then got distracted. What with a body falling from the sky and a wee girl needing her mammie.'

'Age?'

'She was only about ten. Eleven. Twelve tops.'

'The car, you fanny.'

'Looked new or almost new,' Kenny replied, giving Ray a smile. Telling him he knew what he meant.

'You're slipping, man. Round that part of the town, the only people who have big cars are the spunkbuckets dealing in human misery. Drugs. Debt. Prostitution.' He ticked them off one by one on his fingers.

'Yeah,' said Kenny. Subtext: shut up, I know I messed up. He looked at Ray. Saw the gleam in his eyes. 'Look at you getting all cop-ready and everything.'

'Shut it.'

'What now, Columbo?' Kenny asked.

'Alessandra will tear me a new arsehole if I get in touch with her for something like this . . .' Ray leaned on the bar. Elbows on the black marble surface, he drummed his fingers against his pursed lips as he considered his next actions. 'Those tower blocks have lots of CCTV, aye?'

Kenny nodded.

'A few of them have them just for show. Some of them feed into the housing association's own bank of images, but they don't have the staff to examine them. We . . .' Ray paused as if reflecting on how quickly he'd returned to the police "we". Corrected himself. '*The polis* have their CCTV command central kind of place. Maybe . . . just maybe, we can twist someone's arm. Feed them some cash . . .'

'Please don't tell me that former pillar of the community, Ray McBain, is about to contemplate an illegal action?'

Ray made a fuck-you face.

'Don't worry,' said Kenny. 'Let's not dirty your hands until we really need to.' He formed a smug expression. 'I know a guy.'

The next morning, his groin sticky with sex, Kenny received a phone call. He stretched across Christine and picked the phone off his bedside cabinet. As he did so he thought about the wisdom of the previous night's action. He still hadn't got any information from Dimitri about her, and here he was bringing her back to his place. And it wasn't like he was going to get that information soon, now that he'd side-tracked Dimitri once again. This time to try and find CCTV imagery from Dom's tower block.

He read Ian's name on the caller display.

His heart lurched.

Last time he'd seen Ian's phone it was being charged in Dom's flat, not ten minutes before he fell. Had Ian been back there?

'Ian? Mate?' he answered trying to sound blasé.

A female voice responded. 'This is Police Scotland, sir. Could you please identify yourself?'

Kenny cut the connection. Then he pulled the back off his phone and removed the battery and the SIM card.

'Shit,' he said to himself. He remembered he'd asked Ian to save his name on his phone only by his initials. So, they wouldn't know anything about him other than K and O. And that could mean anything.

How the hell did the police get Ian's phone so quickly? Must have searched Dom's flat.

'Mmmm? Everything ok, babes?' Christine asked, lifting her head off the pillow.

Kenny ignored her. Jumped out of bed and walked through to his kitchen. Once there he pulled a plastic box from a drawer above the cooker. Placed it on the worktop and opened it. There was an emergency burner phone inside. One of Dimitri's better suggestions. He pulled out the phone and its charger. Plugged it in.

He heard Christine's feet on the floor tiles.

'Coffee?' she asked.

'I'll get it,' he said and turned to face her. She was wearing the white shirt he had been wearing last night and which, with hard-on urgency he had hung up on the bedroom floor. Before she pulled it closed he caught a glimpse of perky breast and nipple. The man's shirt on an otherwise naked woman was a well-used image in Hollywood, he thought, and for good reason. A picture that shoots straight from the eye to the groin.

'See something you fancy?' she asked, pushing her hair to the side and adopting a cross-eyed expression.

Kenny laughed. 'Eejit.'

She stuck out her tongue. He pulled her to him and kissed the top of her head. Thought: whoa, Kenny. What's up with that?

Christine managed the moment of awkwardness with ease. 'As much as I enjoy looking at your firm backside, why don't you go and put something on while I get the coffees?'

'Aye,' Kenny said. Scratched said arse with a half-smile and walked back into the bedroom where he selected a pair of black jogging pants and a grey t-shirt from the chair in the corner. As was usual when he did this, he thought about a friend who'd said that for someone who took such care with his appearance while out of doors, his house was a mess. He made a mental note: get a cleaner.

He picked his wallet from its usual resting position on the top of his chest of drawers. Stuffed it into his pocket and walked back to the kitchen.

Sliding on to a stool, he pulled out his wallet again and sat it on the worktop as a reminder to pay Christine her dues. From her expression, she read this as his attempt to get things back to their functional relationship basis. He pays. They have sex. Displays of affection to be filed away as mistakes.

'Sorry . . .' he offered. 'I don't mean . . .'

'No problem, Kenny,' she said with a guileless smile. 'I'd fuck you for free, but you know, you offered payment first. And what's a girl to do?'

He couldn't help but smile.

His burner phone was still charging, but the battery was now holding enough of a boost to make the phone functional. He picked it up and sent Dimitri a quick message. Copied in Ray and his aunt Vi.

You can get me on this phone for now.

The coffee machine behind Christine signalled it was ready to deliver their first caffeine hit of the day. Kenny got two mugs from the cupboard and poured.

'So, how did a nice girl like you end up in a place like this?' he asked as he pushed her drink towards her over the kitchen island.

She raised an eyebrow, subtly asking if they really needed to go there.

'Sorry,' he said. 'I'm always curious as to how people make their living. How they . . .'

'Bullshit.' She smiled, blew on the surface of her drink and took a sip. She swallowed. 'Actually I don't mind talking about it. To be honest I'm surprised we haven't talked about this earlier.'

'It comes up often?'

'Yeah. This end of the market is more . . . relaxed. Less wham, bam, thank you, babes.'

Kenny settled himself on the stool again. Asked, 'You must meet some utter twats.'

She cocked her head to the side and raised her eyebrows. 'I couldn't possibly comment.'

'A professional professional.' He raised his mug to her. They clinked.

'If I'm discreet in your presence, you can trust that I'm discreet with my other clients.'

'So. Anyway . . .' Kenny moved to return the subject to her career choice and registered a grumble in his stomach.

'Long story short. I left school. Went to university and studied English. I wanted to be a writer . . .' As she said this she offered an apologetic smile. As if to say, pathetic eh? 'Ended up teaching . . .'

'Really?'

She nodded and continued. 'Got married to a lovely guy. I'll change his name to protect the innocent. Let's call him Pete. The first clue was that he didn't want to have sex until we were married . . .'

'I think I know where you're going with this part of the story.'

'Yup.' She nodded. 'Then when we were married he blamed his lack of sexual response on a prescription for anti-depressants.' She made a face. 'He was the artistic type. An actual published writer. Which is probably what drew me to him in the first place. That and his incredibly long eyelashes.'

'Your second clue.'

'Quite. Then he said it was because he was a diabetic. Poor blood flow to the extremities, don't you know.' She threw her head back and laughed. Kenny wanted to lean forward and kiss the pale expanse of her throat. 'How naïve was I? Jeez! So I tried everything, didn't I? The sexy underwear. Sex toys. Massages.

Porn. You name it and nothing, zilch. Mini Pete was a permanent Mr Softy. Even watched pornos for hours to learn how best to give a blow-job . . .'

'And all that time was well spent,' Kenny said, feeling a charge.

'But I loved him, you know? He was sweet and kind. Just didn't get it on with my lady parts.' She shifted in her seat at this and crossed her legs. Kenny caught a mental image of her lying on his bed displaying said parts and felt a stirring.

'Holy fuck, are you sexy,' he said.

'Down boy.' She grinned. 'So. I had this lovely man. And no sex life. I can't tell you how frustrating that was. I started to go out with the girls. Had a couple of one night stands. I like sex. I like men. I like men to be men, what can I say?' She threw her hands up. Then held them in front of her with fingers pressed into her palms, wrists up. 'Guilty as charged, arrest me, officer.'

'You have cufflinks?'

'Another time.' She stuck her tongue out. 'Then one night I had arranged to meet a friend in the bar of a classy city centre hotel. She stood me up. A handsome older man approached me. Offered to buy me drinks. Once I was half-pissed, he took me to his hotel room and it felt dangerous, you know. A total stranger in a hotel room? I don't know *what* I was thinking. Afterwards, we showered and he asked me to leave 'cos his wife was about to arrive. Then he emptied his wallet into my handbag.' She laughed at the memory. 'I had no idea until that moment that he thought I was a prostitute. And I was standing there in the hotel corridor with my back to his door, thinking, shit that was easy.

'For a moment I was like, what a prick, and almost knocked his door and threw the money back in his face.' She smoothed her hair away from her face. 'I waited until I was in the lift until I counted the money.' She grinned. ''cos I'm a classy bird. And he'd paid me a thousand pounds.'

'You were lucky,' Kenny said. 'He could have been a psycho.'

'Yeah,' she agreed. 'But I had this feeling, you know? Like I had with you. This was a good guy.' She held a hand over her flat stomach. 'I trust my gut. Always have.'

'So you kicked the teaching into touch?'

'Not at first. I went back to that hotel the following week, wearing the same dress and hung about like I was waiting for a pal. And pretty soon I had another offer. After a few weeks of that I realised I could make more money at this than in education. Besides. Kids nowadays? Wee bastards.'

Kenny laughed. His next thought was interrupted by a text alert from his phone.

It was Dimitri.

That CCTV? I'm in.

Kenny looked from the screen to Christine. Her crossed legs. That shirt on her. A peep of cleavage.

'I need to go soon,' he said. Shifted off the stool and stepped up close to her. He opened the shirt and cupped her left breast with his hand. Softly rubbed her nipple with the pad of his thumb. He noted her swallow, open her mouth slightly as her breath caught. 'Fancy a quick shower?' he asked.

26

Ian came to as they carried him back through to the room he'd got prepared in. One person to each limb. They placed him not too carefully on the stone floor, and he just lay there thinking, what the fuck?

Dave appeared above him. Voiced his own question. 'What the fuck, mate?'

Ian propped himself up on to his elbows and then, checking that his head could take him being upright, he managed to get his feet under him and stood up. Found the plastic bucket seat against the wall and sat down.

'You should have had him, mate. Easy.'

The door opened and in strode Specs and Baz. Ian groaned. He hadn't spotted them in the crowd.

'Yeah, you should 'ave 'ad him, mate,' said Specs. Dave's tone was supportive. Specs' wasn't anywhere close to that. Cold and matter of fact.

'cost us a shitload of money, ya spunker,' said Baz.

Ian looked up at Baz. He'd had enough of this guy's Glasgow hard man act. 'Yeah, well, when it's you, I'll make sure I dodge any of your lucky swings, 'cos that's all you've got, ya prick.'

'Now, girls,' said Specs. 'This lover's tiff ain't helping anyone. And we need help, cos we 'ave a problem. Little Dom's debt is still outstanding, and that has just climbed to twelve grand after this carry on today.' He crouched down so that he was on Ian's eye level. 'Whatcha gonna do about that, mate?'

'I'll tell you what he's going to do. He's going to get his arse back in that ring and kick shit out of someone so we can get some money back,' said Baz. He was hopping about from one foot to the other as if he was about to go into the ring himself.

Ian said nothing. Just studied the floor. Two days away, a botched fight and Dom's situation wasn't any better than it was before these arseholes turned up at his door. He shook his head slowly. What the hell was he even doing here? An image of Dom striking at Baz with his walking stick entered his mind. Shit, if the wee man can show that amount of fight, surely he could too.

Specs stood up, groaning as he did so. 'Oh, me back.' Looked over at Dave. 'So, how is he? When can he go again?'

Dave walked over to Ian. Took his head in his hands. Turned his neck from side to side.

'Any dizziness?' he asked.

'Nope,' Ian replied.

Dave asked him to stand up. Then turn round. And turn back to face him.

'There isn't much damage at all,' he said. 'Just got caught with one lucky punch, and that can happen to the best of us.' He winked at Ian. 'A good night's sleep and some decent scran is all this guy needs.'

They went through the same pantomime of the hood and the long drive and dropped Ian off at the same digs he'd slept in the night before.

He climbed out of the car, thinking: I'm pretty sure we're still in Glasgow. Why bother with all this nonsense? Kept the thought to himself. Dave got out too and walked to the front door with him.

'Need anything?' Dave asked.

'Some food that doesn't begin with a "c".'

'Gotcha.' Dave grinned. 'Anything else?'

'Could do with some new underwear. My pants and socks are getting a bit crusty.'

Dave made a face. 'Isn't there a wee laundry in there?'

'Aye, but I can hardly go in there, strip off and sit naked while everything is washed and dried.'

'Leave it with me.' Dave paused. 'I could go to yours and pick up some stuff?' He held out a hand as if asking for Ian's house keys. He recoiled at the thought of these guys looking through his home.

'Nah. Just get yourself to M&S and put the cost on my tab.' He felt his expression sour as the notion of owing these guys *any* money hit home.

Dave put a hand on his right shoulder. 'Don't worry, mate. You'll get all this sorted.'

Ian shrugged the hand off his shoulder. Gave Dave a fuck-you look, turned and walked inside.

Once in his room, he lay on the bed, feet crossed at the ankles, hands under his head and examined the stipple on the ceiling. Well, this is a clusterfuck, he thought. Kenny would be pissing himself. And yet again convinced that he couldn't tie his shoe-laces without making an arse of it.

He replayed the fight. Still didn't see the punch coming.

Fuck.

He felt an itch in his right arm. Gave it some fingernail. For the thousandth time asked himself what the hell he was doing here. Thought about scoring some hash.

That was his pattern. Fuck up. Score some drugs to remind himself what a fuck up he was. Just a little oxy here. Some crack there. He'd take anything. Feel that rush and slide into forgetfulness.

It started with glue sniffing as a kid. Quickly moved on to eccies. And jellies. He didn't know why he was so intent on getting out of his face. Getting swedgered out of his nut.

Kenny, however, got his teenage highs from fighting and

fucking. Hated losing control. When everyone else was getting tanked on Buckfast he would just look at them as if they were losers. Never did give in to peer pressure. And he had the speed, strength and attitude to back that up. Someone might try to give Kenny a hard time for not getting pissed, but they'd be put in their place – firmly.

Other guys did the swagger thing. Puffed up chest, arms wide in that "come ahead" pose. Kenny didn't bother with any of that. He would get that look. And strike. It would be over before the other guy knew what was happening. Tears 'n snot. And the odd broken bone.

To be fair, peer pressure was never what drove Ian. There was a sourness in his mouth. A twist in the gut. A voice in his head that chanted "useless bastard", and the only way through all of that was to chase it from his head with the help of some chemicals.

Lying on the bed, staring at the ceiling, he thought back to that first hit. How the joy centre in his brain sparked and flooded every cell in his body. Rush. Whoever first coined that phrase hit the nail smack bang on the pleasure dome.

Then came the fall.

Feeling even more worthless in those moments when he didn't have access to the highs. The down even more pronounced because he'd never experienced anything like it.

He'd managed to function through most of it. Convinced the powers-that-be he was normal enough to join the army. And then the shit he'd experienced in 'stan was enough to drive him back into the arms of his favourite dealer.

And another fall.

Oxy was great at first. What a buzz. But when he couldn't get a hold of any, the downs were horrific. Vomiting till his ribs felt like they were broken. Headaches so severe they'd make migraines feel like a tickle. And the bone pain. What the hell was that about?

He felt his muscles tremble. His breath shorten.

Just one.

Just a wee hit?

A place like this there's bound to be a few dealers nearby.

Three slow, deep breaths.

The army got him a drug counsellor. Jim was a good guy. He'd been there. Ripped up the t-shirt and wiped his arse with it.

Jim warned him that old habits would try to reassert themselves in times of worry. Get a coping mechanism. Distract yourself, he said. Fill the void with something else.

And he was on the floor. Twenty press ups. Twenty burpees. Repeated until each breath was hard-won. Then he stripped off and took a shower.

As he was drying himself there was a knock on his door. He wrapped a towel round his waist. It had as much cushion as a piece of cardboard.

It was Dave. When he stepped inside he brought with him the chill of the outside and a note of nicotine. He was carrying two bags. One he placed on the bed, and the other he carried to the kitchen-cum-cupboard.

'Got you some corned beef and some bread and butter.'

'Feeling spoiled here,' said Ian. 'And again with the letter "c".'

Dave laughed. 'Shit. Didn't realise.' He pointed at the other bag. It was labelled TK Maxx. 'Didn't know if you preferred boxers or briefs. Got you some of both.' He bent at the knees. 'Like a bit of support round the gonads myself.' He stepped across to the bed and picked out a pair of black t-shirts from the bag. 'Also got you these. That one . . .' he looked at Ian's clothes on the floor, ' . . . will be a bit minging.'

Ian looked at the clothes. Managed a begrudged, 'Cheers.'

'Right,' Dave echoed and clapped both hands on thighs. 'There's a TV room downstairs, I think, if you get bored pulling your wire all day.'

'Aye,' said Ian and walked over to the kettle, filled it and switched it on.

Dave took the not-too-subtle signal and with a nod he left.

Ian dried himself, pulled on a clean pair of briefs. He liked the support himself. And a t-shirt and his jeans. Once the kettle boiled he made himself a cup of coffee and a sandwich. All the while he forced his mind to focus on the simple movements each action required. Fighting the siren call and note of urgency that ran through his mind.

Just one wee hit.

Just one.

27

Dimitri took one look at Kenny when he walked into his office and howled like a dog.

'Should I phone out for some Pedigree Chum, Dimitri?' Kenny asked.

'Wait . . . wait . . . wait.' Dimitri held up a hand, while his face shone in a huge grin. 'Don't tell me. The sex last night was so good even your neighbours had a cigarette?'

Kenny smiled despite himself. 'Where's this CCTV stuff then?'

'Aww, man, let's not do that right now. I've been married for twenty years, I live my sex life vicariously through you.'

'Vicarious? Get you with the big words this morning.'

'Any advice on the, you know, shagging front?' asked Dimitri as he leaned forward on his seat.

'Aye, there's a thin line between cuddling someone and holding them down so they can't get away, you creepy wee bastard. Now, CCTV?'

'Spoilsport.' Dimitri turned back to his screen. *Screens*. He had two giant monitors side by side. 'I managed to get the footage for the day Dom died.' He pointed his mouse at the bottom of the screen and maximised some images. 'This is a still from that morning. Three guys entered the building. Four came back down.' Dimitri did some more fiddling with his keyboard and another imaged filled the other screen. He pressed a button and the image came to life.

Kenny's stomach twisted when he recognised Ian. It looked like his hair was still wet from a shower, but he was walking freely. Not talking to any of the men beside him and not giving anything away as to the relationship he might have with any of the other guys.

The tall speccy guy was not at a good angle on any of the pictures to get a definitive look at. It was as if he was acutely aware of the cameras and how best to avoid them. The stocky guy looked ex-army and like he didn't give a shit if there were cameras. The third guy was tall, wore his hair cropped and looked like he spent every spare moment hefting tractor tyres.

'That means I just missed them,' Kenny said. Looked at the time on the top right of the screen. 'They were there not long before me.'

'Yup,' said Dimitri. He reduced that file and brought up another. 'Here you are walking in the front door . . . then waiting on the lift . . .,' his voice took a little hitch with excitement, ' . . . and this.'

He pressed play.

Kenny could see himself enter the lift. Fast forward and he was coming out of the lift. A man passed him going up, wearing a baseball cap.

'Wait a minute,' Kenny said. 'He . . .'

Then Dimitri moved the film on again and he could see himself and a distraught Myleene enter the lobby. The lift door opened and baseball cap guy came out. Kenny motioned for the guy to keep the lift for them and was ignored. A moment later, just as Kenny and Myleene entered the lift, the baseball cap guy turned.

'That's . . .'

'Aye,' said Dimitri. 'One of the guys who was with Ian leaving the building.'

'So,' said Kenny thinking it through. 'He left. Came back and then left again just after Dom fell.'

Dimitri nodded. Offered a pained sigh. 'I'll bet that bastard threw Dom off his balcony.'

28

Gordon Gallagher had a chin that jutted out just enough to hang your jacket on, and there was nothing his carefully shaped beard could do about that. Take the beard, the high and hard cheekbones, small dark eyes and the once-firm jawline, now starting the slow slide into jowl-dom and you had a face that gave many young men in the Dennistoun area of Glasgow nightmares.

He tried to soften the impact of his stiff gaze with a pair of horn-rimmed spectacles and the determined set of his face with a well-worked, gap-toothed smile, but no one was convinced. If this man's gaze ever fell on you for a reason he determined was the wrong one, then you were in for a shocking time. Quite literally. He always kept a spare car battery and some crocodile clips in his boot. And was more than happy to attach the lot to the testicles of any young man who pissed him off.

Gallagher kept himself to his own part of the city. Ran drugs and counterfeit goods. As far as he was concerned there was an unwritten agreement that every other Glasgow gangster should keep to their own patch, and any excursions into his area were met with swift and painful persuasion to desist and move on.

As other crime families expanded into other areas of the city, then fell apart and others moved in, he managed to keep his streets to himself. And had done so for almost thirty years. McBain told Kenny that in Gallagher's case the police went for the devil they knew. Ok, he was brutal, but only to his own criminal class, and while he was bossing that area, the police knew other, potentially more dangerous types would keep out. Remove him and it would be like hell-gate had opened.

Just like what happened in Libya when the west removed Gaddafi, Ray explained with a rueful smile.

One of Gallagher's strengths was information. He might not get physically involved in other criminals' businesses, but he had paid informants in every part of the city who were as diligent and resourceful as any spy cabal.

Something that Kenny had learned from him over the years. Keep an eye on your competitors. If they're making cash on something, perhaps you can too.

This was why Kenny was sitting opposite him in a booth of a café on Duke Street. He'd dropped that particular ball since McBain tangled with a certain serial killer. Time to pick it back up, but he'd need a few favours first.

'Get you something, son?' asked Gallagher as he leaned back in his seat to allow a young waiter to put down his plate of food.

'Black coffee will do me, thanks, Mr Gallagher,' said Kenny. He looked around himself. Took in the red vinyl seating wide enough for two, black and white photos on walls not taken up by mirrors. They were a mix of Glasgow and some unspecified Italian city in the twentieth century. The space was small, but the corner site with large windows on either side made it feel much bigger. A glass-fronted cabinet displayed a variety of cakes, scones and pastries. He smiled. Not to his taste, but McBain would happily stand at one end of that cabinet and shovel the whole lot in his mouth.

Gallagher smiled at the honorific. *Mr.* Didn't correct him. Clearly, by his expression of content, he thought he was more than deserving of such an acknowledgement.

Their paths had first crossed almost twenty years ago. Kenny was a tangled ball of wire made of surging hormones and attitude, but he took one look into Gallagher's eyes, noted the black spots and instantly calmed down and promised himself he'd never knowingly tread on this guy's toes. And that was before he heard about his trick with testes and an electrical charge.

Gallagher rubbed his hands together and looked at the food on his plate. Two rolls. Well-fired almost to the point of being burned. He opened them up to show that they were filled with braveheart sausage: sausage meat shaped into squares and centred with a heart-shaped piece of black pudding. Like most of the city's population, he was proud of his cheerful disregard for any notion of food as health-promoting.

If food didn't instantly gratify and add plaque to your arteries, why the hell bother?

He reached for the tomato sauce bottle, gave it a shake, took off the lid and gave each black heart a dollop.

'See that paper the other day?' he asked. 'Another of them studies saying red meat was cancer-promoting. Cancer, my hairy hole. Tell that to the cavemen chasing down them mammoths, eh?'

'Aye,' said Kenny, thinking: just agree with everything the old man says. The waiter arrived with Kenny's coffee.

'Anything else, Mr Gallagher?' he asked as he set the cup and saucer down. Kenny looked at the lad. Short, black hair that was just growing out of a buzz-cut and a chin sprouting the odd dab of facial hair. Bumfluff he'd called it as a youth when his mates first tried to grow a beard. The boy had a doleful set to his eyes, as if he'd just read his own early-death diagnosis moments before serving the coffee. And he was tall. Basketball player tall. Which was unusual in these parts.

Gallagher shook his head and continued speaking. 'Eejit scientists. All that money for research and they publish this shit. 'cos that would be a colossal evolutionary fuck-up, eh? An entire species evolves over millennia on eating red meat – along with a few beans and lentils here and there – only to find out in the present day that meat's carcinogenic? Gimme a break.' He picked up one roll, pushed it past his teeth and chomped down on almost a third of it. Chewed, then swallowed as if he was worried the rest of the food would vanish from his plate before he could finish.

He didn't say another word until both rolls were demolished. Then he burped and took a drink of milky tea. He swished the drink about his mouth as if making sure there were no stray bits of meat clinging to his teeth.

'So, what's up, young man? To what do I owe this pleasure?' he asked, going for an avuncular tone.

'Did you hear about the soldier who fell from the tower block?' Kenny asked, acknowledging that whatever the old man gave him would come at a price.

'I did, aye,' said Gallagher and dabbed at his lips with a paper napkin. 'Terrible business. Mind you, so's sending these young boys and lassies out to fight in those hellholes in the first place. More of these kids kill themselves when they get back home than get shot by fundamentalists. How's that for unintended consequences?? Keep the money and build some hospitals over here, eh? Would that not make more sense than sending all these weans out there to get blown up? That arsehole Blair. Ol' Maggie Thatcher must've been right proud of him.' He took another sip of tea. 'Capitalism is ruined. Greed's overcome duty. Forget your responsibility to your fellow man, keep your shareholders drooling over their dividend.' He shook his head. His face grew softer.

'Anyway. What about this boy?'

Kenny chewed down on a grin. Didn't want to offend the man, but it had been a while since he'd come across a street philosopher. Glasgow's pubs were full of men low in erudition but strong in reading. They didn't need a certificate from some weak-wristed academic to tell them they were smart. They read. They debated. They knew shit.

There was also the fact that in Gallagher's rush to decry the rich and powerful, he'd forgotten his own role in pushing down on the heel that kept the ordinary man and woman under control and unquestioning.

Kenny told him about Ian, the black car and the guys as described by Myleene. Gallagher listened, and once Kenny stopped speaking, he sat back in his seat and looked somewhere over Kenny's shoulder as if sifting through each and every one of his memory cells.

'We managed to get some pictures,' Kenny said and reached into his jacket pocket. He pulled out an envelope and the three best images of the men on the CCTV film Dimitri could retrieve.

Gallagher studied them in turn. Looking at each man as if committing him to memory.

'Not ringing any bells, son.' He thought some more. 'The big bruiser guy. He's muscle. Not too bright. Ruled by the thickness of a prospective employer's wallet. I'm pretty sure he's there as back-up. No way he's involved in this in any other capacity. Tall, skinny guy with Harry Potter specs?' Shook his head. 'Nope. Not getting anything.'

Kenny didn't believe him for a second. It used to be said that if Glasgow's Godfather, Arthur Thompson, farted in his gaff, old Gallagher heard and smelled it over in his. Looking at the gleam in his eyes, Kenny thought there was no way he had lost his touch. The old man wanted something from him first.

'It just occurs to me . . .' Gallagher began.

And here it comes.

'We could do each other a wee favour, Kenny my old son. I don't know anything at the moment. But I will do once you come back after having completed a wee job for me.'

'Ok.'

'It's just a wee job. Some stuff going on outside my patch that is leaking on to my streets. And I cannae have that. Cannae have that, son.'

'Aye?'

Gallagher looked down at the space on the seat beside him. Put his hand down and pulled up an iPad. Set it on the table between them, and as he fidgeted with it he kept speaking.

'Excuse me, Kenny. I just need to find something to show you. And I detest it when other people look at their phones and gadgets while they're in company. Shockingly rude.' He paused. Looked at Kenny, his eyes wide with disbelief. 'Here, did you read about that woman who fell off a cliff while taking a selfie? A bloody selfie? That's a waste of evolution right there. Don't bother with red meat, give these eejits a smartphone and a selfie stick.' He barked out a laugh. 'There's a gene pool that could do with some chlorine. Forgive me, I'm getting distracted in my old age, but don't you find there's so much more to get annoyed about these days?'

He fiddled on the screen some more and then turned it round so Kenny could see what he had been doing. He could see a colour photo of two men walking side by side.

'There's these guys. Eastern Europeans. Czechs, Slovaks, Poles, whatever. They're running a shoplifting, burglary operation from the Gorbals, but some of their people are coming into Dennistoun, and I can't have that.' He read Kenny's quizzical expression and pre-empted any question he might come up with. 'I've read their people the riot act. Frightened them off. But others keep finding their way over here.' He paused. 'My guys tell me that the taller one is called Andrei and the other is called Stefan. I need Andrei and Stefan to learn a lesson.'

'Right,' said Kenny. One word. Two meanings. 'I understand. Where exactly do I come in?'

29

Kenny drove back from Dennistoun to his own place in the West End. Dropped the Range Rover off at his lock-up and got in his grey Astra. A set of wheels that would be far less conspicuous when following someone.

Then he drove over to the Gorbals area of the city and parked in the spot as shown in Gallagher's iPad map. The old man had shown a deft touch with technology. Instructed the young waiter that he needed something printed off and that he'd be linking in to the wireless printer.

He'd obviously done this before. Besides, he probably owned the place.

Gallagher also had two copies of a map of the Dennistoun area printed off. Then laminated. And then Kenny was given instructions as to how they might be deployed.

Creative, he thought, and understood why lamination was a necessary part of the process. Also on the passenger seat was a small tool bag, provided by Gallagher.

The man's thought processes were beyond thorough.

Kenny winced at the thought of what he had to do, but if it meant finding Ian he'd do what was needed. In any case these guys were criminals. Idly, he wondered what the Russian, Georgian or Polish word might be for scum.

He settled into his seat and waited for the two men to make an appearance. Looked around himself. The building he was in front of was nothing special, but this whole area had seen a massive amount of regeneration over the years.

Mention "Gorbals" to anyone in the country and the word comes with a virtual smack on the mouth. A reputation that was outdated and hard-won. In the city's rapid race to industrialisation, the Gorbals area was infamous for giving the word "slum" a bad name. Its streets were walked by people with poverty engraved on their faces, and more than a few of them would have borne scars carved by the razor gangs of the day.

In the 60s, much of it was razed to the ground and replaced with tower blocks that quickly suffered from permanent damp and were referred to as "prisons in the sky" by the residents. Glaswegians have never lacked a sense of humour, and the blocks became known as Alcatraz.

Those towers were in turn destroyed, and the buildings Kenny could see around him were built in their place.

Gallagher had a fondness for the area. 'Been over to the Gorbals much, son?' he asked Kenny before he left.

'Can't say I have. I didn't want to carry a knife when I was kid, and the reputation that place had meant it should have been avoided unless you were tooled up.'

'Jeez, it wasn't that bad,' said Gallagher. 'Mind you, we did like a scrap. I remember once, a bunch of us were fighting just off Crown Street. And these Yank tourists walked past. We stopped fighting long enough to help them get back to the nice part of the city – and then carried on getting stuck in.' He laughed. 'Those were the days.' Sigh. 'It's gone all fancy now. Posh people living there and everything.

'One of the older buildings . . . older,' he said with irony. 'It was probably built in the 90s. This building, it was an old council building, has been converted into studio flats and given to a bunch of refugees. Poor bastards, eh? Flee a war zone and end up in the Gorbals. Won't know what's hit them.' This was said with fondness. 'And your Eastern European crims are preying on these poor unfortunates. Forcing them to steal in order to pay for some illusory protection. Pricks. Deserve everything that's coming to them.'

Gallagher looked into Kenny's eyes.

'You've aye had a serious reputation, son. But you sure you're up to this? There's two of them, and I've no idea how handy they are. You needing hauners?'

Hauners.

Kenny grinned. He hadn't heard that term for years. It came from the Scots word for hand: haun. Meant, are you needing a hand? More often than not it applied to a fighting situation.

'Hauners won't be necessary, thanks, Mr Gallagher. I'm sure I'll manage.'

Gallagher looked into his eyes like he was studying the thought behind the words. Then nodded as if finding himself satisfied. 'Take a wee photo on your phone once you're done. Bring that back to me and I'm sure I'll have some information on the guys you're looking for.'

Kenny was certain the man already knew what he needed to know, but went along with the scenario anyway. He'd known before coming here that Gallagher wasn't going to give him the information without some form of reciprocation.

That this meant he would have to get his hands dirty, Kenny welcomed. He had some frustrations that even Christine's skills couldn't reach.

Besides, if he wanted to keep his fighting *street*, he needed to get out of the gym and get into some real, you know, unregulated and nasty shit. He shifted in his seat and reached into the tool bag on the passenger seat. Pulled out a small metal object. Slipped his fingers through the holes and fortified his knuckles. Felt the thrill of the violence to come and thought: this was all the hauners he needed. He looked through the other objects inside. Plastic ties, some rope, a hammer, a small plastic box of nails, a staple gun . . . and, what the hell? Two ball gags? He chuckled. This guy really did think of everything.

He was thrown from his thoughts by his phone ringing.

He read the caller alert. Dimitri.

'Elucidate,' Kenny said.

'Nice,' replied Dimitri. 'Still not as good a word as vicarious.'

'Good for you. You win the big word of the day competition. Why are you calling?'

'Your bird . . .'

'She's not my bird.'

'Whatever. I've been doing some more digging. Got a surname from the phone number. Craven. Which is nice. And she's not on any police databases, so she's never been arrested.'

'That it?'

'Yup,' said Dimitri, utterly uncaring that this was as far as he'd got. 'You need to give me more than a first name and a mobile number. That's not enough to go on, my man.'

'She used to be a teacher.'

'An ex-teacher called Christine Craven. I'm liking the alliteration.'

'Yeah, yeah,' said Kenny, keeping his eyes on the entrance to the building, and absently lamenting the sad little trees on either side of the door. 'Next time I see her, I'll wait till she's sleeping and rifle through her handbag. See what I come up with, ok?'

'Should have an address soon and we'll be cooking wi' gas.'

Kenny cut the connection. Didn't bother with bye-bye. Dimitri was a big boy, he'd get over it.

Two hours later and only a couple of people had entered the building. A black guy wearing shorts and a t-shirt, the dark skin on his forehead slick with sweat. And a white guy. Had the look of a local. Walked with the grace of an athlete and the confidence of a man who could handle himself. He was carrying two plastic bags. One bag was light blue, unbranded. The other had a big red circle and the lettering TK Maxx on it.

Minutes later this guy walked back out, mobile pressed to his face, and got into a silver BMW and drove off.

Interesting, thought Kenny. If this was a refuge for refugees, why was a guy like that, in a car like that, making deliveries? Surely if it was a charitable donation it would be much larger than two small plastic bags' worth.

He was distracted from dissecting this further by the arrival of a white van. As it passed him he could see two men. White. Late twenties. And very similar to the men as pictured on Gallagher's iPad. The van parked in a disabled space by the door and two men climbed out.

Kenny sat upright in his seat. These were the guys. Gelled dark hair. High cheekbones, wide jaws and noses that looked like they were pushing down on their lips. There was little to tell them apart, facially. The driver had a slightly heavier face. The passenger was taller, wider and had a darker beard-growth shadow on his cheeks and chin. Both were wearing light blue denims and black, leather bomber jackets.

Brothers?

They were inside for an hour.

Came back out escorting a young woman. The top of her head reached the collar-bone of the smaller guy. She was pole thin, dark-skinned and wearing grey jogging trousers and a dark blue puffa jacket. Kenny caught a glimpse of world weary and fearful acceptance in her eyes and thought her age could be anywhere between fifteen and thirty. Whatever they were going to do to that poor girl, meant they were deserving of anything that happened to them.

Kenny followed the van into traffic, and without too much difficulty, given that the van provided such a good visual, managed to follow it through the city.

They drove past the Citizens Theatre and from there on to Eglinton Road, past Queens Park, along Kilmarnock Road and then a left into suburbia. The land of yummy mummies and Botox, quinoa and goat's milk, and an inappropriate and entirely wasteful use of 4x4 vehicles.

The white van slowed, indicated and pulled into the drive of a white bungalow. Kenny drove past without looking at the van, and when he judged that he was out of sight, he executed a three-point turn and edged forward until the van was in view.

He looked up and down the street to note that most driveways were absent of cars.

The house was detached. A small two-man wide brick porch in front. A low sloping roof held a dorma window and there were two large bay windows either side of the porch. Both with curtains closed.

Couldn't be better, he thought. Detached house. Everybody at work, school or having their morning coffee and scone down at the local bistro.

Less chance of people hearing the screams.

30

Kenny pulled a black Buff neck warmer over his head and pulled it down around his throat. A black, unbranded baseball cap, black sweat top and glint of knuckleduster completed the look. Wintry, with a hint of approaching storm.

He'd been sitting in the car for two hours, had seen no movement through any of the windows, and no one had left or arrived. There was no way to judge how many people were inside, so he decided he'd just have to deal with whatever he found and get on with the job he'd been asked to do.

Andrei and Stefan weren't going to beat themselves up.

Carrying the tool bag helpfully provided by Gallagher, he walked to the small, brick porch of the bungalow, pulled the neck warmer up over his nose so that only his eyes were visible and knocked. The door was wood, painted white with a small window at head height. A window that was masked with a net curtain.

What is this, the 90s?

He heard a shout. Deep bass. Words incomprehensible. Then a heavy footfall and a clear, *for fuckssake*. The door opened and there stood the taller target, Andrei. His mouth opened in preparation to speak, but the question was already there in his eyes. What the hell? But before he could do anything, Kenny introduced the steeled knuckles of his right hand to his chin.

Pop.

Andrei fell to his knees, but before he reached the ground Kenny caught him and placed him against the wall of the porch.

Deep cushioned carpet in the hall muffled sound. There was little of that, save for the grumble of a television coming from the back of the house. He reached into his bag, and while Andrei groaned and mentally stumbled his way back into consciousness, he cuffed his wrists with a cable-tie. Then he pulled him into the hall where he placed his ankles side by side and bound them with a piece of rope. Then he eased the ball of the gag inside the man's mouth and fastened it behind his neck.

Andrei's eyes opened. Widened. He bucked at his restraints, sounds issuing from his throat that Kenny was sure would offer a threat to his personal safety, if they made any sense whatsoever.

Kenny patted him on the cheek.

'Just hang about here, will you, my good man? I'll be back for you shortly.'

Andrei shot hate at him with his eyes.

Kenny chuckled, picked up his bag, rose from his knees and eased further into the hallway. To his right a closed door. He opened it slightly. A bedroom. Pushed it open further. A large king-sized bed faced him. Empty. He closed the door with a barely audible click.

On the opposite side of the hall was another closed door. He put his ear to it. Silence. Gently turned the handle and pushed it open. The curtains were closed, but were thin enough to let plenty of light into the room. A pair of brown leather two-seater sofas flanked a glass-topped coffee table. A large marble fireplace, topped with a wide mirror. In the corner of the room, the expected large widescreen TV. No people. In fact, the room looked as if it was there for show. The thick pile of the carpet was tracked by hoover marks. Kenny placed a foot in the room, like a child might when faced with a virgin field of snow. Left his mark. Then he closed the door behind him to carry on down the hallway.

A voice from the back of the house. A query. Kenny caught a name and handful of short words. Stefan probably asking what was going on.

There was one more door before the door that Kenny judged would lead to the back of the house, where Stefan's voice and the noise of the TV was coming from.

A bathroom? He put his head to the wood. Someone was singing inside. High, soft and female. He tried the handle. It turned. He opened it slowly. Caught the smell of pine-scented bleach and saw the girl he'd earlier witnessed being shoved into the van, now on her knees with one elbow down inside the toilet bowl. She was wearing a set of earphones, humming along, completely unaware of Kenny's presence.

He looked back at Andrei and indicated he should stay where he was. Andrei mumble-moaned at him, eyes wide with fury. Kenny ignored him and stepped inside the bathroom. Closed the door behind him and pulled the black cloth away from his face.

With a light touch on the girl's shoulder, he let her know he was present. She swung round, turned up to him, mouth open in surprise. Kenny removed the earphones from one side.

He whispered. 'Do you speak English?'

The girl trembled and began to lift up her t-shirt.

'Jesus, no,' Kenny said and stopped her. Made a mental note: *really* mess these bastards up. 'It's okay. I'm not going to hurt you. But I am going to hurt Andrei and Stefan.'

He had no idea if anything that he said made any sense to her, but she seemed to relax a little.

'Please. Lock the door behind me?' Kenny said. Pointed to the lock and made a closing motion. 'Yeah?'

'Ok,' she said and fell back on to her backside and from there slid to the wall, where she pulled her knees up to her chest. 'No hurt me.'

Kenny placed his index finger before his lips and hoped this request for silence was one that was universally understood. He then gave her a thumbs-up sign with a questioning look.

She just looked at him.

Having run out of hand signals, Kenny replaced the cloth over the lower part of his face, stepped out of the room and closed the door. He looked back down the hall to see that Andrei was lying on his front and inching along the carpet as a worm might.

Kenny walked back to him. Placed a foot on his back and pressed down hard.

'Where do you think you're going, mate?'

Thinking he couldn't leave him here, Kenny grabbed him by the ankles. Andrei wriggled, trying to make it hard for him. A punch in the balls stopped that.

Kenny dragged him into the bedroom, dumped him at the side of the bed and closed the door. Try wriggling out of that, prick.

Kenny turned, aware of a presence behind him.

'What the fuck is going on?'

'You'll be Stefan,' Kenny said and cut the distance between them. Fast. Stefan threw a punch. Kenny blocked it with his left. Heard a thunk. Brought up his right fist. Hard. Clocked Stefan on the chin. He fell, his head hitting the side of the door with a meaty thud on the way down. Before he had the sense to curl into a protective position, Kenny kicked his balls. Felt a satisfying connection with the soft tissue there. A half-scream, half-groan issued from his mouth.

Soon, Stefan was bound and gagged in a similar fashion to his buddy, lying side-by-side on the carpet.

Both men were furious. Eyes blazing, strangled sounds bunched in their throats. Probably the Georgian equivalent of: do you know who you are messing with? Kenny decided on Georgian. Had a nicer ring to it than Eastern European.

Neither of them were showing any fear whatsoever. Which was interesting. Probably too thick. Or they'd been in plenty of difficult situations and always came out of them safely.

Always a first time.

Kenny reached into his bag and pulled out a hammer. That shut them up.

'Okay. If you speak English nod your head,' Kenny said.

Both men nodded their head.

His phone vibrated.

'Aw, for . . .' He looked at the caller display. Gordon Gallagher. Kenny answered.

'You're inside, Kenny?'

'I have a feeling you already know that,' Kenny answered, wondering where the camera was and how Gallagher had managed to plant it. How else would he time his intervention so well?

'Someone is going to knock at the door. Please let them in. They are going to carry out the rest of my instructions.'

'What?' Kenny asked. Gallagher rung off without answering.

There was a knock at the door.

He opened it. It was the waiter from the café. He stepped inside with a quiet apology. His arms were hanging uselessly by his side as he walked, like a teenager who'd sprouted overnight and had yet to grow used to his new, longer limbs.

He was wearing the same expression he'd worn as he'd served Kenny his coffee. The world was about to end and he didn't much care either way. The ultimate "whatever".

Kenny looked at his eyes as he tried to judge what the boy's purpose was in the next step. Recognised the shape of the brow, the crease under the bottom lid. A relative of Gallagher's then? Grandson, perhaps.

'Ok, buddy,' said Kenny. 'What gives?'

'Mr Gallagher thinks I need to move into the next step of my development,' he answered with a matter-of-fact tone. He was calm and completely untroubled with thoughts of whatever he had to do.

'Where are they?' he asked.

Kenny led him to the bedroom. Stefan had managed to prop himself up against the side of the bed and caught sight of the new arrival. Dismissed him with a flick of his eyes.

'You have the bag?' the waiter asked.

Kenny pointed to where it lay, just beyond Andrei's bound figure.

'Please explain to the men why we are here,' the waiter said.

Ok, thought Kenny, this couldn't get much stranger. Then did as he was asked.

'Your people are stealing from the streets of an area of Glasgow called Dennistoun. For future reference, we have a map.' Kenny reached into the bag and pulled both of them out. 'Which has been laminated,' he added with a rueful tone. 'Please do not send any of your people in to this area ever again.'

Andrei's throat bulged and sounds came from behind his gag that almost made sense. 'Fuck you.'

'Mr Gallagher was concerned that was how you might react,' said the waiter. 'So, regrettably we have to teach you a lesson.' He looked at Kenny. 'Pick one.'

What the hell, thought Kenny and pointed at Stefan.

The waiter moved towards him and reached to the man's belt and unbuckled it. Then he pulled down his zip and eased down his jeans and boxers to his knees. As he displayed the struggling man's genitals, he kept up a stream of chat. His tone conversational and calm. Completely at odds with the situation.

'These men come from a background that is paternalistic. And brutal. They learn to deal with punishment from an early age. The only thing they understand is superior strength. The one thing they can't abide is a threat to their manhood.' He paused. Thought for a moment. Said to Kenny, 'Would you mind pinning his legs down, please?'

Kenny manoeuvred so that he was holding the man's legs, his view of what was going to happen next completely unimpeded.

As the waiter finished speaking he got a staple gun from the bag. Then he reached out for the man's flaccid penis, pulling at the foreskin as if this was something he did every day, along with dishing up coffees and braveheart sausage. Then he lined up the edge of the map on the foreskin, brought the staple gun in from the side and with a loud click punched it shut, attaching the map to the man's flesh.

Stefan kicked out and screamed. The noise mostly contained by the ball-gag.

Andrei's eyes were bulging from his head. His throat red, tendons like ropes, taut down either side of his neck.

'Unfortunately,' continued the waiter, 'Mr Gallagher considered that this simple humiliation might not be enough for such men.' He reached for the other laminated map. And into the bag for a small plastic box of four-inch nails. He made a smacking noise with his lips as if it might help his thought process.

'This man looks completely unrepentant. So Mr Gallagher left it to me which option I should go for next, if I thought it was necessary.'

Speak normal, kid, thought Kenny. What's with the formality? He gave a mental shrug. He was getting a sense that this was what the young man was really like. If he grew up in the Gallagher household, it was little wonder he was a bit strange.

The waiter placed the map against Andrei's forehead with his left hand. Pursed his lips in thought. Moved the map down to the man's right knee and hefted the hammer in his right hand as if weighing up how much movement was required. Then he pulled a nail from the box and held it between his teeth.

Andrei continued in his rage behind the gag. Leaving no doubt as to what he would do if he ever got out of this situation.

'Thought as much,' said the waiter while gripping a nail, answering his own question. He placed the map back on Andrei's forehead, placed a nail in position and before Kenny could react, drove three inches of steel into the man's skull.

31

Gavin was driven back to the spot where Dave had first picked him up.

'Well, that was fun,' Gavin said and released his seatbelt. 'Don't be a stranger, eh?'

Dave put a hand on his before he could leave the car. 'Wait,' he said and reached into the inside pocket of his jacket. Pulled out an envelope. 'This is yours.'

Without a word, Gavin accepted it.

'We might need you again, so don't be surprised if you see me drive up.'

Gavin pushed open the door and climbed out of the seat. He stood by the kerb and watched the car as it drove away. Turned to face his doorway. It had been swept clean. No sign if anyone had stolen his spot since he'd been off the streets.

He felt a spit of rain on his scalp and looked up at the sky to judge if he needed to take shelter. When he felt more drops spark on his face, he stepped under the shelter of the doorway and crouched in the corner. While part of his mind registered this manoeuvre as hard-won habit, he considered what his next step should be.

A couple walked past, the woman hunched under a small, blue umbrella. The man spotted him, put a hand in his pocket, pulled out a coin and threw it at his feet.

Gavin picked it up. A £2 coin. 'Have a good one, mate,' he shouted at the man's back. Then he felt like chasing the guy down and returning it to him. He had money of his own. For now. Then he dismissed this as foolish. £2 was £2. Who knew how long his cash would last him?

At that thought he pulled out the envelope Dave had given him. Opened it and counted one hundred pounds in fivers. Clever. Dave knew that a guy like him might attract attention if he started to splash twenties all over the place. And that meant, along with the money he'd earned earlier, he had almost three hundred quid.

From what Dave said, there would possibly be scope for more, but who knew how long it would be before that happened and for how long he'd have to eke out this wee stash.

His mind ran through a potential shopping list. Whisky. Whatever pills his dealer had to hand. And a sleeping bag. He'd gone and left his stuff when Dave picked him up. It would either have been trashed or some other poor bastard would have found and claimed it.

On the opposite side of the street, a man walked past trailing a small boy. The child couldn't have been any older than three, and for the entire time they were in his sight, the boy's eyes, large and curious, never left his.

Gavin matched his expression to the boy's and felt himself grow sombre when he disappeared from view. He hoped the boy was loved and cared for. Hoped he might turn out to have none of the anger that coursed through his own veins.

His own kid would have been thirteen by now. Gavin Junior. Not very original, but hey, it suited them. Him and the boy's mother.

She blamed him for the boy's death. In her grief-raddled reason she was certain Gavin Jr wouldn't have been out playing with his pals that night; wouldn't have raced in front of that car for the ball; wouldn't have died on impact, if Gavin Senior hadn't been on tour in Afghanistan.

In his darkest moments, he found her logic irrefutable. His son died. He wasn't there to protect him. That was his job, wasn't it? To protect his family? But he'd been taking the Queen's shilling and protecting other men's children when his own son died.

He would never forget the moment the midwife placed that warm bundle in his arms. Memory had frozen the moment in one image. The baby was swathed in white cotton. All that was showing was a hot pink, pinched, raw face, eyes closed, mouth open as he made a mewling noise while he searched for the nipple and his mother's heat.

His mother was out of it at that point. Exhausted after a twenty-hour labour followed by an emergency C-section, she'd crumpled into sleep.

Gavin never knew what to do with the wean. Couldn't handle the nub of love that bunched in a kernel of hope deep in his gut, waiting for his attention, for permission to bloom into acceptance.

People he loved died.

When he was in his early teens, both his parents died in a house fire while he was having a sleepover at friends. His sister drowned while on a camping trip with the school two years later. Far too much grief for one boy to take.

Proof if it was needed.

If he dared to love this burping, sighing, gummy lump of soft skin then he'd only die, wouldn't he? Withholding that was a form of protection, wasn't it? His own irrefutable knot of grief-ridden logic he'd never escaped from.

Three men walked past. Heads hunched into collars, hands in pockets. One looking pleased with himself as the others laughed at something he must have said out of earshot. That was Glasgow. Humour as social currency.

And Gavin hated them for it.

Laughter was a medicine no prescription pad could fill for him.

Wee Gav died while he was overseas. Protecting the nation's interests overseas.

In frustration he sought a memory that might soothe. He remembered hitting that guy in the underground car park. Swivelling from the hips. A punch that came up from his feet. Now he wasn't protecting anyone. Least of all himself.

32

Kenny was back in the booth of the café on Duke Street, opposite Gallagher. The waiter came over to take his order, didn't acknowledge that they'd spent any time together the previous afternoon.

'Your usual, sir?'

Usual? thought Kenny. Did one visit constitute a habit? To mess with the kid, Kenny asked for a cappuccino.

The youth nodded his acknowledgement of the order with as much enthusiasm as he'd had when driving the nail into another man's skull. Kenny watched him walk behind the counter.

'He's a special kind of kid,' he said and looked at Gallagher, who returned the look as if measuring it for criticism.

'Some children are born with a burden that no amount of holy water or counselling can help. I give him room for his special gifts here at the café,' Gallagher said. His facial expression added no meaning to the words. Kenny raised his eyebrows as if asking for clarification. Gallagher turned to the side and reached for his iPad, indicating that he wouldn't be giving any.

'Why didn't you tell me he would be joining me on the job yesterday?' Kenny asked. He let some of his irritation show in his expression. 'I also don't like that I might now be implicated in a murder.'

'You're a resourceful man, Kenny. I've always been impressed how you manage to adapt to situations. I knew whatever happened at that house, you could deal with.'

'How did you know the right time to call me? If you had called moments earlier you could have put me in danger.' Kenny went for a pissed-off tone. Wanted the old man to feel he owed him more than he did.

'We've had eyes,' he did the air quote thing, 'on these men for a while. Be assured, my timing was not an accident.' Gallagher placed his hands on the table in front of him and clasped them in the manner of a priest about to begin mass.

The waiter returned carrying Kenny's drink. The foam on top was arranged in a heart shape. So the lad did have a sense of humour. Kenny looked up to offer a smile in response, but the waiter didn't meet his gaze, only placed a plate with a croissant in front of Gallagher and then returned to his station, with that same awkward loping gait.

'Does everyone know he's your grandson?' Kenny asked.

Gallagher leaned towards him. His eyes and the line of his lips narrowed. The air between them dropped by several degrees.

'A perceptive man should always be careful how much of what goes on here,' he pointed to the side of his head, 'comes out here.' He pointed to his mouth. 'As far as the world at large is concerned, I have no living relatives.' He looked into Kenny's eyes to check he was understood. Kenny nodded. He got it. Much safer for the boy that way, in case an up-and-coming gangster wanted to take over and was looking for Gallagher's weakness. But he was letting the old man know he had something on him. For the man who held information in such high regard, he would understand instantly where Kenny was coming from. And continue not to take him too lightly.

Kenny leaned back in his chair, took a sip from his drink, placed it back on the saucer and crossed his arms. 'Any fallout from yesterday?' he asked.

Gallagher shrugged. 'I can show you the film of what happened after you guys left the house?'

'Just tell me,' Kenny replied.

'I liked the improvisation the young man displayed. Made me kinda proud. The foreskin and then the forehead. Neat, eh?'

Fucking twisted, was what Kenny wanted to say, but instead just nodded.

'Pierced penis guy carried pierced forehead guy to the car,' Gallagher began, showing a rare slice of humour. He picked up his croissant, tore off a chunk with his teeth. Chewed. Swallowed. 'Presumably to take him to the hospital. But only after he removed the staple and the map from his dick. An hour later, penis guy returned, packed a bag and left. He hasn't been seen since. We phoned round our contacts in the city's hospitals. And found out a guy was indeed dropped off at A&E with a map attached to his head. He was taken in for emergency surgery and the nail removed after four hours. A metal plate was put in his forehead to replace the shattered bone.' Then as an aside, 'The boy has a surprising amount of strength.'

'Mmmm,' said Kenny, not trusting himself to say much more.

'The man hasn't died. Yet. The doctors can't say for sure how much damage will result. The nail went through the frontal lobe and touched the parietal lobe. One affects motor skills etcetera and the other, sensation among other things. But . . .' He rubbed his hands. 'Suffice to say, a lesson has been issued and learned, and I appreciate your help in the matter.' He gave a small nod. 'Now, you'll want to know about the men in the photos you gave me, yes?'

'The photos,' Kenny repeated. 'Yes.'

'The bruiser we told you about already. The guy with the specs? Can't find anything on him. He's new to the scene, so we'll have to keep digging. The other guy . . .' Gallagher set his iPad on its stand. Pressed the screen a couple of times and then turned it round so Kenny could see what he was doing. He was displaying an image of the guy who'd been wearing a baseball cap in the CCTV film. Must have been taken in response to Kenny's request. He nodded his thanks.

It was the guy he'd seen in the foyer of the tower block, and he was completely unaware that eyes and a camera were on him. He was standing in a doorway, side on, talking to another man, heads almost touching. Not that this was a tender moment. It was clear from his stance that he was imposing himself on the other man. Invading his space. Threatening the infamous Glasgow kiss.

'He was christened Barry Gibbs,' said Gallagher. 'Known as Baz, for obvious reasons. Spent a number of years in the army and was given a dishonourable discharge a few years back. Couldn't find out why. The army likes to keep these things out of the public domain where they can. My guy's best guess is that it was mistreatment of prisoners of war.' He looked into Kenny's eyes, trying to impart a warning. 'This guy is your communal garden psychopath.' He gave a little smile to indicate that his verbal slip was an attempt at humour. 'My impression is that violence to you is a tool, Kenny. To this guy it's a way of life.'

'Where was this taken?' Kenny asked, as he studied the image for clues.

'In town,' replied Gallagher in the manner that Glaswegians referred to the city centre. 'That's just off St Vincent Street. The other guy is living rough. Our Baz here is giving him a helping hand.'

'Clearly he is being a concerned citizen,' said Kenny.

'It's more likely he's recruiting him for his underground fight scene.'

'His what?' Kenny asked. As a member of an MMA gym, Kenny had heard whispers about such things going on in the city over the years, but he'd never actually come across anything definite.

'Aye, your man Baz is quite the entrepreneur. Apparently he saw an illegal clip of a fight in New York where some drunk guys out on the town paid a couple of street bums to have a scrap. He imported the idea here, with the subtle change that the scrappers be ex-servicemen.'

'Lovely,' said Kenny. 'The man is full of the milk of human kindness.'

'He's full of something, son, that's for sure. And it ain't white and creamy.' He scratched his cheek. 'That didn't come out right.' He laughed. Actually laughed. 'I feel positively cheery,' he said with an off-centre smile. 'It's amazing what watching a nail being hammered into your enemy's head can do for you.'

Who's the psychopath? thought Kenny.

'So, this fight club thing. You have to know someone in the know to get an invite. There's a ticket price and then you're expected to gamble on the outcome once you're there. There's several levels of fighting going on. The first,' he leaned forward, his face twisted with distaste, 'involves guys with disabilities. They call it Broken Biscuits. You know the thing, lose a leg to a land-mine and we'll further degrade you by having you fight a guy who went through something similar.' He shook his head. 'Pricks. Just having a laugh, eh?' He looked into Kenny's eyes. 'I hope you go in there with a landmine yourself, Kenny son. I'd love to see these arseholes get their comeuppance.'

Kenny nodded. Thinking, can't follow this guy's mood with a radar.

'Next level is guys off the streets, fighters who are more evenly matched, y'know? These guys probably have more emotional than physical problems. Don't believe what that eejit mob, Britain First, say. There's lots of help available for ex-servicemen, but inevitably some fall through the cracks. They're on the street because of their war experiences mingled with drink and drug issues. Some of them feel that going to all of these services is like begging, so they don't accept all the help that's available to them.'

'You seem well informed on this issue,' Kenny said and felt a little shame that he was less so. He was the one with the relative who was ex-army.

'I read stuff,' he said. 'You need to stay engaged in the world, Kenny son.' He raised his eyebrows to stress his meaning. 'So these guys. They get a break from living rough for a night. A square meal. They get to fight and then go back on the street well-funded for their next drug 'n drink binge.'

'Nice,' said Kenny, his tone suggesting he thought this was anything but.

Jeez, Ian, what have you got yourself involved in? Kenny thought about his last training session with Ian. Felt reassured. His cousin . . . brother . . . could look after himself. If they were picking guys off the street – out of condition and probably under-nourished – he was confident that Ian could hold his own.

But why would he get involved in any of this shit? He had a job now. He was no longer homeless. Dom? Did they have something on Dom and Ian somehow got involved that way?

Shit.

Gallagher paused. Pursed his lips. 'I heard that a lot of money passes hands at these things, and because of this some of the interested parties are introducing ringers. Guys who have the look of street living, but who can actually fight.'

Could that be where Ian has come in?

And why hasn't Ian reached out for him? Surely he can't be that pissed off with his mum, Colin and him that he's putting himself in this position? Kenny answered his own question. He was certain that was the case. God forbid he slip back onto the junk as well.

'There's more,' said Gallagher, with a downward cast to his eyes and mouth. 'I'm not sure about the last level, to be honest. Has the ring of urban myth to it, you know?'

Kenny sat up straight in his seat. Interest piqued. 'Aye?'

'Special fights. With themes. Only for the incredibly wealthy.' He leaned forward. His voice a step up from a whisper. 'Gladiatorial stuff. Where the fight is to the death.'

'Nah,' said Kenny. 'I'm not buying it.'

'Telling you,' said Gallagher. 'I trust this source completely. This isn't urban legend. It's real.'

Kenny nodded. Gave it some thought.

'Can you get me in?'

33

'Horseshit,' said Ray McBain after he'd finished chewing on a mouthful of bacon roll. 'No way there's an underground fight scene in Glasgow. And certainly not one that's to the death.' He snorted. 'Your guy's been watching too much crap on Netflix.'

'You're certain about that?' asked Kenny. They were in The Blue Owl, in their usual position at the bar. The only people in the room.

'There was a wee spell of it yonks ago after that shit movie with Brad Pitt. Some students at Glasgow Uni had a go. Taps aff, fists up kinda thing. It was laughable. I saw one of the fighters.' He shook his head. 'Managed to be fat and skinny at the same time.' He laughed. 'You could see his ribs, and he had a wee pot belly.'

'Probably all those pot noodles.'

'See what you did there,' countered McBain. 'They were as intimidating as white kittens wearing pink angel wings.'

'Back to the here and now,' said Kenny. 'You're sure? Really sure?'

'I'd bet my police pension on it,' answered McBain and took a slug of his Irn-Bru.

Kenny laughed. 'I hear they're not worth shit these days.'

'I'd bet my house on it.'

'How much of that is free of equity?'

Ray smiled and held his hand up. Thumb and first finger almost touching. 'Okay,' he conceded. 'I don't have much in the way of financials to back up my argument. Too busy saving society for a living. But,' he read Kenny's open mouth as his attempt to butt in and cut him off, 'I'm pretty sure we'd have heard of it at HQ.'

'From what my guy is saying this is relatively new. Could be just in the last year.'

'While I've been sat on the sofa scratching my arse?' Ray asked. He looked into Kenny's eyes. 'You're not going to let this rest are you?'

'Nope.' He took a sip of his coffee. 'Would you, if it was a member of your family?'

Ray picked up his mobile. Checked the time. 'You can check with DC Alessandra Rossi. She'll be here in ten minutes.'

'Hey,' said Kenny. 'Now that you guys are no longer colleagues, does that mean . . .'

'Shut up, O'Neill,' Ray interrupted. 'People have finally realised, in the modern era, that men and women can be actual friends.'

'Yeah,' Kenny snorted. 'Right. You're telling me you can simply be pals with a woman you find attractive and not try to imagine her naked? Late at night when you're in your sad wee bed, pulling the head off it, your imagination isn't going to go there?'

'You're disgusting, O'Neill. And once you join the grown-ups and have, you know, a real relationship? We can carry this conversation on then.'

They were still arguing five minutes later when the door opened.

'Bugger me, a customer,' Kenny said. 'Get behind the bar, Ray.'

Alessandra Rossi stepped inside the threshold, looked around herself before allowing her eyes to fall on the two men at the bar. She cocked an eyebrow.

'Not sure how I'm going to fight my way through this crowd to get to the bar.' She grinned, her focus on Ray. 'How you doing, big fella?'

She walked towards him. They hugged.

'Looking good, Ray,' she said, stepping back and patting his flat belly. 'Bar work suits you.'

'Don't worry,' said Kenny. 'He's back on the bacon rolls. Fat Ray will be with us shortly.'

'Kenny,' Alessandra said and gave him a nod. There was a hint of warmth there. A *hint*. She had clearly been worried about Ray and in her own way was acknowledging, perhaps, that Kenny was good for him.

'Ale,' Kenny said, mirroring her tone and movement. He knew that if it wasn't for their shared affection for Ray they would never occupy the same space. But hey, he thought, she was easy on the eye. Perhaps even more attractive now than when he'd first met her as a rookie cop. She was wearing a navy trouser suit and white blouse. The trousers tight enough to show the shape of her lean thighs, and there were a couple of buttons loose on the blouse, highlighting the light tan of her skin. Her dark hair was straight, cut to shoulder length, and the only makeup she was wearing was a lip gloss. Kenny imagined her applying it in her car before she entered the bar and wondered if that was what she had done, and if so, was it for herself, or was it for Ray?

Kenny's eyes moved back up to her face and she looked at him, head cocked to the side as if to ask, like what you see?

Kenny grinned. He did like confidence in a woman. 'Good to see you, Alessandra. Have you met my new bar manager?' He held out a hand indicating Ray.

'Aye,' said Ale with a huge smile. 'What's that all about?'

'There's only so much daytime TV a man can take,' Ray answered and walked behind the bar. 'Get you something?'

Ale ordered a coffee.

'Fuckssake,' said Kenny. 'Does nobody in this city drink alcohol anymore?'

'Join me at A&E on a Friday night and I'll answer that question for you,' Ale replied.

'Yeah,' said Kenny. 'Daft comment.'

Ray began to work at the coffee machine, so Kenny and Ale sat on the stools at the bar.

'Sorry to hijack your wee get-together, Ale. I just want to ask you a question and then I'll leave you two alone to catch up,' Kenny said.

'Right,' said Ale, shifting her backside on the stool and crossing her legs. 'What's up?'

Kenny told her. Most of the story. He left out the part about knowing wee Dom, his fall from the tower and the guy in the baseball cap.

Ale made a face. 'An underground fight club? With ex-army guys? To the death?' She looked over at Ray. Snorted. 'Nah. I'm sure we'd have heard of it.'

'Christ, you guys really are up your own arses. Do you really think you know about every illegal activity going on in this city?'

'Aye,' said Ray.

'Pretty much,' Ale said at exactly the same time. They looked at each other. Grinned. Bumped fists.

Kenny groaned. 'Newsflash, guys. There's plenty of shit going on out there you haven't a clue about.'

'Like what?' asked Ale.

Kenny made a pffft sound. 'Like I'm going to suddenly turn into a grass.' He sat back in his stool and crossed his arms. 'Like an underground fight club.'

Ray looked at Ale. 'He doesn't believe us.'

'Guys, I'm telling you. My source is impeccable. I've never known him to be wrong.'

Ale thought for a moment. 'There was that poor guy who fell from one of the tower blocks the other day. He was ex-army.'

Kenny listened and hoped that his body language didn't betray any previous knowledge. He felt Ray's eyes on him, refused to look over at him and willed his friend to keep quiet.

'What?' asked Ale. 'You guys look like you know something . . .'

'Your feminine intuition is over-reaching,' Kenny said, going for a patronising tone. Hoping that if he got Ale annoyed it would throw her off the scent of whatever was pricking her strong ability to read the unreadable.

'Bawbag,' replied Ale. 'I'll have you know . . .'

'What can you tell us about this guy that fell from the tower block?' Ray interrupted.

'Young. Ex-army, as I said. There's nothing to say whether he was pushed or if he fell. But his ex-wife is adamant that he wasn't suicidal. Quite the opposite in fact. He had a wee boy he was desperate to keep in touch with. But . . .' Ale paused in her speech to have a sip of her drink, ' . . . his injuries, I believe, were consistent with a fall. Nothing to indicate he'd been in a scrap.'

Kenny listened, nodded. Caught Ray's eyes and hoped his neutral expression let his friend know that he didn't want a current official of the law to know about his involvement in that particular young man's death.

'There's some CCTV cameras in that block,' said Ale, and Kenny's stomach gave a twist. 'We could put in a request to the housing association to look at the film of that day. See if there's any dodgy characters going in and out.'

'I heard lots of these places have the cameras but never actually film anything,' Kenny said.

'Yeah, well, we'll ask anyway.'

Kenny stood up. 'Need to siphon the python,' he said as he walked to the toilet.

'He'll grow up one day,' Ray said to Ale.

Kenny turned back to the bar when he reached the toilet door and pushed it open. 'Heard that,' he said.

Once inside, he took a quick leak. Zipped up and pulled his phone out of his pocket. Fired off a text to Dimitri.

You need to delete any film of me at those flats.

By the time he had washed and dried his hands there was a reply.

Way ahead of you, boss. Already done it.

Back at the bar, Ray was still standing on the service side of the bar, just in front of the optics. He leaned forward on his elbows.

'Say you had a fight club like that. What would you do with your injured fighters?'

'Take them to A&E,' answered Kenny.

'Right. We ... sorry, the police might be persuaded to check if there have been outpatients presenting with injuries consistent with fighting. If they also happen to be ex-army ...' he clapped his hands, 'Bob's your uncle.' He gave Ale a huge smile.

'Like we haven't enough to do. You heard of the austerity cuts?' she asked.

'What about this fight to the death thing? Let's say it was happening. Where would you get rid of the bodies?' Ray asked.

'Building sites?' said Kenny.

'There's plenty of them in Glasgow,' said Ale. 'But dead bodies do have a habit of turning up.'

'Exactly,' said Ray.

'Eh?' Ale and Kenny said at the same time.

'What you said about the guy from the tower block got me thinking. The best way to hide something is in plain sight, right?'

'Yeah,' said Kenny, mystified.

'The suicide rate among ex-servicemen is pretty high, isn't it? So, if I was involved in this kind of thing I'd be making it look like a suicide. Hiding in plain sight, if you like.' He held his hands out, palms up. 'Easy, peasy.'

'If we look at young male suicides in the ex-army bracket,' Ale continued Ray's thought processes, 'there can't have been that many of late. Surely? But if we look closer, we might be able to tell if it was suicide or something even more sinister.'

'Yeah,' said Kenny feeling hopeful. He'd find these bastards and please God before Ian got hurt.

'If I look into this, you owe me,' Ale said to Kenny.

'Count on it,' Kenny replied.

34

Kenny was on his sofa wearing black jeans and a hoodie. The television was on, blue light flickering as some pasty-faced guy in a suit bleated on about how much rain was on its way. A hurricane with a daft name had hit the Caribbean and was travelling across the Atlantic. Storm Edna would hit our shores sometime during the night. If facial expressions had hashtags, his would be fake sadface.

His aunt Violet had been on the phone earlier. Up to high doh, as they say in Glasgow. Worried sick about her son. And the latest update about her wanker of a husband was that he had apologised about his behaviour and promised to do what he could to make things right.

Which really meant he would do nothing but sit on his arse and watch Jeremy Kyle while drinking tea and scratching his nuts.

Where are you Ian? Why won't you get in touch?

His phone was on a cushion by his side. It sounded an alert. He picked it up and saw that it was a text from Gallagher.

Fight on at midnight. Gate fee is £100. Directions to follow.

Moments later, as promised, a text arrived with the fight site.

Excellent, thought Kenny, getting to his feet and slipping on a pair of black shoes. Going to this would give him an insight into what was going on, and if Baz Gibbs was there that would be a bonus. He put on a sleeveless quilted jacket over his hoodie and then, thinking it would be better if no one recognised him, topped off the look with his black baseball cap.

*　　*　　*

Ten minutes before the fight was due to start, Kenny arrived at a multi-storey car park in the city centre. The streets were empty. Nothing moved. No cars and no pedestrians. Darkness pushed up against the night sky by fluorescent street lighting.

As he walked up to the steel mesh door entrance, he zipped his jacket against the chill. He thought he should have given McBain a call, but dismissed it as being a bad idea. He'd only want to involve his former colleagues, and if they poked their noses in it might frighten the organisers off and drive them further under-ground. And then he'd never find Ian.

A security guard was visible through the mesh. A short guy in a black v-neck jumper and black trousers that were three inches too long. His face was long and lean, his bottom lip swollen and pale. He looked as if he might have all the heft of a wet paper bag. The man made a nodding movement with his head to the side. Kenny took a couple of steps round the corner and a black door there opened.

He walked inside.

The security guard walked over to him and held his hand out. Kenny was tempted to blow on him to see if he fell over. Instead he took the hand and shook it.

'You'll be the comedian for the post-fight party then, eh?' the guard asked. His boredom with the situation infecting his tone.

'How do I know you're the right guy to take the money?' Kenny asked.

'You'll just have to trust me.' Pause. Looked like he considered smiling, then thought, nah, bugger it. 'Besides do I look like I can defend myself if you had to come looking for me?'

Kenny pulled the cash out of his hip pocket and handed it over.

'The stairs.' The guard indicated a stairwell to his right. 'Go down till you can't go down any further. Knock on the door to the tune of Bohemian Rhapsody and they'll let you in.'

'Who's the comedian now?'

'Just messing with you, mate.' This time some nicotine stained teeth were displayed. 'Got to relieve the boredom, eh?'

Kenny walked down the steps with the old Queen tune running through his mind. He reached a black door and to the rhythm of *Scaramouche, will you do the Fandango*, he knocked.

Another security guard opened it. Same uniform. Similar demeanour. Twice the girth of the guy upstairs.

'Whit's wi' the daft knocks the night?' he asked.

Kenny ignored him. Walked past. Suddenly alert and tuned in to the atmosphere. Low greenish-yellow lighting, bare grey concrete floors and walls, dirty white lines on the ground at regular intervals. A couple of parking spots were free of any members of the audience. They were the ones painted yellow which bore the universally understood sign of the wheelchair for disabled drivers.

A knot of men in each corner of the space, hands in pockets, stood chatting in a low hum. Some of them looked at him. Checking him out. He was a new face. What was his business here? Does he have lots of cash? Somebody that will bet and lose big?

Kenny stood on his own, feet planted shoulder width apart. Pulled his baseball cap lower on his brow and discreetly examined the other men. He noted with a pang of disappointment that there was no sign of the guys from the CCTV pictures. Looked at his watch. Five minutes to go. They might yet still arrive.

The door banged shut behind him and he turned to see another couple of men arrive. They were dressed much the same as he was, and judging by the way their eyes darted around the room, large with excitement, they were also new to this.

They stood beside him.

Both were about medium height. One had the look of a fighter: lean muscle, light on his feet, an easy gaze that said whatever happened he could deal with it. His mate was broader, bearing the kind of muscle that was won in front of a mirror with heavy weights in each hand. He looked the more excitable of the two. Lessons to be learned there, Kenny thought. He's probably a pub bouncer and thinks handling drunks gives him some sort of tough guy qualification.

'Awright,' bouncer guy said to Kenny.

Kenny nodded.

'I'm Jay.' Nodded towards his mate. 'This is Russel.'

'Fuckssake,' said Russel. 'This isn't a social club, mate.'

'Come here often?' Jay asked Kenny with a grin, ignoring his buddy.

Russel shook his head and looked away. Mumbled, 'Diddy.'

Despite himself Kenny responded. Found the young man's enthusiasm reminded him of an old, deceased friend. 'First time, mate.'

Jay rubbed his hands together. 'Me too.'

It's like you have a neon sign above your head saying that, thought Kenny.

'What's the drill then, do you know?' Jay asked.

'Two guys try to knock lumps out of each other,' answered Russel. 'We gamble some cash. Probably lose it. The end.'

Kenny opened his mouth to speak but was stopped when he heard the hum around him rise in pitch. He turned and saw that from the far corner of the "arena" a man wearing a dark hood over his head was being led in. He was wearing camouflage trousers and was shirtless. Broad shoulders suggested that the man had been active at some point, but his ribs were showing, his pecs were soft, and he was carrying a belly that looked like it was born in the local pub and grew up on Greggs.

On some silent signal, the men formed a loose circle behind him and began talking about his potential as a scrapper.

'Not sure about this guy,' said Jay.

'Wait till the next guy arrives and we can see who we fancy,' said Russel.

Just then, some men in front of them shifted position to create some space and another fighter was led into position.

Even with the hood on Kenny could see that it was Ian.

35

Ian felt the cool air on the naked flesh of his chest and back. Squinted his eyes against the sudden glare of light when his hood was removed.

Moved his head from side to side and felt the vertebrae in his neck click and loosen. He shook out his arms, rolled his shoulders and bounced from one foot to the other.

The noise from the audience rolled over him. They were a distraction. The other fighter was the only thing he could allow in to his mind. Cropped hair. Thick growth on his face that matched the wiry hair that rampaged across his soft chest and belly.

The other guy opened his mouth wide as if unclicking his jaw. Worked it into a yawn, like he was trying to stress how unaffected he was by the situation.

Not buying that, thought Ian. No one was that relaxed when going into a fight. If they were, they were fools. Maybe he'd been too relaxed the last time and was lulled by the other guy's apparent inexperience. This time he'd be fighting to win. And win quick.

He allowed himself to look at the section of the audience behind the other fighter. Bugger them. To hell with the lot of them. Thought: I don't care about your winnings, or your entertainment. This guy is being brought down fast.

Dave did the introductions this time. He called Ian the Bellshill Bomber and held his right hand up in a salute. Ian tried not to look too embarrassed at the moniker. The other guy got the same treatment. His name: Rampaging Rab.

Give me a break.

Dave motioned them together. Instructed them to bump fists then gave the spiel. No rounds. Last man standing wins.

Ian took a step back, thought, right Dom, this is for you.

Rab held his defence high. Too high. Ian got in a couple of easy shots on his ribs. And then dodged Rab's angry response.

'Wake you up, did I, big man?' Ian shouted at him. First man to get angry loses.

Rab swung at him again. Should have sent a postcard, thought Ian as he ducked it and shot in an uppercut. Caught him on the cheekbone. Nothing that would break a bone, but it would swell nicely in the morning.

Anger getting the better of him, Rab went for the bear-hug approach. Rushed Ian and tried to sweep him up in his long arms. His speed took Ian by surprise and they both fell to the floor, with Rab on top.

Glee on his face, Rab put both hands on Ian's neck and started to squeeze.

Is that allowed? Ian wondered. He pummelled Rab's ribs hoping pain would be settling in from his earlier strikes, but the effect was minimal. Aware that oxygen debt would arrive quickly, Ian managed to remain calm and changed his approach. He daggered the first two fingers of his right hand and, reaching over Rab's arms, he drove them into his trachea.

The effect was instant. Rab leaned back choking. Ian twisted from his hips and managed to unseat him. He got to his feet first and landed a couple of punches to the face before Rab got back onto his.

Ian danced back out of reach. Lungs heaving. He needed to catch his breath before he took this fight back on.

Rab smiled at him, teeth smeared with blood, and returned to his defence position with hands high.

I'll give you something to smile about, buddy. Time to bring this fight to a close. Keeping eye contact, Ian shot out a jab to his face. Connected with Rab's defence. But this was only a decoy.

As the jab connected, Ian immediately pulled his fist back in, planted his feet, lowered his body and re-loaded. Still in eye contact, Rab was sold the lie that another jab to the face was coming. Instead Ian aimed lower. A cross between a left uppercut and left jab, a shovel punch was a thing of beauty. Knuckles coming up to the right side. The floating ribs. And through them to the liver.

Rab folded from the waist.

Poleaxed.

Like the feet had been cut from him.

The liver shot.

Ian knew this was a punch rarely seen in public fights. Viewers want a money shot. Blows to the head were more dramatic. And we all want to protect our face.

A blow to the head is also easier to cope with. Adrenalin and your state of mind often meant that pain caused there was referred until the fight was over. Get clocked in the head, you see stars, but you can't necessarily process the pain.

Nobody gets back up from an effective liver shot. The vagus nerve is impacted and the body folds and closes down. It causes a sudden dilation of all your blood vessels everywhere except for the brain. The victim gets a nerve signal going into the autonomic nervous system, his blood vessels dilate, the heart rate decreases, the blood pressure suddenly drops, and the athlete collapses. He has no control. He's down.

And looking at Rab, Ian could see this guy was out.

'What the fuck was that?' one guy asked.

'What did I miss?' asked another.

Dave walked up to Ian, grabbed his right wrist and held up his arm in the time-honoured winner's salute. As he did so he said, 'Nice one, mate. These numpties have no clue what just happened.'

To shouts of, "I want my money back," Dave led Ian through the circle of gamblers.

Somebody got in Ian's face.

'Want my fucken cash back, prick.'

Ian reared back, thought about nutting the guy.

Realised it was Kenny.

36

As soon as Kenny saw Ian's opponent, he thought, Ian's got this, and he scanned the crowd for the guys who had been in Dom's lobby.

He quickly spotted Baz Gibbs, but a roar from the audience brought his attention back to the fight. Rampaging Rab – what the hell is that about? – managed to get Ian on the floor. But he dealt with it well. Strictly speaking, a blow to the throat like that was illegal in MMA, but this wasn't a regulated fight, and Rab looked like he wouldn't have a clue when a choke might turn into strangulation.

In this situation a fighter might only have thirty second's worth of air in their lungs, and in a proper fight the referee would be quick to stop the fight from going any further. The fighter with the other guy's neck in his hands needs to know that it would only take minutes for brain damage to occur. Or from there you're only a short step from brain death.

And nice one with the liver shot. Kenny wasn't aware Ian knew how to set that up.

He scanned the crowd again for Baz. Saw him turn at the end of the fight and walk towards the exit. Just as he was about to follow him, Ian was led past.

By instinct, he faced up to Ian, copying the behaviour of the men around him. He read Ian's confusion and the subsequent recognition. Some instinct warned Kenny off alerting the other men to his relationship with Ian. He got in Ian's face.

'Want my money back. That was shite. It was just a wee blow and the guy was down. A fucken fix.'

Ian's handler tried to barge in between them, but Ian turned his shoulder so that he couldn't get close to Kenny.

'Need to talk to you,' Kenny mouthed. Before he could say anything about Dom, Ian interrupted him.

'Not interested,' he hissed.

Kenny read the anger in his eyes and took a step back. Guilt scored his gut. He understood why Ian was furious with him, but he needed to know that he'd acted with his best interests at heart.

'Who is this guy?' the minder pulled at Ian.

Ian looked at Kenny. 'Nobody. Just some waster.'

The minder placed himself between Ian and Kenny. 'Listen friend,' he said. 'If you lost money, that's just the way it goes. Now kindly do one and piss off.'

Kenny held his hands up. Looked at the ground. 'Sorry, man. Needed the money for the electric, you know.'

'Not our problem,' the minder said and led Ian away.

Kenny watched them walk towards the far door. Then looked over his shoulder in the direction of the door that Baz was walking toward. Just as he looked across, the man turned and looked towards the group of men at the fight, scanning the crowd. Kenny ducked his head, offering the skip of his baseball cap. Did the guy make him?

He thought about what he should do next, and before he could articulate what he should do, he followed Baz.

Whatever he might say to Ian right now, his brother clearly wasn't in the mood to listen. Did he know about Dom? He's not going to be completely removed from the world, whatever it is he thinks he's doing. An underground fight club, for fuckssakes. What's he playing at?

There was no sign that Ian was back on the drugs, so there was that. He also looked reasonably well rested and well fed. Which he could use to reassure his aunt Vi. If he was going to get to the bottom of what was going on, Ian wasn't the man to offer any information. He'd have to follow this Baz Gibbs character and see what he could find there.

He saw Russel and Jay make a move to the exit and stepped up until he was alongside them. His thinking was that if he had aroused anyone's curiosity, they were less likely to be suspicious of him if he was with other guys. If that meant he had to put up with these guys' nonsense for a little while, so be it.

'Disappointing fight, eh?' said one of them to Kenny. He'd already forgotten which was which.

'You totally missed that, didn't you, Jay?' the slightly taller one said to his mate and looked at Kenny as if to say, what an eejit. He'd be Russel then.

'Ok smartarse, what was I supposed to have seen?' Jay asked.

Russel swung round, faked a punch in to the right side of his mate's torso. 'That's the liver punch, dude. You get hit with that and it's goodnight, Glasgow.'

'Really?' Jay looked to Kenny for confirmation.

He nodded. 'It's like getting it full bore in the nuts. TKO. No way back from that, buddy.' Kenny reached the door, held it open for his two new best friends and followed them as they climbed the stairwell.

Just ahead he could see the lower half of Baz Gibbs' legs, and he skipped up the stairs ahead of Jay and Russel in case he lost him. He stepped out of the side door and onto the street. Rounded the corner. Shot a look up both sides of the street. No sign of Gibbs.

Shit.

The two guys came out the door and flanked him.

'Lost something, mate?' one asked with a smile.

'Nah,' said Kenny. 'Thought I knew that guy.'

A car engine fired up further down the street. The noise echoing in the cold, still night air. Then the car, a long, sleek line of black metal, surged past them. But not before Kenny got a look at the driver. He watched the car till it stopped at a set of traffic lights. Looked further on. The whole length of this street was a stop-go set up. Almost every hundred yards was another set of lights. Perhaps, if Kenny ran to his car, he could catch up.

'You know Baz Gibbs?' asked Russel.

Taken aback, Kenny took his eyes from the car.

'Yeah,' he replied. 'From way back.' He heard his voice trail off with the lie and gave a cough. 'Yeah. Why?' he asked, adding conviction to his voice.

'Were you with him in Afghanistan?' asked Jay, his eyes bright with the need to hear some gossip.

'If I told you, I'd have to kill you.'

'Ha!' said Russel. 'That's you told, loser.' He punched his mate on the arm.

'How do you guys know him?' Kenny asked.

'Sometimes see him down at the Riverboat casino. That's probably where he's headed to now,' said Jay.

'Yeah? Still a big gambler then?' Kenny asked.

'Guess so,' answered Jay. 'And he likes a bit of call girl action as well.'

'They have prozzies down there?' asked Russel.

'You know nothing, dude,' Jay said to Russel.

'Well, in that case why are we standing here like a bunch of spare pricks?' asked Kenny. 'You comin'?'

Jay looked at Russel.

Russel spread his arms wide, palms up. 'Don't mind if I do.'

Jay and Russel agreed to meet Kenny at the entrance to the casino and ran to their car. Kenny moved to his and shucked off the waistcoat. From the last time he'd been down at the Riverboat he knew that the dress code was smart casual. The jeans would do, but the waistcoat and baseball cap would have to go.

When he arrived, as promised, Jay and Russel were standing just inside the tall, glass door at the entrance. Kenny walked past them.

'Where's the bar?' he asked.

'Just follow the noise,' answered Jay.

They walked up to the long, metallic counter. Kenny put his back to it and surveyed the crowd. Couldn't see Gibbs. Turned to the guys.

'Drink?'

'Don't mind if I do,' said Russel. 'Heavy.'

'So's your Ma,' said Jay with a smile. Dodged the punch that was Russel's reply and turned to Kenny. 'And I'll have a lager, mate.'

Kenny waved down a barman. Ordered the drinks as requested and a glass of tonic water for himself. A cheeky wee slice of lemon in it and he hoped he wouldn't get mistaken for being caught in the act of committing the Scottish cardinal sin of Not Drinking.

The drinks arrived and he stood to the side to let the guys pick theirs up.

Both of them took a long sip and groaned with pleasure.

'Needed that,' said Russel.

'Aye,' agreed Jay. 'Watching folk punch the hell out of each other is thirsty work.'

Despite himself Kenny grinned. 'Anybody see Gibbs?'

The three of them turned their back to the bar and looked through the spread of people.

'Mind if I go walkabout, guys?' Kenny asked and picked up his drink. Without waiting for a reply, he walked away.

Fifteen minutes later he located Gibbs with one hand on a pint of lager and the other attached to the handle of a one-armed bandit. With the focus of a zealot he was pushing in coins and pulling on the metal arm. Judging by his expression the fruits – or whatever the hell they were – weren't falling kindly for him.

Kenny approached the counter in the corner. Asked for a bag of change. Then he pulled out his phone. It was answered within a couple of rings.

'Are you available?' Kenny asked.

'I am,' replied Christine. Kenny could hear the sleepy tone in her voice.

'Great.' He told her where he was. 'And bring a pal.'

He cut the connection, took a stool one up from Gibbs and started to pump coins into the machine. Having no idea what he was doing, he simply put the coins in and pulled the lever. When lights flashed he had no clue what buttons he should press.

His ineptitude caught Gibbs' attention, and Kenny could see him looking over at his machine, then looking at Kenny with an expression that had the word "twat" placed firmly at its centre.

A burst of music, some lights and coins flashed out of the mouth at the bottom of Kenny's machine.

'Jammy bastard,' said Gibbs. He took a long slow drink of his pint. 'I've been at this for ages and I've won the square root of fuck all.'

'Sometimes, not having a clue can be a good thing,' said Kenny, giving it his "daft laddie" act. He judged that if he looked and acted gormless, Gibbs would be drawn in and would try to take advantage of him. The man was a predator, there was no way he could pass up such an opportunity. 'Maybe this is a lucky machine. Want to swap?'

Gibbs pursed his lips and blew in a you-know-nothing kind of way. 'Not a chance, mate. I've put a lot of cash into this bastard. If anyone gets the win from all that it will be me.'

'Fine,' said Kenny and shrugged. Put some more coins in his machine. Got nothing. Some lights flashed, he put some more in and again got nothing back.

'What you doin', mate?' asked Gibbs. He looked at the pile of coins in front of Kenny as if to judge how long he might be sitting there.

'Just wasting time, really. Waiting on the girls arriving.'

'Why don't you walk up to the window and throw your money into the river? That would make as much sense.' Gibbs turned back to his machine and fed in some more coins. At what seemed finely judged moments, he pressed some buttons and with a

"Yes", cupped his hands under the coin drop to collect any that might spill out.

'Who's a jammy bastard now?' asked Kenny with a grin.

'Luck's got nothing to do with that, bud. That was sheer skill and judgement,' Gibbs said with a smile. He was transformed with the win. His eyes brighter, head tilted back and his shoulders corrected from their earlier slump.

Kenny drained the last of his drink. Looked at the almost finished glass of lager in front of Gibbs.

'Get you a top up when I'm over at the bar?'

Gibbs looked at him as if assessing him for duplicity. Decided he was just being friendly. 'Aye,' he said. 'Lager.'

Kenny nodded and turned towards the bar. A young man in white shirt and black bow tie was the sole member of staff.

'You on here all night?' asked Kenny.

'Yes, sir,' the man, boy really, replied.

'Do me a favour, eh? My mate over there doesn't know I'm with AA. So it would save some awkward moments if you only gave me tonic water the rest of the night. If he orders a gin and tonic, just pretend to put the gin in, will you?'

'Absolutely, sir,' said the waiter as if he was asked this every night. Kenny slipped him a twenty-pound note and ordered his drinks. He was back at the fruit machines moments later with a glass in each hand.

'Cheers,' said Gibbs, keeping his focus on the machine in front of him. Every couple of seconds he popped another coin in the slot, followed the lights and pressed buttons. Again some lights and music went off, but this time only a handful of coins came out as a prize.

Kenny pretended to mimic what Gibbs was doing and won nothing. Waited until Gibbs looked over at him and shot a glance at his watch.

'I'm shite at this. Hope the girls arrive soon.'

Gibbs said nothing.

'This is what happens when you get divorced, eh? Good riddance.' Kenny held his glass up. 'Cheers, bitch. Hope you enjoy the house I worked a sixty-hour week for.'

Gibbs shot him a shut-up look.

Kenny snorted. Pretending the drink was getting to him. 'You married, mate?'

'Was. Once. Got rid. Fed up with the cold shoulder, if you get my drift.'

'Yeah,' said Kenny, staring into space. Drained his drink in one go. 'She shagged my best mate. When I caught them she said, no wonder, how am I supposed to be satisfied with a pencil dick? Then she gets everything. House, pension, savings, the lot.' Kenny shot the bar a look of longing. 'Want another?'

Gibbs held up his glass, it was still three quarters full.

'A wee whisky chaser then, eh?' said Kenny and walked back to the bar. He worried that he didn't have enough experience of being drunk to sell it, so he settled for amping up his smile and voice instead.

He returned with the next round.

'Pencil dick,' he said to Gibbs with a dismissive expression. Grabbed his crotch. 'Keeps me happy.' He laughed. 'I blame these feminists. Got women thinking they should enjoy a shag as well. Bollocks to that, eh?'

Gibbs turned and took a sip of his drink, his eyes smiling over the rim of his glass.

'Aye. Women. Can't live with them,' Kenny took a sip, 'can't live with them.' He clinked glasses with Gibbs. 'So my wee divorce present to myself is a night in the casino, throw some money down these . . .' he fed another coin into the slot, '. . . bastards. And a night with a couple of special girls.' He winked. 'If you know what I mean.' Sip. 'Always fancied a night with a couple of prostitutes.' Sip. 'Tomorrow I'll be back to working all the hours to keep a roof over *her* head. Tonight it's gambling, booze and getting balls deep in a beautiful woman.'

'Cheers to that, mate.' Gibbs drained his whisky. 'Fancy another?'

'Would be rude not to, mate,' Kenny said and emptied his glass. He turned, looking at the space around them. 'You get them in while I go to the loo. Point pencil at the porcelain.'

Gibbs snorted a laugh. Kenny smiled back, pretending he hadn't noticed that Gibbs was laughing at him, rather than with him.

Putting a hitch in his step, Kenny walked to the corner where the gents' loo was situated. Once inside he sent Christine a text.

When do you expect to get here?

Taxi pulling up outside. Was the almost instant reply.

Kenny started to thumb out his instructions. Thought, fuck this and pressed "call" instead.

'Doing it the old-fashioned way?' Christine said, and he could hear the humour in her voice.

'You got me,' he said. 'My thumbs are too big. When you arrive, we're over at the fruit machines.'

'We?'

'I have a new best friend. I need you to be nice to him.' He passed on some additional instructions.

'Of course,' she replied and hung up. Was that a note of disappointment in her voice?

Back at his position at the machines, Gibbs had delivered on the drinks front.

'Got us both a double,' he said, and with a nod over to the bar added, 'Service here is brilliant. Guy knew what to serve up without being asked.'

Kenny grinned. 'Ya dancer.' Reached forward, picked up the glass. Took a long drink. Faked a hiccup. 'Better watch. It's a school day tomorrow.'

'What do you do?' asked Gibbs.

'I'm a teacher.'

'Eh?'

'Nah, winding you up, mate. I do a bit of this. A bit of that. Buying and selling. Made my first million by the time I was twenty-nine.' Kenny almost went for thirty, but judged that rounding it down to an odd number would be a plausible piece of detail. Then he screwed up his face. 'Sorry. The drink talking there. Sounds a bit like I'm bragging.'

'Don't worry. The demon drink tends to free the tongue.'

Kenny felt a tap on his shoulder. Turned.

'You'll be Kenny?' said Christine. 'Just like your photo. I'm Tina, we spoke on the phone.' She turned to the woman by her side. 'I'd like you to meet my friend, Lexi.'

Lexi smiled, leaned forward and pressed her cheek against Kenny's. She was a taller, leaner and blonder version of Christine.

'Wow, Lexi,' said Kenny looking her up and down. Laying it on for Gibbs, but not having to fake it too much. 'Haven't your genes been kind?'

Lexi flashed white teeth, flicked her hair away from her face. She stepped forward and held on to Kenny's arm. 'My father's fat, bald and as ugly as a leper's crotch. Calls me the family fluke.'

Kenny laughed, then replied. 'Well, your mother must've been a stunner.'

'I didn't realise from your email that there would be two of you,' Christine said with a nod and a smile thrown in Gibbs' direction.

'Well, actually . . .' Kenny pretended a moment of uncertainty. 'We just met. Don't even know this guy's name.'

Gibbs was quick.

'It's Baz, and how are you and your pencil going to keep these two babes happy?' he asked with a grin that Kenny wanted to knock from his face with a chunk of granite.

Kenny disguised his feelings. Snorted. Pushed at Gibbs' arm. 'As long as I'm happy. Right?'

'I'm sure we can accommodate you both,' said Christine with a look at Lexi.

Lexi winked. She nodded at Gibbs, shot Kenny a smile and pecked him on the cheek. 'Let's get this party started,' she said. Then she looked around herself. 'It is a bit public here, right enough.'

Kenny opened his mouth to speak, but was beaten to it by Gibbs.

'Hey, my place is ten minutes away. Just down the riverside.'

Kenny pretended to stumble over a reply.

'Sorry, mate. Don't mean to crash your party,' Gibbs said. 'But it will be fun. And I have lots of booze down at mine. 'He turned to Christine and Lexi. 'How about it girls? Fancy a wee nightcap?'

37

In the taxi to his house, Gibbs sat in the front of the car, giving off a stream of inane chatter. Who he was trying to impress, Kenny had no clue. He knew Gibbs had no real interest in what he thought, and the girls were there because they were being paid. Maybe it was the taxi driver. Maybe he was excited because he was about to get groiny with a beautiful woman.

They drove past a couple of working girls on the streets. One was wearing a large puffy jacket, tiny skirt and impossible heel combination.

'Bet her arse is freezing,' Gibbs said with a chuckle.

Christine looked straight ahead as if terrified to look at her street version. Kenny looked at Christine's profile and felt a pang of something approaching guilt. She appeared to be completely fine with her choice of profession. Was she in denial?

As if aware of his scrutiny, Christine turned to him and smiled.

'Ok?' she asked him quietly.

He nodded and reached for her hand to give it a little squeeze, and then parked his thoughts. There was work at hand here. And he needed Christine to play her part.

Some time later they were all inside Gibbs' top-floor flat. The living room had a black and grey corner sofa large enough to house several parties. The only other pieces of furniture in the room were a giant flat-screen TV and a long black coffee table.

The table was littered with remote controls. Four. And a

Sunday Times newspaper, with the sports section prominent. And a stainless steel coffee mug.

On the way in, through the hallway, they all had to negotiate their way past a clothes horse full of Gibbs' socks, t-shirts and boxers.

'Right, there's champagne, red wine or whisky,' Gibbs said as the other three took a seat. 'Who wants what?'

Lexi sat beside Kenny, put a hand on his thigh and asked for a glass of red. Kenny followed Gibbs' eyes as he watched this action.

Christine asked for the same.

'Gimme a hand with the drinks in the kitchen, Kenny?'

'Sure,' Kenny said as he got to his feet. The room was open plan. The kitchen separated from the living space by a counter that held a double sink.

In the kitchen area, Gibbs handed him a bottle of wine and a corkscrew. 'Do the honours, mate?'

'Sure,' said Kenny and set to work.

'Whisky for yourself?' he asked.

Kenny indicated that would be fine. 'Just with water, ta.' He gave a mental shrug: it would be difficult to limit his alcohol intake now, with Gibbs doing the pouring.

'Just to release the flavours, the smoke and the peat and all that shite,' mocked Gibbs. 'I have mine with coke. To hell with all that crap. I just want the buzz.'

As he spoke, Gibbs brought out a bottle of whisky and a couple of glasses. Gave both glasses a healthy measure. Then he reached into the fridge and brought out a two-litre bottle of coke. He opened it and poured some into his glass. When he opened the fridge to replace the bottle, Kenny got a glimpse of the contents. A head of broccoli sat in the middle shelf like an abandoned New Year's resolution. Apart from that and the coke, and a carton of milk, the fridge was empty.

Kenny finished working out the cork from the wine bottle and poured the wine into two glasses.

'By the way,' Gibbs said in a low voice as he walked past Kenny, holding one wine and his whisky. 'I quite fancy that one, Lexi. She's a babe.'

In the living room, Gibbs held up the red wine to Lexi. 'Me and you babe. We're taking the party into the next room.'

With a smile, Lexi stood up and reached out for the wine. 'Lead on, fine sir,' she said.

When they were out of the room, Christine relaxed on to the sofa. 'You were right.'

'Aye. I had a feeling if Lexi looked more interested in me he'd want her.'

Christine shot a glance at the door. 'Lexi will be safe enough, you think?'

'Yeah. If there's any bother I'll be kicking the door . . .' Kenny's reply was interrupted by a loud peal of laughter. 'She sounds happy enough.'

'She might look young, but she's got plenty of experience in handling men.' She chewed the inside of her lip. 'But there's something not right with that guy.'

More laughter from the other side of the wall. High and happy. Not a fake note in it.

'We'll keep an ear out, eh?' Kenny said and sat back in the sofa. He put an arm over Christine's shoulder. She put a hand on his thigh. The heat shot from there to his groin. 'In the meantime . . .'

Christine took a sip of her wine. 'He might look like a nutter, but he's got good taste in wine.'

'Probably on special down the local Co-op.'

'Is that how you choose your wine?' Christine asked with a grin.

'Of course it is. All that bouquet bollocks. It's really about the pounds and the pennies.' He picked up his whisky glass and downed the contents. Then he leaned forward and kissed her on the lips. 'This is a very large sofa. Would be a shame not to put it to good use.'

Christine smiled. Put her glass on the table. Reached for his zip.

The next few minutes – could have been ten – could have been thirty – passed in a haze of skin, pulse and snapping nerve ends.

He was on his back, Christine straddling him when he realised that someone was watching. Kenny opened his eyes, twisted his head to the side and saw Baz Gibbs standing in the doorway. He was completely naked, stroking the thick hair that covered the ridges of his hard abdomen, his view completely unencumbered to the space where Kenny and Christine were connected to each other.

Kenny felt a twist in his perineum. He was no prude, but this was doing nothing for his mood. He sat up and swung his legs round so he had his back to the cushion of the sofa and his feet on the floor.

'Don't mind me,' said Gibbs as he strode into the room, his semi-engorged penis swinging. 'Just need to top up my drink.' He held up a hand with two empty glasses in it as if to prove his motivation and walked through to the kitchen area.

Christine looked at Kenny as if to ask if he wanted her to invite Gibbs to join them.

Kenny curled a lip.

Lexi appeared in the doorway. She was also naked. 'Hey, is this where the party is?' She squealed and leapt on to the sofa. Kenny looked at Christine with a raised eyebrow. She smiled her assent and giggled when Lexi fed a breast to Kenny's mouth.

He gave himself up to the charge of the moment and time vanished under a swelter of limbs, soft curves and warm parts. At one point he caught sight of Gibbs at the far end of the sofa. He was sitting upright, still naked, absently stroking the skin of his chest, watching them with as much interest as a bored teenager might watch animals at a zoo.

Next moment, Gibbs was in his face, eyes manic wide, handing him a drink. 'Get that down ye, mate.'

What the hell, thought Kenny. Wondered if the drink might be spiked but tossed it back with a mental fuck it. Whatever Gibbs had in store for him he was sure he could handle it.

If he thought the previous session was electric, the next one took it up a notch. He'd never felt so powerful, so charged, so hard. He could fuck all night. Line up a dozen girls and he'd keep them all happy. He might even have roared at one point.

He drank some more.

Fucked a hell of a lot more.

He was all throb, pulse and cock. Immortal.

Didn't even mind when Gibbs positioned himself behind Lexi and joined in. At one point Gibbs pushed his penis at his face. Kenny bared his teeth in warning. Gibbs laughed like he was about to cough up a lung.

Kenny woke up next morning under a tangle of limbs with a pleasant ache in his groin, a wrung-out feeling in his thighs, and a headache that threatened to split his skull. Taking care not to wake up either of the girls, he extricated himself and walked over to the kitchen. He filled a glass with water and took a long drink. Savoured the cold and wet sensation in his mouth and throat. Opened up some of the kitchen drawers to see if there were any painkillers.

Gibbs appeared by his side, wearing a pair of jogging pants. His eyes were red-rimmed and sleep-punched.

'Get one for me, mate?' he asked, looking pointedly at Kenny's glass. Kenny did the needful and handed it over to him. Gibbs gave a groan.

'Just what the doctor ordered.' He rubbed his eyes. 'Man, did I need that.'

'Got anything for a headache?' Kenny asked. 'And what did you put in my drink last night?'

'Did you enjoy yourself?'

'Aye.'

'Then fuck it.' Gibbs' mouth was a hard line.

'Painkillers?' Kenny held his forehead and groaned.

'Hair of the dog?' asked Gibbs.

'This dog's got all the hair he needs, mate. Now he's after some paracetamol.'

'Bathroom cabinet,' said Gibbs and cocked his head to the side. Kenny went to the toilet. Suddenly needed a shit when he was there. Voided his bowels, taking care not to push down too hard because the pain was pretty ridiculous. Finished, washed his hands and then searched in the cupboard above the sink. Found a small blister pack of painkillers. Took two.

Looked at himself in the cabinet mirror.

'Jesus,' he said out loud. If Gibbs looked like shit, he was ten times worse. What did that prick put in his drink last night?

Back in the kitchen, praying for the analgesic to take effect.

'What the hell did you put in my drink last night?' Kenny asked. He wanted it to appear that he had submitted to Gibbs' alpha act, while simultaneously putting up token resistance.

Kenny was suddenly aware of his nakedness. It wasn't an issue the previous night, when it was dark and they were all drunk, but in the bright light of a new day he was now beginning to feel a little self-conscious.

'That was a good night,' said Gibbs, leaning his hip against the black marble work surface. 'The best nights are the ones you don't expect, eh?'

Kenny turned to the side and refilled his glass from the tap. Nodded. Felt a heavy beat of pain across his skull and reduced his movement. 'Aye. I've never done anything like that before. Two birds at once. Fucking amazing, man.'

'So, what's your story, really?' asked Gibbs. As he spoke his eyes narrowed. He looked Kenny up and down. Assessing. Nothing about his attention could be construed as sexual. It was a look a soldier would use to measure a potential combatant. An exercise in risk assessment. 'I'm not buying the act you gave me last night. You didn't find me by accident.' He took a step closer. 'What the hell's your game?'

38

From the corner of his vision, Kenny could see the ladies gathering their clothes and beginning the act of dressing. They were hunched in posture as if some kind of street sense was kicking in, alerting them to some possible danger. Kenny looked at Gibbs and measured the aggression in his tone. And reconsidered the man's intelligence. He'd obviously underestimated him. Or his performance hadn't been strong enough. Whichever it was, if he wanted to get close to whatever Ian was embroiled in, he'd have to improve his act.

'Shit,' said Kenny and indicated his state of undress. 'I seem to have lost my watch. What time is it?' Tried to inject a note of worry into his voice. Let Gibbs think he had the upper hand.

'What's the score, mate?' Gibbs insisted.

'Fancy a bacon roll?' asked Kenny. 'I'm starvin'.' He looked at Christine and gave the door a quick look. A signal she should go. 'Where are you going, ladies?' he asked for Gibbs' benefit. 'Not fancy a wee morning session?'

'Leave the lassies out of this, mate,' said Gibbs. He looked over at them. 'Want me to order a taxi for you?'

'Aye,' said Kenny as he took a step forward. 'I'll just come with . . .'

'You're going nowhere, buddy,' said Gibbs and put a hand on his chest. Kenny imagined snapping one of his fingers back. Swallowed the impulse and leaned back against the wall. He cupped his genitals in his hands. Thought, time for a little kickback. Can't let him think he's going to get it all his own way.

'Fair enough, you want answers. First, let me put some clothes on. Unless you enjoy looking at my junk.'

Gibbs stepped back from the accusation, a sneer on his face.

'Right,' said Kenny. 'Didn't think so.' He padded through to where the girls were standing. Winked at Christine when his back was to Gibbs, to tell her not to worry. Picked his jeans and boxers from a crumple on the floor and put them on. He found his t-shirt behind a cushion and pulled it on. Next, he sat down on the sofa and put on his socks and shoes. If things got heated he didn't want his feet to be unprotected.

'Why don't you wait downstairs for your taxi, girls?' said Gibbs. 'You don't want the driver to go without you.'

Kenny reached into his pocket, pulled out his wallet and plucked from it a bunch of notes. Handed them to Christine. Reached forward and kissed her cheek. 'Great night, last night,' he said. Then he looked at the other girl. Injected some bravado into his tone. 'Lexi, baby,' he said. 'You were awesome last night. Made this old man's dream come true.'

She gave him an extravagant kiss. Using her index finger she drew a line from Kenny's chin down to the buckle on his belt. Then said, 'You don't have bad breath and you've got like five percent body fat. Anytime, baby.'

'Aye, very good,' said Gibbs. 'Time to piss off, hen.'

Both girls picked up their shoes and bags and clutching them to themselves, took short rapid steps to the door. It banged shut, and Gibbs faced Kenny.

'You were sayin'?'

'I could fair go a bacon roll, mate. All that shagging is hungry work.'

'I'll get a bacon roll and shove it up your arse, mate, if you don't tell me what you are fucking up to, ya prick.'

Kenny stood, held his hands up in the universal don't shoot

position. 'I saw you at that fight thing last night . . .'

'You what?' Gibbs' face bunched ugly and he moved closer to Kenny.

'Wait a minute . . .'

'You followed me to the casino?'

'Kinda . . . yes, I did,' Kenny answered, thinking the best lies stick close to the truth.

Gibbs put a couple of fingers on Kenny's chest and pushed. 'This better be good, mate, or you're in serious shit.'

Kenny took a step back. Injected some enthusiasm into his voice. 'That fight, man. It was awesome. And I was watching it thinking: I want some of this action, you know? I saw you leave just ahead of me. Noticed you drive off in the beamer. Thought you obviously had cash. And . . .' here Kenny looked Gibbs up and down, ' . . . you look after yourself. You walk like a scrapper. So I'm thinking you could be a possible partner in this.'

'You what? You want to get into that business? With me?'

'Totally,' said Kenny. 'I'm a business man and although last night was good, I'm pretty sure we could do a better job than those monkeys.'

'Those monkeys?' Gibbs repeated with an incredulous expression.

'Yeah,' said Kenny, getting into his stride, allowing the fake idea to grow. 'I mean, it was a good watch, right, but what if we had guys who could actually fight? Those guys looked like they'd been picked up off the streets, for chrissakes.'

'Off the streets,' Gibbs repeated and shook his head.

'Aye. I'm a member of a gym. I'm just into CrossFit and stuff like that, but there's a few guys who go there who are into that MMA shit. Some of them could probably do with some extra cash, you know?'

'The whole off-the-street thing is the point, you prick,' Gibbs said. 'Not heard of bum fights? But these guys are ex-army, living on the street. We do them a favour and give them a chance to earn some cash. Feed their habit an' that.'

'Wait a minute,' said Kenny as if the penny had just dropped. 'You said "we". You're already involved in this?' He held a hand to his forehead. 'Man, am I the stupidest guy on the block.' He exhaled. 'Jesus.' He made an apologetic expression. 'At least I had the good sense to pick you then, eh? Didn't know you were involved but thought you looked like somebody who could be involved.'

Gibbs shook his head. Appeared to relax.

'What a walloper,' he said.

'So.' Kenny crossed his arms. 'There's some action here.' Pursed his lips. 'You and your guys looking to branch out? Need a new investor?'

'Don't think so.'

'Aww c'mon. I got you your hole last night,' said Kenny. 'We would be a good team.'

'Yeah, 'cos I'm that shallow. I'll go into business with any prick that organises a prostitute for me.'

'Aye, but what a prostitute,' Kenny said, arms wide.

'Wait a minute,' said Gibbs. His eyes narrowed. 'That was all part of the set-up? You saw me at the fight, followed me to the casino and organised a couple of women? Who the hell are you and what are you really after?' As he spoke he edged forward, head low, hands bunched into fists by his side.

'Whoa, steady on, mate.' Kenny stepped back from him. 'The thing with the girls was pure coincidence. I was celebrating my divorce. That's why I was at the fight.' Out of the side of his mouth he added, 'My missus hates all that stuff. And the girls were always something I'd dreamed of. Bucket list kinda thing, you know?' Kenny held a hand up. Didn't see this guy being so paranoid. 'I'm a business man. I told you. I see an opportunity and I go for it. Simple as.' He turned to the side, spotted his jacket on the floor. Picked it up. Put it on. 'You're not interested? Fine. I'll find something else to throw my cash at.'

'Did I say you could go?' asked Gibbs.

'You know, I get you drunk, get you laid. It's not unusual in the world of business to go to those lengths to sweeten up a deal. But I don't appreciate the tone or the . . .' Kenny pretended to be flustered and struggle to complete his sentence, ' . . . so if you don't mind I'll take my offer of a bacon roll and leave.'

'You don't appreciate the tone,' said Gibbs in a camp voice. 'Fuck me, are you in the wrong place at the wrong time.' His phone sounded an alert. He looked at Kenny. 'Aye, why don't you piss off.'

'Fine,' said Kenny in his best prissy, self-important voice. 'I'll just say cheerio and next time I'll keep the girls to myself.' Taking a wide berth, he passed Gibbs on the way to the door and walked along the hallway, aware that Gibbs was following him.

'Cheerio,' Gibbs said in a mocking voice.

Kenny ignored him and pulled the door open. He came face to face with two men. Both of whom he'd seen on the CCTV film from the young soldier's apartment building. One was tall and lean with short hair and round, thick spectacles. The other was the height and width of the door. This guy was holding a gun.

The guy with the specs smiled. 'Hello, Kenny. We've been looking forward to meeting you.'

'Aye?' Kenny was stuck for anything else to say. 'I hope you're better company than your mate here.' He heard a crackle and spark. Looked at the guy's hand. Saw a blue flash. The guy reached out quicker than Kenny could react and pointed a small black object at him.

First the crackle.

A stabbing sensation. A burning smell.

Hot agony.

His knees went from under him and he felt a full body cramp as every muscle in his body seized.

39

Business was so slow in The Blue Owl that Ray McBain, former detective inspector, had taken to reading. Customers were almost as rare as balls on a hen, so rather than count the hairs on the back of his hands again – the nuns did warn him about that – he thought he should take up reading.

There was a small second-hand bookshop just two doors down from the bar, so on his way into work one lunchtime he took a wander in and among the piles of once-loved books, with that particular smell of cigarettes, dust, vanilla and almonds, found a much-thumbed copy of *Zen and the Art of Motorcycle Maintenance*. He opened it at random and read, "When a shepherd goes to kill a wolf, and takes his dog to see the sport, he should take care to avoid mistakes. The dog has certain relationships to the wolf the shepherd may have forgotten."

Rubbed that across his brain cells.

Understood? Nope. But he held on to the book. He could do with stretching the old grey matter. A row of brightly coloured book spines attracted his eye. Read the names in bold print. Crime writers. When he was on the job the last thing he wanted to do was read about the nasty shit people inflicted on each other when he was experiencing it first-hand every day. Now that he was retired, he wasn't sure he wanted to dip his mind back into that cess-pit, even if it was constructed in someone's imagination.

A woman walked past the outside of the shop. Her hair and her gait were so like Maggie that his breath caught in his throat and his heart gave a lurch. He forced air into his lungs. Grief and guilt were ever present. One day it would lessen, people told him. He shook his head and turned back to the books.

One attracted his eye. *The Guillotine Choice*. Shawshank meets Papillon was how the blurb put it. Sounded like the very thing he could escape into. He carried both books to the till point. An old man looked over the top of his specs from behind a barricade of books. His hair was a grey frizz, just two inches short on top from being an afro, and too long down his back. The man's beard was equally full and quite possibly electrically charged. This hairstyle of abandon was offset by a collar, tie and cardigan ensemble that looked like it came in a package. And judging by the slight fraying on the collar, that package was opened a good ten years earlier.

'Right,' he said and looked at both books. 'Can't remember these coming in.' He peered over at Ray. 'You working in The Blue Owl?'

'The new manager,' said Ray.

'That'll be a wee change fae being in the polis.'

'Still means dealing with a lot of drunks,' Ray replied, wondering how the guy knew.

'Bill,' the man said. 'I'd shake your hand but I'm not sure I could reach you past all these books.'

'And you know about . . .'

'You bein' an ex-copper? Don't worry.' He pushed his spectacles back up his nose. 'Not much gets past me.' He winked. 'Quite pleased about it to be honest. We don't get much bother in this street, but if we did it's reassuring to know we've got a man nearby who can handle stuff.'

'Stuff,' repeated Ray, thinking, don't count on it. 'How much for the books?'

'You can have them for free,' said Bill as he made a face. 'We've had them for ages.'

At the bar, Ray made himself his first coffee of the day and settled down on a stool to read *Zen*. As soon as he opened the book, the door opened. In walked a couple of young women, shaking the rain from their hair and jackets.

They were in their mid-thirties, fashionably dressed – at least to Ray's unpractised eyes they were – and laden with bags of shopping.

'Aww, man, my feet are pure throbbing,' the blonde woman said before slumping into a chair.

'We totally deserve a glass of wine,' the brunette replied.

Ray wanted to ask them if they were lost, but bit his tongue.

'Red or white?' he called over.

They answered "Red" in unison.

'Small or large?'

'Large,' was the consensus, followed by a giggle.

'Relax. Take a weight off,' Ray said. 'And I'll bring them over.' Moments later he was serving them their wine.

'You're new,' one said.

'Fresh out the packet,' Ray replied.

'What happened to Margaret?' the other asked. The name was pronounced *Magrit* in that Glasgow way.

'She got fed up listening to Al Jarreau and Sade all day. Got a job in Lidl.'

'Some folk have got nae ambition,' she replied.

'You'll be the ex-polis,' her friend jumped in. 'You're the talk of the steamie.'

'Aye,' said Ray and told them the price of the drinks to distract them from going into that any further.

Then started the Scottish verbal dance that occurred in every teashop, café and bar in the country when women got together.

'Here,' one shoved a £10 note at Ray.

'Naw,' her friend said and pulled her arm away. Then thrust a note towards Ray. 'It's my turn. You bought the scones down at Betty's.'

'That's 'cos you paid the bus fares into town.'

'Aye, but I owed you for those tights you got me in Markies,' the other interrupted, and as they talked at each other they continued to pull at each other's arms while thrusting cash at Ray.

He plucked the note out of each of their hands. 'Life's too short, ladies. Why don't I keep both notes behind the bar and when you run out of money you can top the kitty up?'

'Barman,' the blond one said. 'You are a total genius.'

'That's 'cos he's ex-polis,' her friend said and looked him up and down. 'I do like a man in a uniform.' They both laughed.

'My uniform days are long gone, ladies,' Ray said. Gave a little bow. 'Enjoy your drinks.' He turned and walked back to the bar, aware that they were both checking out his arse. He had enough vanity to be grateful that grief had at least shrunk the flab on his backside. The advice had been to accept small victories on the road through his grief. It might be shallow, but as a yoyo fatty he'd take that.

He got himself comfortable on the stool again and opened his book, and the door opened. Another customer. He should really take up this reading malarkey full time: it's bringing in the customers.

'Afternoon, Ray.'

He looked up. Smiled. 'Alessandra. How are you this fine afternoon?'

She brushed some rain from her sleeves, shook water from her head and grinned. 'If it was warmer I'd take my boots off and give my webbed feet an outing.'

'Red wine seems to be the drink du jour.' A wee cheer from the women in the corner. 'Want one?'

Alessandra looked over her shoulder at the women and gave a small wave of acknowledgement. Back to Ray. 'Nah, I'm an all or nothing kinda girl. One drink never does it for me. Just a coffee, thanks.'

She settled on a stool at the bar, holding her large, wide handbag on her lap.

'What's a nice girl like you doing in joint like this?' Ray asked.

'It's the ambience, innit? And the hunky barman.'

Ray laughed. 'He just popped out for a fag, in the meantime I'll get you your drink.' As he set the coffee machine to work, Ray asked. 'So, what really brings you here?'

'You seen Kenny today?'

'Actually, no.' Ray cocked his head to the side. 'Which is unusual. He's either called or visited every day since I took over. Doesn't quite trust me on my own yet.' The dark liquid poured to a stop. Ray lifted the cup and put it on a saucer with a teaspoon. 'Milk or cream for madam?'

'No cow required, ta.'

He set the drink before her. She took the teaspoon, gave the drink a stir and then took a sip. Swallowed. Gave a sigh. 'Just what the hard-pressed GP ordered.'

Ray had a sip of his own. It was lukewarm. 'Yeah, should be on subscription.'

'Prescription.'

'Same thing.' Ray smiled. Acknowledged the warmth of his affection for Alessandra. Felt a pang for the old job. Quashed it. Working in the police only ever brought him pain. Three years and three near-death experiences was enough for anyone surely. 'Why are you looking for Kenny?'

'We did a search on the deaths of ex-army guys.' Her expression grew sombre. 'You know, there's lots of help out there for these guys, but far too many fall through the cracks. If you want a mood downer just check out some of their files.' She shook her head. 'Anyway. There have been a number of suicides. Too many. None of the post mortems showed anything dodgy. Clear-cut cases of self-harm. Except for one. Luke Crabb. He jumped off the Erskine Bridge. Which would have had the added difficulty of happening given he was already dead.'

'So he was thrown?'

'Give that man a badge. Impact with the water caused so much damage they couldn't be sure how many injuries were inflicted before he died. But given the angle of his entry into the water . . . there were facial injuries that couldn't have been caused by the fall.'

Facial injuries. Could be from a fight?

'Also, one eye had been pecked out by a bird before the body was found, but the other had evidence of strangulation. Or as the PM put it, subconjunctival haemorrhages.'

Blood-red eye. Due to capillary rupture in the white portion of the eyes. Ray remembered his first choking victim. A case of domestic abuse. He could still remember her name: Jackie Craig. Understood the panic she might have felt before death when the police doctor explained that this phenomenon suggested a particularly vigorous struggle between the victim and assailant.

'How far did the murder investigation get?'

'It stalled. Took ages to identify the body. His family were from Fife and they hadn't seen him since just after his discharge from the army nearly two years ago. In fact there were no records of him after that date. No bank activity. No engagement with social services. This guy went completely off the radar.'

'Was probably on the street all that time.'

'Yeah. And the thing is, he had just over ten grand in his bank account. For some reason he didn't go near it.'

'Bloody hell,' said Ray. 'Poor guy. What state must your mind be in that you can't access your own money to buy yourself some creature comforts?'

'Anywho . . .' Ale reached into her handbag, lifted out a manila folder and placed it on the bar. 'The CCTV at Dom Hastie's place.' She opened the folder and displayed some images. She paused and placed a hand on top of them, obscuring Ray's view. 'I really shouldn't be doing this, ex-Detective Inspector McBain . . .'

Ray gave her a small smile and raised his eyebrows with an unspoken *what's new* motion. They had done similar previous, where Alessandra helped him with cases when he was persona non grata with the suits.

'Been here before, eh?' she said and lifted her hand. Got down to business. 'We looked at the film in the lobby of Hastie's building for the day before and the day of his fall. The factor eliminated all of the inhabitants, and she recognised some regular visitors . . . but these guys threw up a warning sign.'

The images were not the easiest to make out because of the poor quality yellowish paper, cheap printers and the bad angles from which the pictures were taken. Still, there was enough to make out a couple of faces.

'This guy,' Ale pointed, 'is on the system for GBH. Judge went easy on him because of his exemplary service in the forces. He picked a fight with some poor random guy in a bar. Kicked him so hard on the side of the head that he'll never hear properly from that side ever again. Reason? He was murdering an Elvis song during a karaoke session.' Ale gave an ironic shrug as if to say, what else can one do when an Elvis song is being ruined? 'Barry Gibbs is the name of this charmer. He's former Black Watch. Now a mercenary. Strikes me as strong contender to be involved in a fight thing.'

'From the sound of it, he'd rather be in the ring than organising the fight.'

'Yeah,' agreed Ale and pushed that image to the side to show another one. 'This guy with the Harry Potter specs is also on the system. Was involved in a spate of car thefts as a teenager down in London. Name's Dan Stewart. Our Dan did some time in a young offender's institution. Nothing more since. I wondered if he'd learned the error of his ways . . .' She gave Ray a look. They both knew how rare that was. Most of these places were breeding grounds for career criminals. 'But my digging sent up a red flag, and I received an interesting call from someone in Organised Crime down at the Met. Seems our Dan has been consorting with some seriously dangerous types, but he's yet to be caught with his hand in the till, if you get my drift.'

Ray understood exactly what Ale was getting at. Dan had gotten older and smarter. Operated at a remove from crime's coal-face. Let younger men take the fall while he raked in the profits.

'This guy at the Met wants to be kept informed. They suspect Stewart's involved in all kinds of nasty. And they're keen to nab him once and for all.'

'Interesting,' said Ray.

'What's more interesting is the times the images were taken. We caught Stewart and Gibbs the day before Hastie fell. And Gibbs the day of the fall.'

'Really?'

'There's not enough to say that Gibbs pushed Hastie, but the evidence is there to show that he was in the building.'

Ray gave it some thought. 'He's the kind who'd think nothing of scaring up an alibi. Pretend he was visiting someone else in the building.'

'Which could be plausible.'

'True. What does your gut say, Ale?'

'They say that more guys kill themselves when they get home than ever the Taliban managed. So suicide can't be ruled out. But the ex-wife is adamant that regardless of how troubled Hastie was, he wasn't suicidal.' She paused. Tapped a finger on Gibbs' photograph. 'But, there's something about this guy . . .' She tailed off and looked at the image again. Ray followed her gaze, studied the body language of Gibbs. His head was low into his shoulders, his back slightly hunched. He was trying to make himself small. Less visible. And that was not the action of an innocent man. Whatever he was doing in that building was not an act of kindness.

They fell into silence again.

'Top up your coffee?' Ray asked.

'Please.'

Ray did the needful. Sat back down.

'I keep thinking about that guy, Crabb,' said Ale. 'What had his time in the forces done to his mind that a life on the street would be preferable to an ordinary life?'

They fell silent as they each considered this man's life. In a job that constantly threw up reminders of life's miseries, neither of them had grown inured to the pain that people might suffer. Ray thought he had been losing the ability to access the sympathy button for people who repeatedly sabotaged their own lives in petty, meaningless acts, but he took some measure of reassurance from the fact that he could still access that common humanity when life was in danger. His ability to empathise was not lost. Perhaps that was due to the shit he'd experienced in his own life. Lead a sheltered life and you can't understand how some people might react in a given circumstance, how they might behave in their own worst interests.

'So,' Ale looked into his eyes, searching,' what's really the story with Kenny and this fight club? If his cousin's involved, are we going to be collecting his body from under the Erskine Bridge?'

40

Ian lay on his back, on his single bed, in his tiny room, hands behind his head, feet crossed at the ankles. These digs were like an exact copy of the previous ones. He stared at the stained stipple on the ceiling and for the thousandth time that morning thought about Kenny and the shock he felt when he recognised him at the fight. How the hell had he found him? He smiled. Daft question. Kenny always was one of the most resourceful people he'd met. If he hadn't become a criminal, he could have become a chief executive of a major bank.

Which amounted to the same thing really.

Why hadn't Kenny made it obvious who he was? Why approach him so secretively like that? What did he know? Ian crossed his arms over his chest in a protective motion. Was he in danger – apart from the obvious?

Was Dom?

He sat up. And how much of Dom's debt had he repaid with last night's fight? On the way back here after the fight, Dave was pretty silent on the issue. Enough of this bullshit, thought Ian. It's time for some answers.

Down the stairs in the area that was ambitiously entitled "Reception", a woman was sitting at a desk. She had short grey hair, was almost as thin as a coat-hanger and when she smiled displayed a mouthful of stained teeth. The badge attached to her black jacket read, "Margo". She had a laptop she was typing into furiously, as if all of her life issues were fuelling her fingers.

'Help you?' she asked without looking from the screen.

'Where are we?' Ian asked.

Her fingers stopped. She looked up at him. 'Where are we?' She looked confused. 'Do you need to know what year it is as well, darling?'

Jesus, thought Ian, the woman thinks I'm permanently zonked. 'Just the location, please?'

'Well, this is Craigie House and . . .' her forehead creased with concern, ' . . . we're in Stirling.' She bit her upper lip then asked, 'You okay, honey? Anything I can get you?'

Ian found a smile from somewhere, hoped it appeared at least half genuine. Stirling? Why would they want to remove him from Glasgow? What did they not want him to know? Just what had he got himself into? He'd been so pissed off with his mum and Kenny and his dad – or the man he always thought of as his father – that he'd just gone along with Dave and Gibbs etcetera without questioning them. He recognised that was part of his army training. Stay in automatic pilot – breathing, eating, sleeping, and shitting – until someone in authority told him where to go and what to do. His time on the streets as a youth had been so chaotic he'd taken to that way of living with a huge sigh of relief, immediately feeling that he'd come home. And here he was doing it again. Albeit, the people he'd currently sanctioned with that authority were dubious as all fuck.

This time his smile was laced with purpose. 'Nah, you're alright. I just need some fresh air, thanks.'

She nodded, her face full of uncertainty. Her right hand moved towards her phone. Ian turned and walked to the exit. As he pushed it open he heard her speak.

'Hi, it's me . . .'

Couldn't care less if she was in cahoots with the fight organisers – in fact, that would make sense, how else would someone like him get in here along with the asylum seekers without raising any questions?

He let the door close behind him and breathed deeply of the cool and crisp air. Someone came out the door behind him. It was the man who'd been his neighbour at the digs Dave had supplied in Glasgow. Name was Mo, and he was wearing a red t-shirt and black shorts. What the hell was he doing here? Was he involved in this fight club stuff as well? Surely not, thought Ian. Looked like he couldn't fight his way out of a sweaty t-shirt.

Mo flashed a smile. 'I go run.' And off he went. Long, ropey, lean muscled limbs covering the ground to the end of the street in a perfectly economic motion. In a couple of blinks, Mo was out of sight.

Ian considered running after him, just for a moment. Snorted. In the time it had taken to think about and discount the action, the man was out of reach. He shivered against the chill, and wishing he'd brought a jacket, he pushed his hands into his pockets and walked to the end of the street. Once there he looked around. He was now on a long road. On the right a high, sandstone wall provided a border to a patch of lawn that led up to a church. On the left side of the street, a row of white, two-storey houses had their front doors on the street. Double yellow lines prevented the locals from parking.

They could have dropped me on Mars for all the good I am here, he thought. What did he know about Stirling? There was a castle, and they held a crime fiction festival here every year.

Also, there were some good pubs in town. He'd spent an evening there with some army mates a lifetime ago. Got royally pissed on some state-sanctioned lager therapy. He remembered the group of them in one bar. Cropped hair, tanned faces and haunted eyes. Moaning about how difficult it was to adapt to life on civvy street. Going from being constantly hyper alert, with the worry that a stray bomb or bullet would catch them, to listening to some halfwit moaning that their favourite singer had been chucked out of X Factor.

Gun was with them that day. He had a massive bruise on his

forehead. Said that he'd stood in front of a brick wall and repeatedly banged his head off it until he "felt woozy". The strange thing about it now was that at the time no one thought this was an odd way to behave. Everyone around the table nodded at his explanation as if to say, yeah, I get that.

As usual when thoughts turned to his ex-army mates, he thought about Gun. Initials GSW – Gun Shot Wound – shortened to Gun. He was the most capable one among them. Calm under fire, always seemed to have a solution to a problem, quick to kick arses when it was needed and even quicker to lend an ear. It was a complete shock when he, the last person they thought would succumb to PTSD, was the first one in the platoon to do so.

Ian forced his thoughts from the past to the present. Looked around himself. Envied the apparent comfort and security of the inhabitants who might live in this part of town. Warmth, shelter and knowledge of where their next meal might come from.

In his mind's eye he saw his mother on her pink sofa, phone in her hand, waiting for a message from him. Guilt twisted the muscles in his jaw. He should get in touch. At least let her know he was safe. Sort of.

A curtain twitched to his right. He saw a soft wrinkled face. Some old dear, her hand clutching her cardigan at her throat. He ducked his head and picked up his pace. Didn't want the old soul to get worried she had a psycho on her doorstep. Felt a twinge of missing for his mother. He could have her fussing over him in a couple of hours. Setting him out a plate of food. Offering him his old bed for the night. He just needed to tell Dave, Gibbs and the Harry Potter specs guy to go fuck themselves. Whatever debt they imagined he owed them he could borrow off Kenny and then work it off, however long that might take.

He wandered aimlessly for the next hour or so, thoughts in a jumble, scraps of meaning passing before his conscious mind then being whipped away like leaves in the wind.

A car slowed behind him. A couple of stones popped under the tyres.

'Ian, get in.'

He turned. It was Dave, and he was climbing out of the driver's seat.

Ian studied his face, reading it for his intention.

'C'mon, mate,' Dave said and indicated the car with a nod of his head.

'Piss off.'

'What's got into you today, buddy?' Dave reached him and put a hand on his shoulder. Ian looked into his eyes, saw this for what it was: an act. Dave was the good guy. The charmer. Kept everyone sweet, but Ian could read the steel there. Friendly old Dave would have no compunction in mixing it if need be. Did he want to test how far he might go?

'I need answers . . . *buddy*.' He invested the word with scorn. 'I've done everything you guys asked of me. Now it's time to go back to my life.'

Dave stood in front of him. Feet wide. Arms crossed. A barrier. 'Here's how it's going to go. One more fight. One biggie. And then the debt's paid.'

'Really? You guys are full of shit. It was only supposed to be *one* fight. I might only be a thick ex-squaddie, but even I can tell that this one would be the third. Take your one more fight and shove it up your arse.'

Dave opened his jacket. Ian saw the glint of metal in an under-shoulder holster and read the warning in Dave's face.

'We have this. Or you fight one more time and hey, the purse on this one is so big you might even come out of it with some extra cash. You pay off Dom Hastie's debt and come out of it with some mullah of your own.'

'Yeah,' said Ian. 'At least you could dab yourself with perfume before you try to fuck me over.'

'No. Really, mate. This is kosher. The organisers loved your last fight. How you took that guy down. They're buzzing with it and want to set up something special. With a real purse. Win this and you could come out of it with a few grand in your pocket.'

Ian turned away. Thought about the gun beneath Dave's jacket. Had that been there all this time? The stick and the carrot. The gun or the cash conundrum.

'Well, when you put it like that . . .' Ian walked to the car.

41

Ray McBain knocked on the white double-glazed door. Realised he'd given it his usual ratatat police knuckle and grimaced. You can take the man out of the job . . .

He heard the rapid, short-spaced footfall of a child before the door opened and a small boy looked up at him.

'Is your mum in, son?' he asked. The boy had large blue eyes, a button nose and one large white tooth showing from behind the plump pink of his lips. It was like life had imitated Disney art. He was as cute as a basket of puppies.

A young woman that McBain took to be his mother appeared at his back. She was tall and lean with dusty blond hair scrapped back from her drawn face.

'Can I help you?' she asked. McBain could see where the boy got his big eyes from and judged that the lower half of his face – nose, mouth, chin – resembled those features found in photos of the boy's recently deceased father.

'Sorry to trouble you, Mrs Hastie . . .' He paused as he gathered his thoughts. He should have rehearsed this before coming here. Should he use his old job to earn her trust? With the thought that the best lies are the ones that stick closest to the truth, he opened his mouth and allowed the words to flow. 'My name is Ray McBain. I'm looking into the disappearance of a former army colleague of your husband's.' He didn't say why he was looking into this, knowing that his manner and bearing were informed by the years he spent working in the police.

The boy shifted position and he moved behind his mother, peering up at Ray from her side.

'I'm sorry,' she said and moved to close the door. 'I didn't know too much about the guys my *ex*-husband was in the army with. Not sure I can be any help to you.' Sorrow pulled down the corners of her mouth. She looked dimmed with lack of sleep.

'No, *I'm* sorry,' Ray said and took a step back, to show her he wasn't a threat. 'It's just that we know this guy was one of the last people to see your husband. Sorry, ex-husband. And since your . . . since Dom . . .' McBain took a look at the boy and modified the language he was about to use. ' . . . since Dom passed, this guy has completely disappeared. We're concerned that the two events are linked and that there is more to all of this.' He knew that his use of "we" along with his bearing would make the woman think he was from the police. But he never actually said he was.

If Alessandra Rossi heard him trying to justify this, she would tear strips off him. So be it. He couldn't just sit by and not do anything. Another day and no word from Kenny. In normal circumstances he could go for weeks without hearing from him, but all of his instincts were telling him that Kenny was caught up in something that even he might have trouble dealing with.

'You think it might not be suicide after all?' asked Mrs Hastie as she placed a hand on her son's head. At the thought, a little light leaked into her eyes. As if a little slice of guilt might be eased.

'Mind if I come in, Mrs Hastie?' asked Ray. 'This is not the best place to be talking.'

She looked over his shoulder at the door across the landing behind him. 'Aye, that old bat, Mrs Macpherson will be standing there with her ear trumpet wondering why the police are at my door.' She stepped back. 'C'mon in.'

The small flat was scoured to a sparkle, and McBain wondered if cleaning was this woman's coping mechanism. Keep busy, keep scrubbing, and it will hold the feelings at bay. That's an impulse he well understood.

In the living room he sat on a brown leather armchair while the woman, girl really, and the boy sat on the sofa.

'Can I get you a cup of tea?' she asked as if just remembering that's how society was oiled.

'No thanks,' said Ray. 'I've been drinking tea and coffee all day. Think my bladder is about to burst.'

She looked down at her son. 'Away and play with your toys, baby.' McBain looked at the corner where the boy's toy box rested. It looked like it hadn't been disturbed in days. The boy walked over, picked up one toy and wordlessly returned to his mother's side, where he leaned closer, as if trying to burrow into the cushion of her grey fleece top. She made a face at Ray. 'He's barely left my side since his dad died. And that's the only toy he'll play with. His dad gave it to him the other week.'

Ray looked at the small plastic figure now caught in the prison of the boy's fingers. He could see enough to recognise a toy from his own boyhood. 'A ninja turtle?' He tried to inject enthusiasm into his voice. 'Cool. I used to have one of them.'

'He's barely made a sound since his dad died,' she said and shook her head with a weariness that seemed to come from the deepest part of her. Then she leaned down and kissed the top of his head. 'Poor wee lamb. The world of adults is a totally messed up place.'

'Mrs Hastie . . .'

'It's Theresa.'

'Theresa, can you tell me what you know about your husband's last movements? Who his friends were? What old army mates he kept in touch with?'

She looked away from him: stared at the black, shiny rectangle of the silent television as if there was a film on show there that only she could see. Shook her head. Looked at Ray and then down at the floor. 'You must think me a horrible bitch. My husband goes to war, comes back a basket case, and I abandon him.'

'That's none of my . . .' Ray paused as he wondered how best to respond.

'I *know* that it wasn't him. It was the bullet. But still . . . the mood swings, the mad mental screaming, the fury . . .' She bit her lip. Took her son's hand in hers and lightly stroked the back of his small hand. 'It was terrifying. He was impossible to live with, and I know the wee fella was one of the things that helped, but I was scared shitless that he'd do something when he got into one of his rages, you know?'

'I'm not here to judge, Theresa . . .'

'He had a couple of respite visits to that Combat Stress place down in Ayrshire. They gave him physiotherapy, armchair yoga and that mindfulness stuff. And it helped. For a wee bit. But I used to wonder about the wives, you know? Where's our therapy? We have to deal with the broken men that return to us from their bullshit wars. What support do we get?' She looked away. Closed her eyes as if damming a threatened flow of tears. 'I know he found it difficult – not seeing the wee man every day – but I did my best. I needed to protect my son from him, while still making sure they had time together.'

'I can't imagine how difficult all of that would have been for you, Theresa,' Ray said, wondering how he could get her off the subject of her troubles. Then he realised how self-serving this was and resisted the thought. If she needed to talk, why not let her? He held a hand out to the boy. 'Can I see your ninja turtle?'

The boy looked at him, with the wide-eyed solid gaze of the guileless and the judgement of the blameless. Ray was unsettled for a moment. No one could appear to look into your depths and find you wanting like a small child could.

'On you go, Darren. Let the nice man see your toy,' said Theresa.

The boy held the toy tight to his stomach.

'My favourite turtle's Donner Kebab. Who's yours?'

The boy's features squeezed together as he tried to stifle a smile. 'It's Donatello, silly,' he said in a quiet voice. His mother gave Ray a wide-eyed look and tears shone in her eyes.

'That's what I said.' Ray slipped from the chair and sat cross-legged on the carpet. 'Donner Kebab.'

Darren snorted. 'You're silly.'

Bugger me, thought Ray, I'm a child whisperer. 'Grown-ups are *all* silly. Haven't you realised that already?'

Darren looked up at his mum and pursed his lips as if thinking this notion through.

'Can I watch TV now, Mum?' he asked.

She gave him a look of fake admonition. 'Ok then. Just for a wee while, ya wee scamp.'

He slipped from the sofa, walked over to the TV and the remote that sat on the table under it. Moments later, the high-energy music and voices of cartoons filled the room. Darren returned to his mother but sat on the floor at her feet. One of his shoes nudging against Ray's as if the boy craved the solidity of another male. Given that his father was no longer available, Ray would do for the moment.

He felt a surge of sympathy for the boy. Offered him a smile. Nudged his foot in return. Darren nudged it back. Although his eyes fixed on the screen, they brightened with the beginnings of a smile.

'I don't know much about the guys that Dom was spending time with. There was one guy . . .' she searched her thoughts for a moment, ' . . . his name might have been Ian. He'd been down in Ayrshire with Dom and he'd kept in touch. Felt like he was one of the good guys, you know?'

Ray nodded his head.

'And . . .' She looked as if the thought had just occurred to her. 'Dom was buying stuff he couldn't afford. Toys for the wee fella.' She made a face. 'And some wacky baccy. It was the only thing that helped with the pain. His doctor gave him some painkillers, but they made him woozy.' She leaned forward towards Ray, her elbows on her knees. 'Who he was getting the drugs from, I have no idea. He could barely get out of his house.' She paused. 'Do drug pushers offer a home delivery service?' She shrugged. 'I know there was some ex-army guy who Dom . . . he hated this guy actually . . . but this guy could get him the cannabis, so he put up with him.'

The noise from the television temporarily increased in pitch. A cartoon car chase. The boy squirmed with excitement. Theresa shot him a look of love and relief. Then she turned back to Ray.

'Maybe I've been watching too much cop and robber stuff on telly, but I wonder if he got in too deep with these guys, couldn't or wouldn't pay up and they threw him . . .' She stopped speaking. Pressed the fingertips of her right hand against her lips. Her eyes wide and bright with fear as if she was imagining Dom's terror in that moment before he fell from his balcony.

Ray said nothing. From what she just told him, and now knowing the men involved, he was sure she was uncomfortably close to the truth.

They spoke some more before Ray rose to his feet in order to leave. At the front door he offered a smile of thanks. 'If you can think of anything else . . .' He paused as he realised he couldn't give her his business card. 'DC Alessandra Rossi down at Stewart Street station is who you should get in touch with.'

'Sure,' she said as she crossed her arms across her chest. 'I . . . eh, thanks for listening. I don't usually talk so much to – you know – cops.'

Just then, a flurry of footsteps and Darren appeared at her side. Now that Ray was at the front door, he had returned to his previous silent self. He held out a hand, offering Ray a gift. Ray picked it up. It was a miniature ninja turtle, a smaller version of the one he'd been playing with, like one that might come from a kid's junk food meal.

'Donna Kebab,' Darren said with the ghost of a smile.

Ray felt a stab of emotion. Ever since Maggie died, it felt like he was only ever a breath away from losing control. He swallowed. Bit his lip. Felt a sting in his eyes. Wanted to lean down and give the boy a hug. Wanted to promise him that everything would turn out okay. That all of this would ease in time. But he knew this was a lie he couldn't sell, so he kept his counsel to himself.

Instead, he put a hand on the boy's shoulder, and before the tears could flow in earnest, he turned and left.

42

The shock from a taser can last for up to five minutes, and while Kenny's muscles screamed in protest and then eventually relaxed, he was trussed up like a turkey for the oven. With duct tape tight around both his wrists and ankles, he was picked up by Gibbs and his mate and deposited on a chair in a room at the back of the flat.

'Right, supposing you tell us who you really are?' asked the guy with the specs.

'What the hell is going on here?' Kenny shouted. 'I was at that fight thing last night. And I tried to get your mate here into another fight deal. Let me out of these.' He held up his arms in front of him to indicate the tape.

Gibbs stepped forward and lashed out, striking Kenny on the right side of his face. Kenny blinked against the pain.

'Time for the bullshit is over, Kenny,' said Gibbs. 'While you were out of it last night, I took your photograph with my phone and sent it off to my friend Dan here, who did some digging.' He bent down and peered into Kenny's face. 'Your first mistake. Pretending to be some kind of businessman and then allowing me to see you with your top off. That's the build of a fighter, not a market trader.' Gibbs held his phone up with his left hand. 'I got some interesting answers back, Mr O'Neill.'

'Yeah,' interrupted Dan. 'Seems like you have quite the reputation around these parts, Kenny. A man not to be messed with.'

Kenny probed the inside of his mouth with his tongue to assess if there was any damage after Gibbs' punch. He moved his jaw from side to side. There would be swelling, but other than that nothing. Thankfully, the thug was holding back, but how he would love a couple of minutes one on one with the prick. His defiance must have shown in his eyes because Dan then said, 'Whatever you're thinking of doing, save us the trouble and don't.'

'Your man there killed Dom Hastie. Threw him off his balcony. The police are on to him and you by proxy. So, why don't you let me go, leave Gibbs here for me to deal with and you can scurry back to your manor in London. Or wherever it is you come from.'

Dan pretended not to be affected by this accusation, but Kenny could see a moment of surprise in his eyes and the bunching of muscles in his jaw before he recovered enough to sing the party song. 'Nice try,' he said.

'Bullshit!' shouted Gibbs.

'Course it is,' said Dan, turning to square off to Gibbs. ''cos if you had the effrontery to kill someone who owed me cash before he had the chance to pay it back to me, there would be hell to pay, Mr Gibbs. You know that don't you?'

'You're going to listen to this wanker?' Gibbs' face was an ugly street snarl.

Dan said nothing. He simply looked Gibbs in the eye and pushed his specs back up his nose. Then he turned to Kenny.

'So, what's the deal, O'Neill?' Then he grinned. 'Hey, I'm a poet.'

'You're also getting way over your head here,' said Kenny. 'Why don't you let me out of these restraints and we can talk like men.'

'Tut, tut, Kenny. We both know that as soon as you're free from that tape you'll go all ninja on our arses. No. I'm happy to equalise things till we get to the bottom of this.' He crossed his arms and looked down at him. Kenny studied him. Saw a lean build spare of muscle, but read a low cunning and able calculation in the man's eyes. He was all about the brain, leaving the muscle-work to the likes of Gibbs.

Kenny looked around the room. The only features were the door and a wide window that looked down on to the Clyde. The walls were cream and the carpet a chocolate brown. The only piece of furniture was the chair he was sitting on. A very spare room.

'Poor wee Dom was a friend of a friend,' Kenny said and scowled at Gibbs. 'I was to check this prick out and report back.'

'To who?' asked Dan.

'Aye. Who?' demanded Gibbs leaning forward on to his toes as if getting ready for a fight.

Kenny adapted his position on the chair into a relaxed slouch with his hands in his lap and his legs stretched out in front of him. He was saying, who's really in charge here?

'An interested party,' answered Kenny.

Dan stood in front of Kenny, getting inside his space, letting him know his attempt to assert himself in the room wasn't working. He studied Kenny's face. Kenny gave him nothing back.

'I watched Gibbs for a wee while. Thought, this guy's clearly got street smarts . . .' There's no harm in blindsiding the prick with a compliment, thought Kenny. ' . . . and hit upon a different approach. A wee party with a couple of gorgeous girls. Who's going to refuse that? Then the plan was to see if I could get you talking about Dom.'

Dan looked at Gibbs and made a motion towards the door with his head. 'Outside,' he said. Then he looked at the walking wall who Kenny was sure would still be packing a gun. 'Stay,' he commanded.

'You're not going to listen to this prick, for fuckssake?' demanded Gibbs, but followed the other man out of the room. Gibbs continued to talk at Dan as they left, closed the door and walked down the corridor towards the living room.

Then it fell silent. Kenny strained his ears to try and work out what was being said, but their speech was nothing but a meaning-less low rumble. He gave up trying to work out what was going on. Better to try and think of a way out of this shit.

Speaking of which, he felt a twist low in his bowel. Drink always affected his gut. Clearly, alcohol was not a friend to his system.

He looked at his guard, who was standing to the side of the door, chewing on the inside of his cheek as he coolly regarded him. Kenny winked. Grinned. Said, 'Awright, handsome?' Thought, how's that for irony. The guy looked like he'd had his face re-arranged by a large, blunt instrument, using only a passing reference to symmetry.

He simply stared back, impassive. Nothing registered.

This guy was huge: gym huge. Sure he could probably crush your skull, but only if you stood in the one place and allowed him to place a paw on either side of your head. A nimble, strong guy could take him easy.

Kenny shifted his feet, testing the tape. Did the same with his wrists. Both were set tight. Thought out several plays. All of them risky.

'Mate.' Kenny screwed his face. 'I need a piss. You going to hold it for me?'

Nothing.

'Buddy,' Kenny said more loudly, injecting some urgency into his tone. 'And a shit. You going to wipe my arse as well?'

His guard cocked his head to the side as if listening for move-ment from down the corridor.

'You'll have to wait,' he said.

'Jee-zuz,' said Kenny. 'I'm touching cloth here. There's going to be an almighty stink in here just directly.'

Nothing.

Kenny shifted a buttock, allowed the release of the gas that was building. It trumpeted off the hard plastic of his seat. You use whatever weapon you can, right?

The guard cocked an eyebrow as if to ask, really, that's the best you can do?

Then the smell hit him.

'Aww, man. That's rank.' He held a hand up to his nose. Breathed in through his mouth. 'What did you eat last night, ya prick?'

'C'mon,' Kenny said with some urgency. 'Things are about to get a lot worse if you don't let me get to a loo.'

The big guy looked unsure what to do and moved his head closer to the door. From his expression, he heard nothing. With a muttered, 'For fuck's sake,' he put the gun in the back of his trouser waistband and walked across to Kenny. 'Nae funny business.' He got to his knees and reached down to the tape around Kenny's ankles. He worried at the loose end and pulled some of it off. When he was at just the right height, Kenny braced his feet on the floor and powered up his thighs so that his knee struck the guy's chin. Right on the knockout spot.

The big man fell like a tree.

Kenny got to his feet, raised both hands above his head, and with a silent thank you to a short video on YouTube, he brought them down and apart with as much power as he could muster. The tape split easily.

He leaned forward and finished pulling the tape from his ankles. Once he was done, he pulled the gun from the back of his erstwhile guard's trousers and walked to the door. He pressed his ear against it and hearing nothing, he twisted the door handle as silently as he could and pulled the door open. He paused to listen.

Nothing.

He exited the room, and with the gun held in front of him, he walked up the corridor. When he reached the open-plan space of the living room and kitchen, he saw Dan and Gibbs looking at someone else who was out of Kenny's line of sight. Dan was the first to notice him.

Kenny held the gun out.

'Mr O'Neill, you're living up to your reputation,' said Dan. He was completely unruffled, which unnerved Kenny slightly.

'For chrissakes, O'Neill,' said Gibbs and took a step towards him.

Kenny waved the gun at him by way of deterrent. 'Your man wouldn't let me go to the loo.'

'I hope he's in one piece?' asked Dan.

'He'll live,' Kenny replied. 'Now if you don't mind, I'll be going.'

'What about your detective thing? Still trying to solve a murder?' Dan took a seat on one of the kitchen stools. Cool as you please.

'Not sure there's enough evidence.' Kenny stole a look at Gibbs and shuffled, pretending he was giving up on Gibbs as a suspect.

'Anywho.' Dan said in a dramatic tone. 'Your gun?' Dan reached into his jacket pocket and pulled out one of his own. 'Is for decoration. This is the one with the bullets.' He smiled. A display of teeth bereft of humour. 'Come in. Have a seat,' he said, his voice brooking no argument. Then he looked at Gibbs, sent him a silent message. Gibbs walked forward, grabbed the gun out of Kenny's hand.

With a broad, fuck-you grin, Gibbs said, 'Fud.'

'Prick,' replied Kenny. Yeah, it was childish, but it made him feel temporarily better. With a sigh, he walked into the living room towards the giant corner sofa. Stopped when he saw who was already sitting there.

The lanky, awkward figure of Gordon Gallagher's grandson. He looked up at Kenny with the same expression that hung on his face while he was hammering a nail into another man's skull.

'Hello, Mr O'Neill,' he said in that strange sing-song voice of his. 'Mr Gallagher sends his apologies, but Mr Stewart and he have come to . . . an understanding.'

'Yeah,' said Dan Stewart. 'By way of apology for sending you to sort out my Russian guys, he told me everything.'

43

Gavin was down to his last fiver when Dave reappeared, a grim smile on his face.

'Awright, buddy.' Dave said.

Gavin looked at him, ignored the question and burrowed into his sleeping bag. How long had it been since he'd last seen Dave? He had no idea. In the meantime he'd had the odd mouthful of food and a bellyful of booze and pills. Not so much chasing the dragon as keeping him in a somnolent state.

It had gotten worse in the last few days. The booze and pills were weakening his mind, but they were the only thing that worked when that wind began to course through his brain. If he stuck his nose in the air, he could smell the burning flesh of Iraqi soldiers in the breeze. When he closed his eyes, he heard them screaming. A bottle of vodka for breakfast was the only thing that kept all of that at bay.

'We've got a big show coming up. A real show this time. Similar to your first one.' Gavin read the meaning behind the words. The last time, he killed someone for the entertainment of a bunch of rich strangers. He gave a mental shrug. What was one more death on his hands? He felt the adrenalin surge at the thought of his hands around another man's throat. Him or me. Or he could just let the other guy kill him this time. What did his life matter after all?

He gave nothing of his thoughts away. Let the prick work for it.

'But, mate, you look like shit. We need you to be in better shape this time. You're going to be up against a guy who knows his way around a fight. There's going to be some very rich people flying in from all over the world. This is going to be special.'

'Aye?'

'Aye. There's a twenty-five-grand seat fee for this one. The brains behind it want to go for a jailhouse theme. They're going to build a kind of jail on one side of the stage, a shower scene on the other. Get some girls in for some lezzy action. Get the audience warmed up with some pussy, you know? Then the blood-letting can begin. It's going to be mental.' He rubbed his hands together fast. 'So, first thing is, we get you dried out. Feed you up for a couple of days and then let you loose.'

44

Ray thought about letting his phone ring out when he saw that it was Alessandra Rossi on the line. Surely she hadn't already worked out that he'd been covering for Kenny? His instincts said that this was the case. All of their recent contact had been by text, why else should she choose to phone him this time? Could he just ignore her for a couple of days? Nah, she'd hound him.

After a long boring day at the bar, he could do without Ale's pressing him for information. The bar had been empty from about 7pm, after the workers had supped their pre-face-the-wife-and-family pint. Sadly, it showed no sign of picking up, so at nine he'd closed up and left for home.

He looked at the time on his phone. Ten-thirty.

He pressed *Accept.* 'Ale, what kind of time is this to be calling?'

'Don't "Ale" me,' she said. 'You big prick. You sent me chasing this knowing Kenny was involved. When were you going to let me know?'

'Ale. Ale,' Ray said. 'I can explain.'

'You better. I'm coming to see you now, and I want to know everything. Everything, understand me?'

She hung up without saying goodbye.

Half an hour later she was at the front door of his flat. He let her in. She walked past him and through into the living room without a word. Once there she sat down and looked around herself. Her anger at him was doused for a moment as she took in the energy of the space.

'It's the first time I've been here since . . .' she said.

'What's up?' Ray asked and sat beside her.

Her mouth was a thin, tight line as she wondered what to say first. She looked into his eyes. 'You know, it was bad enough when you were a maverick when you were an actual cop. But don't be doing this bullshit when you're a civilian, Ray. I can't protect you.'

'What do you know?' he asked, thinking he couldn't defend himself until he knew what was going on.

'One of our technicians was studying the footage from the flats where Dom Hastie died. He realised it had been tampered with. Tracked the IP address – or some such technical shite – and found one Dimitri Ianotti . . .'

'Nice Greek-Italian combo.'

Ale gave him a look. It said: not in the mood. 'Mr Ianotti has a record. Cyber crime. The condition on his parole is that he doesn't use a computer or go online. So, we had him over a barrel. He had to tell us what he was up to or face a return to the Bar-L.'

'Right?' Ray made a motion as if to say, and why are you telling me all this?

'It appears that Dimitri was acting on the behalf of one Kenny O'Neill.'

Kenny. For chrissakes, thought Ray. 'Right,' he said, delaying for time to work out what his answer to all of this might be.

'Don't "right" me, Ray McBain. You're in this up to your sticky-out, pointy ears.'

'What's with the Dr Spock allusion? And what the hell are you on about? I've never come across this guy Ianotti.'

'Don't give me that, McBain.'

'Scout's honour.'

'You're a bloody liar. His office is above a certain pub in town.'

Ray thought this through. 'The Blue Owl? Really? You're messing with me.'

'Ray, this is not a time for messing about. This is a possible murder investigation, and your mate is armpit deep in it. And by proxy, so are you. Spill the beans, Ray. If this goes up the line, I can't protect you. There's a number of people at HQ who would like nothing more than to hang you and yours out to dry.'

'I swear, Alessandra, I don't know this Ianotti fella.' He gave this some more thought. 'There's an office above The Blue Owl?'

She nodded.

Ray thought: Kenny, you wanker, you obviously didn't trust me enough after all.

'And what does this guy do in this office above The Blue Owl?' Ray asked.

'Not sure what he does most of the time, but on this occasion he hacked into the computer of the people who run the CCTV for those flats and tampered with the footage.'

'By tampered, you mean . . .' Ray made a tell-me-the-rest motion with his right hand.

'Removed any sight of his boss from the recording of the day of Dom Hastie's fall.'

'Right.' Ray sat forward on his seat in a request for more information.

'As Mr Ianotti tells it, he'd had a falling out with his cousin, Ian. Tracked him down to there, but missed him. Ian left that morning – escorted, I should say, by the guys he had us looking for, Gibbs and Stewart.'

'Fuck,' Ray whispered.

'There's more, I'm sure of it,' said Ale and leaned forward. 'But I need you to go to our friend Dimitri and weasel it out of him.'

'Your wish is my command, bossy lady.'

'Bet your life it is, McBain.' She stood up. 'Let's go.'

'What? Now?'

'You've got your toenails to cut?'

Ray shrugged. Stood. Walked through to the hallway, while Alessandra followed him. He picked a black jacket from the coat stand there. Once he put it on, he plucked his keys from the lock and opened the door. Before he walked out into the landing, he turned to Alessandra.

'I really have sticky-out, pointy ears?'

In the car, Ray closed his eyes and prepared himself. If he didn't tell Ale about his visit to see Theresa Hastie, she would be even more pissed off at him.

She looked over from the driver's seat. 'What?'

'What do you mean, "what"?' Ray asked, playing for time.

'You did that thing as if you were about to start talking, and then you stopped.'

'I went to see Theresa Hastie this morning.'

'Ray. I could bloody kill you. I could crash into that bloody wall there just to spite you.'

'Aye, ok,' said Ray in a conciliatory tone. 'I'm an eejit, but you can't be surprised? I don't do sitting back and doing nothing. Besides, Kenny's pulled me out of a few holes over the years.'

'I'm worried that in the future those holes will be the ones he helps you dig.'

'What's that supposed to mean?'

Ale studied the road in front of them. Stopped at a red light. 'Don't go over to the dark side, Ray.'

Ray crossed his arms. Tried to damp down a surge of irritation. 'For chrissakes, Ale. I'm hardly likely to start running an illegal goods operation.'

Ale made a face. 'Kenny's a big personality. And he's loaded. And over time he could encourage you to compromise on your standards. A wee thing here, something else there, and before you know it . . .'

'Not going to happen, Ale. You can relax on that score. Kenny does his thing. I'm working in his bar until something better comes along.' Feeling annoyed, his voice rose in pitch and speed as he finished his sentence. 'Fucking dark side, my hairy hole.'

Ale said nothing, her silence louder than words. She wasn't in the least concerned that she'd pissed him off, and she was happy that she'd said her piece. 'So, you were about to say. Theresa Hastie?'

'Fucking dark side,' Ray repeated. Took a couple of deep breaths. Acknowledged that she was only speaking to him like that out of a genuine concern for his well-being. 'Right. Theresa.' He gathered his thoughts. 'She's finding the idea of suicide a difficult one to deal with. And these CCTV images are backing that up. She told me that he was overspending. Toys for his son. And weed, as it was the only thing that he could manage his pain with.'

'Right,' Ale processed this. 'So he could have been in to these guys for some money. They charge him like a million per cent. He can't pay, so they send him flying?'

'As a theory it works for me.'

'So, where do Ian and Kenny come into it all?'

When they arrived at The Blue Owl, Ale parked at the front door and pulled her phone out of her pocket. Dialled. Spoke. 'We're here.'

She listened to some instructions. Hung up.

To Ray, 'Let's go.'

They both climbed out of the car and stepped into a silent, dark street. The roads were devoid of cars and people, prompting Ray to question, for the thousandth time, why would anyone open a bar in this location? All that was missing was the tumbleweed. Or an urban fox.

'That lane down the side.' Ale pointed. 'There's a door that leads up to an office on the first floor. Ianotti says he'll be waiting for us there.'

They walked into the lane, and a few footsteps later it was as if someone had turned off the lights. Ray automatically stepped in front of Ale as if to protect her. She snorted.

'Shut it,' he said with a smile.

Their footsteps echoed in the cool air, and from somewhere Ray caught the scent of Asian food. Probably someone's after-drink repast of chips and curry sauce. Which they'd dropped after going for a piss.

Just as he was about to bring out his phone and activate the torch app, a door opened, flooding the lane with light. A chubby, bald guy with an apologetic expression stepped out.

'In you come, guys,' he said as he held the door open. They followed as he wordlessly climbed the stone stairs and then led them through a white door into a large room at the top. The walls were chipboard that had yet to be painted, with dowel holes at regular intervals as if shelving had been removed. The carpet was worn and stained. Lighting was provided by a bare bulb hanging from a ceiling that looked like the ingress of water was an occupational hazard. Against the far wall, in contrast to the remainder of the room was a shiny cornucopia of newness. Geek heaven. Like a scene fresh out of a computer maternity ward.

Ianotti walked to the plump, black leather swivel chair in front of a pair of widescreen monitors. He sat, swung the chair round and looked at Ray.

'You'll be Mr McBain then,' he said.

Ray looked around himself. Tried to judge where he was standing in relation to the bar downstairs. He reckoned he was above the toilets.

'You recognise me?' he asked, realising it was important that Ale could judge from this conversation that he knew nothing whatsoever about this set up.

Ianotti pointed at one of his screens then pushed a couple of keys on his ergonomic keyboard. The screen lit up and he could see the bar downstairs. 'If I get bored I sometimes look and see who's in. Feels like I know you, actually.' He grinned.

'Why have you never come down and introduced yourself?' Ray asked.

'I'm usually pretty busy,' he answered. 'And then I need to fire off home to ferry my daughters here there and everywhere. They're into gymnastics,' he added, looking at Ale. He was demonstrating his worth as a human being, praying that Ale wouldn't have him sent back to prison. 'Amazing what these wee things can do with their bodies. Defies gravity actually.'

'Very nice,' said Ale, with her whatever tone. 'Sorry to drag you away from your family at this time of night,' Ray heard the no apology in her tone whatsoever, 'but we just need to clarify what you know about Kenny and Ian. Who they might be with? Where they might be?'

'Actually, I'm getting kind of worried about Kenny. I usually hear from him at several points in the week, but he's been silent for a few days.'

This chimed with Ray's thoughts. Something was definitely wrong here.

'Tell me what you know,' Ale said.

'I already told you everything,' Dimitri replied.

'Tell us again.'

Dimitri turned to his computer screen. Brought up the images he'd taken from the CCTV cameras and ran through the timeline of events.

'Ian was led away by Gibbs, Stewart and one other man,' Ale said out loud to herself. 'And didn't come back. So, clearly he had nothing to do with Hastie's fall.' They looked at some more images. 'Ah, here's our Kenny,' she said with more than a hint of sarcasm. 'And Gibbs walking back in. Kenny leaving. Then he's coming back in . . . with a small girl?' She looked at Ray as if asking for an explanation.

He shrugged. 'Fucked if I know.' Then he wondered why he just didn't admit how much he knew. Was Kenny pulling him in, making him compromise on his standards? He gave a shudder.

'And then Gibbs comes slinking out,' said Dimitri.

Ray motioned for Dimitri to pause the screen. It would be diffi-cult to prove from that angle that it was Gibbs, but he recognised the man's movement from the previous slice of film and hoped this might be enough to sway a jury, if we ever got this to trial. We? There is no "we" any more, Ray, he told himself.

'Who's the girl?' Alessandra asked Dimitri.

'Name's Myleene,' answered Dimitri. 'She's a wee character according to Kenny. He thinks she was helping Hastie. Running errands, that kind of thing.' He paused. Adopted what Ray thought might be his fatherly tone. 'From the way Kenny's helping her in to the lift, it looks like she saw more than a wee girl should.'

Ale leaned her hip against the desk. 'Then what?'

'What do you mean?'

'No way Kenny's going to leave things like that,' Ray interrupted. 'He'll want to track down the guys who've led Ian away, at the very least.'

Dimitri leaned back in his chair, eyes fastened on to the ceiling. Then he sat up, rubbed at his forehead. 'Please don't make me do this.'

'Need I remind you of the condition of your parole, Mr Ianotti?' asked Ale.

He exhaled. Looked at Ray. 'Have you heard of Gordon Gallagher?'

'Who hasn't?' Ray asked.

Ale made a face for his benefit only. It read, *Who the hell is he?* Ray made a "tell you later" motion.

'Gallagher has made it his mission, over the years, to keep informed about everything nefarious that is going on in Glasgow. As you know, he runs the Dennistoun area, and to protect his interests there, he trades in information,' Dimitri said.

'So, Kenny went to him to see if he could name the characters in the film?' asked Ale.

Dimitri nodded. 'But our Mr Gallagher does nothing for free. He asked Kenny to sort out a wee burglary problem he was having in the area from incomers.'

'Incomers?' asked Ale.

'A couple of Eastern European types were running a gang of pickpockets and thieves. They were encroaching into Dennistoun, so Gallagher wanted to send them a message.'

'A message?' Ray was almost afraid to hear the answer.

'Seems Kenny was about to deliver said message when one of Gallagher's men interrupted and increased the severity of said message.'

Both Ray and Ale just looked at him.

'A nail in the forehead kinda deal.'

'Jeezus,' said Ale.

'Whatever happened to a simple knee-capping?' asked Ray.

'Then next I heard, Gallagher tells Kenny that Gibbs and Stewart are involved in some underground fight scene, and Kenny got Gallagher to arrange entry for him into one of their fight nights. And then nothing. Kenny disappears.'

Ray looked at Dimitri. Then at Ale.

'Looks like Mr O'Neill has bitten off more than he can chew,' said Ale.

'You're the geek,' said Ray to Dimitri. 'Kenny didn't ever get you to put some tracking device on his person, did he?'

Dimitri shook his head slowly. 'His previous phone was an iPhone and he had me activate the tracker on that, but he was forced to bin the phone when the police called him on it from Hastie's flat.'

'You're joking?' asked Ale, eyes wide. She pursed her lips. 'That was me. I phoned the last number dialled from a phone I found in Hastie's flat. It was still on a charger.' She looked at Ray. 'Who goes anywhere without their phone these days? We assumed it was Hastie's.'

'That must have been Ian's phone,' said Ray. 'Where is it now?'

'In evidence,' Ale replied.

'Any chance there's any more wee titbits on that phone?'

'Our tech guys had a right good scour through it. There were few contacts. Only three regular . . .'

'The phone's not important,' Ray interrupted. 'Let's piece all of this together.' He thought some more. 'Ian befriends Hastie. Offers him support. Gets tangled up in his problems with Gibbs and Stewart. Along comes Kenny.'

'What would Gibbs and Stewart want with Ian?' asked Ale.

Ray made an intuitive leap. 'Say Hastie couldn't repay his debt, and Ian offered to do it for him? Gibbs gets him to fight?'

'Jesus, this just gets worse and worse,' said Ale. She crossed her arms. Made a leap of her own. 'Then Kenny jumps in. Gets a fight night of his own.'

'This Gallagher guy,' Ray said to Dimitri. 'Can you reach out to him?'

'He doesn't know me from Adam,' Dimitri answered, his face going pale. That reaction told its own story. Mr Gallagher's reputation preceded him.

'*We* can't go to him,' said Ale. 'He won't talk to cops. Or ex-cops for that matter. It has to be you, Mr Ianotti.'

'Shit,' he replied. Rubbed his head. And repeated, 'Shit.'

'Do you know where Kenny met him?' asked Ray.

'He has a café over on Duke Street.'

'Right, let's go.' Ray took a couple of steps back.

'What? Can't we send an email or something?' Dimitri asked, going even paler, if that was possible. 'Won't it be closed anyway?'

'For this one, you're going to have to step away from your computer, Mr Ianotti,' said Ale with a grim expression. She looked at his screen. 'Probably best to check his opening hours.'

With a dexterity that Ray found impressive, Dimitri's fingers flew over the keyboard, and some web pages appeared then vanished from the screen. One stayed.

Dimitri read with some relief, 'It's closed.'

'Aye, but it opens at seven tomorrow morning,' said Ale as she read from the screen. 'And you're going to be his first customer.'

45

Kenny's bindings were reset, under gunpoint. This time, Gibbs was more thorough, attaching each of his legs to the leg of a chair and each arm to a thigh. Kenny was grateful that they allowed him to visit the toilet first.

Once he was trussed up, they saw to the guard that he'd knocked out. A face-full of cold water was enough to bring him back to his senses. After which he sat up and threw a baleful glare at Kenny. It promised retaliation. Kenny just grinned back in return. He was telling the guy, in an even fight I've got you. See what I can do even when I'm tied up.

Gibbs had no sympathy. When the guy wiped the water from his face, he said, 'You're fired, ya big prick. Piss off out of my sight.' Then he looked at Kenny. 'What are we going to do with you, eh? We had a good thing going with those Eastern European guys.' He scratched the side of his face. 'And word has to get out on the street that if things happen, we handle them. You get me?'

Kenny just stared. Gave him nothing. Instead he tried to work out what was going on here. What was Gallagher's play? He'd gone into bed with these wankers to protect his precious Dennistoun. He'd told them about his involvement in closing down Andrei and Stefan, but left out the fact that it was his grandson who drove the message home – literally – and trusted that Kenny wouldn't spill that particular bean.

Then it occurred to him that Gallagher hadn't disclosed why Kenny had been involved: his drive to find Ian. If Gibbs and

Stewart knew about that relationship, you can be sure they'd have crowed about it. And then used it to their advantage.

What was the old fox up to?

He was thrown from his musings by a slap from Gibbs.

'Hey, prick, I'm talking to you.'

Kenny flexed his jaw, working out the moment's pain. 'Sorry, I was somewhere else. What were you saying?'

'Aren't you the cool customer, Mr O'Neill?' said Stewart. 'From what Gallagher tells us, you can look after yourself . . . you're calm under pressure. Never been in the military?'

'Nope,' replied Kenny. 'Being a sheep was never my thing.' Saw from Gibbs' reaction his words stung. He stepped forward as if to give Kenny another slap. Stewart put out a hand to stop him.

'Far too cocky, mate,' said Stewart. 'You need to be brought down a peg or two. And if we send out a message to our colleagues on the street at the same time, then 'appy days.' He rubbed his hands together. Then steepled his fingers and pressed them in that position against the underside of his nose, as if in prayer. 'I'm getting the impression that you can withstand a fair amount of pain. So we'll see what else we can come up with.' His smile was vulpine, displaying long white teeth and nothing but ill intent.

Kenny sent him a silent fuck you, his eyes saying: give me a couple of minutes on our own together, man to man, and I'll knock the superior attitude out of you. He knew his aggressive expression was ultimately futile, but again, it made him feel better for the moment.

'Yes, you're a dangerous man, Mr O'Neill, and don't worry, we won't underestimate you again.' Stewart signalled to Gibbs and they both left the room.

They returned a good while later with an iPod and a pair of large earphones.

'Isn't the internet a wonderful fing? By all accounts the yanks used this on the poor saps in Guantanamo. Apparently, if you're forced to listen to music like this over a twenty-four hour period, your brain and body functions start to slide, your train of thought slows down, and your will is broke.' Dan grinned. 'How cool is that? Why don't we see if it works?'

'Bloody love it,' said Gibbs on the verge of a giggle, as he put the fat leather cushions over each of Kenny's ears. 'Meet Barney. He's a purple dinosaur with a chuckle that is *painful*, man.'

Music filled Kenny's ears. He looked at Gibbs as if to say: really? Gibbs mouthed – just you wait – and put a black canvas bag over Kenny's head.

I love you, you love me.
We're a happy family

The merry tune went on. And on. And on. And on. The same song on a loop. At first Kenny sang along, shaking his head to the rhythm. Then he grew tired of that and tried not to listen but it was just *too* loud. Barney's friendly laugh soon become wearing and then just short of demonic.

Kenny couldn't think about anything but the words to the song, the goofy voice of the singer and that fucking laugh.

'I'll give you a hug, you purple dinosaur prick.' he shouted. For some reason this made him laugh, and he giggled until he was breathless. A giggle that felt like it was bordering on hysteria.

He gathered his thoughts. This was playing in to the hands of these guys. He needed not to give them a reaction. But why were they bothering? Why make him feel this uncomfortable? Petty revenge? They were right, he would be able to handle plenty of physical pain, was this a replacement for that?

Again, why bother?

The song stopped. And the intro began again.

'Aw, for fuckssakes, guys,' he shouted. 'Enough, eh? What do you want from me?'

He got nothing back.

Kenny lost track of time. His world was reduced to the sound in his ears. A cartoon voice and a chuckle that grated on the inside of his skull. He exhaled. Felt his irritation build and build. He drummed his fingers against his thighs, moved his feet so that they were resting on his toes and began to move his thighs up and down in a rapid beat.

'Jesus Christ.' he roared. 'Enough. What do you want?'

In his imagination, he saw Gibbs grin in response to his discomfort and fought to rein in his reaction. He couldn't let the bastard win. He breathed once. Twice. Three times. Took the air in deep till he felt his lungs fill and then let it out slowly. Thought about the advice of his old fighting sensei. Sent all of his attention to the in-breath.

. . .we're a happy fam-i-lee . . .

Barney doesn't exist. There's only Kenny O'Neill and his breath. Air cool on the linings of his nostrils, passing the fine hairs there. Chest filling, stomach expanding . . .

. . . I love you, you love me . . .

Nothing but the heat of his exhalation on the inside of the cloth bag. Out for a slow count of nine. In for nine. He yawned. His lack of sleep the previous night catching up with him. Thoughts turned to Christine and Lexi. He was glad they were out of the clutches of Gibbs. He's not the kind of client he'd wish on any working girl.

Then the music stopped.

Blessed relief. The sweetest sound. Silence.

Then the bag was pulled from his head and he blinked rapidly to allow his eyes to adjust to the light. Wished he hadn't bothered when he was confronted by a naked Barry Gibbs, his chest red and sweat-patched.

Gibbs leered down at him and thrust his fingers under Kenny's nose.

'Get a load of that, mate. Sweet, sweet pussy.' His eyes were wide. Probably stoned, thought Kenny. 'While you're in here getting it on with Barney, I'm in the next room getting all hot and sweaty with your girls. Man, do they know how to fuck. Thanks for the introduction.'

Then he stretched forward, pressed play on the iPod and put the bag back over Kenny's head, having easily disrupted his hard-won moment of peace.

46

Ray met Dimitri outside the café on Duke Street as arranged. Ray took in Dimitri's pale face and the way his jowls wobbled as they shook hands and thought, thank Christ I'm here. This guy won't get much out of Gallagher.

Ray pushed open the door and walked in, Dimitri followed. The place was empty apart from a couple of waiters, so they sat at the first booth on the right as they walked in. Once seated, Dimitri stretched for the menu and started reading. When he caught Ray looking at him, he shrugged.

'Might as well, seeing we're here.'

A waiter appeared. Tall, heroin-skinny and looking like he'd just been starched into his white shirt and black apron. He stood, pen poised over his small pad of paper. Said nothing. Waited for them to speak first.

'Black coffee, please,' said Ray.

'Me too,' said Dimitri. Then he paused as if debating with himself. 'And a croissant, please.'

'And could you tell Mr Gallagher that friends of Kenny O'Neill would like to speak to him,' added Ray.

The waiter met his eyes for the first time. 'I'm sorry, sir. We don't have a Mr Gallagher here.'

'Sure you do,' said Ray. 'Just tell him we're here.'

The coffees and Dimitri's breakfast pastry arrived. Ray sipped. Dimitri tore chunks off his croissant, spread jam on the underside and got chewing. Finished the thing off like he hadn't eaten for a month.

'Hungry?' asked Ray.

'When I get nervous I eat,' Dimitri replied.

'Get nervous a lot?' asked Ray with a smile.

'Aye, chubby,' Dimitri replied, returning the grin. 'You too?'

'Hey.' Ray patted his relatively trim stomach. 'I'm on the light side of the yo-yo diet cycle at the moment. And thanks very much for destroying my fragile ego. I'm going to eat an entire box of Tunnocks teacakes when I get home and it will be all your fault.'

Dimitri laughed, and Ray was relieved to see that his attempts at humour had relaxed the man. From what he knew of Gallagher, he was the kind of guy who could smell fear, the way sharks home in on the scent of blood. If they were to get anywhere here, they would both have to play this very cool indeed.

Ray felt a presence at his side and turned.

'You're looking for me?' the man said. He was average height and build, wearing a dark green cardigan and brown cords. His chest broad and solid under the nondescript clothing. A pair of spectacles hung from his neck on a piece of black string. His was a face that was not so much lived in but one that had suffered through a series of squatters. The eyes held a deal of pain. Whether that was his pain or yours, would become clear in any subsequent conversation.

'Mr Gallagher, I'm . . .' began Dimitri.

'I know who you are, Mr Ianotti.' His eyes didn't leave Ray's. 'And if I'm not mistaken, this is the recently medically retired Detective Inspector Raymond McBain.'

'Why don't you pull up a chair?' said Ray.

'I won't be staying long enough to warrant that, Mr McBain.'

'We wondered if you might . . . that is . . . Ray and I hoped you . . . following your recent . . .' Dimitri stumbled through what he wanted to say.

'Where's Kenny?' Ray interrupted.

'Kenny?' asked Gallagher. 'I'm not sure I know who you mean.'

'Don't insult me, Mr Gallagher. We both know you know exactly who I'm talking about.'

Gallagher said nothing. He simply unbuttoned each cuff of his sleeves and started to roll them up, revealing thick corded muscle that a man half his age would be happy to develop.

'I make it a rule not to give people anything they want unless I get something back in return, Mr McBain. Are you prepared to pay that price?'

Ray sat back in his chair, crossed his arms and studied the man. Knew he was wasting his time, but that he still had to play his part. He stood up.

'C'mon, Dimitri. This is a waste of time.'

'But, but . . .' Dimitri stood as if his thigh muscles only worked in concert with McBain. He reached forward, picked up his cup and drained the last of his coffee as if this was an act of defiance.

'Mr Gallagher,' Ray said before he turned to walk to the door, his eyes drilling into those of the older man. 'Anything happens to Kenny O'Neill, I will hold you personally responsible. You do not want me as an enemy.'

Gallagher smiled, and a darkness swept across his face. 'I've been hearing threats like that for over fifty years, Mr McBain. Feel free to return when you think you are able to deliver.'

Ray snorted. Looked at Dimitri. 'Pay the man. I'm out of here.'

On the street, about twenty yards from the café, Ray waited for Dimitri. He left the shop a couple of minutes after him and walked down to meet him. His face pink and flustered.

'What the hell was that all about?' Dimitri asked. 'You just blew any chance we had of getting any information out of him.'

Ray dismissed his words with a look. 'What did he give you?'

'Eh?'

Ray thought for a moment. Held a hand out. 'Receipt?'

Dimitri put a hand in his pocket and pulled out a piece of paper that he'd crumpled. He handed it to Ray.

'He couldn't talk to me. I'm ex-polis,' Ray explained. 'Doesn't matter that there was no one else in the room, a certain form has to be maintained.' He smoothed out the small piece of paper and read. 'For fu . . .' he shook his head and looked back up towards the café. 'The old prick is playing with us.'

'What?' asked Dimitri. 'Show me.' He pulled the paper from Ray and read.

Do not tell secrets to those whose faith and silence you have not already tested.

47

Barry Gibbs was all but burning up with excitement. Tonight was going to be the night of his life. People would be talking about it for years. He stood in front of the marble-framed mirror, running his hands under warm water, and studied his face. *They won't be laughing at you any longer, Bazza son.* He shut off the spotless chrome tap and, stretching over the glass bowl of potpourri, picked up a small rectangle of towelling to dry his hands. Then he fussed at the knot on his tie, making sure it was resting plumcentre in his collar. He'd even gone designer for this suit: he who was never out of combat trousers and t-shirts. And he had to admit, he thought, as he ran a hand down the fine wool of his dark, perfectly cut suit jacket, it was all well worth the effort.

They couldn't have picked a better place to showcase his organisational skills. Of course, the old duffers who ran the Grand Western Gentlemen's Club had no idea what was about to happen. A twenty-five-grand donation for the use of their conference hall was enough for them to hand over the keys and not ask any questions.

No damp and dingy car park for their event of the year. Of the *fucking decade*, he crowed at his reflection.

The owners of the club were very proud of their history, and almost everywhere Gibbs looked among the oak panelling and ankle-deep-piled carpets were various signifiers of their rich history. Portraits of glassy-eyed, ruby-cheeked city fathers and traders who'd sanitised the slave trade out of their achievements and set themselves up as the servants of capitalism and Christianity.

The Great Western was an attempt to bring the grand gentlemen's clubs of London to the second city of the Empire. Here they would self-congratulate and allow others to celebrate a success that was unparalleled in the history of this small country. A smoking room and library were the first of their concerns. Next came opulent rooms that members could hire as a home from home. In other words, thought Gibbs, a place for the old reprobates to exercise their various lusts away from the rest of gimlet-eyed Victorian society.

He phoned Dan Stewart and hoped the speccy prick was as on the case as he was.

'Dan,' he said. 'Everything in place?'

'Yeah,' Stewart replied, sounding bored. 'We're sorted.'

'Listen, fuckface,' said Gibbs. 'There's no room for complacency here. We need to be on this.'

'And we are, Barry. Chillax. Everyone's in place. The staging's all set an' tested . . .'

Chillax. If Stewart was in front of him he'd slap seven colours of shit out of him.

He managed to contain his irritation at the man. Promised himself that once this was over there would be some well-earned retribution. All the crap he'd put up with over the last few weeks? Doling out a kicking was the least he was owed. And surely then the big boys down in London would see he could be trusted and deserved to be handed the keys of this particular kingdom.

'The dog owners know when to bring in the mutts?' he asked.

'Yup.'

'The girls are set?'

'Oiled and lubed. Had a bit of an 'and in that myself, if you catch my drift.' He laughed. And at that noise, Gibbs thought he might have caught a glimpse into what that poor bastard O'Neill had gone through after a full day of listening to Barney. 'The bed is on the stage. And it's on wheels so it can be pulled away quickly before the main event begins,' Stewart continued.

'The fighters?'

'Getting pulled out of cold storage and into their *costumes* as we speak.'

'Listen, you don't think we've gone a wee bit OTT on that do you?' Gibbs asked, displaying a rare moment of uncertainty.

'We've gone for a jailhouse shower theme, Baz. Who goes for a shower in their jail uniform? And the little towel things will mean that any delicate flowers in the audience won't be too upset by any naughty bits.'

'Yeah, let's amp up the violence, and then protect them all from the sight of a cock or two.' He shook his head and thought: hypocrites. 'What about the audience? Anyone arrived yet?'

'Bazza, my old son. Relax,' Stewart chimed in his ear. 'Ain't no thing but a chicken wing. Everything's peachy.'

Ain't no thing, thought Gibbs. Where did that prick get that sort of shite from? He really deserved a mauling. He closed the connection. Stared at his image in the mirror, admiring this new version of himself. Rubbed his hands slowly. Stewart, once tonight is over I'm paying you a wee visit.

48

Ian was led to the car as usual, and he submitted to the black bag over the head. As usual. After an hour's drive, as he was led out into a building, he could sense that tonight was going to be different. The air around him was warmer for one thing. And the surface he found himself walking on was much softer. Carpet for once instead of the concrete he was used to.

What was going on?

At one point he thought he heard the bark of a dog, followed by a whine. Then a door opened and he caught an excited thrum of noise before it was closed again. He stopped walking to try and work out what it was and where it might be coming from, but Dave had a firm grip of his bicep and pushed him along.

After a few more minutes of walking he heard a door open, he took a couple of steps and then it was closed behind him. The bag was pulled from his head. He blinked and then narrowed his eyes until he was used to the light.

He looked around himself. He was in a small dressing room. There was a mirror above a Formica desk. A red plastic bucket chair. And in the corner a shower cubicle.

He noticed that a white towel was over the back of the chair. Dave pointed at it. Said, 'That's your costume.'

'Sorry?'

'Strip off down to your underpants and put that on.'

Ian picked it up. The towel was about three feet long and two of its ends were connected by a short piece of elasticated material, meaning it would stay around his waist without needing to be tied.

He held it up. 'For real?'

'Yeah, sorry, mate.' He made a face. Then, 'As you can see . . .' he held his hands wide, ' . . . things are a wee bit different tonight. None of your shitty wee car parks for you, my boy.'

'What's the deal?' Ian asked. Even Dave was different tonight. Sure, he was doing the good guy act as well as he ever did, but there was an energy to him that was usually missing. Ian felt a twist in his gut and a tremble in his thighs as adrenalin surged into his system.

'Fight night,' answered Dave. 'We've gone big time for this one. Rich folk have flown in from all over the world for some extra-special entertainment. Think of it as a modern take on the Roman Coliseum . . .'

'People fought to the death in the Coliseum,' interrupted Ian.

'That's why I said it was a modern-day version,' Dave answered smoothly. Too smoothly. 'First we have the fighting dogs. You heard them on the way in, aye?' Without waiting for Ian to answer, he continued. 'Then they've decided to go for a jailhouse theme. So, there's a girls' prison,' he said with a wide grin. 'And a couple of girls will be giving each other a very nice time, if you get my drift. They've set up a big, king-sized bed behind a set of bars and everything. Looks amazing, to be fair. Then once the girls have done their thing they change the set and it's the jailhouse shower scene. A guy's having a shower and another guy comes in – that's you with your wee towel round your waist – and they start fighting.' He rubbed his hands on the side of his trousers. 'Sounds awesome, eh?'

Ian looked at him. Looked at the towel. Wondered why Dave was rubbing his hands on his trousers. Was he nervous?

'That's really what's going on?' he asked.

'Aye, totally,' said Dave. 'Scout's honour.'

'Rich people, you said. Where are they from?'

'Everywhere, I believe. And they're paying a fortune, by the way, which is why we are sure that this is your last fight. Your chance to pay off wee Dom's debt once and for all.'

'They're paying a fortune? How much?'

'Don't concern yourself with that, mate. That's our business. Just concentrate on the fact that it means your connection with Gibbs and Stewart will be over.' He looked into Ian's face, his own a model of sincerity. 'Here. Put your wee costume on and then I'll get your fists wrapped.'

Ian allowed himself to be swayed by the mention of money. It would be good to pay this off once and for all. And then he'd make sure Hastie never borrowed another cent unless it was from a bank. He stripped down to his white underpants and, feeling slightly ridiculous, stepped into the cotton circle of the towel and pulled it up to his waist.

'There,' said Dave. 'I'd put my money on you, mate. You look fearsome.' Then he started to bind Ian's fists.

'Wait,' said Ian and pulled his hands back. 'This doesn't feel right. What's the truth, Dave? What's really going on?'

'I promise you, mate. It's just as I described it to you.'

'These rich folk. Flying in from all over? What's attracting them, really? Can't they get dogfights, a lesbian love-in and a bum-fight where they come from? What's so special about this one here tonight?'

'Mate,' Dave cajoled. 'Who knows how these crazy rich people think? Probably one of them's got a mate among the organisers, and he tells the rest of them that this is so bad it's cool. And you know, you do have a bit of a reputation.'

'What? Me? Fuck off,' said Ian.

'For real. Somebody at your last fight filmed it and posted the whole thing on YouTube. Last time I checked you've had over three million hits.'

'Yeah, sure,' said Ian, his head reeling. Disbelieving, but wanting to believe. Would add some meaning to all of this nonsense. Could this be true? 'Piss off.'

'Honest to God, mate.' Dave reached into his pocket and pulled out his phone. 'Here. Let me show you.' He fiddled about with it. Swore. Looked disappointed. 'Sorry, mate, the signal in this place is shite. All these thick walls.'

'Three million hits?'

'Yeah,' said Dave, his face large with admiration. 'And everyone wants to see the guy off the street who put another guy down with just one kick.' He put a hand on Ian's shoulder. 'You're an internet sensation, old pal.'

Three million? Bloody hell, thought Ian. Isn't that something? Wonder if Kenny's seen it. He hoped he had. His younger cousin . . . brother, he still couldn't quite get his head round that . . . his younger brother had given him plenty of drubbings over the years. Perhaps this was a chance to show Kenny that Ian Ritchie wasn't such a loser after all.

49

They came for Gavin, drove him to a posh building and deposited him in a dressing room. It was only when he was stripped and in the shower that Gavin realised they hadn't bothered with the bag over his head this time. He shrugged at the realisation: so what. They trusted him now and besides, what did it matter? Who was he? A homeless drunk with nothing to show for thirty years of life but a wet-through sleeping bag and scarring through his soul like the lines of a cat's cradle.

He stepped out of the shower, dried himself and then put on the daft wee towel they left for him. Then he crouched in the corner, much in the same position he used in his doorway while day moved into night. As he waited for Dave to come back and bind his wrists he thought about what the evening might bring. That he would be expected to kill someone didn't matter to him. What was one more dead body on his conscience? Sure, those other ones were mostly in war, but this was a form of war, wasn't it?

His life had been one long series of battles, since the moment he was forced from his mother's womb.

In his mind's eye he caught an image of himself fading into the distance as if through a series of mirrors. In each one he was crouching, light falling on his head, shoulders and bloody knees. His eyes deep in shadow: nothing but black holes. Each copy of him drawing away from sight before he faded as if into a worn and torn irrelevance.

Sorrow was a stone, sinking through his heart down into his stomach. An indelible blemish. Let's get this over with, he thought. This was the only time he was worth something, the only time when life had meaning.

When he was killing.

50

Ian felt like a bit of a chump standing in the middle of the changing room wearing nothing but the towel. Dave left. Said he would be back and just to stay put. He'd come back and guide him into the, he paused and with a laugh said, the coliseum.

Time moved on and Ian felt himself grow impatient. How long was this going to take? Maybe the crowd were enjoying the girls too much and begged for them to go another round? Whatever it was, it needed to hurry up. He wanted this over with.

He paced up and down the room. Feeling the charge grow in his stomach. Adrenalin beginning to do its job. He exhaled. Felt his breath shorten. Took this as a good sign. If he wasn't nervous he wouldn't perform. And it wouldn't do to lose this fight. He had the wee man to look after. He imagined him and Dom standing out on the balcony. Dom thanking him for getting rid of the debt and then excitedly imagining the next time his son came to visit.

This thought cheered and energised him. Savouring the feeling, he walked to the door. Put his ear to it. Heard nothing.

Then he put his hand to the door, expecting it to be locked, but it opened easily. He stuck his head out and looked up and down the corridor. Nothing. Nobody. He stepped out. Caught the sound of a small crowd. A meaningless melee of noise, with a strong undercurrent of excitement. He followed the sound, picking up his pace, and corrected his earlier impression. Not excitement: bloodlust. He'd never heard anything quite like it, even in a war. There was something uncanny about it: other-worldly.

He saw a lit sign above a door. It read "Stage". He pulled it open and came face-to-face with a sight that would haunt his dreams for the rest of his life.

51

This fight was going to be too easy, thought Gavin. The black fella they put him up against was more suited to running. He recognised him. Of course he did. But he'd worked himself up for this and only one outcome would do.

When Gibbs pulled off the black guy's hood, he did so with relish. And it dawned on Gavin that they'd always been watching him and knew that he'd come to this guy's rescue in the hostel. This was their way of paying him back. A great big fuck you, Gavin.

What did that matter? Really? Gavin understood the impulse. Somebody does one over on you, you get him back. The law of the battle zone.

Gibbs probably ran those two Eastern Europeans and, it occurred to him, by proxy the whole thieving operation.

The two men stood facing each other while the crowd bayed for action from their rows of tiered seating. Gavin had eyes only for the runner, Mo. He was a gentle soul, as he'd shown back at the hostel. So he should make this quick. Do the guy a solid.

He was full foot taller than Gavin, and Gavin was taller than your average fighter. As if reading that thought, Mo bent at the knees, moving into a sort of crouch. His skin was glistening with sweat, his eyes wide with fear.

'No, please. What I do here?' he said.

'You're in the wrong place, buddy,' Gavin said. 'Wrong time.' And moved in.

The next few minutes were a blur as he set his body to cause as much damage to this guy as he possibly could. While his fists struck meat, his mind soared above him and watched as fragmented parts of him shifted, coalesced and reformed to strike. And strike again.

A small knife came from Gibbs' direction. Landed at his feet. He picked it up.

The voices of the crowd stopped as if everyone was holding their breath: waiting for that final strike. And who was he not to oblige?

52

The stage was set as if it was a shower room, with a row of shower heads high on a white tiled wall. They even had soap dispensers.

Ian took this in even as his mind rebelled against the rest of the image.

Two men.

One black.

And behind, straddling him, pulling his head back with one hand so that he could strike with the hand that held a knife.

Ian recognised both of them.

The black guy was Mo from the hostel. The runner.

The white guy: an old friend. One of the best guys he'd ever had the pleasure of meeting. Before he knew what he was doing, Ian ran onto the stage and shouted, 'Gun!'

The knife went in the man's neck. Once.

'Gun!' Ian shouted as he ran. 'What the hell are you doing?'

At the second shouting of the name, the man Ian called Gun stopped. Looked at Ian. Drew his mouth back in a feral snarl.

'Gun . . .' From somewhere, God knows where, a name thrust itself into his mind. 'Gavin. Stop.'

Gavin looked at him. Really looked.

Recognition.

He mouthed the word. 'Ritchie?'

Then looked down at the man in his grip. Stepped back with alacrity as if moments earlier he'd been standing before an abyss. His eyes full of horror.

Gibbs arrived on stage. His tie flying behind him like a pennant, his face bright with fury.

'What the hell are you doing? End him. Now.'

The crowd began to roar again. Their noise filling Ian's ears with their urgency.

Gavin, known to Ian as Gun, released his grip on Mo's head and retreated away from the scene. Small steps. Until he reached the shower wall where he fell into a crouch, staring at the space in front of him as if it held all the terrors of the universe. His mind displaying a movie of every horror he had ever witnessed.

Gibbs reached him, pulled a gun from his jacket pocket, pressed it against the side of Gavin's head. 'What are you doing, you fuckwit? Kill the skinny big bastard.'

Ian reached Mo's side. Fell onto his knees. Saw that the man's neck and chest were covered in blood. Yet, beneath one swollen eye, a light. Ian bent down as if testing his pulse. Whispered urgently. 'Pretend you're dead.' Prayed that the man understood. Then he stood up, shouted at Gibbs over the noise of the crowd. 'What are you on about, Gibbs? The guy's already dead. You can't kill him twice.'

To prove his point, he lifted up one of Mo's arms and dropped it. It fell like a deadweight.

Gibbs turned to the crowd and roared like he'd been the one to complete the coup de grace. The crowd went crazy in response. Gibbs motioned to a guy offstage to come and pull Mo out of view. He climbed up, grabbed both his feet and began to pull him away. Ian prayed that his erstwhile neighbour had the good sense to keep up the act.

'Right, cunt. Wait there.' Gibbs, charged with the sense of his own drama, marched over to Ian. He motioned the crowd to silence. He had them. They obeyed.

'Now for the main event!' he shouted. Pointed behind Ian. Ian turned.

Kenny.

53

Kenny was completely disorientated. Barely knew which side was up, which was to the right or left. The bag was pulled from his head and the earphones silenced with a suddenness that made his stomach lurch.

The first sound he recognised was his name.

Kenny. That was him, wasn't it?

He opened his mouth, his lips all but gummed together. By Christ, he could do with a drink. And a sleep. He felt his feet on the ground. Fought for a connection. For something to make sense.

There was his name again.

A man in front of him.

Kenny smiled like a drunk. *Ian*. Mouthed the name. And again. *Ian*? Something else. Whatever it was slipped away from his conscious mind like a bar of soap in the bath. He looked down at himself. Realised he was naked apart from a small piece of towelling. What was that all about?

He saw a man with a tie staring at him. Instantly wanted to punch him. Who was he? Gibbs. A thought. Series of images. This man needed to be put down.

Then sense came crashing in like a tsunami.

He fell to his knees. Cradled his head.

Gibbs was in his ear, 'For fuckssake, O'Neill. Get a grip. You've got a job to do here.

From his position on the floor, Kenny twisted his head to the side. Read the situation. There in the front row, Dan Stewart, and beside him as if he was watching nothing more exciting than a flower show, sat old man Gallagher's grandson.

'Water,' he said, as if it was taking all his strength to speak. Gibbs motioned someone behind him and shouted Kenny's request.

The crowd fell silent as if waiting to see what drama would next develop. Kenny heard Ian behind him. Urgency in his voice.

'Dave, what the hell, man?'

'So sorry, dude. I had no idea. Honest to Christ. I swear.' A male voice, presumably Dave.

Kenny lifted his head up, maintained the idiot mind-drunk act. Looked at Dave to assess his threat. Ian was in Dave's face. Dave was acting like he was deeply embarrassed: uncertain.

'Here.' Gibbs arrived with a bottle of water and thrust it into one of Kenny's hands. Kenny took it, keeping his eyes on Gibbs' weapon. Then he drank slowly. Just a sip at first. Sluiced it round his mouth. Felt his tongue loosen and relax. Drank some more. Savoured the cool of it as it filled his mouth, and from there down his throat.

'Where the hell am I?' he asked Gibbs, keeping the act going.

Gibbs exhaled with relief. The fight wasn't over. He didn't reply to Kenny, instead he turned away and looked at the crowd.

'Three stout warriors,' he announced like a ringmaster. 'Last man still breathing receives a get-out-of-jail-free card.'

The crowd cheered.

'Are you insane?' shouted Ian. 'No fucking way.'

Gibbs walked over to him and pressed his pistol against his forehead. 'Aye, fucking way,' he said. 'Only one of you pricks is leaving this stage alive. Best get used to that idea, pretty quickly.'

Ian's mouth was open in disbelief. Looking as if he was on automatic pilot, he moved back away from the weapon. Then, as if realising he was moving towards the other combatant, Gun, he edged the other way closer to Kenny.

Kenny had the presence of mind to take another sip of water. He was fast coming back to his self. Adrenalin flooding his system.

'Ian,' he hissed. His brother looked over at him. 'It's all a lie. Dom Hastie's dead.'

Gibbs heard the exchange. Grinned. Then looked at Kenny with a question in his eyes. You know these guys? What am I missing here?

Ian reared back. 'What?'

'Dom's dead. Gibbs threw him off his balcony the day they took you away,' Kenny hissed.

'What?' Ian's face was a mask of disbelief. This was too much. Too much information. He looked over at Gun, still in his crouch. Back to Kenny. Then to Gibbs. 'He's dead?'

'Wee prick didn't have a parachute,' said Gibbs with a wild smile.

Ian launched himself at him. Gibbs stood to the side smartly, brought his gun down on the side of his head. Ian crumpled to the floor.

Kenny shuffled to his side. Looked into his eyes. 'Keep it together, brother,' he whispered. 'Get even. Then you can get angry.'

'Once you two boys have finished with your love-fest, can we get on with this fight?' Gibbs shouted. Kenny watched as he motioned to Dave behind him, to back him up. He looked at Dave and saw that the fight was all but out of the guy. This wasn't what he'd joined up for.

'Right,' said Gibbs. 'Last man breathing. You, Ritchie, stand up. You, Gavin, Gun or whatever the fuck your name is, get away from that wall and get over here.'

To their surprise, Gun got up, keeping his eyes on the floor, and stood so that he, Ian and Kenny formed a triangle.

'Right, you twats, fight,' said Gibbs and stepped back.

Kenny looked at Gun. Assessed his potential to cause damage. Saw a shell. There was nothing there. His arms were by his side.

His eyes on the floor. Then he watched as Gun looked down at his right hand as if seeing the knife there in his grip for the first time.

'Get on with it!' shouted Gibbs, his face getting brighter by the second. 'Or I'll shoot the lot of you.'

Gun looked up. His eyes sought Ian's. They were full to brimming with shame and self-loathing. There was no apology ever so profound. Kenny felt scoured by that look. All the pain that ever existed in the world was in the man's eyes.

But how much of a risk was he? Kenny judged the distance, braced himself to dive in and protect his brother. Before he could move, Gun mouthed 'Sorry' and pulled the knife across his own throat, filling the air in front of him with a geyser of blood.

54

'No!' shouted Ian and fell at his old friend's side. 'No.'

Kenny shifted his view from Gun. Looked at Ian. Then watched Gibbs as his mind raced through the variables. He still had two fighters. That they knew each other probably pleased him in some twisted way, but by the set of his face he was clearly still determined to get his last fight to the death.

Gibbs looked towards the crowd. Held his hands out, palms up. Made a what-the-hell face. Kenny followed his line of sight and watched Dan Stewart as he smiled at Gibbs' discomfort. A smile that said, this clusterfuck is all your doing, mate, and I'm having a great time watching you sweat. Beside him, Gallagher's grandson stared impassively at the phone in his hand, his thumb moving over the keyboard.

Kenny dismissed the boy from his thoughts. The youngster was clearly deranged.

'Fight, you crazy fucks!' Gibbs shouted, close to losing it altogether. He stomped over to Ian, like a child who's been refused a toy in the supermarket, and pushed him away from Gun's body.

Ian fell back. As he fought to right himself, he looked down the length of his body as if realising for the first time that he was covered in his friend's blood: dark, thick, arterial. He scrambled back in a crab-walk, away from Gun, stood up and pulled the towel from around his waist. And then, chest heaving as if each breath was reaching his lungs through a withered channel, he attempted to wipe the blood from his body. Horror large in his eyes.

Kenny saw Gibbs raise his weapon. Judged that the man was close to his edge. Realised that he had to take back an element of control. So he stepped forward and punched Ian in the face.

'Jesus Christ!' shouted Ian, focus returning to his eyes. 'What the hell?'

There was a build-up of noise from the crowd. Things were about to get interesting again.

'Yes,' roared Gibbs. 'That's what we want.'

Without waiting for Ian to react, Kenny jumped. Wrestled him to the floor, realising that as he did so, his strength was waning rapidly. No food, no drink, no sleep for a couple of days. Fatigue was inevitable. This situation had to be resolved, and resolved soon.

'Go with it, Ian,' he whispered urgently. 'We have to get that gun away from Gibbs.'

Ian grunted in his ear and held on to his head so tight that Kenny wasn't sure he'd gotten through to him. Next thing he knew, Ian had coiled a foot round his and pushed so that Kenny fell with Ian on top.

'Yes,' shouted Gibbs moving close, as if he was desperate to get in on the action. 'This is more like it.'

On automatic pilot, Kenny shifted so that Ian fell to the side. But his brother was stronger than him. He had eaten and slept over the last couple of days. With a dexterity that would have made him proud, if he hadn't been on the receiving end of it, he felt himself being flipped in return, and in the next moment Ian was behind him and was holding his head in a lock.

Kenny slapped at Ian's forearm. Felt the strength there. Knew that in this state oxygen debt wouldn't take long in coming. He fought for breath. Nothing. Slapped at Ian's arms. The bristles of his brother's chin scraped his ear.

Couldn't.

Breathe.

Then he felt Ian's grip shift. His head was still held tight, but the blood flow to his brain was no longer being restricted. What was Ian up to?

Kenny saw Gibbs moving closer and made a face as if he was desperate for breath. Gibbs moved closer still. Both of his feet in the middle of a wide puddle of blood. Kenny kicked out. Gibbs shifted. Slipped. Fell.

Ian released Kenny, and Kenny was on Gibbs in a second. While Gibbs fought to reorient himself, Kenny slapped the gun from his hand. It fell with a dull clang on to the floor.

'Right,' a voice said from the crowd. 'Fun's fun and all that, but fuck this for a game of soldiers.' It was Dan Stewart. He was standing, pointing a gun of his own at the men on the stage. 'We're stopping this now.'

At this the young Gallagher stood up, pulled a large knife from his pocket and in one easy motion plunged it into Stewart's chest.

People sitting in the seats around them screamed. Ran from their seats. People behind them stood up and craned their necks trying to see what was going on.

Gallagher leaned over Stewart's body, pulled the knife back out and plunged it back in for good measure. He turned to the stage. Caught Kenny's eye. The young man winked, held up his phone in some sort of warning, pulled the knife back out, turned and walked away. Everyone around shrunk from him as if he was carrying some terrible disease.

While Kenny was distracted, that moment's delay was enough for Gibbs to dive for his gun, but Kenny read the movement and managed to get there first. Besides, he wasn't slowed down by the vague worry that he needed to protect his new suit from all this blood. Kenny reached the gun. Brought it crashing down on Gibbs. Hit him on the shoulder.

Kenny got to his feet. The gun in his hand. Looked to Dave as if to ask, want any of this? Dave held his hands up and walked off the stage. Signalling his intent. He was out of here.

Gibbs was on his hands and knees. Face smeared in blood. The whites of his eyes almost the only part of him not stained red.

Kenny looked at Ian. 'Will you do the honours, or will I?'

Ian didn't bother to reply. He simply stepped forward and lashed out with his foot. Catching Gibbs on the chin. Then he was on him. Head in a lock. Repeating how he'd held Kenny.

'I'm going to kill you, Gibbs,' Ian hissed in his ear. His face was strained with a terrible determination and effort. Gibbs' face was bright with the need to breathe. He scrabbled for purchase. Frantic for oxygen, his feet slid in Gun's blood, his face a mask of fear and desperation. His hands flapping uselessly at the steel bars of Ian's arms.

Kenny watched on, debating whether or not he should stop his brother. Did he want him to have murder on his conscience?

Ian's hands were clasped palm to palm. One arm like a noose under Gibbs' chin, the other braced against his back, giving Gibbs nowhere to go.

Gibbs' eyes were large with panic. The need for oxygen.

Ian shot his right hand deep behind Gibbs' neck and locked it into place using pressure from his head. His left hand was now clutching his right bicep. Kenny could see the muscle enlarge as Ian squeezed down, in and up in a hooking motion under the jaw.

Gibbs' movements slowed. His face was almost purple . . . and he was out of it.

Ian continued with the hold.

Kenny knew if his grip was reduced now, the blood flow to Gibbs' brain would resume, he'd remain unconscious for a few more seconds and no damage would ensue.

Ian maintained his death grip.

'Ian,' Kenny said. Leaned forward and patted his cousin's arm. 'Enough.'

Ian ignored him.

Kenny knew that a couple more minutes of this and the lack of blood flow to Gibbs' brain, such as it was, would cause permanent damage. Only a few more minutes after that and Gibbs would die.

Sure, the prick deserved everything he got, but did Kenny want Ian to be the executioner? His brother had enough to deal with, would he be able to handle all that comes with a death by your own hands?

Kenny stepped forward, tried to put a hand in between Ian's grip and Gibbs' neck. But there was no space.

'Ian,' Kenny said. But there was no response. Ian was locked in, mentally and physically. Kenny looked about for something he could use on Ian. A weapon of some sort. He spotted Gibbs' weapon, almost submerged in Gun's blood. He reached for it.

Then the lights in the hall went on full. Blaring. And a voice echoed harsh in the space: demanding obedience.

'Police. Stop.'

55

Ray McBain had his phone in front of him, on the bar. He was willing it to ring. Kenny. Ale. Dimitri. Anybody. Somebody phone me. He'd been sitting here for hours and nothing.

What the hell was going on?

Where was everyone?

He wasn't used to this. He was the one who took action. He was the one who sorted things out.

Someone walked in the door of the bar. A small, bald man in a too-large, tweed jacket.

'We're closed,' he shouted at him. 'Piss off.'

'Piss off, yursel,' the man said and walked back out.

Ray looked at his phone again. Ring, for chrissakes. Ring. Nothing.

Then an alert. It was from Dimitri.

Great Western Gentlemen's Club. NOW.

Between the lines? A fight was happening right at this moment. His friend's life could be in danger.

What to do? He couldn't do much on his own. But he couldn't just sit here on his arse and do nothing.

He picked up his phone and called Ale. Told her everything. Her calmness and willingness to act reassured him.

'Right. We're on it.' Before she hung up on him, she said, 'If I see your skinny arse down there, Ray, I'll arrest you.'

Yeah. You'll need to catch me first.

He ran out the door, not bothering to lock up, and jumped in his car.

Ray had been at any number of crime scenes in his career as a policeman, but few of them came close to the sight that greeted him at the Great Western.

One blood-covered corpse on the stage.

One in the front row.

One tall, skinny black guy lying in the corridor at the back of the stage, barely breathing.

And unconscious on the middle of the stage, one Barry Gibbs.

Standing over him, Detective Constable Alessandra Rossi looked at Ray with a thunderous expression. 'What the hell, McBain? I told you to stay away.'

'Where's Kenny?'

Ale looked around herself. Shook her head. 'Nowhere to be seen.'

Ray exhaled. Relief flooded him. That was a good thing, right?

56

'Ashes to ashes, dust to dust . . .'

The priest spoke, but Kenny was elsewhere. Less concerned with the dead than he was with the living. He looked along the short row of people at the graveside and gave thanks for each of them. His second funeral in as many days. Gun had been buried the day before. The only attendees were Kenny and Ian. Thinking of Ian, Kenny turned to his side.

There he was, offering a solid reassuring presence, actually looking healthy. Ian caught his look and nodded. Kenny responded to the nod with a wink. They were good. They'd had Sunday dinner back at Vi's, and Colin was like a changed man. He was all over Ian. A hand on his shoulder. Offered more potatoes. Put the football on the telly for him. As if hearing about the danger Ian had been in reminded him that he did actually care about him.

Ray, on his other side, stood hands clasped in front of him, head bowed like a professional mourner. Before they'd arrived at the graveside, Kenny took a moment to ask Ray about his involvement in the incident. Would D.S. Alessandra Rossi be knocking on his door any time soon? With a half-smile Ray let him stew for a moment, then shook his head, said the police were happy to have Gibbs in custody and were doing him, for among other things, Dom's murder. But perhaps Kenny should keep his head down for a while. Like, a decade?

Beyond Ian, at a safe distance of a few steps, stood Dom Hastie's widow, one hand over her mouth as if to contain her gulps of grief, the other down by her side holding her son's hand. Big-eyed and bewildered, he was looking around himself, trying to process events but lacking a reference that would help any of this make sense.

The boy caught Kenny's gaze and stared at him. Who are you? that stare asked. Can you help sort this out? You're a grown up. Isn't that your job? Kenny could do nothing but offer a smile of reassurance and send a silent prayer to the gods of childhood that this wee boy would never experience anything like this again.

The aftershock of the Great Western Bloodbath, as the press were calling it, was still rumbling on. A police spokesperson was saying that there were a couple of players they were still looking for, but they were happy that the main culprits had been accounted for. One of the men at the scene survived his wounds: a Somalian refugee called Mohammed. But the leader of the whole fighting operation, Barry Gibbs, would be going away for a long time and his action closed down for good.

A photo of Gibbs in his blood-stained suit, in handcuffs, being pushed into the back of a police van had been on the front page of pretty much every newspaper in the country.

Back at the Great Western, as soon as Kenny heard the command "Police. Stop." he knew he had to get Ian out of there. While the audience rushed to escape official attention, he grabbed Ian's arm and pulled him out the stage door.

Dave had the same idea. When he saw them move in the same direction as him, he waited for them. 'This way,' he said with quiet urgency.

He guided them back to the changing rooms, found their clothes, helped them clean up as best and as quickly as they could, and helped them get dressed.

While he was pulling on his jeans, Ian looked at Dave.

'Why you helping us?'

Dave shook his head slowly. He was back there on the stage.

'Seeing Gavin . . .' He looked at Ian as if searching for

forgiveness and understanding. 'His eyes, man. I've never . . .'

'A bit fucking late, mate.' Ian was in his face. Fist cocked. Kenny pulled him away.

'Wrong time and place, Ian.'

Dave stood with his arms by his side. His stance saying, go ahead, I deserve it.

'Wrong time and place,' Kenny repeated with urgency.

Dave shook himself. 'The car's out the back,' he said and led the way to his black vehicle, and from there drove to Kenny's flat in the west of the city. For the entire length of the journey no one spoke. Each of them lost in a mental maze, trying to make sense and come to terms with what they had seen and done.

'I'm going to kill that bastard,' Ian said at one point. He looked Kenny in the eye. Certain and vengeful. 'I'm going to kill him.'

Kenny said nothing.

When the car stopped at Kenny's, Dave looked over his shoulder at Ian on the backseat. He was scoured by his own dishonour. 'Anything I can do, just let me know,' he said, knowing there was nothing he could do, but he had to make the offer.

'I want nothing from you,' Ian replied, staring him down.

'I had no . . .'

'Can it,' Ian said. 'Not interested.' And climbed out of the car.

The service ended, and huddled against the cold and the weight of their sorrow, everyone present took time to have a word with the grieving family before shuffling off to find solace in some sort of reminder that life does indeed go on.

Kenny watched as Ian got into a crouch, eye-to-eye with Dom's son. He had no idea what Ian said to the child. What could you say that would make any sense? One of the most important figures in his life had vanished. His physical body put in a box and buried in a hole in the ground. Make sense of that.

Ian stood, patted the boy's head. Had a word with his mother.

'Anything I can do,' Kenny heard. She bit her lip and nodded her silent thanks. Ian turned, motioned to Kenny that they should leave, and walked down the gravel path back to the car park.

There he stopped when he saw a small girl, standing beside a young woman he thought would be her mother.

'Myleene,' Ian said. 'What you doing here, honey?'

Myleene bristled at the word "honey". Her look said it all. She was one of the gang. How dare he call her honey? Kenny grinned. Wished he had this girl's gumption when he was her age.

Her mother answered for her. 'When she heard Dom's funeral was today she wanted to come down.' She looked over Ian's shoulder at the dispersing mourners, with a poorly disguised look of relief. 'Is it all over then?'

Ian nodded.

'Sorry, darlin',' she said to Myleene. 'We can come back when the grave has been filled. Bring some nice flowers, eh?'

'Sure,' Myleene said and kicked at a stone. Then she looked at Kenny. 'I remember you,' she said. 'You helped me.'

'I did,' replied Kenny.

'You did?' asked Ian.

Kenny sent him a look. Tell you later.

Myleene looked at Ian. Looked over at the graveyard behind him. 'Dom was my pal,' she said, and her face darkened, her small mouth forming a tight pout of anger. 'Did you get the guy who did it?'

Her mum. 'Myleene!'

Myleene was unrepentant. 'Did you?' Her eyes demanding, shining with unshed tears. Her small fists were clenched by her side, every inch of her wanted to see the bad man who did this hurt. Her need for retribution was biblical in scope, unleavened by life and the experience that teaches innumerable shades of grey. Her friend was dead. He was a good friend. A kind man, a little boy's father, and he died for no good reason and in a terror that she couldn't begin to imagine. The man who did it needed to pay.

'We did,' said Ian. 'We got him good.'

THE END

ACKNOWLEDGEMENTS

With thanks to…

My fellow crime scene-ers, whether you are a reader, writer, publisher, bookseller or reviewer. Your camaraderie and your enthusiasm for the (dark) written word make this a vibrant and fun area to be working in and I thank my lucky stars for you all every day.

CONTRABAND ☮

Contraband – the crime fiction imprint from Saraband – publishes an eclectic range of crime, mystery, noir and thriller writing, from dark literary titles to pacy detective novels. Contraband books have proved to be incredibly popular with critics and readers alike since the imprint was launched in 2014. Graeme Macrae Burnet's *His Bloody Project* was shortlisted for the Man Booker Prize 2016 and won the Saltire Society Fiction Book of the Year Award, and two further books were shortlisted for the Bloody Scotland Crime Book of the Year (in 2014 and 2015 respectively): *Falling Fast* by Neil Broadfoot and *DM for Murder* by Matt Bendoris. Several of these titles have already been translated into a number of different languages. Saraband was the inaugural Saltire Society Scottish Publisher of the Year in 2013, and was also shortlisted in 2015 and 2016, as well as being shortlisted for the Independent Publishers' Guild Trade Publisher of the Year Award for 2016.